Plain & Fancy

**Center Point
Large Print**

This Large Print Book carries the Seal of Approval of N.A.V.H.

Brides of Lancaster County
3

Plain & Fancy

Wanda E. Brunstetter

CENTER POINT PUBLISHING
THORNDIKE, MAINE

This Center Point Large Print edition is published
in the year 2009 by arrangement with
Barbour Publishing, Inc.

All Scripture Quotations are taken from
the King James Version of the Bible.

All German–Dutch words are taken from
the *Revised Pennsylvania German Dictionary*
found in Lancaster County, Pennsylvania.

Plain & Fancy was first released in 2002 in the Heartsong
Presents series and later in Lancaster Brides anthology.
This edition has additional story scenes never published.

The text of this Large Print edition is unabridged.
In other aspects, this book may
vary from the original edition.
Printed in the United States of America.
Set in 16-point Times New Roman type.

ISBN: 978-1-60285-417-8

Library of Congress Cataloging-in-Publication Data

Brunstetter, Wanda E.
  Plain & fancy / Wanda E. Brunstetter.
    p. cm. — (Brides of Lancaster County)
  ISBN 978-1-60285-417-8 (library binding : alk. paper)
  1. Amish—Pennsylvania—Lancaster County—Fiction. 2. Lancaster (Pa.)—Fiction.
    3. Large type books. I. Title. II. Title: Plain and fancy. III. Series.
  PS3602.R864P58 2009
    813'.6—dc22
2008047597

And this is his commandment,
That we should believe on the
name of his Son Jesus Christ,
and love one another,
as he gave us commandment.
1 JOHN 3:23 KJV

CHAPTER 1

Laura Meade opened her laptop, entered the correct password to put her online, and began the e-mail she had been meaning to write for the past week:

Dear Shannon,
I'm finally settled in at the Lancaster School of Design. I think I'm going to like it here. Not only is the college rated in the top ten, but the area is beautiful, and the Amish I've seen are unbelievable! I haven't met any of them up close and personal, but from what I've seen, the women wear simple, dark-colored dresses, with little white hats on their heads. The men wear cotton shirts, dark pants with suspenders, and either a straw or black felt hat with a wide brim. They drive box-shaped, closed-in buggies pulled by a horse.
Tomorrow, I'm going to the farmers' market. I hear it's a great place to get good buys on handmade Amish quilts. I may even be able to acquire some helpful decorating ideas there.
I hope you're doing well and enjoying your

new job. I'm looking forward to seeing you at Christmas and hearing about those preschoolers you teach.

Your friend,
Laura

Laura thought about sending an e-mail to her parents, but she had talked to them on the phone just an hour ago, so there wouldn't be much to write about now. Moving away from the desk, she picked up a brush from the dresser and began her nightly ritual of one hundred strokes through her long, thick tresses.

She glanced around the room with disdain. Even the smallest room at home was bigger than this dinky dorm room. Fortunately, she would only be here two years. Then she could return to Minneapolis and redecorate to her heart's content—starting with her own bedroom at home.

"It's stifling in here." Laura dropped the hairbrush onto the bed and went to open the window. A slight breeze trickled through the screen, but it did nothing to cool the stuffy room. Here it was the first week of September, and the days were still hot and humid. To make matters worse, the air-conditioning wasn't working right and probably wouldn't be fixed until later in the week, according to what she'd been told.

Fall had always been Laura's favorite time of year. Someday, she hoped to decorate her own home with harvest colors. The kitchen windows would be outlined with sheer yellow curtains. The living-room, dining-room, and bedroom floors would be covered with thick, bronze carpets. She wanted to decorate with Early American furniture and to hang plenty of paintings from that era on the walls.

Mom and Dad had allowed her to travel halfway across the country to attend the Lancaster School of Design, despite the fact that several good schools were closer to home. When Laura had heard about this one so near to the heart of Amish land, she'd known she had to come. She'd read about the interesting culture of the Plain People on a few Web sites and was sure she could gain some unique decorating ideas here in Lancaster County.

Laura glanced at the photo of Dean Carlson, set in a gold frame on top of her dresser. Dean was the newest member of her father's law firm, and he had given her the picture soon after they'd started dating three months ago. Dean hadn't been too happy about her moving to Pennsylvania, even though she had assured him it would only be for a couple of years. She wasn't sure if his reluctance to see her go was because he cared so much or if he might be worried that she would find someone else and end up staying in Pennsylvania.

A loud knock jolted Laura out of her musings.

9

With an exasperated sigh, she crossed the room and opened the door.

A young woman with short, curly blond hair stood in the hallway. "Hi. I'm Darla Shelby. I have the room next to yours."

Laura smiled. "I'm Laura Meade."

"Nice to meet you. Where are you from?"

"Minneapolis. How about you?"

"I grew up here in Lancaster, moved to New York with my folks when I was sixteen, and came back here again to attend this school." She grinned. "But my favorite place to be is Philadelphia. In fact, since tomorrow's Saturday, I thought I'd drive into Philly and do some shopping. Would you like to go along?"

"So you must have your own car?"

Darla nodded. "It's a little red convertible—got it for my birthday last year."

Laura thought about her own car parked in the garage at home. She wished she could have driven it here, but her parents had insisted that she fly to Pennsylvania and lease a car during her stay.

"I realize we've only just met," Darla continued, "but I figure what better way to get acquainted than during a shopping spree."

Laura leaned against the doorframe as she contemplated the tempting offer. "I appreciate the invitation, and I'd love to go with you some other time, but I had planned to go to the farmers' market at Bird-in-Hand tomorrow. I understand some of the Plain People go there to shop and sell some of their wares."

Darla nodded. "Those Amish and Mennonites are quite the tourist attraction around here."

"Why don't you go to the market with me, and we can do some shopping there?"

Darla wrinkled her nose. "No way! I'd rather be caught in the middle of rush-hour traffic on the turnpike than spend the day with a bunch of farmers."

Laura giggled. "Those farmers do look pretty interesting."

"Maybe so, but they're not interesting enough for me to give up a day of shopping in Philly." Darla turned toward her own room, calling over her shoulder, "Whatever you do, Laura, don't let too much of that Amish culture rub off on you."

As Eli Yoder left Strasburg, where he worked at a store that made handcrafted Amish furniture, he thought about the conversation he'd had with Pauline Hostetler after church last Sunday. He had made the mistake of telling her that he planned to rent a table at the farmers' market this Saturday to sell some of the items he'd created in his wood shop at home.

"Oh, Eli," he could still hear her say, *"I was planning to go to the market on Saturday, too.*

Maybe the two of us could meet at noon and eat lunch together."

"Pauline's after me to court her," Eli mumbled, as he headed down the road toward home in his buggy.

His horse whinnied as if in response and perked up his ears.

"Are you sympathizing with me, boy?" Eli chuckled and flicked the reins to get his horse trotting a bit faster. It was fun to ride in his open buggy and go a little faster than usual. It made him feel free and one with the wind whipping against his face.

I won't be free for long if Pauline has anything to say about it. I think she's in cahoots with Mom to see me join the church so I can get married and settle down to raising a family. Eli frowned. It wasn't that he didn't want to get married someday. He just hadn't found the right woman yet, and he was sure it wouldn't be Pauline. He was in no hurry to be baptized and join the church until he felt ready to settle down. So Mom would have to learn to be patient.

"Why'd I agree to meet Pauline for lunch?" Eli fretted. "She's likely to take it to mean I have an interest in her, and then she'll expect me to start officially calling on her."

He gripped the reins a little tighter. "I'll have lunch with her on Saturday because I promised I would, but I'll have to figure out some way to let her know there's no chance of us having a future together."

A ray of sun filtered through the window, causing Laura to squint when she opened her eyes. She peeked at the small clock on her bedside table. It was nearly nine o'clock. She had slept much later than she'd planned.

Jerking the covers aside, she slipped out of bed and headed for the shower. A short time later, as Laura studied the contents of her closet, she had a hard time deciding what to wear. She finally opted for a pair of blue jeans and a rust-colored tank top. She pulled her long, auburn hair into a ponytail and secured it with a navy blue scrunchie.

"Nothing fancy, but I'm sure I look good enough to go to the farmers' market," she said to her reflection in the mirror. "Amish country, I hope you're ready for me because here I come!"

Mary Ellen Yoder had just begun supper preparations when her husband, Johnny, stepped into the kitchen, holding a pot of pansies in his hands. He grinned at her and placed the pot on the counter. "These are for you. I got 'em from the Beachys' greenhouse."

She turned from her job of cutting vegetables for a stew and smiled. "Such a thoughtful husband I have. *Danki*, Johnny."

His smile widened, and he leaned over to kiss her cheek. "I still remember the first bouquet of flowers I bought for my special girl. Do you?"

She nodded. "That was way back when you were doing everything you could to get me to allow you to come courting."

He slipped his arm around her waist and gave her a squeeze. "And it worked, too, didn't it? We not only started courting, but you agreed to marry me, and now we've got ourselves four of the finest *kinner* around."

"*Jah*, I agree." Mary Ellen smiled and resumed cutting her vegetables.

"And let's not forget that spunky little *kindsbuh* our daughter gave us a few years back."

"Now if we can just get our three *buwe* married off so they can add more grandchildren to our family," Mary Ellen said.

"I think the chances of Lewis and Jonas finding wives might be pretty good since they've already joined the church, but Eli's another matter."

Mary Ellen sighed and glanced at Johnny over her shoulder. "It's hard for me to understand why he keeps saying he's not ready to settle down when he's got a fine woman like Pauline Hostetler interested in him. Eli's twenty-three years old already and has gone through his *rumschpringe* long enough. Wouldn't you think

14

he'd be eager to end his running-around years and start courting a pretty girl?"

Johnny shrugged. "I don't want to get your hopes up, but I heard Eli talking to Jonas last night, and he mentioned that he's got plans to meet Pauline for lunch on Saturday when he goes to the farmers' market to sell some of his handmade wooden items."

Despite her husband's warning, Mary Ellen's hopes began to soar. "Really? You heard that?"

"Heard it with my own ears, so it's not just say-so."

She smiled. "Now that is good news. Jah, the best news I've had all day."

When Laura stepped out of her air-conditioned car, a blast of heat and humidity hit her full in the face. She hurried into the market building and was relieved to find that it was much cooler than the outside air had been.

The first table Laura discovered was run by two young Amish women selling an assortment of pies and cookies. Both wore their hair parted down the middle, then pulled back into a tight bun. They had small, white caps perched on top of their heads, and their long-sleeved, dark blue dresses were calf-length, with black aprons and capes worn over the front. One of the women smiled and asked Laura if she would like to sample something.

She stared longingly at a piece of apple pie. They did look delicious, but she'd had breakfast not long ago and didn't think she needed the extra calories.

"No thanks. I'm not really hungry right now." The truth was Laura was always counting calories, and she figured one bite of those scrumptious pastries would probably tip the scales in an unfavorable direction. She moved on quickly before temptation got the better of her.

The next few tables were run by non-Amish farmers. The items they offered didn't interest Laura much, so she found another table where an elderly Amish woman sold handmade quilts.

"Those are gorgeous. How much do they cost?" she asked.

The woman showed her each one, quoting the prices, which ranged from four hundred to nine hundred dollars.

"I'm definitely going to buy one," Laura said without questioning the price. "I don't want to carry it around while I shop, though. Can you hold this one for me?" She pointed to a simple pattern that used a combination of geometric shapes done in a variety of rich autumn colors.

"Jah, sure. I can hold it."

"Great. What's this one called, anyway?"

"It's known as 'Grandmother's Choice.' " The Amish woman's fingers traveled lightly over the material.

Laura smiled. "I like it very much. I'll be back for it before I leave, but I can pay now if you'd like."

"Pay when you come back; that'll be fine." The woman placed the quilt inside a box, then slipped it under the table.

It was getting close to lunchtime, so Laura decided to check out one more table, then look for something nonfattening to eat.

The next table was loaded with a variety of hand-carved items. Laura glanced around for the person in charge but didn't see anyone. She picked up one of the finely crafted birdhouses and studied the exquisite detailing. When a young Amish man popped up from behind the table, she jumped, nearly dropping the birdhouse. He held a box filled with more birdhouses and feeders. His sandy brown hair was cut in a Dutch-bob, and a lock of it fell across his forehead. His deeply set, crystalline blue eyes met Laura's gaze with such intensity it took her breath away. Her cheeks grew hot, and she quickly placed the birdhouse back on the table. "I—I was just admiring your work."

A hint of a smile tweaked the man's lips, revealing a small dimple in the middle of his chin. "I'm a woodcarver and carpenter, and I'm thankful God has given me the ability to use my hands for something worthwhile."

Though Laura had been to church a few times

in her life, she wasn't particularly religious. In fact, the whole church scene made her feel kind of nervous. Nibbling on the inside of her cheek, she merely nodded in response to the man's giving credit to God for his abilities.

"Are you looking for anything special? I also have some wooden flowerpots and ornamental things for the lawn." He lifted one for her inspection.

Laura stared at the small, decorative windmill in his hand, and her gaze traveled up his muscular arm. Below his rolled-up shirtsleeve, his tanned arms were feathered with light brown hair. She moistened her lips and brought her wayward thoughts to a halt. "I . . . uh . . . live in a dorm room at the Lancaster School of Design, so I really don't have a need for birdhouses or whirligigs."

His dark eyebrows drew together. "Don't think I've ever heard of that school."

"I'm learning to be an interior decorator," she explained, drawing her gaze to his appealing face, then back to the items on the table.

When he made no comment, she looked up again and saw that he was staring at her with a questioning look.

"My job will be to help people decorate their homes in attractive styles and colors."

"Ah, I see. So do you live around here, then?"

She shook her head. "I'm from Minneapolis,

Minnesota. I've already studied some interior design at one of our local community colleges, and I'm here to complete my training."

There was an awkward silence as they stood staring at one another.

"Eli, well, there you are! I thought we were supposed to meet for lunch. I waited outside, but you never showed up so I figured I'd better come looking."

A young, blond-haired Amish woman, dressed similarly to the Plain women Laura had seen earlier, stepped up to the table.

"I'm sorry, Pauline," he said. "I got busy talking with this customer and forgot about the time." He considered Laura a moment. "Is there anything you're wantin' to buy?"

"No. I . . . uh . . . was just looking."

"Eli, if you're finished here, can we go have lunch now?" Pauline took a few steps closer, brushing her hand lightly against Eli's arm.

"Jah, Pauline." Eli glanced back at Laura. "It was nice chatting with you, and I wish you the best with your studies and all." He turned away, leaving his wooden items unattended.

Laura shook her head. *That man is sure trusting. And how in the world could someone as simply dressed as him be so adorable?*

As Eli and Pauline exited the building, he glanced over his shoulder. The young English woman still stood beside his table. *She's sure a fancy one. Fancy and very pretty. I wonder why someone like her would be interested in birdhouses?*

"Eli, where do you want to eat lunch?"

Pauline's question and her slight tug on Eli's shirtsleeve brought his thoughts to a halt.

"I thought you carried a picnic basket," he said peevishly.

"I did, but I wasn't sure where you wanted to eat it."

He shrugged. "It makes no difference to me."

"Let's go to the picnic tables out back."

When Eli gave no response, she grabbed his sleeve again. "What's wrong? You're acting kind of *naerfich*."

"I'm not nervous. I've just got a lot on my mind."

Pauline slipped her hand through the crook of his arm. "After you've had a few bites of fried chicken, you won't be thinking about anything but my good cooking."

Eli feigned a smile. "Kissin' wears out, but cookin' don't." Truth be told, he wasn't really in the mood to eat just now, but he was sure Pauline had worked hard making the picnic lunch, and he'd promised to eat it with her. Besides, a few drumsticks and a plate of potato salad would probably make him feel a whole lot better.

Pauline smiled and set the wicker basket she'd filled with chicken, baked beans, cut-up vegetables, and chocolate cake on the picnic table. "You're right about cooking never wearing out. My *mamm* and *daed* have been married twenty-five years, and Dad's still complimenting Mom on her great cooking."

Eli's only reply was a quick shrug. Then he bowed his head, and she did the same. When their silent prayer was over, Pauline opened the basket and set out the food, along with paper plates, napkins, and plastic silverware. "I brought a jug of water for us to drink," she said. "I hope that's okay."

"Jah, sure; it's fine for me." Eli helped himself to a couple of drumsticks and some baked beans, and Pauline followed suit, only she added some cut-up carrots to her plate.

"I was sorry to learn that you hadn't taken the membership classes this summer so you could be baptized and join the church a week from Sunday," she said.

He gave a noncommital grunt and kept on eating.

"Will you take the classes next summer?"

"Maybe. It all depends on how I feel about things by then."

Pauline pursed her lips. "You're twenty-three years old already. Haven't you had enough rumschpringe by now? Don't you think it's past time for you to join the church and settle down?"

"Now you sound like my mamm." Eli frowned. "Maybe one of the reasons I haven't made the decision yet is because she's always hounding me about it."

Pauline flinched, feeling like he'd thrown cold water in her face. Eli obviously thought she was hounding him, too.

Eli reached into the plastic tub filled with chicken and retrieved another drumstick. "Don't get me wrong. I'm not refusing to join the church because I have any ideas about leaving the Amish faith. I just can't see the need of joining when I'm not ready to get married yet."

Pauline felt as if her heart had sunk all the way to her toes. If Eli wasn't ready to get married, then he obviously had no thoughts of marrying her. But he'd taken her home from a couple of singings, and he'd agreed to meet her for lunch today. Didn't that mean anything at all? Wasn't that a ray of hope worth clinging to? Pauline knew she would have to be careful not to push Eli too hard, but if she had her way, by this time next year they'd be planning their wedding.

When Laura returned to her dorm room later that afternoon, she placed the Amish quilt she'd

Laura hung around for a while, looking at various items and keeping an eye out for Amish people. She soon got tired of waiting, so she bought a few more postcards and left the store.

Outside on the sidewalk, she spotted two little Amish girls walking hand in hand behind their mother.

They're so cute—I just have to get their picture. Laura pulled her digital camera from her purse, focused it on the children, and was about to snap the picture when someone grasped her shoulder.

"Would you mind not taking that picture?"

Laura spun around. A pair of penetrating blue eyes bore down on her, and her heart skipped a beat. It was the same Amish man she'd met at the farmers' market a few weeks ago.

"I remember you. You were at the market, looking at my birdhouses, right?"

Laura nodded and offered him what she hoped was a pleasant smile. "Why did you stop me from taking those little girls' pictures?"

"The Amish prefer not to have their pictures taken."

"Oh? How come?"

"We believe it's a form of pride, and some in our church say it goes against Bible teachings reminding us not to make any graven images."

"What about all the pictures on postcards?" She withdrew one from her purse. "Isn't that an Amish man working in the fields?"

"Some folks don't care how we feel about being photographed, and they just snap pictures of us anyway," he said without even glancing at the postcard. "And some people use close-up lenses so they can take pictures without us knowing. I'm sure the man in the postcard didn't actually pose for the picture."

"Well, you don't have to worry about me offending anyone." She slipped the camera back into her purse, then held out her hand. "I'm Laura Meade."

He seemed kind of hesitant at first, but then he shook her hand and smiled. "My name's Eli Yoder."

"It's nice to meet you, Eli." She laughed, feeling suddenly self-conscious. "I guess we did meet before—just no formal introductions."

He motioned toward a wooden bench in front of the building. "Would you want to sit awhile? I'll take my birdhouses inside; then we can have a cup of cold root beer. That is, if you'd like one."

Laura nodded eagerly. Of course she would like a root beer—especially when it would give her more time to talk to this good-looking Amish man. She dropped to the bench and leaned forward with her elbows resting on her jean-clad knees, as she watched Eli head to the parking lot, where his horse and buggy stood waiting. He made two trips into the store, shouldering large cardboard boxes. When he emerged for the last time, he held two Styrofoam cups full of root beer. He gave one to Laura and sat down beside her.

"I noticed your buggy is open—sort of like a carriage," she remarked. "Most of the Amish buggies I've seen are closed and kind of box-shaped."

Eli grinned. "That's my courting buggy. My daed gave it to me on my sixteenth birthday."

"Your *daed*?"

"Jah, my dad."

"Oh. So what's a 'courting buggy'?"

"English boys get a driver's license and sometimes a car when they turn sixteen. We Amish get an open buggy so we can start court-ing—or dating, as you Englishers like to call it."

She smiled. "Have you been dating very long?"

"Are you wanting to know my age?"

Laura felt the heat of embarrassment creep up her neck as she nodded. She did want to know how old he was—and a whole lot more besides.

"It's okay. I don't mind you asking. I'm twenty-three, and my folks think I ought to be married already." Eli lifted the cup of root beer to his lips.

So, he's single and just a year older than me. Laura wasn't sure why, but that bit of informa-tion gave her some measure of satisfaction.

27

"How come you're not married?" she ventured to ask.

"For one thing, I haven't joined our church yet, and that's a requirement before marriage." Eli shrugged. "I haven't met the right woman yet, either."

Laura thought about the Amish woman who had been with Eli at the market. She'd seen the way that Plain girl had looked at him.

Eli smacked his lips. "*Umm* . . . this is sure good root beer. Thomas Benner, the store owner, makes it himself."

Laura took a sip. "Yes, it is very good." Her gaze traveled across the parking lot. "Your buggy's sure nice-looking. Does it ride well?"

Eli rewarded her with a heart-melting smile, and his seeking blue eyes mesmerized her. "Would you like to find out?"

"Oh, I'd love that!" Laura jumped up; then, thinking he might have only been teasing, she whirled around to face him. "Would it be all right? It's not against your religion or anything?"

Eli's smile widened, causing the dimple in his chin to become more pronounced. "There are some other Plain sects who offer buggy rides to tourists. So if someone should see us, they'll probably just think you hired me for a ride."

Eli helped Laura into the left side of the open buggy; then he climbed up on the right and gathered the reins. With a few clucks to his faithful horse, they were off.

A slight breeze caught the ends of Laura's golden bronze hair, whipping them around her face. Eli's chest constricted. *This English woman is sure appealing. Why, it's almost sinful to be so beautiful. I'm wondering why she would want to be seen with someone as plain as me.*

Eli felt a twinge of guilt for allowing himself the pleasure of admiring her beauty, but he couldn't quit thinking how much fun it would be to get to know her better.

"This is so awesome! I never would have dreamed riding in a buggy could be so much fun." Laura's tone revealed her excitement, and her green eyes lit up like a sunbeam.

He glanced over at her and grinned. "Jah, it's wonderful good."

When they had gone a short distance, Eli turned the buggy down a wide, dirt path, where there were no cars, just a carpet of flaxen corn on either side.

"Where are we going?"

"There's a small lake down this way." Eli flashed her another smile. "I think you'll like it there."

Laura leaned back in her seat, breathed deeply of the fresh air, and drank in the rich colors of the maple trees lining both sides of the dirt road. "I think the temperate hues of autumn make it the most charming, loveliest time of the year," she murmured.

Eli raised his dark eyebrows. "Such fancy words you're using."

She laughed. "Should I have said it's 'wonderful good'?"

"Jah, sure." Eli pulled the horse to a stop in a grassy meadow near the small lake. "Here we are."

"You were right. It is beautiful here."

Eli grinned like a child with a new toy. "In the summer, it's a great place for swimming and fishing. We like to skate on the lake when it freezes over in the wintertime, too."

"It looks like the perfect place for a picnic."

"My family and I have been here many times." Eli glanced over at Laura. "Would you like to get out and walk around?"

"That sounds nice, but I rather like riding in your courting buggy." She released a sigh of contentment. "Can't we just keep driving?"

"Sure, we can." Eli got the horse moving again.

As they traveled around the lake, Laura began to ply him with questions about his way of life. "Can you tell me why the Amish people wear such simple clothes?"

"We feel that wearing plain clothes encourages humility and separation from the world. Our

30

clothes aren't a costume, like some may believe, but they're an expression of our faith."

"I see." A gentle breeze rustled the trees, and Laura's heart stirred with a kind of excitement she had never known before. She wasn't sure if it was the fall foliage, the exhilarating buggy ride, or the captivating company of one very cute Amish man that made her feel so giddy. One thing was for sure: A keen sense of disappointment overcame her when Eli turned the buggy back to the main road.

"Do you like wearing men's trousers?" he asked suddenly.

She glanced at her blue jeans and giggled. "These aren't men's trousers. They're made for a woman, and they're really quite comfortable." When Eli made no comment, she decided it was her turn to ask another question. "What's your family like?"

"I have a wonderful family. There's Pop and Mom, and I have an older sister, Martha Rose. She's married to Amon Zook, and they've got a three-year-old son. I also have two younger brothers who help Pop on the farm while I'm working at the furniture shop near Strasburg."

"I think it would be interesting if I could see where you live." The unexpected comment popped out of Laura's mouth before she had time to think about what she was saying.

When Eli's brows drew downward and he

31

made no response, she wondered if she had overstepped her bounds. As much as she would like it, she knew she would probably never get to see Eli's house, meet his family, or have another opportunity to ride in an Amish buggy.

It seemed like no time at all before they were pulling into the variety store's parking lot. Eli jumped down and came around to help Laura out of the buggy. When his hands went around her waist, she felt an unexpected shiver tickle her spine. "Thanks for the ride," she said breathlessly. "If I live to a ripe old age, I'll never forget this day."

Laura started across the parking lot and was surprised to see Eli walking beside her. They both stopped when they reached the sidewalk, and Laura glanced at her watch. "I'd better call my friend. We're supposed to meet for supper soon." She pulled her cell phone from her purse.

"Your friend is some lucky fellow."

She smiled. "It's not a man I'm meeting for supper. It's just a girlfriend from school."

"Ah, I see." Eli stared at the ground for a few seconds, then looked back at her. "Say, I was wondering—would you be interested in going back to the lake with me next Saturday? We could take a picnic lunch along, and if you have more questions about my way of life, I'll have a little more time to answer them."

Laura could hardly believe her ears. Had he really asked her on a date? Well, maybe not a date exactly, but at least it was another chance to see him.

"That would be nice," she said, forcing her voice to remain steady. "What should I bring?"

"Just a hearty appetite and a warm jacket. I'll ask Mom to fix the lunch, because she always makes plenty of good food."

"It's a date." Laura felt the heat of a blush creep up the back of her neck and spread to her cheeks. "I mean—I'll look forward to next Saturday. Should we meet here in front of the store, around one o'clock?"

"That'll be fine," he answered with a nod.

"Until next Saturday then." Just before Laura turned toward her car, she looked back and saw him wave as he was walking away. She lifted her hand in response and whispered, "Eli Yoder, where have you been all my life?"

CHAPTER 3

As Laura drove back to Lancaster, all she could think about was Eli. She pictured his twinkling blue eyes, sandy brown hair, and the cute little chin dimple that made him look so irresistible. Eli was full of humor and had a fresh, almost innocent way about him. It was something she'd never seen in Dean Carlson, who had a haughty attitude and seemed to think he was every woman's dream.

She clenched the steering wheel until her knuckles turned white. *What am I thinking here? I can't allow myself to fantasize about Eli or start comparing him to other men. He's off-limits—forbidden fruit for a modern English woman like me.* She grimaced as she pulled up to a stop sign and spotted a closed-in Amish buggy with two little tow-headed boys peeking out the back. *Then why am I reflecting on the time we had together today? And why did I agree to go on a picnic with him next Saturday?*

As hard as Laura tried, she seemed unable to squelch the desire to see Eli one more time. She could learn a bit more about the Amish; they would enjoy a nice picnic lunch and soak up the beauty of the lake; and it would be over. They'd probably never see each other again. She would have pleasant memories of the brief time she'd spent with an intriguing Amish man, and her life would return to normal. It would be a wonderful story to tell her grandchildren someday. She smiled and tried to visualize herself as a grandmother, but the thought was too far removed. The only thing she could see was the face of Eli Yoder calling her to learn more about him and his Plain way of living.

All the way home, Eli thought about Laura and the conversation they'd had on their way to and from the lake. She had asked a lot of questions about his way of life, but he hadn't asked that many about hers. He would have to do that next Saturday, because there were so many things he wanted to know. How long would she be in Lancaster studying at the interior design school? How old was she? Did she have any brothers or sisters? Did she have a boyfriend? That was the one thing he wanted to know the most, and it troubled him deeply, because it shouldn't matter so much.

He could still picture Laura sitting in his buggy, her long auburn hair glistening in the sun like golden shafts of wheat. *I shouldn't be thinking about her, much less worrying over whether she has a boyfriend. Probably shouldn't have invited her to have a picnic with me next Saturday, but I just want to see her one more time. I'd like the chance to answer a few more of her questions and ask a few of my own.*

The family-style restaurant where Laura was to meet Darla seemed crowded, and after checking her watch, Laura knew she was late. She stood in the clogged entryway, craning her neck to see around the people in front of her. Was Darla already in the dining room? Sure enough, she spotted her sitting at one of the tables.

When the hostess seated Laura, she couldn't help but notice Darla's impatience as she tapped her fingernails against her place mat and squinted with obvious displeasure. "It's about time you got here."

"Sorry. I tried to call, but you must have had your phone turned off." Laura pulled out a chair and sat down.

"Were you caught in traffic, or do you just like to make people wait?"

"I went for a ride in an Amish buggy this afternoon, and I guess we lost track of time."

Darla's pale eyebrows furrowed. "I wouldn't think any buggy driver would lose track of time. I mean, they charge you a certain amount, and when the time's up, it's up."

Laura shook her head. "I didn't take a commercial buggy ride. I was with Eli Yoder."

"Who?"

"Eli's that cute Amish guy I met at the market a few weeks ago. I'm sure I mentioned it."

Before Darla could comment, Laura rushed on. "I had such a good time today. The fall colors at the lake were gorgeous." She glanced down at her purse and frowned. "I had my camera with me the whole time, but I forgot to take even one picture."

Darla stared out the window a few seconds;

then she looked back at Laura. "I can't believe what I'm hearing."

"What do you mean?"

"You're obviously starstruck, and I hope you realize that you're making a huge mistake."

"What are you talking about?"

"I can see you're infatuated with this Amish guy, and you'd better not tell me that you plan to see him again, because it can only lead to trouble."

"I'm not *infatuated* with him!" When Laura noticed several people staring, she lowered her voice. "I did enjoy his company, and the buggy ride was exciting, but that's all there was to it. I hardly even know the man."

"Well, good. That means you're not planning to see him again then, right?"

"We did talk about going on a picnic next Saturday." Laura shrugged. "But it's no big deal."

"No big deal? Laura, do you have any idea of the trouble that could come from an Amish man dating an English woman?" Darla leaned across the table. "Don't do it. You need to cancel that date."

Laura's mouth dropped open. "It's not a real date. It's just an innocent picnic. Besides, I can't cancel. I don't have his telephone number, so I have no way of getting in touch with him." She grabbed her menu, hoping this discussion was finally over.

"Some Amish do have telephones now," Darla said, "but usually only those who have businesses. Do you realize that the Plain People live almost like the pioneers used to? They don't use electricity, or drive cars—"

Laura held up her hand. "I get the picture. Can we change the subject now?"

Darla's voice lowered to a whisper. "I want to say one more thing."

Laura merely shrugged. Darla was obviously not going to let this drop until she'd had her say.

"I told you before that I used to live in this area before my folks moved to New York, so I know a little something about the Amish."

"Such as?"

"They don't take kindly to Englishers dating their children, and I'll bet Eli's folks don't know he was with you today, do they?"

Laura hated to be cross-examined. None of this was Darla's business. "I don't know what Eli told them when he went home, but today was the first time we've done anything together."

"The Amish are private people. They live separate, plain lives. They don't like worldly ways—or worldly women for their men." Darla shook her head. "You'd be smart to nip this in the bud before it goes any further."

Laura remained silent. She didn't need Darla's unwanted advice, and she knew exactly what she was doing.

* * *

"Say, Mom, I have a favor to ask," Eli said, when he stepped into the kitchen and headed toward the table where Mary Ellen sat tearing lettuce leaves into a bowl.

She smiled, thinking her oldest boy looked happier than usual this evening. "Oh? What favor is that?"

"I'm going on a picnic to the lake next Saturday, and I was wondering if you'd mind packing a picnic lunch for me to take along."

"How much food did you need?"

He grinned. "As much as you want to fix, I guess."

"For how many people, Eli?" she asked with a groan. *Johnny's silly ways must be rubbing off on our son. He thinks he's a practical joker now.*

"Uh . . . there will be two of us, Mom," Eli mumbled, his face turning red.

She nodded, feeling quite pleased with that bit of news. Eli obviously had a date, and she figured it was probably Pauline, since he'd gone to lunch with her awhile ago when they'd met at the farmers' market. "Anything special you'd like me to fix?"

He shrugged. "Just the usual picnic things, I guess."

"All right, then. I'll put together something that I'm sure both you and your date will like."

The color in Eli's face deepened, and he looked away. "Danki, Mom. I really appreciate that."

When Wesley Meade entered the living room, he found his wife curled up on the couch, reading a book. "Hi, hon. How was your day?" He bent down to kiss her forehead.

"It was all right, I suppose," Irene replied without looking up from her novel.

He set his briefcase on the coffee table and took a seat in the recliner across from her. "Did you do anything special?"

"Helen and I went shopping at the mall, got our nails done, and had lunch at Roberto's. Then on the way home, I stopped at our favorite catering place and ordered the food for the hospital guild's annual charity dinner."

Wesley's gaze went to the ceiling. It seemed all his wife did anymore was shop for new clothes she didn't need and flit from one charity organization to another, planning dinners, parties, and elaborate balls. Not that there was anything wrong with charities. He knew that most of the organizations she was involved with did a lot of good for those in need. However, Irene's emphasis seemed to be more on the social side of things rather than on meeting the needs of people who were hurting or required financial or physical help.

"I got an e-mail from Laura today," he said, changing the subject to something he hoped might interest her.

"Really? What did she have to say?"

"So you didn't check your e-mail?"

Irene's hand fluttered as if she was swatting a fly. "Wesley, you know I rarely use the computer you bought me for Christmas last year."

"Why not? It's got all the whistles and bells anyone could want."

"Maybe so, but every time I go online, I end up either getting booted off or everything freezes on me." She sighed. "I don't think that computer likes me."

He chuckled. "You just need to go on it more. Practice makes—"

"I know. I know. If I practiced more, I'd have it mastered." She swung her legs over the sofa and sat up. "So tell me . . . what did our daughter have to say in her e-mail?"

"She said she's getting settled in at the school and thinks she's going to like it in Lancaster County, where she can study the interesting Amish people."

Irene's perfectly shaped eyebrows drew together, and she reached up to fluff the sides of her shoulder-length auburn hair. "Amish people? Our daughter didn't go to Lancaster to study Amish people; she went to learn how to be an interior designer."

41

"Laura thinks she can get some design ideas from the Plain People."

She clicked her tongue. "That's ridiculous. From what I know of the Amish, they live very simply, without any decorations in their homes that don't serve some sort of purpose. So I don't see how studying the Amish can help Laura with her studies."

"Knowing our enterprising daughter, she'll figure out something about their way of life that she can use in her decorating classes." Wesley stretched his arms over his head and yawned. "Think I'll head upstairs and change into something more comfortable before we have dinner. It'll be a relief to get out of this suit." He undid his tie and slung it over his shoulder as he stood. "Never did like wearing a suit. Wish I could get out of putting one on every day."

She clicked her tongue again. "What kind of lawyer would you be if you didn't wear a suit?"

"A comfortable one."

Irene opened her mouth as if to say something more, but he hurried out of the room. He'd become a lawyer just to please her anyway, and if wearing a suit made her happy, then he'd probably end up wearing one until the day he died.

CHAPTER 4

Laura had been sitting on the wooden bench in front of the variety store for nearly an hour. Still no sign of Eli. *Where is he? Maybe he isn't coming. Maybe Darla's right and he's decided it's best not to have anything to do with a "worldly" woman. I'll give him another five minutes; then I'm leaving.*

She scanned the parking lot again. Several Amish buggies sat parked there, but they were all the closed-in type. Eli's courting buggy was nowhere in sight. She watched as an Amish family went into the store. *I wonder how those women deal with wearing long dresses all the time. If Eli ever shows up, I'll have to remember to ask him why they wear those little white caps on top of their heads.*

She glanced at her watch again—1:45.

Finally at 1:50, his buggy pulled into the parking lot. Laura felt such relief, she was no longer angry. She waved and skittered across the parking lot.

Eli climbed down from the buggy. "Sorry to be so late. I had to help my daed and brothers with some chores at home, and it took longer than expected."

"It's okay. You're here now; that's all that matters."

Eli gave her a boost up into the buggy, then went around and took his seat. He glanced up at the sky. "There's not a cloud in sight, so it should be a fine day for a picnic." He grinned at Laura, and her heart skipped a beat. "Did you bring a jacket? Even though the sun's out, it's still kind of chilly."

Laura shook her head. "I'm wearing a sweater, so I'll be fine."

Eli picked up the reins and said something in Pennsylvania Dutch to the horse.

"What'd you say just then?"

His face turned crimson. "I told him I was taking a beautiful young woman on a ride to the lake so he'd better behave himself."

Laura's heart kept time to the *clip-clop* of the horse's hooves. "Thank you for such a nice compliment."

Eli only nodded in response.

They traveled in silence the rest of the way, but Laura found being in Eli's company made words seem almost unnecessary.

The air snapped with the sharpness of autumn, and soon the lake came into view. If it was possible, the picturesque scene was even more beautiful than it had been the week before. Maple leaves lay scattered about, reminding Laura of the colorful patchwork quilt lying on her bed.

The sun cast a golden tint against the surrounding hills, and a whippoorwill called from somewhere in the trees. Laura relished the sense of tranquility that washed over her like a gentle spring rain.

As Eli helped her out of the buggy, she slid effortlessly into his arms. Raising her gaze to meet his, her breath caught in her throat at the intensity she saw on his face. Her pulse quickened, and she grabbed her camera, hoping the action would get her thinking straight again. She photographed the scenery, being careful not to point the camera in Eli's direction, but it was a sacrifice not to snap a few pictures of his handsome face. How fun it would be to download them to her laptop and send them on to her friend Shannon back home. Shannon would probably get a kick out of seeing how cute Eli looked wearing a pair of dark trousers, a pale blue shirt peeking out from a dark jacket, and a straw hat.

Eli pulled a heavy quilt and a wicker basket from under the buggy seat. After they'd stretched the quilt on the ground, they both took seats. When Eli opened the lid of the basket, Laura was shocked to discover more food than two people could possibly eat. She figured she would have to count calories for the rest of the week.

Eli spread a tablecloth over the quilt, then set out several containers that held fried chicken, coleslaw, dill pickles, wheat bread, Swiss cheese, baked beans, and chocolate cake. He smiled as he handed Laura a glass of iced tea, some plastic silverware, and a paper plate.

"Thank you."

"You're welcome." His face turned a light shade of red. "Uh . . . will you bow your head with me for silent prayer?"

She gave a quick nod, and Eli immediately bowed his head. Having never believed much in prayer, Laura sat quietly, waiting for him to finish.

When he opened his eyes again, she smiled. "It was nice of your mother to prepare this. Especially since she doesn't know me."

Eli's face turned even redder as he reached for a drumstick. "I . . . uh . . . didn't tell Mom about you."

"Why not?"

He removed his straw hat and placed it on the quilt. "Even though I'm still going through my rumschpringe, my folks wouldn't take kindly to the idea of me seeing someone outside our faith."

"Rumschpringe? What's that?"

"Rumschpringe means 'running around.' It's a time in the life of an Amish young person before he or she gets baptized and joins the church. It's a chance for him to explore the outside world a bit if he chooses."

"Ah, I see."

"My folks think I'm too old to be running around still, and as I mentioned last week, they've been pressuring me to join the church and get married."

She gave him a sidelong glance. "If you didn't tell your mother about me, then why did she pack such a big lunch?"

"I told her I was going on a picnic, but I'm sure she thought it was with someone else." Eli reached for another piece of chicken. "Is there anything more you'd like to know about the Amish?"

Laura sighed. Apparently Eli wasn't that different from other men. If he didn't like the way the conversation was going, he simply changed the subject. "When did your religion first begin?" she inquired.

"Our church got its start in the late sixteen hundreds when a young Swiss Mennonite bishop named Jacob Amman felt his church was losing some of its purity," Eli began. "He and several followers formed a new Christian fellowship, later known as 'Amish.' So, you might say we're cousins of the Mennonites."

Laura nodded as Eli continued. "The Old Order Amish, which is what my family belongs to, believes in separation of church and state. We also expect Bible-centeredness to be an important part of our faith. A peaceful way of life and complying with all nonworldly ways

47

are involved, and we believe it's the way Christ meant for the Church to be."

"Life among your people sounds almost idealistic."

He shook his head. "It may seem that way to outsiders, but underneath the joys and blessings of being Amish lie special challenges and the hardship of keeping separate in an ever-changing world."

"I guess that makes sense." Laura ate in silence for a time, savoring the delicious assortment of food and trying to absorb all that Eli had shared. She knew about some Protestant religions and had attended Sunday school a few times while growing up. The Amish religion was more complex than anything she knew about, but she found it rather fascinating.

"Now it's your turn to answer some of my questions," Eli said suddenly.

"What do you want to know?"

He shrugged. "Guess you can start by telling me how old you are and whether you have any brothers or sisters."

"I'm twenty-two, and I'm an only child."

"How long will you be staying in Lancaster County?"

"Just until I finish my studies, which should take no longer than two years. Unless I mess up and flunk some classes, that is," she added with a frown.

"You seem real smart to me. I'm sure you'll do okay."

"Thanks, I sure hope so." She smiled. "Anything else you'd like to know?"

Eli's ears turned pink as he stared out at the lake. "I imagine a pretty woman like you has a boyfriend—maybe more than one, even. Am I right about that?"

Laura snickered. "You're really direct and to the point, aren't you, Eli?"

"My folks would say so." He turned back to look at her and chuckled.

She toyed with the edge of the quilt a few seconds, then stared into his seeking blue eyes. "I've dated several men, but none have ever captured my heart." *At least not until you came along.*

Was that a look of relief she saw on Eli's face? No, it was probably just wishful thinking on her part.

The wind had picked up slightly, and Laura shivered, pulling her sweater tightly around her shoulders.

"You're cold. Here, take my coat." Eli removed his jacket and draped it across her shoulders.

Laura fought the impulse to lean her head against his chest. The temptation didn't linger, because the sound of horse's hooves drew her attention to an open buggy pulling into the grassy area near their picnic spot.

A young Amish woman, wearing a dark bonnet on her head and an angry scowl on her face, climbed down from the buggy. Laura thought she recognized the girl, and her fears were confirmed when Eli called, "Pauline, what are you doing here?"

"I was looking for you, Eli. I stopped by your farm, but Lewis said you had gone to the lake for a picnic. I couldn't think who you might be with, but now I see who has taken my place." Pauline planted both hands on her hips as her frown deepened. "I'm mighty disappointed, Eli. How could you bring this Englisher here?"

Eli jumped up and moved toward Pauline. He placed one hand on her shoulder, but she brushed it aside. "She's that woman you were showing birdhouses to at the market, isn't she?"

Eli glanced back at Laura, his face turning redder by the minute. "Pauline, this is Laura Meade."

Pauline's lips were set in a thin line, and she glared at Laura as though she were her worst enemy.

Laura didn't feel much like smiling, but she forced one anyway. "It's nice to meet you, Pauline."

"You're involved in something you shouldn't be, Eli," Pauline said without acknowledging Laura's greeting. *"Wann der gaul dod is, drauere batt nix."*

50

Eli grunted. "You're being ridiculous, Pauline."

"I don't think so, and you'll see what I mean if you don't wake up soon and join the church."

"That's my business, not yours."

Pauline turned away in a huff. "And to think, I came all the way out here for this! I deserve much better." She rushed back to her buggy and scrambled inside. "Enjoy your *wunderbaar schee* picnic!"

"Jah, I will," Eli called back to her.

Laura sat too stunned to speak and struggled to analyze what had just happened.

Pauline drove out of sight, leaving a cloud of dust in her wake. She was obviously Eli's girl-friend.

As Pauline drove away, she clamped her teeth together so tightly that it caused her jaw to ache. *How could Eli have made plans for a picnic with that Laura person, who isn't even of our faith? I thought Eli and I were drawing closer. After two rides home in his courting buggy following singings and having had lunch together recently at the farmers' market, I thought we were officially courting.*

She snapped the reins and got the horse moving faster. Maybe some wind in her face would help her think more clearly.

What I should do is drive over to Eli's place and see if his folks know where he is right now.

51

I'll bet they have no idea he's having a picnic with a fancy English woman who wears sweet perfume and way too much makeup.

Pauline continued to fume as she drove down the road, but by the time she neared the cross street that would take her to Eli's place, she had calmed down enough to think things through a bit more. *If I run tattling to Eli's folks, Mary Ellen will probably say something to Eli about it, and then he'll be angry with me. If that happens, I might never have a chance at winning his heart.*

She shook her head and directed the horse to keep going past the road to Eli's house. If she was ever to win Eli over, she would have to find some other way to do it.

As Eli dropped to the quilt, Laura offered him a tentative smile. "Guess I owe you an apology."

"For what? You did nothing wrong."

"I caused a bit of a rift between you and your girlfriend."

Eli shifted on the blanket. "Pauline's not my girlfriend, although I think she'd like to be. We've been friends since we were kinner."

Laura tipped her head. "Kinner?"

"Children."

"If you've been friends that long, then it's obvious to me she was jealous."

"How do you know that?"

52

"You saw how upset she got. Only a woman in love shoots sparks the way she did."

Eli shrugged. "I'm sorry if she's jealous, but I've done nothing wrong, and neither have you."

"Nothing but have a picnic with an Englisher. I couldn't understand the Pennsylvania Dutch words you two were speaking. What were you saying?"

Eli fiddled with the end of the tablecloth. "Let's see. . . . She said, 'Wann der gaul dod is, drauere batt nix.' That means, 'After the horse is dead, grieving does no good.' "

"I don't get it."

"I think she meant that I made a mistake in asking you to have a picnic with me and that it will do no good to grieve once I find out how wrong it was."

Laura wrinkled her nose. "Is having a picnic with me really so wrong?"

"In Pauline's eyes it is." Eli grunted. "My folks would probably think so, too."

"She said something else I didn't understand. I think it was 'wonderbar' something or other."

He nodded. "Wunderbaar schee. It means 'wonderful nice.' "

"It's obvious that Pauline doesn't like me."

He frowned. "How can you say that? She doesn't even know you."

"That's true, but she knows you, and she's

clearly in love with you. I think she's afraid I might be interested, too."

The rhythm of Eli's heartbeat picked up speed. "Are you?"

"Yes, I am interested. You're different from any other man I've ever met." Laura scooted across the quilt and stood. "I don't want to make trouble for you, so maybe it would be better if we say good-bye and go our separate ways." She took a step back and tripped on a rock. The next thing Eli knew, Laura had a face full of water.

As Laura sputtered and attempted to sit up, Eli rushed forward, reaching for her hand and helping her stand.

"I—I can't believe I did that." She stared down at her soggy, wet clothes and grimaced. "Look at me. I'm a mess!"

Eli's lips twitched as he struggled not to laugh. "You are pretty wet, and you might get sick if you don't get your clothes dried soon." He nodded toward his buggy. "How about I take you to my place so you can get dried off?"

"Are . . . are your folks at home?" Laura's teeth had begun to chatter, and goose bumps erupted on her arms.

"Probably so—at least Mom."

"How do you know your family won't disapprove of you bringing me there?"

Eli shrugged. "Guess there's only one way to find out."

Laura held her stomach and took a deep breath, as though she were having trouble getting enough air.

"Are you okay? Did you swallow some water?"

She nodded. "A little, but I'm more worried about meeting your mother than anything else. What if she doesn't like me? What if she throws me off your property or disowns you because you brought me there?"

Eli snickered. "I hardly think either of my folks would throw you off the property or disown me." He motioned to the food. "Let's put the leftovers away and head over to my place before you freeze to death."

"Okay. I—I think I do need to get warmed up a bit."

CHAPTER 5

As they traveled down the road in Eli's buggy, Eli explained that his father's farm was situated on sixty acres of dark, fertile land, and as they approached the fields he spoke of, he mentioned that they had been planted in alfalfa, corn, and wheat.

"They remind me of a quilt—rich, lush, orderly, and serene," Laura said, as she snuggled beneath the quilt Eli had wrapped around her before they'd left the lake.

Eli smiled. "You sure do have a way with words, you know that?"

She shrugged. "I'm just expressing the way I see things."

An expansive white house came into view, surrounded by a variety of trees and shrubs, while an abundance of autumn blooms dotted the flower beds. Laura spotted a windmill not far from the home, turning slowly in the breeze as it cast a shadow over the tall, white barn directly behind the house. There were no telephone or power lines on the property, she noted, but a waterwheel grated rhythmically in the creek nearby, offering a natural source of power. There was also a huge propane tank sitting beside the house. Laura assumed it was used for heat or to run some of the Amish family's appliances.

"This is it," Eli said with a sweeping gesture. "This is where I live."

Laura's gaze traveled around the neat-looking farm. Sheep and goats stood inside a fenced corral, and chickens ran about in a small enclosure. On the clothesline hung several pairs of men's trousers, a few dark cotton dresses, and a row of towels pinned in orderly fashion.

"Here you go; this should help." Eli grabbed a towel from the line for Laura and led her around the house and up the steps of a wide back porch.

When they entered the kitchen, Laura's mouth fell open. She felt as if she'd entered a time warp and had stepped back in time. The sweet smell of cinnamon and apples permeated the room, drawing Laura's attention to the wood-burning stove in one corner of the room. No curtains hung on the windows, only dark shades pulled halfway down. Except for a small, battery-operated clock and one simple calendar, the stark white walls were bare.

A huge wooden table sat in the middle of the kitchen, with long benches on either side, and two straight-backed chairs, one at each end. A gas lantern hung overhead, with a smaller kerosene lamp sitting in the center of the table. Against one wall stood a tall, wooden cabinet, and a long counter flanked both sides of the sink. Strategically placed near a massive stone fireplace sat a sturdy-looking rocking chair.

Eli motioned to the stove. "Why don't you stand over there? The heat from the stove will help your clothes dry."

Like a statue, Laura stood as close to the stove as she dared. "Do all Amish live this way?"

Eli moved across the room. "What way?"

"So little furnishings. There aren't any pictures on the walls and no window curtains. Everything looks so bare." Laura rubbed her arms briskly with the towel and then did the same with her stringy, wet hair.

"The Old Order Amish believe only what serves as necessary is needed in the home. Although I must admit that my folks live more simply than some in our community."

This home was like no other Laura had ever seen. Here was a group of people living in the modern world yet having so little to do with it.

Eli looked a bit uncomfortable when a slightly plump Amish woman entered the room. Her brown hair, streaked with a bit of gray, was parted down the middle and worn in a bun at the back of her head. A small, white head covering was perched on top of her head, just like all the other Amish women Laura had seen in the area. The woman's hazel-colored eyes held a note of question when she spotted Laura.

"Uh . . . Mom, I'd like you to meet Laura Meade." Eli motioned to Laura, then back to his mother. "This is my mamm, Mary Ellen Yoder."

Eli's mother gave a quick nod in Laura's direction. Her forehead wrinkled as she looked back at Eli. "What in all the world?"

She doesn't like me. The woman's just met me, and she's already decided that I'm the enemy. Laura forced a smile. "It's nice to meet you, Mrs. Yoder."

Mary Ellen grunted and moved toward the stove, where she began to stir the big pot of simmering apples. "Do you live around here, Laura?"

"No, I . . . uh . . ."

"Has your car broken down, or are you lost and in need of directions?" She stared at Laura and squinted. "And why are your clothes all wet?"

"Laura's from Minneapolis, Minnesota, Mom," Eli said, before Laura had a chance to respond. "She attends a designer school in Lancaster, and she fell in the lake while we were—"

Mary Ellen whirled around to face Eli. "You know this woman?"

"We met at the farmers' market a few weeks ago. Laura was interested in my birdhouses, and I've been showing her around."

Mary Ellen's gaze went to the wicker basket in Eli's hand. "You two have been on a picnic at the lake?"

"Jah."

"It's beautiful there," Laura put in. "The lunch you made was wonderful."

Before Eli's mother could respond, the kitchen door flew open, and two young Amish men sauntered into the room. They spoke in their native tongue but fell silent when they noticed Laura standing beside Eli and Mrs. Yoder near the stove.

"These are my younger brothers, Lewis and Jonas." Eli motioned to the rowdy pair. "Boys, this is Laura Meade. We met at the farmers' market, and I took her on a picnic today, but she ended up falling in the lake."

Lewis removed his straw hat, revealing a thick crop of dark, Dutch-bobbed hair. Then he nudged Jonas and chuckled. "It looks mighty nice around here, jah?"

Jonas nodded and removed his hat as well. "It sure does."

Laura felt their scrutiny all the way to her toes, and she knew the heat of a blush had stained her cheeks. "It's nice to meet you."

Turning to his mother, Jonas said, "Pop will be right in. Have you got any lemonade? We've worked up quite a thirst out there in the fields."

Mary Ellen nodded and moved across the room to the refrigerator.

Jonas, who had light brown hair and blue eyes like Eli's, pulled out one of the benches at the table. "Why don't you set yourself down and talk awhile, Laura?"

Laura glanced at Eli to see if he approved, but he merely leaned against the cupboard and smiled at her. His mother was already pouring huge glasses of lemonade, while her two youngest boys hung their hats on wall pegs and took seats at the table.

Laura would have expected Eli's brothers to have reacted more strongly to a stranger in wet clothes standing in their kitchen, but maybe they were used to having uninvited guests show up out of the blue.

She had the distinct feeling that Mrs. Yoder would be happy to see her leave, however, and she was about to decline the invitation when Eli spoke up. "I think Laura could probably use something hot to drink, and some of those ginger cookies you made yesterday would be nice, too, Mom."

With a curt nod, Mary Ellen scooped several handfuls of cookies from a ceramic jar, piled them on a plate, and brought it over to the table. Then she poured some coffee from the pot at the back of the stove into a cup and handed it to Laura without even asking if she would like some cream or sugar.

"Thank you."

"Welcome."

Lewis and Jonas dropped to one bench, and Laura sat beside Eli on the other one. Her hair and clothes were somewhat drier now, and since the table was near the stove, she figured she would be nearly dry by the time she finished her coffee.

Eli made small talk with his brothers about the weather and their work in the fields, and occasionally Laura interrupted with a question or two. She was getting an education in Amish culture that rivaled anything she had ever read about or seen on any postcard.

They were nearly finished with their refreshments when the back door swung open, and a tall, husky man with grayish-brown hair and a full beard lumbered into the room. He slung his straw hat over one of the wall pegs near the door, then went to wash up at the sink. All conversation at the table ceased, and Laura waited expectantly to see what would happen next.

The older man dried his hands on a towel, then took a seat in the chair at the other end of the table. He glanced at Laura but said nothing. Maybe he was used to seeing strangers in their house, too.

Eli decided he needed to break the silence. "Laura, this is my daed, Johnny Yoder. Pop, I'd like you to meet Laura Meade."

Laura nodded. "Hello, Mr. Yoder."

Pop gave a quick nod, then turned to Mom, who was now chopping vegetables at the kitchen counter. "What's to eat?"

Mom's face was stoic as she replied in Pennsylvania Dutch, "Our guest is having coffee, and the rest are having lemonade and cookies. What would you like?"

Pop grunted. "Coffee, please."

Mom brought the coffeepot and cup to the table and placed it in front of Pop.

"Danki," he muttered.

Eli turned to his father again. "Laura's from Minneapolis, Minnesota. She's attending some fancy school in Lancaster, and I've been showing her around the area."

"The wisdom of the world is foolishness," Pop grumbled in his native language.

Eli grimaced. "There's no need to be going rude on my guest."

"Ah, so the Englisher can't understand the *Deitsch*. Is this the problem?" Pop asked with a flick of his wrist.

"What kind of fancy school do you go to, Laura?" Lewis questioned.

"I'm learning to be an interior decorator."

"It's so she can help folks decorate their homes," Eli interjected.

Mom placed another plate of cookies on the table. "It wonders me so that anyone could put such emphasis on worldly things."

"As I said before, Laura and I went to the lake for a picnic," Eli said, changing the subject to what he hoped was safer ground. "It's sure beautiful there now. Some of the leaves are beginning to fall."

"I'll be glad when wintertime comes and the lake freezes over," Jonas added. "I always enjoy goin' ice-skating."

Eli noticed that Laura's hand trembled as she set her cup down. He wasn't the least bit surprised when she hopped off the bench and announced, "Eli, my clothes are drier now, so I think I should be going."

He sprang to his feet. "I'm gonna drive Laura back to Paradise so she can pick up her car. I'll be home in plenty of time for chores and supper."

When no one responded, Eli opened the back door so he and Laura could make a hasty exit. "That didn't go so well, did it?" he mumbled a few minutes later, as he helped her into the buggy.

"No, it didn't, and I'm sorry for putting you through all that. Your parents obviously don't approve of me."

"Don't worry about it. We're just friends. I'm sure they know that."

Laura twisted the ends of her purse straps, biting down on her lower lip. "Maybe it would be better if you never saw me again."

"No," Eli was quick to say. "I want to be your friend, and I'll be glad to show you around more of the area whenever you like."

"Even if your parents disapprove?"

He shrugged. "Pop and Mom are really fun-loving, easygoing folks, and since we're not courting or anything, there's nothing for them to be concerned about."

Laura looked a little disappointed. Was she hoping they could begin courting? No, that was about as likely as a sow giving birth to a kitten.

"How about next Saturday?" she asked. "Could you show me around then?"

He nodded. "Jah, I think I could."

　＊ ＊ ＊

As the door clicked shut behind Eli, Mary Ellen turned to Johnny and frowned. "This isn't good. Not good at all."

Johnny glanced at Lewis and Jonas, then nodded toward the living room, across the hall. "Why don't you two go in there awhile? Your mamm and me need to talk."

Jonas grabbed a handful of cookies and his glass of lemonade, then headed out of the room. Lewis did the same.

"Now let's talk this through," Johnny said, turning his chair to face Mary Ellen.

She moaned and let her head fall forward into her hands. "What are we going to do about Eli and that fancy English woman?"

"Since Eli's not joined the church yet, I doubt there's much we can do except look the other way."

Mary Ellen lifted her head. "We can't just stand by and let him be led astray."

Johnny reached over and took hold of her hand. "Now don't go borrowing trouble. Maybe Eli has just been showing Laura around, like he said. Might not be anything more to it than that."

"I hope you're right. It would break my heart if any of our kinner were to leave the Amish faith."

Eli returned home an hour later, just in time for supper. He was glad when neither of his parents

65

brought up the subject of Laura, but just as they were finishing with the meal, Jonas spoke up.

"That English woman you brought home is sure pretty, Eli. Too bad she isn't Amish, because if she was, I'd be tempted to court her."

Mom let out a little squeal and pushed away from the table, and Pop just sat there with his eyes squinted, looking kind of befuddled.

"She's not trying to make you go fancy, is she, Eli?" The question came from Lewis, and it was followed by a jab to Eli's ribs.

"Of course not. Laura's just a friend who wants to know a little something about the way we live. I only brought her home after her fall in the lake so she could get dried off a bit."

"You play with fire, and you're bound to get burned," Mom mumbled from across the room, where she stood in front of a sink full of soapy water. "There's always trouble somewhere, and that Englisher had trouble written all over her pretty face."

Eli shook his head. "I'm old enough to make my own decisions, don't you think?"

Jonas grinned. "I'm thinkin' my big brother might be in *lieb*."

"I'm not in love! As I've already said, Laura and I are just friends, and I don't see how it could hurt for me to spend a little time showing her around the countryside and sharing a bit about our ways."

"Why would she need to know our ways?" Mom asked.

"She's just curious about our lifestyle, and I think—"

"A few questions here, and a few trips around the country there, and soon that woman will be trying to talk you into leaving the faith."

Eli felt his face heat up. "No way, Mom!"

"I'm sure our son is secure in his faith," Pop interjected. "He needs some time to think about what he's doing. If I know my boy right, he'll soon realize that it's time to get baptized, join the church, and find a nice Amish wife." He thumped Eli on the back. "Ain't that right, son?"

Eli swallowed the last bit of food in his mouth before he answered. "Are you forbidding me to see Laura again?"

Pop shook his head. "No, you have the right to choose, and since we haven't raised any *dummkepp*—dunces—I'm sure you'll choose wisely."

Eli pushed away from the table and stood. "I think I'll go out to my shop awhile." He made a hasty exit out the back door before anyone could respond.

Laura collapsed onto her bed. She felt as if she hadn't slept in days. By the time Eli had dropped her off in front of the variety store where she'd left her car, all her energy had been zapped. The thrill she had felt earlier when she'd been alone with Eli at the lake had diminished some, too.

Until today, Laura had usually been able to charm anyone she met. Not only had she not charmed Eli's parents, but she was quite sure that she'd probably alienated them. If they had known that she was hoping to see Eli again and had even fantasized about asking him to leave the Amish faith and join her in the modern English world, she was sure they would have told her to leave their home at once.

Laura looked forward to her date with Eli next Saturday, but she knew she would have to take things slow and easy. She didn't want to scare Eli off by making him think there was more to their relationship than friendship. That's all there was at this point, but she was hoping for more—so much more.

Chapter 6

Saturday dawned with an ugly, gray sky and depressing, drizzling rain. Laura groaned as she stared out the window of her dorm room. She figured Eli probably wouldn't show up for their rendezvous now. If they went for another buggy ride, they would be drenched in no time, and she doubted that he would want to pass the time sitting in some restaurant or wandering through a bunch of tourist-filled souvenir shops with her. They weren't supposed to meet until two o'clock, so with any luck, maybe the rain would be gone by then.

Laura turned from the window and ambled over to her desk, fully intending to get in a few hours of study time. Her mind seemed unwilling to cooperate, however, so she pushed the books aside and painted her fingernails instead.

By noon, the drizzle had turned into a full-fledged downpour. Laura could only hope Eli wouldn't stand her up.

She hurried downstairs and was almost to the door, when Darla showed up in the hallway.

"From the way you're dressed, I'd say you're going out. What I'd like to know is where you're heading on a crummy day like this."

Laura offered a brief smile and held up her green umbrella. "I'm going to Paradise."

Darla's forehead wrinkled. "I figured you would be up in your room studying for that test we'll be having on Monday."

Laura shrugged. "I can't concentrate on school-work today. Besides, I'm supposed to meet Eli at the variety store."

Darla's frown deepened. "Are you chasing after that Amish fellow?"

"Of course not. Eli and I are just friends, and

he's offered to show me around the area. That's all there is to it."

"Yeah, right."

"It's the truth."

"Well, do whatever you want, but don't come crying to me when you get your toes stepped on."

Laura turned toward the door. "I've got to go. See you later, Darla."

"Where are you heading?" Mary Ellen asked as Eli started for the back door. "Out to work in your shop?"

He turned to face her. "Thought I'd go to the farmers' market today."

"Did you rent a table again?"

"Nope. Figured I'd just browse a bit. See if there's anyone else selling handmade wooden items and maybe pick up an idea or two."

Mary Ellen motioned toward the refrigerator. "We're about out of root beer. If you see some of the good homemade kind, would you pick up a couple of jugs?"

"Jah, sure. Anything else you'd like me to get?"

She contemplated a moment, then shook her head. "Guess not, but knowing me, I'll think of something after you've gone."

He chuckled and headed out the door. "I'll be home by suppertime, Mom. See you then."

Mary Ellen moved over to the sink with the last of the breakfast dishes. She would let them soak while she drank a cup of coffee and read the Amish newspaper. "Sure hope that boy of mine isn't meeting the fancy English girl he brought over here last week," she muttered as she ran water into the sink. "The last thing this family needs is for Eli to fall in love with someone outside our faith and decide to leave."

As Pauline stepped onto the Yoders' back porch, she had second thoughts about her decision to see Eli. What if he became irritated with her for coming over? Would he still be angry because she'd interrupted his picnic at the lake last Saturday? She had to know. She had to work things out with Eli. She needed to make him realize that she was right for him, not some Englisher who probably wanted to try and change him.

Drawing in a deep breath, Pauline opened the door and stuck her head inside. "Anyone to home?"

"I'm in the kitchen," Eli's mother called in return.

Pauline stepped into the kitchen and spotted Mary Ellen sitting at the table with a newspaper spread out before her and a cup in her hand. "Are you busy?"

"Just reading *The Budget* and having a cup of

71

coffee. Come join me." Mary Ellen smiled and motioned Pauline to take a seat.

Pauline pulled out a chair across from Eli's mother and sat down.

"It's good to see you. Did you come to visit with Eli or me?"

Pauline's cheeks warmed. Apparently Mary Ellen knew she had an interest in her son. "I came to see Eli. Is he here?"

Mary Ellen shook her head. "Left a few minutes ago for the farmers' market."

"Does he have a table again today?"

"Not this time. Said he just wanted to browse around."

"I see. Did he go there alone?"

"He left here by himself, but I'm not sure what happened after that." Mary Ellen's eyebrows drew together. "I may be speaking out of turn, but I'm a bit *bekimmere* about my son, and I'm thinking maybe you can help."

Pauline leaned forward, her elbows resting on the table. "How come you're concerned, and how can I be of help?"

Mary Ellen's voice lowered to a whisper, although Pauline didn't know why, since they were alone in the kitchen. "Eli has an English friend. He brought her here last Saturday."

"Does she have long reddish brown hair and a pretty face?"

"Jah."

72

"Her name's Laura, and Eli met her at the farmers' market a few weeks ago. She was at his table looking at birdhouses when I went there to see if he was ready to have lunch." Pauline nibbled on her lower lip as she contemplated whether to tell Eli's mother about her encounter with Eli and Laura at the lake. As she thought it through, she came to the conclusion that if Mary Ellen had already met Laura and had some concerns, she might already know about the picnic.

Pauline sat up straight. "I saw Eli with Laura at the lake last Saturday. They were having a picnic."

Mary Ellen nodded. "He told us about that, and I wasn't pleased with the news. When I fixed a picnic lunch for him that morning, I figured he was taking you to the lake."

"I had thought Eli and I were drawing close —that we were officially courting." Pauline swallowed around the lump that had lodged in her throat. "Now I'm afraid I might be losing him to that fancy English woman."

Mary Ellen reached across the table and patted Pauline's outstretched hand. "We can't let that happen. If we work together on this, I believe we can get my son thinking straight again." Her lips curved into a smile. "Are you willing to help me?"

"Jah, sure." Pauline would walk across the

country and back again if it meant getting her and Eli together.

Laura stepped out of her car just in time to witness a touching scene. Eli stood in front of the variety store, holding a black umbrella over his head. The minute he spotted Laura, he stepped forward and positioned the umbrella over her.

She smiled up at him, her heart pounding with expectation. "I'm surprised to see you."

"I said I'd meet you here."

"I thought the rain might keep you from coming."

"We Amish don't stay home because of a little rain." Eli steered her across the parking lot. "I brought one of our closed-in buggies today, but if you'd rather we take your car, that's okay, too."

Laura's heart beat a staccato rhythm, and when she felt the warmth of his hand on her elbow, she realized his touch was something she could easily become accustomed to. "The buggy's fine with me."

Eli helped her into the left side of the gray, box-shaped buggy, then went around to the driver's side.

"Where are we going?"

"The farmers' market is open today. I thought maybe we could go there."

"That sounds like fun." Laura glanced over at

Eli. Her heart felt light, and she was content just being with him, so it didn't really matter where they went.

"How come you're not selling your wooden things there today?"

"Because I'm here with you." He grinned and gathered up the reins. "I don't rent a table every week, and it will be fun just to look around."

She smiled. "Maybe I'll get some more decorating ideas, too."

When they entered the farmers' market a short time later, Laura noticed a host of people roaming up and down the aisles. "The rain didn't keep anyone at home today, did it?" she whispered to Eli.

"Nope, it sure didn't." He motioned to a table on their left. "Let's start over there."

Laura noticed several people staring at them. *What a strange-looking couple we must make: Eli dressed in his plain Amish clothes, and me wearing designer blue jeans and a monogrammed sweatshirt.* "Well, let them stare," she murmured.

"What was that?" Eli asked, as he moved close to a table where a man sold small wooden windmills.

"Nothing. I was talking to myself."

Eli let out a low whistle as he picked up one of the windmills. "Finely crafted—jah, very nice."

"It is nice," Laura agreed.

"Are you hungry? Want something to eat or drink?" he asked when they finally moved on.

"No, but if you're hungry, I'll drink a diet soda and watch you eat."

Eli gently pinched her arm. "A diet soda for someone so skinny?"

"I am not skinny. I'm merely trying to keep my figure."

Eli's ears turned red as he looked her up and down. "Your figure looks fine to me."

Laura giggled self-consciously. "Thanks for the compliment, but for your information, this shape doesn't come easy. I have to work at staying slender, and that means watching what I eat."

Eli raised his dark eyebrows as he continued to study her. "One so pretty shouldn't be concerned about gaining a few pounds. Mom's pleasantly plump, and Pop says he likes her that way."

"You'll never catch me in any kind of plump state—pleasantly or otherwise."

"Someday you'll meet a great guy, get married, and have a whole house full of kinner. Then you probably won't even have a figure, much less have to worry about keepin' it." Eli chuckled and steered her toward the snack bar at one end of the market.

"I told you, I'm not hungry."

"Oh, sure you are." He sniffed the air. "Don't those hot dogs and sausages smell good?"

She wrinkled her nose. "They smell fattening to me."

"If you ask me, you're way too concerned about your weight."

"I don't recall asking you."

Eli jerked his head as though he'd been slapped. "Maybe today wasn't such a good idea after all. Might be better if I take you back to Paradise."

"No, I don't want to go back." Laura clutched at his shirtsleeve. "I'm sorry if I sounded snappish."

They had reached the snack bar, and Eli turned to face her. "Our worlds are so different, Laura. I'm plain, and you're fancy. I see things differently than you do, and I'm afraid it will always be so."

Laura shook her head, her eyes misting with tears. "We're just getting to know each other. It will take some time for us to understand one another's ways." She smiled up at him. "I can teach you things about my way of life, and you can teach me more of the Amish ways."

"I already know all I need to know about the English ways, but if you're still wanting to know more about the Amish way of life, I'm willing." Eli motioned to the snack bar. "Can I interest you in a glass of root beer and a giant, homemade pretzel?"

Laura nodded and released a sigh. "Oh, all

right. I guess I can count calories some other time."

Pauline wandered up and down the aisles inside the market building, searching for Eli. There was no sign of him anywhere, and she wondered if he had even come here today. Maybe he'd just told his mother he was going to the farmers' market, when in fact he'd made plans to meet that English woman again. Maybe they'd gone on another picnic at the lake.

She shook her head. No, that wasn't likely since it had been raining all morning.

"*Wie geht's*—how are you, Pauline?" Anna Beachy asked as she strolled up to her.

"I'm fine. And you?"

"Oh, fair to middlin'. Are you here alone, or did you come with your folks?"

"I'm alone. Came by to see if I could find Eli Yoder. Have you seen him around the market anywhere?"

Anna nodded. "Saw him over at Amos Hilty's root-beer stand about ten minutes ago. He was with some English woman, which I thought was pretty strange."

"Did you speak to him?"

"Just long enough to say hello, but then before I had a chance to say anything more, Eli said he was on his way out. He grabbed two jugs of root beer and rushed off like he was in a big hurry."

Pauline felt as if her heart had sunk all the way to her toes. Not only had she missed seeing Eli, but her fears had been confirmed—he was with Laura again.

"I was just heading over to the snack bar to get a German sausage," Anna said. "If you haven't had lunch yet, maybe you'd like to join me."

Pauline shook her head. "Thanks anyway, but I'm not so hungry." She turned toward the exit door as a feeling of defeat threatened to weigh her down. At the rate things were going, she would never get Eli to marry her.

That evening, Laura lay on her bed, replaying the events of the day. As strange as it might seem, she was glad she and Eli had experienced the little disagreement about her weight. Despite the dissension it had caused, for the remainder of the day, Eli had been quite compromising.

A knock on the door stirred Laura from her musings. "Who is it?"

"Darla."

Laura crawled off the bed and opened the door. "If you've come to give me another lecture, you can save your breath."

Darla shook her head. "I wanted to apologize and see how your day went."

Laura motioned her inside. "Actually, it went well. Eli and I drove to the farmers' market in

Bird-in-Hand, and I got a few more decorating ideas while we were there."

Darla flopped onto the bed. "The Amish don't believe in fancy decorations or adornments in their homes, Laura."

"That's what makes it so unique."

"I don't follow."

Laura dropped down next to Darla, and her fingers trailed across the edge of the quilt covering her bed. "Take this, for example. It's plain, yet strikingly beautiful. A quilt such as this is in high demand, which is why it was so costly."

Darla shrugged. "To be perfectly honest, Amish decor doesn't do much for me. Neither do Amish men."

Laura clenched her jaw. She had a feeling this conversation might lead to another argument, and she wasn't in the mood for one. "It's been a long day, and I'm tired. Besides, I think it's time to end this little discussion."

"Sure, okay." Darla stood and started for the door. "Oh, I almost forgot—you had a phone call while you were out exploring Amish land."

"Who was it?"

"Mrs. Evans took the call, and she just told me it was some guy asking for you."

"Hmm . . . maybe it was Dad. But then why wouldn't he have called on my cell phone?"

"I really couldn't say, but I think Mrs. Evans left a note in your mailbox."

"I'll go check." As soon as Darla disappeared into her own room, Laura ran down the steps and found the note in her mailbox. It read:

A man named Dean Carlson called around two o'clock. He said he had tried to call your cell phone several times and only got your voice mail. He wants you to call him as soon as possible.

Laura sucked in her breath. *Is Dean really missing me, or is he just checking up on me? Should I call him first thing in the morning or make him wait a few days?*

"You ought to keep your cell phone charged and check your voice mail once in a while, Laura. I tried for two days to get you and finally had to call your school and leave a message."

Laura held the cell phone away from her ear and grimaced. She knew she had made a mistake calling Dean so early in the morning. She should have remembered he was a bear before his third cup of coffee. "Well, you've got me on the phone now, so you don't have to make such a big deal of it."

"Yeah, okay."

"What did you want, Dean?" she asked, tapping her foot impatiently.

"I thought that I'd come to Lancaster to see you next weekend."

"What?" Laura's mouth went dry. "Coming here is not a good idea."

"Why not?"

"I'm busy, that's why."

"But I miss you, Laura, and I—"

Laura lifted her gaze to the ceiling. She and Dean had only begun dating a few months before she'd left Minneapolis to come here, but he acted like they were practically engaged. "It's not that I don't want you to come. It's just that—well, I'll be coming home for Christmas soon, and—"

"Christmas? That's three months away!"

Laura could almost see Dean's furrowed brows and the defiant lift of his chin. He was a handsome man with jet black hair that curled around his ears, and eyes as blue as a summer sky, but he was way too possessive. "It would be nice to see you, Dean, but I always have a lot of homework to do on the weekends."

"Were you studying when I phoned yesterday?"

Laura knew she couldn't tell Dean about her Saturday date with Eli Yoder, but she didn't want to lie to him, either. "I went to the farmers' market."

"What's that got to do with homework?"

"I was researching the Amish culture."

"Sounds real interesting." Dean's tone was sarcastic, and it irritated her.

"Actually, it's very interesting. I've been studying their quilts and getting some ideas for my next design project." *I've been studying a fascinating Amish man, too.*

Dean cleared his throat. "How about next weekend? Can I come or not?"

Laura chewed on her lower lip. She liked Dean . . . or at least she had when they were seeing each other socially. So why was she giving him the runaround now? It took only a few seconds for her to realize the answer. She was infatuated with Eli and wanted to spend her free time with him. Dean would only be a distraction, and if Eli found out about her English boyfriend, it might spoil her chances with him.

"Laura, are you still there?"

Dean's deep voice drew Laura back to their conversation, and she sighed. "Yes, I'm here."

"What's it going to be?"

"I'd rather you didn't come."

"Is that your final word?"

"Yes, but as I said before, I'll be home for Christmas, so I'm sure we'll see each other then."

Dean grunted and hung up the phone without even saying good-bye. Laura breathed a sigh of relief.

CHAPTER 7

Over the next several weeks, Eli saw Laura as often as possible. In fact, he could hardly get her out of his thoughts. The vision of her beautiful face, smooth as peaches and cream, inched its way into his mind on more than one occasion. When he'd told his folks he was still seeing Laura, the news hadn't gone over so well, especially with Mom.

"She'll try to change you," she admonished one Saturday as Eli hitched the buggy for another trip to meet Laura. "Why, the first thing you know, that woman will be asking you to leave the faith."

"*Ach*, Mom, you worry too much. No one could ever talk me into something I don't want to do."

His mother pursed her lips. "I wouldn't be so sure about that. Love does strange things to people."

Eli's eyebrows shot up. "Love? Who said anything about love? Laura and I are just friends."

Mom gave him a knowing look. "I've seen the face of love before. Every time you come home after being with that fancy woman, I can see the look of love written all over your face, and it scares me, son."

Eli's face heated up. He would never admit it, especially not to Mom, but he was beginning to wonder if his fascination with Laura might be more than curiosity or friendship. What if he were actually falling in love with her? If she felt the same way about him, would she expect him to leave the faith? Since he hadn't yet been baptized or joined the church, the decision to stay or leave was still his to make. However, there were too many things about his way of life that he would miss if he left home and became English. Besides, there were too many things in the modern world that he didn't particularly care for.

"You have no call to be worried or scared," he said, giving her arm a quick pat. "I know exactly what I'm doing."

"I hope so."

Eli climbed into the buggy and gathered up the reins. "See you later, Mom."

"Say, Eli . . . I was wondering if you could do me a favor."

"What's that?"

"Selma Hostetler has been laid up with a bad back for the last couple of days."

"Sorry to hear that. Nobody likes back pain."

Mom nodded. "I baked some zucchini-banana bread yesterday, and I thought maybe you could drop a loaf by to her. It might help cheer her some."

"Can't Lewis or Jonas do it? I don't want to be late meeting Laura."

Mom's eyebrows drew together. "They're both out in the fields with your daed, which is where you really ought to be, don't you think?"

Eli shook his head. "This is my day off from work, and even though I sometimes help Pop on my day off, he said he didn't need me this morning."

"I see. Well, can you drop off the bread to Selma then?"

"Jah, I suppose, but—"

"I'll go get it now." Mom rushed off before Eli had a chance to say anything more.

A few minutes later, she was back wearing a smile that stretched ear to ear. She handed him the bread, which she had enclosed in some plastic wrap. "Danki, son."

"You're welcome."

As Eli clucked to the horse, his mother waved and called, "Don't be too late for supper tonight. And remember that I love you."

"I love you, too."

When Pauline heard a horse and buggy pull into the yard, she hurried to the back door, not wanting her mother to be disturbed. Mom had taken some aspirin for the pain in her back and had returned to her bed soon after breakfast was over.

When Pauline saw Eli step down from one of their closed-in buggies, her heart skipped a beat. Had he come to see her—maybe invite her to go someplace with him today? She waited on the porch with sweaty palms and shaky legs as he headed to the house. When he reached the porch, he stopped and held out a loaf of bread.

"Mom asked me to deliver this to your mamm. I hear her back's been acting up."

Pauline nodded as a sense of disappointment flooded her soul. She took the bread and mumbled, "Danki. That was thoughtful of your mamm."

Eli shuffled his feet a few times as he stared at the ground. "Well, I—"

"Would you like to come in for a cup of coffee?" She motioned to the door. "I just made a fresh pot, and it might help take the chill out of your bones on this frosty morning."

"I . . . uh . . . appreciate the offer, but I can't stay."

"Are you working today?"

"No, it's my day off."

"Then surely you have time for a quick cup of coffee."

He shook his head. "I'm meeting a friend in Paradise, and I'm already late, so I'd better go."

Pauline clenched her teeth. *I'll bet it's that fancy English woman Eli's meeting. Should I come right out and ask?* She was about to, when

87

Eli turned toward his buggy and started walking away.

"See you at church tomorrow," he called over his shoulder.

"Jah, see you then," she muttered as she went back into the house. *Will I ever get through to Eli? Will he ever see me as anything more than a friend?*

"I'm sorry I was late picking you up," Eli said as he helped Laura into his buggy. "I had to make a delivery for my mamm."

"That's okay. You're here now, and that's all that counts." Laura drew in a deep breath. "It feels and smells like winter is coming, doesn't it?"

Eli nodded. "It's a lot warmer inside my daed's closed-in carriage, but I sure do miss my courting buggy."

"Don't you use it in the winter months at all?"

He shrugged. "Sometimes on the milder days, but it's much nicer inside this buggy today, don't you think?"

"Jah." She giggled and flipped the end of her ponytail.

Eli grinned. "You look real schee today."

"Nice. You said I look nice today, right?"

He nodded. "You're catching on fast to the Deitsch."

Laura's heart fluttered. "Thanks for the compliment."

Eli only nodded again and made the horse go a bit faster.

"Where are you taking me today?" Laura asked.

"I thought you might like to see one of our schoolhouses."

"Schoolhouses? You have school on Saturdays?"

He chuckled. "No, but Saturday's the best day for a tour of the schoolhouse. There won't be any kinner about, and no teacher wearing a stern look or carrying a hickory switch."

"Eli Yoder, you're such a tease." Laura reached across the short span between them and touched his arm. "Maybe that's why I like you so well."

"Because I like to kid around?"

"Yes. I find your humor and wholesome view on life rather refreshing. It's like a breeze on a sweltering summer day."

Eli scrunched up his nose. "I don't believe I've ever been compared to a breeze before."

She withdrew her hand and leaned back. "I've learned a lot from you."

"Is that good or bad?"

"It's good, of course." Her voice lowered to a whisper. "I could teach you a lot about English ways, if you'd let me. We could take in a movie sometime, or—"

Eli held up his hand. "No, thanks. I think I know more than enough about the fancy life."

"How can you say that? Have you ever given yourself a chance to find out what the modern world really has to offer?"

"I'm not blind, Laura," he muttered. "I see what's out there in the world, and even though I haven't felt ready to join the church, I'm not all that interested in electrical gadgets, fancy clothes, or thinkin' I don't need God."

Laura's mouth dropped open. "Who said anything about not needing God?"

"I'm sure lots of English folks do love God," Eli said. "But I've seen many people who seem too self-centered to give Him anything more than a few thoughts, and then it's only when they're in need of something."

"Where did you hear that?" she asked, her voice edged with irritation. Was this going to turn into a full-fledged disagreement? If so, she wasn't sure it was a good idea to give her opinion. After all, she was trying to appease, not aggravate, Eli.

He shrugged. "It doesn't matter where I got the notion. The important thing is, I'm happy to be a child of God, and I don't need any worldly things to make me complete."

"My father says religion is a crutch for weak men, and I'm inclined to believe him." The words were out before Laura had time to think, and she could have bitten her tongue when she saw the look of irritation on Eli's face.

Eli pulled sharply on the reins and eased the horse and buggy to the shoulder of the road. "Are you saying I'm a weak man, Laura?"

She turned to face him. "No, of course not. I just meant—"

"Maybe we've come too far," Eli said, his forehead wrinkling.

"Too far? You mean we missed the schoolhouse?"

He shook his head. "Too far with this friendship we probably shouldn't be trying to build."

Laura's heart began to pound, and her throat felt like she'd eaten a bunch of hot peppers. If Eli broke things off now, there would be no chance for them. She couldn't let that happen. She would not allow him to stay angry with her for something so ridiculous as a difference of opinion on religious matters.

She touched his arm and was glad when he didn't pull away. "Eli, I respect your religious beliefs, but can't we just agree to disagree on some things?"

"It's kind of hard to have a friendship with someone when we keep arguing."

She nodded. "I know, so let's not argue anymore. In fact, if it would make you feel better, I'll just sit here and listen to you narrate. How's that sound?"

He reached for the reins and gave her a side-long glance. "You're a hard one to say no to, you know that?"

Laura smiled. "That's what my father says, too."

"Your wife called five times while you were in court today and left messages for you to call her back as soon as you could," Wesley's secretary told him when he entered the reception area of his office.

"Did she say what she wanted?"

"No, just that it was important and she wanted you to call as soon as you could."

"I can imagine how important it was," he grumbled as he headed to his office. "Probably some major crisis over a broken fingernail."

Wesley had no more than taken a seat behind his desk, when his phone rang. He picked it up on the second ring, recognizing the caller ID. "Hello, Irene. I heard you called a few times while I was in court."

"Yes, I did, and I'm very upset."

His gaze went to the ceiling. Irene was always upset about something it seemed. "What's the problem?"

"It's Laura. I got an e-mail from her today, and she's in real trouble."

Wesley's heart began to race. "Is she sick? Has she been hurt?"

"No, no. She's all right physically, but I think she's taken leave of her senses."

He shifted the receiver to his other ear. "What's that supposed to mean?"

"Our daughter's been seeing some Amish man. She's gone out with him several times, and—"

"Whoa! Hold on a minute, and calm down. You're not making any sense."

"Laura's e-mail said she's involved with an Amish man named Eli. I think his last name is Yoder, or something like that. She said they've gone on a couple of picnics, to the farmers' market, and for rides in his buggy." After a brief pause, Irene released a shuddering sob. "We've got to put a stop to this right away, Wesley. Can you fly out to Pennsylvania and speak to her about this?"

"Me? Why can't you go? I'm tied up in court for at least another week, and then I've got—"

"I can't go, either. I'm involved with that benefit dinner I'm helping plan for the historical society, and then there's the country club luncheon I'm in charge of."

"So you're not that worried about Laura, are you?"

"Of course I am."

"Well, you needn't be. Our daughter is old enough to make her own choices about whom she sees and when. I think if we try to interfere, it will only make things worse." Wesley reached for the cup of coffee his secretary had just placed on his desk and took a drink. "Besides, Laura will be home for Christmas in a few weeks. I'll talk to her about this Amish fellow then, and if I think she's in over her head, I'll try to dissuade her."

"All right. I guess that would be best. Oh, I've got a call on the other line. I'll see you when you get home." Irene clicked off without saying good-bye.

Wesley shook his head. "Like mother, like daughter."

CHAPTER 8

It was only the first week of December, but Lancaster County had been hit with a heavy blanket of snow. Laura figured it would mean the end of her enjoyable rides with Eli . . . at least until spring. She would be going home for Christmas soon, so that would put an end to their times, anyway.

Leaving Eli, even for a few weeks, wasn't going to be easy. However, she had promised her parents and friends that she'd be coming home for the holidays, and she didn't want to disappoint them. Besides, even if she stayed in

Pennsylvania, Eli would spend Christmas with his family, and she, the fancy English woman, would not be included in their plans.

Laura stared out her dorm-room window at the falling snow. If only she had some way to get in touch with Eli. If they could just meet somewhere for lunch before she had to leave.

She finally curled up on her bed with a romance novel, surrendered to the fact that this Saturday would be spent indoors without Eli.

Laura had only gotten to the second page when a loud knock drove her to her feet. "Who's there?"

"Darla. Are you busy?"

Laura opened the door. "What's up?"

Darla was dressed in a pair of designer jeans and a pink sweater. A brown leather coat was slung over one arm, and a furry little cap was perched on top of her short, blond curls. "I thought I'd drive into Philadelphia. I still have some Christmas shopping to do, and only the big stores will have what I want."

"You're going shopping today?"

Darla nodded. "I was hoping you'd come along."

"In this weather?" Laura gestured toward the window. "In case you haven't noticed, there's a foot of snow on the ground."

Darla shrugged. "I'm sure most of the main roads have been cleared." She nudged Laura's arm. "I'll treat you to lunch."

"I'm on a diet."

"So, order a salad."

Laura released a sigh. "Oh, all right." It wasn't the way she wanted to spend the day, but she figured it would be better than being cooped up in her room all day.

"I'm going out for a while," Eli said, as he left the kitchen table and slipped into his heavy woolen jacket.

"Where you heading?" Lewis called to him.

"I've got some errands to run . . . not that it's any of your business, *schnuppich* brother." Eli plopped his black felt hat on his head and closed the door, curtailing more comments from his snoopy sibling.

Mary Ellen clicked her tongue against the roof of her mouth and turned to face Johnny. "Seems like our oldest boy is hardly ever home anymore."

Johnny shrugged. "Guess that's his choice."

"I'll bet he's sneakin' off to see that English woman again," Jonas said as he grabbed a hunk of shoofly pie.

"Don't you ever fill up?" Johnny's eyebrows drew together. "That's your third piece now, isn't it?"

"He's probably lost count," Lewis said with a chuckle.

Jonas smacked his lips. "Shoofly is my favorite

breakfast pie. Never have been able to get enough of it."

"No, but you sure have tried." Mary Ellen pushed her chair away from the table and gathered up some of the dishes. As she placed them in the sink, she glanced out the window and caught sight of Eli hitching his horse to the sleigh. She couldn't help but wonder if Jonas was right about Eli meeting Laura today. He hadn't said much about her lately, but Mary Ellen knew from her last conversation with Selma Hostetler that Eli sure wasn't courting Pauline.

On more than one occasion, Mary Ellen had tried putting in a good word for Pauline, and from what she'd heard, Pauline had made several attempts at getting Eli to invite her somewhere. So far all efforts had failed, and Mary Ellen knew all she could do was pray—and she'd been doing a lot of that lately. If enough prayers went up on Eli's behalf, he might see the light and quit spending time with Laura. Or she might get bored with him and find a nice English man to take her places. Better yet, maybe the fancy English woman would leave Lancaster County and never return.

The ride to Philadelphia went well. They took the main highway, and just as Darla had predicted, it had been plowed and treated. The bad weather hadn't kept many people home, for the stores were crowded with holiday shoppers.

Laura and Darla pushed their way through the crush of people and fumbled through the racks of clothes and stacks of gift items until they'd both purchased enough Christmas presents for everyone on their lists. Everyone except for Eli. Laura wanted to get him something special, but since he lived a much simpler life than she did and was opposed to most worldly things, she couldn't find anything that might be suitable.

They had a late lunch and left the city around four o'clock, and by the time they reached the turnpike, it was snowing again.

"I know it's a little out of the way, but would you mind stopping at the variety store in Paradise on our way home?" Laura asked Darla.

"What for?"

"I want to get a Christmas present for Eli. I couldn't find anything appropriate in Philadelphia, but I'm sure I can find something there."

Darla squinted. "I don't mind stopping, but I do mind what you're doing."

Laura looked away. "What are you talking about?"

"I can see that no matter how much I've warned you about this, you've decided to jump into the deep end of the pool without even looking."

"Huh?"

"Don't be coy, Laura. I've warned you about

getting involved with that Amish man, and you've forged ahead anyway. It doesn't take a genius to realize you're head over heels in love with this Eli fellow."

"In love? Don't be ridiculous! Eli and I are just friends."

Darla gave the steering wheel a few taps with her gloved fingers. "Sure . . . whatever you say."

When they arrived at the store in Paradise, no cars or buggies were in the parking lot, and it appeared to be deserted. However, the sign in the window said they were open, so Darla parked her car, and Laura went inside.

She soon realized that choosing a gift for an Amish man, even in a Plain store, wasn't going to be easy. Shelves were full of men's black felt hats, suspenders in all sizes, and a large assortment of white handkerchiefs. Laura wanted something more special than any of these things. It had to be a gift that would cause Eli to remember her whenever he looked at it.

She was about to give up, when she spotted a beautiful set of carving tools she was sure Eli could use. She paid for them and left the store feeling satisfied with her purchase. Now if she could only get the gift to Eli before she went home for Christmas.

As Laura returned to Darla's car, her foot slipped on the walkway, and she realized the snow had begun to freeze.

"This isn't good," Darla complained as they pulled out of the parking lot a few minutes later. "I should have gone directly back to Lancaster and stayed on the main roads."

Laura grunted. "I'm sure we'll get back to the school in time for your favorite TV show."

"I wasn't thinking about TV. I'm concerned about staying on the road and keeping my car intact."

No sooner had she spoken the words than they hit a patch of ice. The car slid off the road, coming to a stop in the middle of a snow-bank.

"Oh, great!" Darla put the car in REVERSE and tried to back up. The wheels spun, but the car didn't budge. She tried several more times, but it was no use. They were stuck, and it was obvious that there was nothing either of them could do about it.

"Maybe I should get out and push," Laura suggested with a weak smile.

"I'd better make a call for help." Darla reached into her purse for the cell phone and started to dial but dropped it to the seat with a moan.

"What's wrong?"

"The battery's dead. I forgot to charge it last night." Darla opened the car door and got out. Laura did the same.

"Now we're really in a fix." Darla kicked at the front tire with the toe of her boot. "I should have checked my phone before we left Lancaster this morning."

"I guess it's my fault. If I hadn't asked you to go to the variety store—"

Laura stopped speaking when she heard the *clip-clop* of horse's hooves approaching. "Do you need some help?" a man's voice called out.

She whirled around, and her heartbeat quickened as Eli stepped down from an open sleigh. "Are we ever glad to see you!"

Eli joined them right away, and Laura introduced Darla. Then, offering Eli a wide smile, she asked, "Would it be possible for you to give us a ride to the nearest town? We need to call a tow truck to get Darla's car out of that snowbank."

Eli surveyed the situation. "I think I can pull you out with my horse."

Darla shook her head. "You've got to be kidding."

"My horse is strong as an ox."

"Okay," Darla said with a shrug. "You may as well give it a try."

Laura and Darla stepped aside as Eli unhitched the horse and hooked a rope around the animal's neck, then fastened the rope to the back bumper of Darla's car. He said a few words in Pennsylvania Dutch, and the gelding moved forward. The car lurched and was pulled free on the first try.

"Hooray!" Laura shouted with her hands raised.

Darla just stood with her mouth hanging open.

"Why don't I follow you back to the main road where it's cleared?" Eli suggested. "That way I can be sure you don't run into any more snowbanks."

"Thank you," Darla murmured, as though she could hardly believe her car had been freed by a horse.

Laura turned to Eli. "Would it be okay if I rode in your sleigh for a while? I've always wanted to ride in one." She touched his arm. "Besides, I have something for you."

His brows arched upward. "You do?"

She nodded. "I'll get it from Darla's car and be right back." Laura raced off before Eli had a chance to reply. When she grabbed Eli's gift from the car, Darla, already in the driver's seat, gave her a disgruntled look but said nothing.

Laura made her way back to where Eli waited beside the sleigh. After he helped her up, she pulled the collar of her coat tightly around her neck. "Brr . . . It's sure nippy out."

Eli reached under the seat and retrieved a quilt. He placed it across her lap, and she huddled beneath its warmth, feeling like a princess on her way to the ball.

As they followed behind Darla's car, Laura snuggled closer to Eli and said, "I'm glad you came along when you did. I'm leaving for Minneapolis in a few days, and I didn't think I'd get the chance to see you before I left."

"I went to the variety store in Paradise this morning," Eli said. "You weren't there, so I thought maybe you'd already gone home for the holidays."

Laura frowned. If she'd had any idea Eli was going to venture out in the snow just to see her, she would have moved heaven and earth to get to Paradise this morning. "I guess fate must have wanted us to meet today after all."

Eli raised one eyebrow. "Fate? You think fate brought us together?"

She nodded. "Don't you?"

He shook his head. "If anyone brought us together today, it was God."

"I have something for you," Laura said, feeling a bit flustered and needing to change the subject. She lifted the paper bag in her hands, and her stomach lurched with nervous anticipation. "Merry Christmas, Eli."

"You bought me a gift?"

She nodded and smiled.

"But, I—I don't have anything to give you."

"That's okay. I didn't buy you a present so I would get one in return."

Eli's eyebrows lifted and almost disappeared under the brim of his black hat. "What is it?"

"Why don't you open it and find out?"

"If it's a Christmas present, shouldn't I wait 'til Christmas to open it?"

She shook her head. "I'd like you to open it now, so I can see if you like it or not."

"All right then, but let's wait 'til we get to the main road and have stopped so you can get back in your friend's car again."

Laura felt a bit disappointed, but she didn't want to start an argument, so she merely shrugged and said, "Okay."

They rode in silence until Darla's car slowed and came to a parking lot. Eli guided his horse and sleigh in behind her.

"Here you go." Laura handed the sack to him.

Eli opened it and pulled out the carving set. He studied it a few seconds before he spoke. "It's a nice gift—much better than the carving set I use now." He fidgeted kind of nervously, and Laura was afraid he was going to hand it back to her.

"What's wrong? Don't you like it?"

"It's very nice, but I'm not sure I should accept such a gift."

"Why not?" she asked, looking deeply into Eli's searching blue eyes.

"It doesn't seem right, since I have nothing to give you in return."

Laura reached for his hand and closed her fingers around his. "Your friendship is the only present I need this Christmas. Please say I'm one of your special friends."

Eli swallowed so hard she saw his Adam's apple bob up and down. Several seconds went by; then he finally nodded and offered her a smile that calmed her fears and warmed every inch of her heart.

CHAPTER 9

Laura's first few days at home were spent visiting with her parents and thinking about Eli. When she closed her eyes, she could visualize his friendly smile, little chin dimple, and those clear blue eyes calling her to him.

Ever since Laura had returned, her mother had been trying to keep her occupied. "Why not join me for lunch at Ethel Scott's this afternoon?" she suggested one morning.

Laura was lying on the couch in the living room, trying to read a novel she had started the day before. She set it aside and sat up. "I need to get my Christmas presents wrapped."

Mom took a seat next to Laura. Her green eyes, mirroring Laura's, showed obvious concern. "I'm worried about you, dear. You haven't been yourself since you came home for the holidays." She touched Laura's forehead. "Are you feeling ill?"

Laura shook her head. "I'm fine. Just a bit

bored. I'm used to being in class every week-day."

"That's precisely why you need to get out of the house and do something fun while you're here." Mom tipped her head, causing her shoulder-length auburn hair to fall across one rosy cheek. Even at forty-five, she was still lovely and youthful looking.

"Ethel's daughter, Gail, is home from college, and I'm sure she would be thrilled to see you," Mom continued. "In fact, she'd probably enjoy hearing about that boring little town you're living in now."

Laura moaned. "Lancaster isn't little, and it sure isn't boring."

"The point is you've been cooped up in this house ever since you got home. Won't you please join me today? It will be better than being home by yourself."

"I won't be alone," Laura argued. "Foosie is here, and she's all the company I need." She glanced at her fluffy, ivory-colored cat sleeping contentedly in front of the fireplace. "After I'm done wrapping gifts, I thought I might try to call Shannon again."

Mom stood. "I would think it would be Dean Carlson you'd be calling." She shook her finger at Laura. "Dean's called at least four times in the past two days, and you always find some excuse not to speak with him."

Laura drew in her bottom lip. How could she explain her reluctance to talk to Dean? She sure couldn't tell her mother that she had been comparing Dean to Eli. "I'll be seeing him on Christmas Day. That's soon enough."

Mom finally shrugged and left the room.

Laura puckered her lips and made a kissing sound. "Here, Foosie, Foosie. Come, pretty lady."

The ball of fur uncurled, stretched lazily, and plodded across the room. Laura scooped Foosie into her lap and was rewarded with soft purring when the cat snuggled against her. "I've missed you. Too bad cats aren't allowed in the dorm rooms at school. If they were, I would take you back with me."

The telephone rang and Laura frowned. "Just when we were getting all cozy." She placed the cat on the floor and headed for the phone that was sitting on a table near the door. "Meade residence."

"Laura, is that you?"

"Yeah, it's me, Shannon."

"When did you get home?"

"Last Saturday. I've tried to call you a couple of times, but you're never home."

"I've been busy planning my preschoolers' Christmas party and the program they'll put on for their parents. My answering machine isn't working right now, either, so I'm sorry you couldn't leave a message."

"That's okay. I've been busy, too." *Busy thinking about Eli and wishing I could spend the holidays with him.*

"Is it all right if I come over?"

"Sure, I'd like that."

After Laura hung up the phone, she headed for the kitchen. She had two cups of hot chocolate ready by the time her friend arrived.

"Have a seat, and let's get caught up," Laura said, handing Shannon a mug.

Shannon sniffed her drink appreciatively. "Do you have any marshmallows?"

Laura went to the cupboard to look, while her friend placed her mug on the table, then took off her coat.

"I think it's going to be a white Christmas," Shannon commented. "We usually have some snow by now, but I'm sure it's not far off, because I think I can actually smell snowflakes in the air."

Laura tossed a bag of marshmallows on the table and took the seat across from Shannon. "We've already had a good snowstorm in Lanaster."

"Really? Were you able to get around okay?"

"Oh, sure. In fact, I—"

"Say, you haven't said a word about my new hairstyle." Shannon pulled her fingers through her bluntly cut, straight black hair. "Do you like it?"

Laura feigned a smile as she searched for the right words. "You . . . uh . . . look different with short hair."

Shannon blew on her hot chocolate, then reached inside the plastic bag and withdrew two marshmallows. She dropped them into the mug and grinned. "I like my new look, and so do my preschool kids."

"I'm surprised you cut your hair. I thought you would always keep it long."

Shannon shrugged, then took a sip of her drink. "Long hair is too much work, and it takes forever to dry." She set the cup down and snapped her fingers. "Why don't you get your hair cut and styled while you're home for Christmas?"

"I don't think I could ever cut my hair. It took me too long to grow it."

Shannon poked at the marshmallows with the tip of her finger. "Have you met any cute guys out there in Lancaster County?"

"Eli Yoder. I sent you an e-mail about him."

"You mean that Amish fellow?"

"He's the one."

"I thought that was just a passing fancy. Surely you're not seriously interested in this guy."

Laura felt the heat of a blush creep up the back of her neck and spread quickly to her face. "I've been fighting my attraction to Eli, but I'm afraid it's a losing battle." She drew in a deep breath and let it out in a rush. "To tell you the truth—and I can't believe I'm actually saying this out loud—I think I might be in love with him."

Shannon nearly choked on her hot chocolate. "You can't be serious!"

"I am."

"Does he know how you feel?"

"I don't think so. We've agreed only to be friends, and I don't see how it could work for us to have a romantic relationship."

Shannon nodded. "Makes sense to me."

"Eli's family is really religious, and we're worlds apart, with him being a plain kind of guy and me being a fancy English woman." Laura laughed dryly. "At least that's how Eli sees me."

Shannon drummed her fingers along the edge of the table. "Hmm . . ."

"What?"

"Maybe he will leave the Amish faith and become fancy."

"I've thought about that—even hoped for it," Laura admitted. "Eli's religion and his plain lifestyle seem very important to him. I doubt he would be willing to give it up, though I might ask—when I get up the nerve."

Shannon reached across the table and patted Laura's hand in a motherly fashion. "This is a fine fix you've gotten yourself into. Maybe you'll end up going over to the other side before it's all said and done."

Laura's eyebrows furrowed. "Other side? What are you talking about?"

"I was thinking you might join the Amish faith. People have done a lot stranger things in the name of love."

Laura's frown deepened. "I don't think I could do that, Shannon. It would be hard to give up everything I've become used to, and—"

The kitchen door opened just then, and Laura's father entered the room, carrying an overstuffed briefcase. From the way his shoulders sagged and the grim look he wore, Laura figured he must either be exhausted or agitated about something.

Her father was a small, thin man, with dark brown hair and a matching mustache. His mahogany eyes looked unusually doleful as he shuffled across the room and collapsed into a chair.

"Dad, is something wrong?" Laura asked, feeling concern. "You look so tired."

"It's just this fast-paced world we're living in," he answered, lowering his briefcase to the table. "On days like today, I wish I could pull a magic handle and make everything slow down. Maybe the pioneer days weren't so bad. Life in the fast lane is pretty hectic, but I suppose I'll survive." His forehead wrinkled as he looked at Laura. "Whatever you do, young lady, never let 'all work and no play' become your motto."

"I'll try not to, Dad."

"By the way, your mother mentioned that you've become friendly with an Amish man, and I've been meaning to talk to you about it."

Laura nodded and swallowed hard. Was her father going to give her a lecture about Eli in front of Shannon?

Dad smiled. "Well, if you ever see that fellow again, be sure to tell him that I envy his simple lifestyle." He glanced over at Shannon then. "Nice to see you."

"It's good to see you, too, Mr. Meade."

He turned his attention back to Laura. "Where's your mother?"

"She was supposed to have lunch with her friend Ethel today, and I think they planned to do some shopping afterward." Laura released a sigh of relief. Maybe Dad wasn't opposed to her seeing Eli. Maybe there would be no lecture.

"I can only imagine what kind of unnecessary things she'll bring home this time." He shook his head. "Your mother spends more time shopping than any other woman I know."

Laura nodded. "She does like to shop—when she's not busy with all her charity functions."

"There's nothing wrong with helping out, but the kinds of things she does make me wonder if she's more interested in making herself look good rather than helping others." He grunted. "I doubt that your mother knows how to relax anymore, she's so busy flitting from one charity benefit to another. What we both really need is a vacation from the rat race of city life."

"Maybe you should take a trip to Hawaii or go on a cruise to the Bahamas," Laura suggested.

"Maybe so." He moved across the room toward the door leading to the hallway. "Guess I'll head out to the living room and unwind a bit before your mother gets home."

"Okay."

"Your dad seemed pretty uptight, didn't he?" Shannon said after Laura's father had left the room.

"Yes, he did, and I was surprised he didn't lecture me about seeing Eli."

Shannon laughed. "Parents. Who can figure them out?"

"Not me." Laura took a drink of her hot chocolate as she reflected on her father's words. The things he'd said about wanting to slow down had made her think of Eli and his Amish family. They worked hard, but they weren't really a part of the fast-paced world. From all Eli had told her, she knew that he and his family took time out for fun and relaxation. She wondered if Dad were given the chance, whether he might trade in his briefcase for a hoe and the quiet life among the Plain People. She chuckled softly. *No, that could never happen.*

* * *

Wesley wandered into the living room, leaving his briefcase in the kitchen, along with his cares of the day. He had a splitting headache and wanted to spend the rest of his day relaxing and not thinking about anything that pertained to his latest court case.

Wesley discovered Laura's lazy cat lying in front of the fireplace, but the minute he took a seat in his recliner, the cat was in his lap.

"You've got life made, you know that, Foosie?"

The cat responded with a quiet *meow*.

He reclined the chair and closed his eyes as he allowed his mind to wander back to the days when he'd been a boy growing up on his dad's farm in Montana. Life had been so much simpler then. They had worked plenty hard on the farm, but they'd always taken the time to enjoy the simple things in life, and their focus had been on family and friends, not "things."

Wesley had given up that life to please Irene, and now he felt as if he were caught in a trap from which there was no escape. Someday when he retired, maybe he would sell this place and move to the country again, where he could raise some chickens, a few pigs, and some cats . . . lots of cats.

Eli meandered toward his woodworking shop at one end of the barn. He didn't know why, but

114

he wasn't in the mood to carve or build a single thing.

When he reached his workbench, he looked down at the woodworking set Laura had given him and groaned. He wished she hadn't presented him with such a fine, expensive gift. In fact, he wished she hadn't bought him anything. He'd given her nothing in return, and accepting Laura's present only made it that much harder to distance himself from her, which he knew he must do if he was ever going to join the church.

He thought about Pauline and wondered if he could have been content to court her if Laura hadn't come along when she did. It was hard to explain, but being with her made him feel alive and whole.

Eli sank to the metal folding chair by his workbench and leaned forward until his head rested in the palms of his hands. "If only I hadn't started seeing her. If I could just stop the feelings I have whenever we're together. It just isn't right."

"What isn't right?"

Eli jerked upright at the sound of his younger brother's voice. "Jonas, what do you think you're doing, sneakin' up on me that way?"

Jonas chuckled and sauntered over to the workbench. "I thought you came out here to work on a Christmas present, not talk to yourself." He gave Eli's shoulder a couple of thumps.

Eli frowned. "I was planning to finish up the planter box I'm making for Martha Rose, but I can't seem to get in the mood to work on it right now."

Jonas pushed a bale of straw over to the bench and plopped down on it. "Christmas is only a few days away. How do ya think our big sister will feel about not gettin' a gift from you?"

Eli grabbed the planter in question, along with a strip of sandpaper, and began sanding it with a vengeance. "It'll be done on time."

Jonas touched Eli's arm. "Take it easy. Now you're gettin' all worked up."

"I'm not worked up," Eli snapped, as he continued to run the coarse paper over the edges of the wooden box.

Jonas eyed him intently. "Is that so? Well, ya sure could've fooled me."

"Quit your staring."

"I was just checkin' to see if my big brother is in lieb."

Eli slapped the sandpaper down on the bench and stood, nearly knocking over his wooden stool. "I'm not in love! Now, if you don't have anything sensible to say, why don't you go bother someone else?"

"It's that fancy English woman, isn't it? You're all worked up over her, I'm guessing."

Eli's forehead beaded with sweat, and he knew it wasn't from heat, for there was at least a foot of snow on the ground. If only he could get Laura out of his mind.

"You're not denying it, so it must be true," Jonas persisted. "She's gotten under your skin, huh?"

Eli whirled around to face his brother. "Laura and I are just friends." His right eyelid began to twitch. "Even if I wanted it to be more, it could never happen."

"How come?"

"She's English."

"I know, but—"

"There are no buts." Eli felt his patience begin to wane. "I don't want to leave our faith, and I sure couldn't ask Laura to become one of us."

"Why not?"

Eli folded his arms and drew in a deep breath. He was getting frustrated with this ridiculous conversation. "Let's put it this way—would you throw a newborn *bussli* into the *seischtall*?"

Jonas tipped his head and looked at Eli as if he'd gone daffy. "Huh? What's a little bitty kitten and a pigpen got to do with Laura Meade?"

Eli shook his head. "Never mind. You're probably too *verhuddelt* to understand."

"I'm not confused! Just say what ya mean, and mean what ya say!" Jonas's forehead now dripped with sweat.

"Calm down. This is a dumb discussion we're having, and I say we drop it."

Jonas stuck out his chin. "Want to know what I think?"

Eli blew out his breath and lifted his gaze toward the rafters. "No, but I'm sure you won't scram 'til you've told me."

"I think you're in love with Laura, but you know she's not good for you. I'm thinkin' the best thing for everyone is for you to hurry and get baptized, and then join the church so you can marry Pauline Hostetler."

Eli clenched his fists. If Jonas didn't leave soon, he couldn't be sure what he might do. "Just go now before I drag you outside and push your face into a pile of snow."

"Jah, right."

"I mean it, little brother."

"You think you're big enough?" Jonas planted his hands on his hips and stared at Eli as though daring him to make a move.

Eli didn't hesitate. He lunged for Jonas, and Jonas darted for the door. When they bounded into the snowy yard, all thoughts of Laura vanished as Eli focused on catching his nosy brother and giving him a good face washing in a mound of frigid snow.

CHAPTER 10

Christmas Day turned out to be pretty much the way Laura had expected it to be. Her father had invited several people from his law firm to dinner, and most of them spent the whole time talking about trial dates, briefs, and who they thought might get out of going to jail.

Dean Carlson was among the guests, seated next to Laura. She studied him as he droned on about the new computer system they'd recently installed at the office. There was no denying it —Dean was one of the most handsome men Laura had ever met. The funny thing was Laura used to enjoy Dean's company. Now he seemed superficial and self-absorbed. She kept comparing him to Eli, whose warm, sincere smile could melt her heart and whose infectious laughter seemed genuine, not forced like Dean's. She didn't know why she'd never seen it before, but Dean's whole mannerism was brash, and he was certainly the most egotistical man she had ever met. Eli, on the other hand, was gentle and genuinely humble.

"Laura, are you listening to me?" Dean nudged her arm.

She managed a weak smile. "I think Dad may

have mentioned the new computer system."

"You *weren't* listening. The computer system was not the last thing I said."

She blinked. "It wasn't?"

"I was asking if you'd like to go to the New Year's Eve office party with me."

Laura stared at Dean. How could she even consider dating a man like him? Oh, sure, he had money, a good education, great looks, and a prestigious job, but he simply wasn't Eli Yoder.

"I want to take you to the party," Dean said again. "Will you go with me or not?"

Every fiber of Laura's being shouted *no!* She reached for her glass of water and took a few sips, hoping to buy some time.

When Dean began tapping the side of his glass with the tip of his spoon, she finally answered. "I appreciate the offer, but I hadn't planned on going to the party."

"Why not?"

Laura wasn't sure how to respond. She really had no legitimate reason for staying home. "I . . . uh . . . I'm leaving for Pennsylvania the day after New Year's, and I need to get packed."

Dean leaned his head back and roared. It was the first genuine laugh she'd heard out of him all day, but it didn't make her smile. "You have a whole week between now and the party. Surely that's time enough to pack a suitcase."

When Laura made no reply, he reached for her hand. "Come on, honey, please say you'll go with me. After all, I do work for your dad, and I'm sure he would approve."

Laura inwardly groaned. She knew she was losing this battle, and she didn't like it one bit.

Dean leaned closer, and she could feel his warm breath against her ear. "If you don't have a wonderful time, I promise never to ask you out again."

She finally nodded in defeat. "Okay, I'll go."

All during dinner, Wesley kept glancing across the table at Laura. She looked uncomfortable, as if she would rather be anyplace else but here. Didn't she enjoy being with her family and friends? She'd always seemed to before. Surely she wasn't anxious to get back to her studies in Pennsylvania. Maybe she was just tired.

He looked over at his wife, sitting so prim and proper at the other end of the table. She seemed to be in her glory—chatting, smiling, soaking up every compliment that had come her way. He didn't know why. She really couldn't take credit for any of it. The meal had been catered. The house had been cleaned by their housekeeper. Irene's flowing, peach-colored dress had been bought at one of the most expensive shops in town. Her hair and nails had been done by her beautician. She hadn't done much of anything to prepare for this meal except tell others what to do.

Wesley inwardly groaned. It was all superficial. There probably wasn't a person sitting at this table who gave a lick about the person next to them. Except maybe Dean, who kept nuzzling Laura's neck and whispering in her ear. Could Dean be the reason Laura seemed so fidgety today?

"Wesley, did you hear what I said?"

He looked over to his wife again. "What was that, dear?"

Irene smiled sweetly. "I asked if you were still planning to host your office's New Year's Eve party at the country club. Ethel wanted to know."

"Yes, it will be there again this year." Wesley forced a smile. He would never have admitted it to his wife, but the truth was, he would much rather stay home on New Year's Eve and watch TV or read a good book instead of dishing out the money for a party that no one would remember the following day. But he knew it was expected of him, and the gleam in Irene's eyes was a reminder that at least one of them was looking forward to the gala affair.

"What are you doing out here in the cold?" Eli's sister, Martha Rose, asked, as she stepped out the back door and joined him on the porch.

Eli shrugged and leaned against the railing.

"It was getting kind of stuffy in the house, so I decided to get some fresh air."

Martha Rose shivered and pulled her heavy shawl around her shoulders. "This air is downright frigid—that's what it is."

He smiled. "So what are you doing out here in it?"

"Same as you—getting some fresh air." She nudged him playfully with her elbow, but then her face sobered. "You've been quiet all day, and I was wondering if there's something bothering you."

Eli pulled his fingers through the back of his hair. Of course there was something bothering him. Ever since he'd met Laura, he had been bothered. He'd been thinking about her off and on all day, wondering how she was spending her Christmas, wishing they could be together, and fretting because he was having such thoughts. He was tempted to share his feelings with Martha Rose, because the two of them had always been close, but he wasn't sure she would understand. She might even reprimand him, the way Mom had done when she'd learned he was seeing Laura—a fancy Englisher.

"I'm feeling kind of down today," he finally mumbled.

"On Christmas?"

He nodded, keeping his focus on the snowy yard, because he knew if he looked right at

123

Martha Rose, he was likely to give himself away.

"Mom's worried about you, Eli."

"I'm fine. A little chilly weather never hurt anybody."

She touched his arm. "She's not worried about you being out here in the cold."

His only reply was an exaggerated shrug.

"She's worried that you might be thinking about leaving the Amish faith."

Eli bristled and whirled around to face his sister. "Did Mom send you out here to try and talk some sense into me? Is that it?"

Martha Rose shook her head. "Coming out here was my idea. I've seen how sullen you've been all day, and I was worried that it might have something to do with the English woman you've been seeing lately."

"Laura and I are just friends. Mom has nothin' to worry about."

"It might help ease her concerns if you got baptized and joined the church."

"I don't think calming Mom's fears is a good enough reason to become a member of the church, do you?"

"Well, no, but—"

"I've told Mom and Pop, too, that I'm not leaving the faith, and there's nothing serious going on with me and Laura." Eli grunted. "So everyone, including you, can quit hounding me about this."

Martha Rose winced as though she'd been slapped. "I—I didn't mean to sound as if I was trying to tell you what to do. I only want your happiness."

"Sorry. I shouldn't have snapped at you that way."

She gave him a hug. "I want you to know that if you ever need to talk, I'm willing to listen, and I promise not to be judgmental."

Eli smiled and patted her on the back. "Danki. I appreciate that."

"Are you too full from dinner to finish your dessert?" Pauline's mother motioned to the half-eaten piece of pumpkin pie on Pauline's plate.

Pauline shook her head. "Not really. I'm just not so hungry right now."

Dad wrinkled his forehead. "You barely ate any dinner. As a matter of fact, you've been actin' kind of sulky all day. What's the problem, daughter?"

"Nothing. I'm fine."

"She's probably wishing she could be with her boyfriend today," Pauline's younger sister, Susan, piped up.

"I have no boyfriend. Not anymore."

"I thought you and Eli Yoder had been courting," Dad said, reaching for another slice of mincemeat pie.

"I thought so, too, but I was wrong." Pauline couldn't keep the bitterness out of her voice.

Mom poured herself a cup of coffee from the pot sitting in the center of the table. "I was talking to Eli's mamm a few weeks back, and she seemed concerned because he's not joined the church yet."

"He hasn't joined because he's seeing some fancy English woman with long, auburn hair," Sam, Pauline's brother, interjected.

Pauline glared at him. "Can't we talk about something else?"

He shrugged his broad shoulders and smiled. "Guess we could talk about Joseph Beachy. He's had a crush on you ever since we were kinner."

Pauline wrinkled her nose. "Joseph's three years younger than me, for goodness' sake."

Dad chuckled. "So what of it? Your mamm's a whole year older than me."

Mom shook her head as she lifted her gaze to the ceiling. "And you're never gonna let me live that down, are you, Ben?"

He grinned and tickled her under the chin. "Nope, but it don't make me love you any the less."

She reached for his hand. "I love you, too, even if you are just a big kid."

Feeling the need to be alone, Pauline pushed away from the table. "I'm kind of tired, so if

126

you don't mind, I think I'll go upstairs to my bedroom."

"Sleep well," Mom called as Pauline started out of the room.

"Danki." Pauline trudged up the stairs, and with each step she took, she felt more discouraged. Even if Eli did quit seeing the Englisher and decided to join the church, she feared he might never be interested in her. And if she couldn't have Eli, then she didn't want any man.

CHAPTER 11

Mom had insisted that Laura buy a new dress for the New Year's Eve party. Laura couldn't understand what all the fuss was about, but she decided she might as well enjoy the pampering. After all, she would be leaving soon. Then it would be back to the grindstone of school, homework, and . . . Eli. She hoped she would be able to see him again.

Standing before her full-length bedroom mirror, Laura smiled at the lovely young woman looking back at her. *If Eli could only see me now, maybe he'd be tempted to go "fancy."*

Mom stood directly behind her, and she smiled into the mirror, as well. "You look exquisite. I'm glad you decided to buy this beautiful silk gown. That shade of green brings out the color of your eyes so well."

Laura merely shrugged in response. She knew she looked nice, but her heart wasn't in going to the party tonight or in spending the evening with Dean.

"I'm sure your date will be impressed," her mother continued. "Dean seems like such a nice young man."

"I suppose—just not my type."

"Not your type?" Mom's eyebrows furrowed. "How can you say that, Laura? Why, Dean is nice looking, has plenty of money, and—"

Laura turned away from the mirror. "Do you think my hair looks all right this way, or should I have worn it down?"

"Your hair looks lovely in a French roll," her mother responded. She gave Laura's arm a gentle squeeze. "I'm sure Dean will think so, too."

The New Year's Eve party was already in full swing by the time Dean and Laura arrived a little after nine o'clock. He'd been nearly an hour late picking her up, which had put her in a sour mood right from the beginning.

They had no sooner checked their coats, than Dean pulled Laura into a possessive embrace. "You look gorgeous tonight. I'm glad you decided to come."

Laura wished she could reciprocate with a similar remark, but the truth was she wasn't glad to be here. In fact, she felt a headache coming on, and if it didn't let up soon, she knew she would have a good excuse to leave the party.

"Would you like something to drink before we check out the buffet?" Dean asked, pulling her toward the bar.

She merely shrugged in response.

"What can I get for you?"

"Nothing, unless they have some diet cola."

"You're not driving," Dean reminded. "And if you're concerned about me drinking and driving, you shouldn't worry your pretty little head. I won't have more than a few drinks, and I can handle those with no problem at all."

Laura gnawed on her bottom lip until it almost bled. If Dean was planning to have a few drinks, she could only imagine how the evening might end. She had to do something to get away from him now. "There's my friend Shannon," she said, motioning across the room. "I'm going over to say hello."

"Okay, I'll get our drinks. I'll meet you at the buffet table in a few minutes." He sauntered off toward the bar like he owned the place.

Laura saw Shannon carrying her plate to one of the tables, and she hurried over to her. "I'm glad to see you here." She pulled out a chair and took a seat beside her friend.

"Why wouldn't I be? Need I remind you that my boyfriend works for your dad?" Shannon glanced at the buffet table and smiled. "Clark's still loading up on food, but he'll be joining me soon."

Laura shrugged. If Shannon's comment was meant to chase her away, it wasn't going to work. "Listen, can you do me a favor?"

"Sure, if I can."

"If you see my folks, would you tell them I came down with a headache so I called a cab and went home?"

Shannon's eyebrows lifted high on her forehead. "What about your date?"

"When Dean comes looking for me, which I'm sure he will, would you tell him the same thing?"

"You can tell him yourself. He's heading this way right now." Shannon pointed across the room, and Laura groaned.

"What's wrong? Did you two have a disagreement?"

"Something like that." Laura decided it would be pointless to tell her friend the real reason she wanted to get away from Dean. She wasn't just worried about his drinking. She didn't like the gleam she'd seen in his eyes when he picked her up tonight. She was sure he wanted more than she was willing to give, and her best line of defense was to leave now—alone.

"Here's your diet cola." Dean handed Laura the cold drink and nodded at Shannon. "How's it going?"

Shannon smiled. "Fine. How's everything with you?"

Laura set her glass on the table and tuned them both out as they engaged in small talk. Her thoughts turned to Eli, and she couldn't help wondering how he was spending his New Year's Eve. Did the Amish celebrate with a party, or would tonight be just like any other night for Eli and his family?

Laura cringed when Dean pulled her to his side and whispered, "Tonight's going to be a great evening." When he stroked the back of her neck with his thumb, she stood up so quickly, she knocked her soft drink over, spilling some of it down the front of her new dress. "I—I'm not feeling well, Dean. I'm going to call a cab and go home."

Obvious surprise registered on Dean's face, and his eyebrows furrowed. "You can't be serious. We just got here, and I haven't had a chance to eat yet, much less show you off to my friends."

I don't want to be shown off, and I don't want to be with you. Laura thrust out her chin and stared up at him. "I'm going home."

Dean set his drink on the table and steered her toward the coat closet. "Sure, no problem. I'll get my car."

"I'm calling a cab. There's no point in both of us missing the party. You stay and have a good time."

His eyes clouded over. "If you're dead set on going, then I may as well collect that stroke-of-midnight kiss." Before Laura could say anything, Dean bent his head and captured her lips in a kiss that would have left most women reeling with pleasure.

Laura drew back and slapped his face.

"What was that for?" He grimaced as he touched the red mark she had left on his cheek. "I thought you wanted that kiss as much as I did. Always did before."

Laura's face was so hot she felt as though she were the one who had been slapped. She wasn't in control of her emotions tonight, and that really bothered her.

"I'm sorry, Dean," she apologized. "Your kiss took me by surprise."

Dean's eyelids fluttered, and he backed up a few steps. "I don't know what's come over you, Laura, but you haven't been the same since you returned to Minneapolis after attending that stupid school in Pennsylvania for a few months. If I were your father, I would never have allowed you to go there, and I would have insisted that you finish your design courses right here in town."

Laura's hands trembled as she held them at her

sides. If Dean kept goading her, she was liable to let him have it on the other cheek. "Good night, Dean," she said through her clenched jaw. "Don't bother walking me out."

The day after New Year's, Laura said good-bye to her parents at the airport. She was more than anxious to be on her way. It wasn't that she hadn't enjoyed being with them, but she wanted to get back to her studies . . . and she hoped to see Eli again.

Mom and Dad had no idea she'd fallen in love with an Amish man, only that she'd gone out with him a few times. She had no intention of informing them, either. At least not today.

Laura hugged her parents and thanked them for the beautiful leather coat they'd given her for Christmas. Then, without so much as a backward glance, she boarded the plane, welcoming the butterflies doing a tap dance in her stomach.

Her time on the plane was spent thinking about Eli. She couldn't decide if she should be straightforward and tell him that she'd come to realize how much she loved him or if she should try to draw a declaration of love from him first.

By the time the plane landed in Harrisburg, Laura was a ball of nerves. As soon as she picked up the car she had leased, she headed for the main road, knowing the drive to Lancaster would be slow since snow still covered the ground.

When she got back to the school, it would be dark and too late to try and find Eli's house. But come tomorrow, she hoped to see him and bare her soul.

CHAPTER 12

Laura awoke in her dorm room the following morning with a pounding headache. A warm shower and a cup of tea helped some, but when she knocked on Darla's door to see if her friend would like to ride with her to Eli's farm, Laura's headache worsened.

"I have other plans today," Darla said with a scowl. "Besides, I wouldn't consider being a party to you ruining your life."

"How can seeing Eli again ruin my life?" Laura had hoped Darla would be willing to go with her. She needed the added courage.

Darla opened the door wider and motioned Laura inside. "Have a seat, and I'll see if I can explain things a little more clearly."

Laura pulled out the desk chair, and Darla sat on the edge of her bed.

"I know you've got a thing for this guy, but the more you see him, the further your relationship will develop." Darla pursed her lips. "One of you is bound to get hurt, and I'm guessing that you're going to be the one."

"What makes you think I'll get hurt?"

"We've been through this before. You and Eli are from completely different worlds, and even if one of you were willing to try the other's way of life, it most likely wouldn't work."

"How do you know?"

"Trust me on this," Darla asserted. "You're living in a dream world if you think you can get Eli to leave his faith."

"Why is that so impossible? People change religions all the time."

"Has Eli joined the Amish church yet? Because if he has and he decides to leave the faith, he'll be shunned. Do you understand what that means, Laura?"

She nodded. "Eli's told me quite a bit about the Amish way of life, but this isn't a problem because he hasn't joined the church yet."

Darla's eyebrows drew together. "Even so, if he were to leave, it would be a difficult adjustment for him."

"I'll help him adjust."

Darla shrugged. "Whatever. But think about this: Maybe he doesn't want to leave. Then what?"

"I—I don't know. I suppose I'll have to convince him that he does want to leave." Laura stood. "So are you going to help me find the Yoder place or not?"

Darla shook her head. "I'm afraid you'll have to do this on your own."

"Fine. I will."

Laura spent the next couple of hours driving around the back roads near Paradise, searching for Eli's house. Since she'd only been there once before and hadn't paid close attention to where Eli was going, she wasn't sure she was heading in the right direction.

Suddenly, she spotted a one-room schoolhouse. It was the same one Eli had pointed out on one of their rides. *I've got to be getting close to his house.*

Laura continued up the road another mile or so until she spotted a mailbox with the name Yoder on it. She drove up the driveway, and the minute she saw the house, she knew it was Eli's. She stopped the car, turned off the engine, and stepped out.

Walking carefully up the slippery path, she headed for the Yoders' front porch. She was almost to the door when a sense of panic gripped her like a vise. What if Eli wasn't home? What if he was home but wasn't happy to see her?

She thought about turning around and heading back to Lancaster, but the desire to see Eli

136

won out, so she lifted her hand and knocked on the door.

A few moments later, Eli's mother answered. She held a rolling pin in one hand, and with the other hand, she swiped at a wisp of hair that had fallen loose from her bun. Laura couldn't read Mary Ellen's stoic expression, but the woman's silence was enough to remind her that she was on enemy territory.

"Is . . . uh . . . Eli at home?"

Mary Ellen stood quietly a few minutes before she finally answered. "He's out in the barn in his woodworking shop."

Laura nodded and forced her lips to form a smile. "Thanks." She stepped quickly off the porch before Eli's mother had a chance to say anything more. If the older woman's sour expression was meant to dissuade her, it hadn't worked. She was here now and even more determined than ever to speak with Eli.

Eli was bent over his workbench, hammering a nail into the roof of a small birdhouse, when he heard the barn door open. He didn't think much of it, knowing his brothers were still busy with chores, but when a familiar female voice called out to him, he was so surprised, he smashed his thumb with the hammer.

"Laura! How'd you get here?"

She moved slowly across the room until she

137

stood directly in front of him. "I drove."

"When did you get back from Minnesota?"

"Last night."

Eli wished she would quit staring at him. It was hard to think. Hard to breathe. He swallowed a couple of times. "How . . . how was your holiday?"

"It was okay. How was yours?"

"Good." *Though it would have been better if you'd been here.* Eli shook his head, trying to get himself thinking straight again.

"I've missed you," Laura said, leaning toward him. "Did you miss me?"

A warning bell went off in Eli's head, but it was too late. Laura touched his arm, as she gazed into his eyes in a way that made his heart slam into his chest. How could he tell this beautiful woman that it wasn't right for her to be here?

Eli couldn't voice any of his thoughts. He couldn't even think straight with her standing so close and smelling so nice. He took a step back and bumped into his workbench, knocking a hunk of wood to the floor. He bent to retrieve it, feeling more frustrated by the minute.

"So this is where you make your birdhouses, huh?"

He nodded. "And many other wooden items, as well."

She glanced around the small room, as if she

were scrutinizing it. "How can you do this kind of work without the aid of electricity?"

"Some time ago, my daed installed a diesel engine that not only provides power for some of my saws and planers but also powers the compressed air pump that brings water to our house." Eli pointed to a small drill lying beside a handsaw. "Of course I do many things by hand, too."

"I see." Laura took a step closer to him. "Have you been back to the lake lately?"

"The lake's completely frozen over now." He tipped his head as an uncensored thought popped into his mind. "Say, would you like to go ice-skating?"

She pointed to her boots. "Ice-skating? Eli, in case you haven't noticed, I have no skates."

"I think my sister, Martha Rose, left her skates here in the barn when she married Amon Zook, and I'm sure she wouldn't mind if you wore them."

"If your sister's skates fit, I'd be happy to go ice-skating with you."

Eli nodded and smiled. So much for his resolve to keep Laura at a distance.

"Always trouble somewhere," Mary Ellen muttered as she returned to the kitchen, where Johnny sat at the table with a cup of coffee in his hands.

"What's the problem? Who was at the front door?"

"That English woman."

"Which English woman? There are several living nearby, you know."

Mary Ellen dropped into the chair beside her husband with a groan. "I'm talking about Laura Meade. She was looking for Eli."

"What'd you tell her?"

"Said he was out in the barn, in his shop." She pursed her lips. "Couldn't hardly lie now, could I?"

Johnny shook his head. "No, but you could have sent her packing."

"I'd like to think Eli will tell her to leave, but I'm not holding my breath on that one, either."

Johnny set his cup down and reached for her hand. "We need to keep on praying and trusting that God will open our son's eyes."

She nodded. "Jah, but that's easier said than done."

When Eli pulled his sleigh into the open area near the lake, Laura was surprised to see that it was covered with a thick layer of shimmering ice. She thought it was even more appealing than it had been in the fall, and she drank in the beauty of the surrounding trees, dressed in frosty white gowns and shimmering in the morning sun like thousands of tiny diamonds.

They took a seat on a fallen log, and Eli helped Laura into his sister's skates, which were only a tad too big.

"If I ever get the chance to meet your sister, I'll have to be sure and thank her for the use of these skates."

"I'll thank her for you." Eli grinned. "You'd like Martha Rose. She's the best sister any fellow could possibly want, and we've been good friends since we were kinner." He stood and held out his hand. "Should we give those skates a try?"

"Jah, let's do."

Hand in hand, they made their way slowly around the lake. After a time, Eli set off on his own, doing fancy spins and figure eights.

Laura shielded her eyes against the glare of the sun as she watched in rapt fascination, realizing with each passing moment how much she really had come to love Eli. She tried skating by herself, but it was hard to concentrate on anything except the striking figure he made on the ice.

Her heart hammered in her chest when Eli waved and offered her a flirtatious wink. He wore a pair of black pants, a light blue shirt, and a dark gray woolen jacket. He had removed his black felt hat, and his sandy brown hair whipped against his face as he appeared to become one with the wind.

Laura decided to try and catch up to Eli, hoping she could convince him to take a break so they could talk. She needed to tell him what was in her heart.

Pushing off quickly with her right foot, she lost her balance and fell hard on the ice. Eli was at her side immediately, his blue eyes looking ever so serious. "Are you okay? You didn't break anything, I hope."

"My knee hurts, but I don't think my leg's broken."

Laura shivered as Eli pulled up her pant leg and gently probed her knee. "It looks like a bad sprain. You probably should put some ice on it."

She giggled. "I think I just did."

Eli helped Laura to her feet and put his arm around her waist as she hobbled over to the sleigh. "I'd better get you back to my place so you can rest that knee and get out of the cold."

Impulsively, Laura gripped Eli's shoulders with both hands and kissed him on the cheek.

His face flushed, and he smiled at first, but then he jerked back like he'd been stung by a bee. "Wh–why'd you do that?"

"Just my way of saying thanks for being such a good friend."

His gaze dropped to the ground, and an awkward silence followed as Eli helped her into the sleigh. She wondered if she had said or done something wrong.

"I—I think it would be best if we didn't see each other anymore," he mumbled as he picked up the reins.

"Why? Haven't you enjoyed yourself today?"

He nodded soberly. "That's the problem: I had too good of a time."

Her hand trembled as she touched his arm. "I don't see how enjoying yourself can be a problem."

"I told you once that I wanted to be your friend, but now things have changed."

"How?" Her voice rose, and her heart started to pound. "Why?"

"I can't be your friend because I've fallen in love with you, Laura." He didn't look at her, just stared straight ahead.

"Oh, Eli, I love you, too!" She buried her face in his jacket, relishing the warmth and his masculine smell.

"What we feel for each other isn't right," he mumbled.

"It feels right to me."

"It won't work for us. I think we need to end this before we both get hurt."

"Nothing could hurt worse than never seeing you again," Laura said with a catch in her voice. "We can be together if we want it badly enough."

He eased her gently away. "I don't see how."

"You could leave the Amish faith. You're not a member yet, so you won't be shunned, and when we both feel ready for marriage—"

Eli's eyebrows arched. "Marriage? Are you saying you want to marry me?"

Laura swallowed hard. Was that what she was saying? Did she really love Eli, or was he simply a prize she wanted and thought was out of her reach?

"After we've dated awhile, we might be ready for marriage," she amended.

Eli sat there several seconds, staring at the reins in his hands. "The only reason I haven't joined the church yet is because I was waiting until I felt ready for marriage."

"Wh–what are you saying?"

"I'm saying that despite my feelings for you, I don't believe I could be happy living and working as an Englisher."

"Why not?"

"To my way of thinking, a newborn calf, freshly plowed soil, and the ripening of grain are all manifestations of God's power. Farming to many Amish men in this area isn't just a job, it's a way of life blessed by God and handed down from one generation to another. If I left the Amish faith or moved away from God, I wouldn't feel like a whole person anymore."

She grasped the collar of his jacket and gazed at his handsome face. "I'm not asking you to leave God. You can worship Him in any church. I'm only asking you to give up your

Plain lifestyle so we can be together."

"Could you give up your modern way of life to become Plain?"

She shook her head. "I—I don't think so. It would be too hard for me to adjust."

"Exactly. While it is possible for outsiders to join the Amish community, it seldom happens because it would be too big of a change." Eli leaned away from her. Snapping the reins, he shouted, "Giddap there, boy. It's time to go!"

Laura's eyes stung with unshed tears. As the horse moved forward and the sleigh began to glide across the snow, she felt as though her whole world had fallen apart.

Why wouldn't Eli listen to reason? What had gone wrong with her plan?

Eli gripped the reins so hard his fingers ached. *I wish I'd never met Laura. I should have never invited her to take that first ride in my courting buggy. I was stupid for asking her to go skating with me this morning, too. It only made both of us hope for the impossible.*

As much as Eli hated to admit it, he had come to care for Laura, but he didn't think he could give up his way of life in order to marry her. At the same time, he knew it would be impossible for her to give up the only way of life she had ever known to be with him.

They rode in silence all the way back to his

145

house, and when Eli guided the sleigh into the yard, Laura leaned close to him, sending shivers up the back of his neck. "Won't you at least think about what I said earlier? Maybe there's a reason you haven't joined the church yet. Maybe we're supposed to be together."

Eli shook his head as he swallowed around the lump in his throat. "We've let this go on too long, Laura. You and I both know that neither of us could be happy living in the other person's world. So the best thing is for us to say good-bye now, before one or both of us get hurt."

Tears filled Laura's eyes, and Eli was tempted to pull her into his arms and kiss them away. Instead, he stepped out of the sleigh and skirted around to the other side to help her down. Laura leaned down and picked up Martha Rose's skates. "Tell your sister I said thanks for giving me the opportunity to spend a few more hours with you before we had to say good-bye."

"Jah, I will."

"And you were right, Eli. It wouldn't have worked for us."

Before Eli could respond, she hopped down without his assistance and limped toward her car. Every fiber of Eli's being screamed at him to go after her, but reason won out. He turned his attention toward the horse, vowing that no matter what it took, he would forget he had ever met a fancy English woman named Laura Meade.

Chapter 13

January and February were cold . . . so cold and dreary Laura thought she would die. It wasn't just the weather making her feel that way, either. Her heart was broken because Eli had rejected her. If he really cared, he should have agreed to leave his world and join hers.

Two months had passed since their final good-bye, but Laura still longed for something she couldn't have. Visions of the happy times they had spent together danced through her mind. Losing Eli hurt so much, and she couldn't seem to do anything to ease the pain. Shopping for new clothes didn't help. Throwing herself into her studies made no difference. Even an occasional binge on hot-fudge sundaes and chocolate milkshakes did nothing to make her feel better. The barrage of e-mails and phone calls from Dean Carlson didn't soothe Laura's troubled spirit, either. She cared nothing for Dean, and she told him so.

As winter moved into spring, Laura finally began to move on with her life. At least she thought she was moving on until one of her teachers gave the class an assignment, asking each student to decorate a bedroom using something handmade by the Amish as a focal point.

Laura had her Amish quilt . . . the one she'd purchased at the farmers' market the first day she'd met Eli. However, when she and Eli broke off their relationship, she had boxed up the quilt and sent it home, unable to look at it any longer. She supposed she could call Mom and ask her to mail it back, but the assignment was due early next week, and there wasn't enough time for that. There was only one logical thing to do —go to the farmers' market and buy another quilt.

"If you can spare a few minutes, I'd like to talk to you about Laura."

Wesley halted in front of his office door and turned to face Dean. "What about her?"

Dean nodded toward the office. "Can we talk in there?"

"I guess so." Wesley stepped into the room and motioned to one of the leather chairs near his desk. "Have a seat."

Dean sat down, and Wesley took a seat in the larger chair behind the desk. "Now what did you want to say about my daughter?"

"I was wondering if you'd heard anything from her lately."

"Laura calls at least once a week, and we get e-mails nearly every day. Why do you ask?"

Dean rubbed his fingers along the edge of his

chin and grimaced. "She won't answer my phone calls or any of my e-mails."

"Any idea why?"

"She turned off to me the night of the New Year's Eve party and wouldn't even let me take her home when she said she wasn't feeling well."

Wesley leaned forward with his elbows on the desk. "So you've had no contact with her since she went back to Pennsylvania?"

"Just one phone call, and she told me she didn't want to see me again."

"Then I guess you'd better take Laura at her word. She's a lot like her mother in many respects."

"How so?"

"Once my daughter makes up her mind about something, there's no changing it."

"Has she found someone else? Is that the problem?"

Wesley shrugged. "You'll have to ask her that question." He motioned to the door. "Now if you don't mind, I have work to do, and I'm sure you do, as well."

Dean stood. "The next time you talk to Laura, would you give her a message for me?"

"That all depends on what the message is."

"Tell her I'm not giving up on us, and when she finally comes to her senses, I'll be here waiting."

Before Wesley could respond, Dean sauntered out of the room.

"I'll give Laura a message all right," Wesley mumbled. "I'll tell her the best thing she ever did was drop you flat on your ear." He tapped the end of his pen against the desk a couple of times. "If you weren't such a crackerjack lawyer, I'd drop you flat, too."

As Eli headed to the farmers' market in his horse and open buggy, he kept thinking about Laura and how interested she'd seemed in his birdhouses that first day when he'd met her at the market. It had been two whole months since they'd said good-bye after their ice-skating date, and a day hadn't gone by that he hadn't thought about her.

He glanced over at his date sitting in the seat beside him. *Here I am with Pauline again. Is it fair to lead her on? Is it possible for me to learn to love her?* It wasn't a case of Pauline not being pretty. She just wasn't as pretty as Laura. It wasn't that he didn't enjoy Pauline's company. She simply wasn't as much fun to be around as Laura. But Eli had decided to give Pauline a chance, thinking it might help him forget Laura, and knowing it would please his folks if he settled down, got baptized, joined the church, and took a wife. He just wasn't sure that wife could be Pauline.

"Spring's just around the corner, jah?" Pauline said, cutting into Eli's private thoughts.

He nodded. "Many of the trees have blossoms already, and some flowers are poking their heads through the soil."

She sighed. "Won't be long and it'll be warm enough for picnics."

"Jah."

"If this warm weather holds out, maybe we could go to the lake next Saturday."

"We'll have to see how it goes."

She reached over and touched his arm. "Guess I'll have to pray for sunshine."

He gave no reply as he guided his horse and buggy into the market parking lot.

Laura was glad Darla had agreed to go with her to the farmers' market. She didn't relish the idea of going there alone. Too many painful memories lived inside that building. Too many reminders of the day she'd met Eli.

They had taken Darla's car this morning, and as soon as it was parked, Laura hopped out and headed for the building. She knew from what Eli had told her that Saturdays were always busy at the market, and she didn't want to miss out on the best deals.

"Hey, wait for me," Darla shouted.

Laura halted. "Sorry. Guess I'm in too big a hurry to look at those beautiful quilts."

"I might just buy one myself this time."

They stepped into the building, and Laura led the way.

"I'm beginning to see why the country look fascinates you so much," Darla commented, as they browsed through a stack of colorful quilts. "The vibrant hues and various shapes in these are actually quite pretty."

Laura nodded as she fingered a monochromatic blue quilt with a Double Wedding Ring pattern. The middle-aged Amish woman selling the quilts mentioned that it was an old patchwork design, and that as the name implied, two rings interlocked with each other.

"Some quilters use their scraps of material for the Double Wedding Ring because the pieces are quite small." She smiled and lifted one edge of the quilt. "Others plan their quilt with great care, alternating light and dark rings."

"I think I'll buy this one," Laura said. "I love the variance of colors and the interlocking rings."

"And I believe I'll keep looking awhile." Darla chuckled. "No sense picking the first one I see."

When Laura didn't answer, Darla poked her in the ribs. "Did you hear what I said?"

Laura stood frozen in her tracks. Her heart pounded like a pack of stampeding horses, and her throat felt so dry she could barely swallow.

"Laura, what's wrong? You look like you've seen a ghost."

"It's . . . it's Eli . . . and that woman." Laura's voice cracked. "I—I had no idea he would be here today. If I'd known, I wouldn't have come."

Darla craned her neck. "Where is he, and what woman are you talking about?"

"She seems really possessive and thinks she's Eli's girlfriend—and maybe she is now that I'm out of the picture. They're right over there." Laura pointed toward the root-beer stand several feet away. "I shouldn't be surprised to see them together, but it hurts, nonetheless."

Darla grabbed hold of Laura's arm. "Come on. We've got to get you out of here right now."

Laura jerked away. "I'm not going anywhere. This is a free country, and I have as much right to be here as they do."

"I'm sure, but you don't want Eli to know you're here. Do you?"

Laura dropped her gaze to the floor and shrugged. "Maybe."

"What? The guy threw you over for someone else, and you want to grovel in the dirt in front of him?"

"He didn't throw me over, and I wasn't planning to grovel. I was just thinking I should probably say hello."

"Now that's a real brilliant idea." Darla turned

back toward the stack of quilts. "You can do whatever you like, but I came here to look at handmade Amish items. That *was* our assignment, you know, not saying hello to some cute Amish guy."

Ignoring her friend's comment, Laura took a deep breath and marched straight up to the root-beer stand. "Hello, Eli. How are you?"

"Laura? What are you doing here?" Eli's eyes were wide, and his mouth hung slightly open.

"I'm looking at quilts," she answered, fixing her gaze somewhere near the center of his chest. "I—I have an assignment to do, and—"

"Come on, Eli, let's go."

Laura turned her gaze to Pauline. She stood beside Eli with one hand on his arm in a possessive gesture, and she offered Laura an icy stare.

Laura's legs felt like rubber, and tension pulled the muscles in her neck. She had a deep sense that she had done the wrong thing when she'd asked Eli to leave his Amish faith, and she couldn't ignore it a moment longer. She took a guarded step forward. "Eli, could we talk? I need to tell you something." Her mouth went dry with trepidation as she stared into his blue eyes and recognized hesitation.

A few seconds ticked by. Then he shrugged. "I guess it would be all right." He glanced over at Pauline. "Could you wait for me at the hot dog stand? I won't be long."

154

Pauline scrunched up her nose. "Are you kidding me?"

He shook his head. "I'll just be a minute."

She glared at Laura, then stalked off, muttering something in Pennsylvania Dutch.

Eli turned back to Laura. "Should we go outside?"

She nodded and followed as he led the way to the nearest exit. When they stepped outside, he motioned to a wooden bench near the building.

Once they were both seated, Laura felt a bit more comfortable. At least now she could gulp in some fresh air, which she hoped might tame the brigade of bumblebees marching through her stomach.

"What did you want to talk to me about?" Eli asked.

"Us. I wanted to talk about us."

"There *is* no *us*, Laura. I thought you understood that I'm not going to leave my faith. In fact, I've decided to—"

"I do understand, and I'm sorry for asking you to give up your way of life."

"Thank you for understanding. Someday you'll meet the right man, and—"

Laura lifted her hand and covered his mouth with her fingers. "I've already found the right man."

His eyebrows raised in obvious surprise. "You have? That's good. I wish you all the best."

155

She compressed her lips in frustration. Was Eli deaf, dumb, and blind? Couldn't he see how much she wanted to be with him? She grasped both of his hands and gave them a squeeze. "The man I've found is you. I want no other, and I never will."

"But, Laura—"

"I know, I know. You won't leave the Amish faith and become a fancy Englisher." She swallowed hard and drew in a deep breath. "That doesn't mean we can't be together, though."

He tipped his head and looked at Laura as if she'd lost her mind. "It doesn't?"

"No, it doesn't. Not unless you've found someone else." She leaned closer to him. "Have you, Eli? Are you in love with Pauline?"

He shook his head. "We're still just friends, but—"

"Do you still have feelings for me?"

"Jah, but you know—"

"Well, good. I can solve our problem by coming over to the other side."

A deep frown creased Eli's forehead. "I'm afraid I don't get your meaning."

"I'll join the Amish faith and become Plain."

"What?"

"I said—"

Eli held up his hand. "You don't know what you're saying, Laura. A few folks have joined our faith, but not many. It's not all cakes and pies, you know, and there would be much to learn—classes to take."

"I'm sure it wouldn't be an easy transition, but I can do it, Eli. I can do anything if I set my mind to it."

Eli couldn't believe Laura was offering to join his faith. During the time they had been seeing each other, he'd often found himself wishing for just such a turn of events, but after she'd asked him to join her world, he was certain she would never consider becoming Amish. Now she suddenly wanted to become Plain? It made no sense at all. He studied her intently. She seemed sincere, but truth be told, Laura didn't have any idea what she was suggesting.

"I do love you," he admitted, "but—"

"I'm glad to hear that." She leaned her head on his shoulder. "I was afraid you might turn me away."

Eli breathed in the strawberry scent of Laura's hair and reveled in the warmth of her touch. How could he make her understand, yet how could he say good-bye to her again?

"These last few months have been awful," Laura said with a catch in her voice. "I need to be with you."

"But you might not be happy being Amish, and then what? As I said, it would be a hard thing to change over and give up all the modern things you're used to having. You would have to learn our language and accept our religious views."

She nodded. "I know it won't be easy, but with your help, I can do it. You will help me, won't you, Eli?"

Eli filled his lungs with fresh air as he struggled to make a decision. He lifted Laura's chin with his thumb and stared into her sea green eyes, hoping to find answers there. He wanted to be with her more than anything. Yet he didn't see how it could ever work out.

When she smiled at him the way she was now, it was hard to think. Hard to breathe. Hard to know what was right and what wasn't.

"Eli, what's your answer?"

Pushing the niggling doubts aside, he finally nodded. "You'll need time to adjust, but I'll help you in every way I can."

CHAPTER 14

Once Laura made her decision to become Amish, the purchase of a second quilt was completely forgotten. The first order of business was to find Darla and tell her what she planned to do. Then she would need to go back to the interior design school and withdraw. After that, she would call her parents. That was going to be the hardest part, because she was sure they wouldn't understand. Eli's job was to tell Pauline the news, and also his parents, and she was sure that wouldn't be easy, either.

Eli stood from the bench where they had been sitting. "As soon as I leave the farmers' market, I'll head over to my sister's place and see if she would be willing to let you live with her."

Laura stood, too. "Do you think she would do that?"

"Jah. Martha Rose and I are close." He chuckled. "It's always been hard for her to tell me no, and I'm sure she would be a big help in teaching you everything you'll need to know about our way of life."

Laura gripped his arm. "I'm a ball of nerves, Eli. What if Martha Rose says I can't stay there? What if your folks don't accept me? What if—"

Eli held up his hand, halting her words. "Tomorrow I'll hire a driver to pick you up at the school in Lancaster, and we'll drive over to Amon and Martha Rose's place so you can meet them."

"That's okay," she said. "I'll need to turn in the car I'm leasing, so I'll have someone from the rental company drop me off in front of the variety store in Paradise. You can pick me up there, if that's all right."

"Jah, sure." He smiled, and it gave her a sense

159

of reassurance. "I'm sure everything will work out okay."

"I still can't believe what you're planning to do," Darla said, as she and Laura drove back to their school. "Don't you realize what you'll be giving up? Don't you know how hard the transition from English to Amish will be?"

Laura nodded. "I know it won't be easy, but I can do it. I can do anything if I want it badly enough, and this is something I really want."

"You want to live the Plain life, without all the modern conveniences you've become used to?"

"Well, I—"

"Think about it, Laura. You won't be able to use your computer to send e-mails anymore. You won't be allowed to wear makeup, jeans, or any fancy clothes. You'll have to trade in your leased car for a horse and buggy."

Laura shrugged. "I'm sure it won't be easy, but I can do it for Eli—because I love him and hope to be his wife someday."

"Can't you talk him into leaving the Amish faith? You told me once that he's not joined the church yet, so he wouldn't be shunned if he were to become English."

"I did ask him about leaving once, and it wasn't long after that he said we should go our separate ways." Laura clenched her fingers tightly together in her lap. "I was miserable those months we were apart, and I won't let Eli walk out of my life again, no matter how many sacrifices I might need to make."

Darla gave the steering wheel a couple of taps. "Suit yourself, but don't come crying to me when things don't work out."

"I won't. You can be sure of that."

As Pauline waited near the root-beer stand for Eli to return, she became increasingly anxious. What had that English woman wanted to speak with Eli about, and why had he agreed to talk to her? She hoped he hadn't given up his plans to take membership classes this summer and join the church in the fall. Surely he wasn't thinking about leaving the Amish faith and going English.

"Oh, good, I'm glad you're still here. I need to speak with you."

Pauline whirled around at the sound of Eli's voice. She felt relief to see that the English woman wasn't with him. "Is everything all right, Eli? You look kind of flushed."

He drew her away from the table and over to one corner of the room. "I need to tell you something."

"What is it?"

Eli stared at the concrete floor as he shifted his weight from one foot to the other. "I—I've tried to tell you this before, but there's really no way it could work for us to be together."

Her forehead wrinkled. "Why not? We've been courting for a couple of months now, and I thought we've been getting along fairly well."

He lifted his gaze to hers. "There's no easy way for me to say this, but I'm in love with Laura."

"The Englisher?"

"Jah."

"You're going to leave the Amish faith to be with her?"

He shook his head. "Laura wants to become Plain."

Pauline tried to let Eli's words register in her brain while fighting the tears pushing against her eyelids. This couldn't be true. It had to be some kind of horrible joke. No one just up and decided to join the church—to her knowledge very few ever had.

"You're a nice person, and I'm sorry if I've led you on or hurt you in any way." Eli touched her arm. "I thought I could forget about Laura and move on with my life, but after seeing her today, I realized that she's the one I love and want to be with."

Pauline shrugged his hand away. "It won't work, Eli. That fancy woman will never become one of us. I doubt she could last one week as an Amish woman." Pauline's heart felt like it was breaking in two, but there was no way she would admit to Eli how much he had hurt her, or that she'd hoped to become his wife someday. She lifted her chin and stared right into his blue eyes. "You're verhuddelt if you think things are going to work out for you and Laura, but if she's what you want, then don't expect any sympathy from me if things go sour." Pauline turned on her heels and stalked off.

"Where are you going? Don't you need a ride home?"

She shook her head and kept on walking. She would find her own way home, even if it meant phoning one of their English drivers for a ride.

As Eli left his sister's place and headed down the road toward home with his horse and buggy, he reflected on the conversation he'd had with Martha Rose and felt relief that she'd agreed to let Laura stay with her and Amon while she took her training to become Amish. Martha Rose had also been willing to instruct Laura in cooking, sewing, and many other things she would need to know in order to become part of the Amish community.

Eli was sure that once his sister met Laura in person and saw how nice she was and realized that she wanted to become Amish, everything would work out fine and dandy. Now all he had to do was break the news to Mom and Pop.

163

Mary Ellen was just putting lunch on the table when she heard a horse and buggy come into the yard. She glanced out the kitchen window and saw that it was Eli. "I wonder what he's doing home so soon," she said to Johnny, who had just finished washing up at the sink. "I thought he and Pauline were going out to lunch after they left the market, and I figured he would be gone most of the day."

Johnny shrugged. "Guess there must have been a change of plans."

"I hope they didn't have a disagreement. Eli can be kind of headstrong sometimes."

Johnny chuckled and flicked a little water in her direction. "Wonder where he gets that trait from?"

She wrinkled her nose. "Maybe you'd best look in the mirror."

"Ha! I'd say we both tend to be a bit headstrong at times."

"I guess you're right about that." She glanced out the window again. "Eli's putting his horse away, so he'll probably be in shortly. Did Lewis and Jonas say when they were coming inside?"

Johnny dried his hands on a towel before answering. "They had a couple of things to do in the barn, but I'm sure they'll be in soon, too."

"I'll go ahead and serve up the soup. By the

time they come in, it will probably be cool enough to eat."

"Makes sense to me." Johnny kissed Mary Ellen's cheek, then ambled across the room and took a seat at the table.

A few minutes later, Jonas and Lewis entered the kitchen, followed by Eli, whose face was all red and sweaty.

Mary Ellen felt immediate concern, and she placed the ladle back in the pot of soup and rushed to his side. "Is there anything wrong, son? You look kind of flushed."

"That's what Pauline said right before I told her the news." Eli flopped into a chair and let his head fall forward into his hands.

Pop reached over and touched Eli's shoulder. "What news is that? What's got you so worked up?"

Eli looked up and blew out his breath. "There's something I need to tell you."

"Are you and Pauline gettin' hitched?" The question came from Lewis, who had also pulled out a chair and sat down.

Eli shook his head. "I think it might be good if everyone took a seat. What I have to say will probably be quite a shock."

Mary Ellen's heart slammed into her chest. Was Eli going to announce that he'd decided not to join the church in the fall, after all? With a sense of dread, she took the chair closest to him.

"So, tell us what's on your mind," Johnny said, after Jonas took his seat.

"You all remember Laura Meade, right?"

"The pretty redheaded woman you brought by the house a few months back?" Lewis asked with a grin.

Eli nodded. "The thing is—I saw Laura today, and she wants to join the Amish church."

"What?" Mary Ellen could hardly believe her ears. Eli hadn't mentioned the English woman in some time, and this made no sense at all.

"I've just come from Martha Rose's place, and she's agreed to let Laura stay there."

"She'll be staying with Martha Rose and Amon?"

"Jah, Mom."

"It just doesn't seem right, her being so fancy and all," Jonas said with a shake of his head.

"Jah," Lewis agreed. "It's not gonna be easy for Laura to give up all the modern things she's been used to and start livin' as we do."

"If Laura stays with Martha Rose, she can teach her all the things she'll need to know about being Amish, and Laura and I can both take the membership classes this summer. Then by fall, we'll both be baptized and join the church."

"Whose idea was this?" Johnny asked, leaning his elbows on the table.

"The part about joining the church was Laura's idea, but I'm the one who thought of asking

Martha Rose to help her." Eli scrubbed a hand down his clean-shaven face. "Laura wants it, and so do I. She knows what she's giving up, and it's her decision to do this. So won't you please give her a chance?"

"It will take a lot of gumption for her to make all the sacrifices needed to join the church," Johnny put in. "If she can do it, then I'm willing to give her a chance."

"How about the rest of you?" Eli looked around the table.

Lewis and Jonas both nodded, but Mary Ellen couldn't seem to find her voice. If Laura wanted to join the church, and Eli wanted them to take classes and be baptized together, then in all likelihood, he had plans of marrying the girl soon after that. Mary Ellen didn't like the idea, but she knew if she voiced her concerns it might drive Eli away. They had waited a long time for him to reach a decision about joining the church, and she wouldn't do anything to discourage him. She finally nodded and forced her lips into a smile. "I'll give Laura a chance, too."

As soon as Laura returned to the school, she went straight to the admissions office and told them she would be withdrawing and would try to move her things out in the morning. Then she went to her room to call her parents.

She felt relief when Dad answered the phone,

167

because she was sure the news of her decision would be harder for Mom to handle. "Hi, Dad, it's me," she said, drawing in a quick breath for added courage.

"It's good to hear from you, Laura. How are things going with your studies?"

She shifted the phone to her other ear. "I . . . uh . . . need to tell you something."

"Oh? What's that?"

"Starting tomorrow morning, I'll be done with school."

"Done? What do you mean? You haven't even finished your first year there yet."

"I'm . . . uh . . . not planning to finish, Dad."

There was a pause, then, "Irene, you'd better pick up the phone in the kitchen. Laura's on the line."

Laura held her breath as she waited for her mother to come on. Maybe it was better this way. She could tell them both the news at the same time and be done with it.

"Hello, Laura. How are you, dear?"

"I—I'm okay."

"Our daughter has some news she wants to share with us," Dad said before Mom could add anything more.

"What news is that?"

"I've withdrawn from school, and tomorrow morning, I'll be moving in with Eli's sister so I can join the Amish church."

"What?" Mom and Dad shouted in unison.

"I'm planning to join the Amish church."

"This is not April Fool's Day, Laura," Dad said with a chuckle. "Now quit fooling around."

"I'm not kidding. I'm in love with Eli Yoder, and the only way we can be together is if I join his faith."

"Why can't he leave the Amish faith and join our world?"

"Because, Mom, his roots are deep, and he's committed to his family as well as to his religion."

"Oh, and you're not committed to your family?"

"I am, but you and Dad have your own busy lives, and you've raised me to be independent and make my own decisions." Laura paused as she groped for the right words. "This is the decision I've chosen to make."

"Laura, do you know what you're saying?" Mom's voice had risen at least an octave, and Laura had to hold the phone away from her ear. "I'm catching the next flight to Pennsylvania so I can talk some sense into you."

"You may as well save your money, because nothing you can say will make me change my mind. Besides, by the time you get here, I'll be moved out of my dorm room and into Martha Rose's house, and you don't know where that is." Laura sucked in her bottom lip. The truth was, she had no idea where Eli's sister lived, either. For that matter, she wasn't even sure Martha Rose would agree to take her in. What if the woman had said no to Eli's request? What if Laura had quit school for nothing and now had no place to go?

She shook her head, trying to clear away the troubling thoughts. It would all work out. It had to work out. Eli had said it would.

"What about Dean?" Mom asked. "I thought the two of you were—"

"It was over between me and Dean months ago. The last time we talked, I told him so, too."

"Laura, your mother and I want you to be happy," Dad said. "But is giving up the only way of life you've ever known and becoming Amish really going to make you happy?"

"Being with Eli will make me happy, and if I have to make a few sacrifices along the way in order for it to happen, then I'll learn to deal with it."

"She's got a determined spirit, this daughter of ours, and it took a lot of courage for her to make a decision such as this. I think we should give her our blessing."

Laura knew Dad was talking to Mom now, so she waited to hear what her mother's response would be.

"I don't see how you can expect me to give Laura my blessing when I know she's making the biggest mistake of her life. She won't be happy living without electricity and many other modern conveniences. She might think she's in love with this Amish man, but a few months from now, she'll change her mind; mark my words."

Laura released an exasperated sigh. "I've got to go now. I need to pack. I'll give you a call on my cell phone after I get moved so I can give you my new address. Maybe you can send me that quilt I bought at the farmers' market. It would be nice to have it in my possession again."

Mom released a couple of sobs and hung up.

"If you change your mind about this or ever need anything, don't hesitate to call," Dad said.

"Thanks, I'll remember that."

"Be happy, and please keep in touch."

"I will, Dad." Laura clicked off her cell phone and flopped onto the bed. Mom had reacted to the news pretty much the way she'd expected her to, but her father's reaction had been a complete surprise. Had he been so compliant because he wanted her to be happy, or was it possible that some part of Dad could actually identify with Laura's desire to go Plain?

CHAPTER 15

As Laura sat on a bench in front of the variety store in Paradise, she began to worry. She had turned in all of her books at the school, sent everything home that she didn't think she would need in her new life, and dropped off her rental car. Now she was waiting for Eli to pick her up. But what if he didn't show? What if he'd changed his mind about asking his sister to take Laura in? Maybe his folks had talked him out of his plans. Or maybe his sister had said no to his request.

She drew in a deep breath and tried to calm her nerves. The last time she'd waited on this bench for Eli and had been worried he wouldn't show, he'd only been running late. That was probably the case this time, too. At least she hoped it was.

She leaned her head against the wall behind her and tried to focus on something else. It was useless. All she could think about was Eli and how much she wanted to be with him. If he didn't show up, she would be devastated, and she'd never be able to face Darla again.

Darla had tried again this morning to get Laura to change her mind about joining the Amish faith. She'd reminded her of how hard it was going to be and said that Laura needed to give it more thought.

Ever since the day Laura had met Eli, he'd never been far from her thoughts. She dreamed about him at night, compared him to Dean during the day, and imagined what it would be like to be Mrs. Eli Yoder.

The *clip-clop* of horse's hooves drew Laura's attention to the parking lot, and a feeling of relief flooded her soul. Eli was here. He had come for her just like he'd promised. Everything would be okay now.

As Eli led Laura up the steps to his sister's home, her insides quivered with anticipation. She'd been relieved when Eli had told her that Martha Rose had agreed to let her stay, but that was only half the battle. Laura still had lots to learn, and she worried about whether she would be accepted among Eli's friends and family.

"Don't be nervous now," Eli whispered as he opened the back door. "You'll like it here, I promise."

Laura forced a smile. "I—I hope so."

When they entered the kitchen, they were greeted by a tall, large-boned woman with a flawless complexion, hair the color of chestnuts, and dark brown eyes. She offered a warm, friendly smile. "You must be Laura."

Laura's only reply was a quick nod.

"I'm Eli's sister, Martha Rose."

Laura extended her hand. "It's nice to meet you, and I appreciate your letting me stay here."

Martha Rose glanced over at Eli and smiled. "I'd do most anything for my little brother."

Eli chuckled. "Should I bring in Laura's things while you show her around?"

"Jah, sure." Martha Rose motioned toward the door leading to a hallway. "Why don't we start with the upstairs, since that's where Laura's bedroom will be?"

Eli disappeared out the back door, and Laura followed Martha Rose up the stairs.

"This will be yours," Martha Rose said, opening the door to the second room on the left. "It's right across the hall from the bathroom."

Laura breathed a sigh of relief. At least this Amish farm had indoor plumbing, and for that she felt grateful. Darla had told her that most Amish in the area used diesel or propane-operated generators, so they had indoor bathrooms with hot and cold running water, but a few homes still used outhouses.

As Laura stepped into the bedroom where she would soon take up residence, a shockwave spiraled through her. It was even smaller than her dorm room at the school had been. Plain . . . so very plain. There was a double bed, a chest of drawers with a washbowl and pitcher sitting on top, and a small cedar chest at the foot of the bed. Dark shades hung at the two windows, and except for a small, braided throw rug, the hardwood floor was bare. Instead of a closet, a row of wooden pegs was connected to a narrow strip of wood lining one wall.

"Here are a few dresses you can wear." Martha Rose handed Laura two long, cotton frocks. One was navy blue, the other a dark shade of green. "You're a bit shorter than me, so they might be kind of long." She grinned. "Better too long than too short."

Laura was too dumbfounded to even speak. In her excitement to join the Amish faith and win Eli's heart, she had almost forgotten that she would be expected to wear such plain, simple clothing.

"I have a white head covering for you. And you'll need a dark bonnet to wear over it when you go out at certain times."

Laura nodded mutely as she was given the rest of her new wardrobe. *What have I gotten myself into? Can I really exchange my jeans and T-shirts for long, plain dresses?* She inhaled deeply, reminding herself that she could do this and that it was for a good cause. Her determination and love for Eli would see her through.

"We'll go to the boot and harness shop tomorrow and buy you some black leather shoes for church and other special occasions," Martha

Rose said. "If you already own a pair of sneakers, you can wear them for everyday." She looked down at her bare feet and smiled. "Of course, most of us just go barefoot around home, especially during the warmer weather. It saves our shoes, and it's much cooler."

Laura shifted from one foot to the other. Barefoot? Sneakers and black leather shoes? Were those her only choices? "Don't your feet get dirty and sore, running around barefoot?"

"Jah, but they toughen up, and I always wash my feet before going to bed."

Laura shrugged. What could she really say? She'd gotten herself into this predicament, and it was of her own choosing that she had decided to go Plain. She would simply draw from her inner strength and do whatever was necessary in order to convince Eli and his family she was worthy of being part of their clan.

The next few weeks were busy . . . busier than Laura ever imagined. She had so much to learn about cooking, sewing, baking, and doing laundry and other household chores, not to mention the outside jobs. Gathering eggs, slopping the hogs, and cultivating the garden were all things she had never done before. It was dirty, backbreaking work, and she made so many foolish mistakes at first.

One morning after breakfast, as Laura was in

her room getting ready for a date with Eli, she glanced at herself in the hand mirror she'd found in the drawer and dug underneath her underwear for the satchel of makeup she had stashed away. She knew Amish women didn't wear makeup, but she wasn't ready to part with those things, so she hadn't mailed them home with all her clothes.

Today was Saturday, and Eli would be coming soon to take her for a buggy ride. They planned to go into Paradise and do some shopping, then stop for a picnic on the way home.

Laura stared longingly at the tube of lipstick she held in her hand. *What would it hurt to apply a little color to my pale lips so Eli will find me attractive? I wouldn't want him to lose interest in me and go back to Pauline.*

Laura blended the coral lipstick with the tips of her fingers, then reached inside the makeup case for some blush. A little dab blended on each cheek made her look less pale. She added a coat of mascara to her eyelashes and filled in her brows with a soft cinnamon pencil.

"There now," she whispered to her reflection. "I almost look like my old self—not nearly so plain." She glanced down at her plain green dress and scowled. "What I wouldn't give to put on a pair of jeans and a T-shirt." She slipped her head covering on and sighed. "Guess I'd better get used to this if I'm ever going to fit in here."

Downstairs in the kitchen, Laura found Eli's

sister and his mother sitting at the table, drinking a cup of tea and eating shoofly pie. Just the smell of the molasses-filled pastry made Laura's stomach churn. She didn't think she would ever acquire a taste for this particular dessert.

"Guder mariye," Martha Rose said cheerfully when Laura joined them.

"Good morning," she responded with a slight nod. Learning Pennsylvania Dutch was another challenge for Laura, along with studying the Bible and learning the church rules, which the Amish called the *Ordnung*. She glanced over at Eli's mother. "I didn't realize you were here, Mary Ellen."

"Came to help Martha Rose do some baking." Mary Ellen studied Laura intently, making her feel like a bug under a microscope. "What's that you've got on your face?"

Laura shrugged and reached for an apple from the ceramic bowl sitting in the center of the table. "Just a little color to make me look less pale," she mumbled as she bit into the succulent fruit.

"Makeup's not allowed. Surely you must know that."

Laura blinked a couple of times as she stared at Mary Ellen. "What harm is there in trying to make myself a bit more attractive?"

" 'Favour is deceitful, and beauty is vain: but a woman that feareth the Lord, she shall be praised,' " Mary Ellen quoted.

178

Laura squinted her eyes. "Where'd you hear that?"

"It's in the book of Proverbs," Martha Rose answered, before her mother had a chance to respond.

Mary Ellen looked right at Laura. "Face powder may catch some men, but it takes baking powder to hold them."

Martha Rose giggled, and her mother chuckled behind her hand, but Laura sat stony-faced. She didn't see what was so funny. Besides, she had the distinct impression these two Plain women were laughing at her, not at the joke Eli's mother had just shared.

Laura felt foolish for doing something she knew was wrong, but it irritated her that Mary Ellen had made a joke at her expense. She was sure the woman didn't like her. With a sigh of frustration, she pushed her chair away from the table and stood. "Sorry about the mistake. I'll go wash the makeup off my face now."

Eli whistled as he hitched his horse to the open buggy. He was looking forward to his date with Laura, but he still couldn't believe she had actually agreed to become Plain. She was beautiful, talented, and smart. He was sure she could have any man she wanted, yet it was him and his way of life she had chosen. It almost seemed too good to be true.

"I'll make her happy," he said aloud. The horse whinnied and nuzzled the back of Eli's arm.

"At least *you* aren't givin' me a hard time. If Mom and Pop had their way, I'd be married to Pauline by now, not courting Laura."

Eli knew his parents had his best interests at heart, but they didn't understand how much he loved Laura. Even though his folks had agreed to try and make her feel welcome, he was sure it was only to please him. Deep in his heart, Eli felt they were just waiting for Laura to give up and leave so they could say, "I told you so."

He was glad Martha Rose seemed to be on his side and had agreed to let Laura stay there. It was a comfort to know his sister was willing to mentor his fancy English woman who wanted to become Plain. Mom and Pop were another matter. They were no more thrilled about the idea of Laura joining the Amish faith than they had been about Eli seeing her when she was still English. It was hard to understand how Mom, who normally was so pleasant and easygoing, had seemed almost rude to Laura when she'd first visited their home. Even now, as Laura prepared to become Amish, there was a coolness in the way his mother spoke to Laura. He hoped things would change once Laura took her training and was baptized into the faith.

Eli climbed into the driver's seat and gathered up the reins. He knew Mom had gone over to

Martha Rose's this morning so she would see Laura before he did.

He clucked to the horse, and it moved forward. "Let's hope things went well between Laura and Mom, for if they didn't, I'm likely to have a cross woman on my hands for the rest of the day."

When Laura greeted Eli at the back door, he thought she looked like she'd lost her best friend. "What's wrong? Aren't you happy to see me this morning? Do you still want to go to Paradise and then on a picnic?"

"Of course I want to go."

"Would you like to come in and have a piece of shoofly pie?" Mom asked.

Eli glanced at his mother, who sat at the kitchen table with Martha Rose. "Jah, sure."

"I think we should be on our way," Laura said, stepping between Eli and the table.

He frowned. "What's your hurry?"

"I've got quite a bit of shopping to do, and we don't want to get to the lake too late." She rushed past him, pulled a dark blue sweater from the wall peg by the back door, and grabbed the wicker picnic basket sitting on the cupboard.

Eli looked at Laura standing by the door, tapping her foot. He glanced back at the table, and his mouth watered just thinking about how good a hunk of that pie would taste.

As though sensing his dilemma, Martha Rose

said, "Why don't you take a few pieces along? You and Laura can have it with the picnic lunch she made."

Eli shrugged. "I guess I can wait that long to sample some of your good cooking, sister."

He reached for the pie, but Martha Rose was too quick for him. She had already begun slicing it by the time he got to the table. "If you really want to help, get some waxed paper from the pantry," she instructed.

He did as he was told, not caring in the least that his big sister was bossing him around. He'd grown used to it over the years. Besides, she really didn't mean to sound so pushy. Martha Rose had always been a take-charge kind of person. She was pleasant and kind, so he could tolerate a little ordering about now and then.

"You two have a good day," Martha Rose said as Eli and Laura started out the back door.

"Jah, and be sure to be home in time for chores and supper," Mom called.

"I will," Eli said, closing the door behind them.

Laura stopped at the bottom of the stairs, and Eli nearly ran into her. "What'd you stop for? I could have knocked you to the ground."

She scowled at him. "You're henpecked. Do you know that?"

His eyebrows furrowed. "You don't know what you're saying, Laura."

Her nose twitched as she blinked rapidly.

"Those two women have you eating out of the palms of their hands."

Eli started walking toward his open buggy. "They do not. I just happen to like pleasing them, that's all. I love Mom and Martha Rose, and they're both mighty good to me."

"Well, they're not so good to me."

Eli whirled around to face Laura. She looked madder than one of his father's mules when a big old horsefly had taken a bite out of its ear. "How can you say they're not good to you? Martha Rose took you in, didn't she?"

Laura opened her mouth, but before she could respond, Eli rushed on. "She gave you some of her dresses to wear, took you shopping for shoes and the like, and both she and Mom have taken time out of their busy days to teach you about housekeeping, cooking, Bible reading, and so many other things you'll need to know before joining the church."

Laura's lip protruded as she handed Eli the picnic basket. "I should have known you wouldn't understand. You're one of them."

"What's that supposed to mean?" Eli asked, as he climbed into his rig and took up the reins.

Laura stood on the other side of the buggy with her arms folded. "It means you're Amish and I'm not. I'm still considered an outsider, and I don't think anyone in your family will ever accept me as anything else."

"Of course they will." He glanced at her out of the corner of his eye. "Are you getting in or not?"

"Aren't you going to help me?"

He groaned. "I might have, if you hadn't been naggin' at me. Besides, if you're going to be Amish, then you'll need to learn how to get in and out of our buggies without any help when you're going someplace on your own."

Laura was so angry she was visibly shaking. If she hadn't been sure she would be expected to help with the baking, she would have turned around and marched right back to the house. It would serve Eli right if she broke this date!

"Time's a-wasting," Eli announced.

She sighed deeply, lifted her skirt, and practically fell into the buggy.

Eli chuckled, then snapped the reins. The horse jerked forward, and Laura was thrown against her seat. "Be careful! Are you trying to throw my back out?"

Eli's only response was another deep guffaw, which only angered her further.

Laura smoothed her skirt, reached up to be sure her head covering was still in place, then folded her arms across her chest. "I'm glad you think everything's so funny. You can't imagine what I've been through these past few weeks."

"Has something bad happened?" Eli looked over at her with obvious concern.

She moaned. "I'll say."

"What was it? Did you get hurt? How come I didn't hear about it?"

She shook her head. "No, no, I wasn't hurt. At least not in the physical sense."

"What then?"

"I've nearly been worked to death every day since I moved to your sister's house. It seems as though I just get to sleep and it's time to get up again." She frowned. "And that noisy rooster crowing at the top of his lungs every morning sure doesn't help things, either."

"Pop says the rooster is nature's alarm clock," Eli said with a grin.

How can he sit there looking so smug? Laura fumed. *Doesn't he care how hard I work? Doesn't he realize I'm doing all this for him?*

"In time, you'll get used to the long days. I bet someday you'll find pleasure in that old rooster's crow."

"I doubt that." She held up her hands. "Do you realize that every single one of my nails is broken? Not to mention embedded with dirt I'll probably never be able to scrub clean. Why, the other morning, Martha Rose had me out in the garden, pulling weeds and spading with an old hoe. I thought my back was going to break in two."

"You *will* get used to it, Laura."

She scrunched up her nose. "Maybe. If I live to tell about it."

185

CHAPTER 16

Laura's days at the Zook farm flew by despite her frustrations. As spring turned quickly into summer, each day became longer, hotter, and filled with more work. Instead of "becoming used to it," Laura found herself disliking each new day. How did these people exist without air-conditioning, ceiling fans, and swimming pools? How did the women deal with wearing long dresses all summer instead of shorts?

Laura and Martha Rose had gone wading in the creek near their house a few times, while Amon taught little Ben how to swim. The chilly water helped Laura cool down some, but she missed her parents' swimming pool and air-conditioned home.

Another area of Amish life Laura hadn't become used to was the three-hour church service held every other Sunday in a different member's home. She had gone to church only a few times in her adult life—mostly on Easter and Christmas—but she'd never had to sit on backless, wooden benches or been segregated from the men. The Amish culture still seemed strange to her and very confusing. She couldn't visit with Eli until the service was over, lunch had been served, and everything had been cleaned up. If Laura had ever thought life as an Amish woman was going to be easy, she'd been sorely mistaken. She couldn't even keep her cell phone charged because Amon's farm had no electricity. On days like today when she was hot and tired, she wondered if she had made a mistake by asking to join the Amish church.

"It's not too late to back out," she muttered as she set a basket of freshly laundered clothes on the grass underneath the clothesline that extended from the porch into the yard. "I can go back to the school in Lancaster or home to Mom and Dad in Minneapolis. At least they don't expect me to work so hard."

A pathetic *mooo* drew Laura's attention to the fence separating the Zooks' yard from the pasture. Three black-and-white cows stood on the other side, swishing their tails and looking at her.

"Just what I need—a cheering section. Go away, cows! Get back to the field, grab a hunk of grass, start chewing your cuds, then go take a nice, long nap." She bent down, grabbed one of Amon's shirts, gave it a good shake, then clipped it to the clothesline. "At least you bovine critters are allowed the privilege of a nap now and then. That's more than I can say for any of the humans who live on this farm."

"Kuh," a small voice said.

Laura looked down. There stood little Ben,

gazing up at her with all the seriousness of a three-year-old. He'd said something in Pennsylvania Dutch, but she wasn't sure what he was talking about. She'd been studying the Amish dialect for a few months, but she still encountered many unfamiliar words.

"Kuh," the child repeated. This time he pointed toward the cows, still gawking at Laura like she was free entertainment.

"Ah, the cows. You're talking about the cows, aren't you?" She dropped to her knees beside the little boy and gave him a hug.

Ben looked up at her and grinned. He really was a cute little thing, with his blond, Dutch-bobbed hair, big blue eyes, and two deep dimples framing his smile. He studied the basket of clothes a few seconds as his smile turned to a frown.

"Loch," he said, grabbing one of Amon's shirts.

Laura smiled when she realized the child was telling her about his father's shirt with a hole. She patted the top of Ben's head. "No doubt that shirt will end up in my pile of mending."

Ben made no comment, but then, she knew he didn't understand what she'd said. He would be taught English when he started school. With an impish grin, the boy climbed into the basket of wet clothes.

Laura was about to scold him, but Ben picked

up one of his mother's dark bonnets and plunked it on top of his head. She sank to her knees and laughed so hard that tears ran down her face. The cows on the other side of the fence mooed, and the little boy giggled.

Maybe life on this humble, Amish farm wasn't so bad after all.

Pauline sat on the front porch, staring at the flowers blooming in her mother's garden but not really seeing them. She'd been miserable ever since Eli had told her they had no future together and had begun dating that fancy English woman. Not that Laura looked so fancy anymore. She wore the same plain clothes as the other Amish women in their community, but there was something about the way she walked, talked, and held her body so prim and proper that made her seem out of place among the other women in their district.

Every time Pauline saw Laura at church or some other community event, it made her feel sick to the pit of her stomach. She didn't know if she would ever get over the bitterness she felt over losing Eli to someone outside their faith.

She won't be outside the faith once she's baptized and joins the church, Pauline reminded herself. *She'll be one of us, and I'll have to accept her as such, no matter how much it hurts.*

"What are you doing sitting out here by your-self?" Pauline's mother asked as she seated herself on the step beside Pauline. "I figured you'd be anxious to get some baking done before it gets too hot."

"I don't feel much like baking today. Can't it wait for another day?"

"I suppose, but we're almost out of bread, and you know how much your daed likes those ginger cookies you make so well."

Pauline made no comment; she just sat there breathing in and out, feeling as though she couldn't get enough air.

"Are you okay? You look kind of peaked this morning."

"I'm fine. Just tired is all."

Mom laid a gentle hand on Pauline's arm. "Still not sleeping well?"

"Not since . . ." Pauline couldn't finish the sentence. It pained her to think about Eli, much less speak his name.

"You've got to put your broken relationship with Eli Yoder behind you, daughter. You can't go through the rest of your life pining for some-thing that's not meant to be."

Pauline released a shuddering sob. "It was meant to be, until *she* came along and ruined things. Eli and I were getting closer, and I was sure he would ask me to marry him after he finished his membership classes at the end of summer." Tears slipped from her eyes and rolled down her cheeks. "It's not fair, Mom. It's just not fair."

"Many things in life aren't fair, but we must learn to accept them as God's will and move on."

"I'm not sure I can do that. Not when I have to see Eli and that woman together all the time."

"Maybe you should go away for a while."

Pauline wiped her eyes with the backs of her hands and turned to face her mother. "Go away? Where would I go?"

"Maybe you could stay with your daed's sister, Irma, in Kidron, Ohio."

"I'll have to think about it."

Mom patted Pauline's hand. "You do that. Think and pray about the matter."

Laura sat at the kitchen table, reading the Bible Martha Rose had given her. Why did it seem so confusing? She had been to Sunday school and Bible school a few times when she was a girl. She'd even managed to memorize some Bible passages in order to win a prize. Why couldn't she stay focused now?

"You've been at it quite awhile. Would you like to take a break and have a glass of iced tea with me?" Martha Rose asked, pulling out a chair and taking a seat beside Laura.

Laura looked up and smiled. She really did need a break. "Thanks, I'd like that."

Martha Rose poured two glasses of iced tea and piled a plate high with peanut butter cookies.

"Are you trying to fatten me up?" Laura asked when the goodies were set on the table.

Martha Rose chuckled. "As a matter of fact, you are pretty thin. I figured a few months of living here, and you'd have gained at least ten pounds."

"Your cooking is wonderful, but I'm trying to watch my weight."

"You need to eat hearty in order to keep up your strength." Martha Rose pushed the cookie plate in front of Laura. "Please, have a few."

Laura shrugged. "I guess two cookies wouldn't hurt."

"How are your studies coming along? Has little Ben been staying out of your way?"

"He's never been a problem. Your little boy is a real sweetheart."

"Jah, well, he can also be a pill at times." Martha Rose shook her head. "This morning I found him playing in the toilet, of all things. Said he was goin' fishing, like he and his daed did last week."

Laura laughed. "Where's the little guy now?"

"Down for a nap. I'm hoping he stays asleep awhile, because I've got a bunch of ripe tomatoes waiting to be picked. Not to mention fixing lunch and getting a bit more cleaning done. Church will be here this Sunday, you know."

"I'd almost forgotten. Guess that means we'll have to do more cooking than usual." Laura reached around to rub a tight muscle in her back, probably caused from standing long hours at the stove.

"Not really. I'm just planning to fix a pot of bean soup and some sandwiches."

"Isn't the weather kind of hot to be having soup?"

"We enjoy soup most any time of the year, and my daed always says, 'A little heat on the inside makes the outside heat seem cool.'" Martha Rose chuckled. "Dad has lots of sayings like that, and plenty of jokes to tell, too."

Laura bit into a cookie and washed it down with a sip of cold tea. She hadn't really seen a humorous side to Eli's father and wondered if he held back because of her. She had a feeling Mary Ellen wasn't the only one in Eli's family who didn't care for her, and she had to wonder if she would ever truly feel a part of them.

"How's the Pennsylvania Dutch coming along?" Martha Rose asked. "Do you feel like you're understanding the words better yet?"

"I can figure out what many words mean, but I'm still having trouble speaking them."

"Practice makes perfect. I think it might help if we spoke less English to you."

Laura nearly choked on the second bite of cookie she had taken. "You're kidding, right?"

Martha Rose shook her head. "I think you need to hear more Deitsch and less English. It will force you to try saying more words yourself."

Laura groaned. Wasn't it enough that she had to wear plain, simple clothes, labor all day on jobs she'd rather not do, conform to all kinds of rules she didn't understand, and get along without modern conveniences? Must she now be forced to speak and hear a foreign language most of the time?

As if she could read her thoughts, Martha Rose reached over and patted Laura's hand. "You do want to become one of us, don't you?"

Tears gathered in Laura's eyes, obscuring her vision. "I love Eli, and I'd do anything for him, but I—I didn't think giving up my way of life would be so hard."

"You say you love my brother, but what about your love for God? It's Him you should be trying most to please, not Eli."

Laura swallowed hard. How could she tell Martha Rose that, while she did believe in God, she'd never really had a personal relationship with Him? She wasn't even sure she wanted one. After all, what had God ever done for her? If He were on her side, then wouldn't Eli have been willing to leave his religion and become English? They could have worshiped God in any church.

"Laura?" Martha Rose prompted.

She nodded. "I do want to please God. I just hope He knows how hard I'm trying and rewards me for all my efforts."

Martha Rose's forehead wrinkled as she frowned. "We should never have to be rewarded for our good deeds or service to God. We're taught to be humble servants, never prideful or seeking after the things of this world. There's joy in loving and serving the Lord, as well as in ministering to others."

Laura thought about that. The Amish people she was living among did seem to emanate a certain kind of peaceful, joyful spirit. She couldn't figure out why, since they did without so many things.

Martha Rose pushed away from the table. "I think we should end this discussion and get busy picking in the garden, don't you?"

Laura eased out of her chair. While she had no desire to spend the next few hours in the hot sun bent over a bunch of itchy tomato plants, at least she wouldn't have to listen to any more sermons about God and what He expected of people.

A short time later, as Laura crouched in front of a clump of rosy, ripe tomatoes, she thought about home and how she'd never had a fresh out-of-the-garden tomato until she'd come here. Yesterday, she'd gone over to the Petersons, who were Martha Rose's closest English neighbors, to call her parents. Dad had been gone on a fishing trip, which was a surprise since he rarely did anything just for fun; and Mom had mentioned that she would be hosting a garden party this weekend and was having it catered.

Probably won't have anything this fresh or tasty to eat, Laura thought as she plucked a plump tomato off the vine.

Her thoughts went to Eli. Martha Rose had told Laura that Eli liked homemade tomato ketchup, which Laura hadn't learned to make yet. There were so many things she still didn't know, and even though she disliked many of the chores she was expected to do and still hadn't gotten used to wearing a dress all the time, she never got tired of spending time with Eli. The more they were together, the more she was convinced she had done the right thing when she'd decided to become Amish. Despite the fact that Eli could get under her skin at times, he treated her with respect—nothing like Dean had done when they were dating.

Laura wasn't looking forward to another long church service this Sunday, but the promise of attending a singing that night gave her some measure of joy. It would be held in the Beachys' barn, and Eli had promised to take her. Since he would be coming to Amon and Martha Rose's for the preaching service, he would probably stick around all day, then later escort Laura to the singing. If things went as planned, she should be baptized into the Amish church by early fall, and she hoped she and Eli could get married sometime in November. Of course, he needed to propose to her first.

Eli felt a mounting sense of excitement over his date with Laura, and even though he'd told her awhile back that she should learn to get into the buggy herself, he helped her in this time, not wishing to cause another rift between them. Truth be told, Eli worried that Laura might not like the Amish way of life well enough to stay, and he didn't think he could deal with it if she decided to return to her old life.

"I've been looking forward to tonight," Laura murmured as she settled against the buggy seat.

"Jah, me, too." Eli glanced over at her and smiled. "You're sure pretty, you know that?"

Laura lifted her hand and touched her head covering. "You really think so?"

He nodded. "I do."

"But my hair's not long and beautiful anymore."

"Your hair's still long. You're just wearing it up in the back now."

"I know, but it looks so plain this way."

He reached over to gently touch her arm. "You may become one of the Plain People, but you'll never be plain to me."

* * *

When they arrived at the Beachy farm a short time later, the barn was already filled with young people. The huge doors were swung open wide, allowing the evening breeze to circulate and help cool the barn.

Soon the singing began, and the song leader led the group in several slow hymns, followed by a few faster tunes. There were no musical instruments, but the young people's a cappella voices permeated the air with a pleasant symphony of its own kind. Laura got caught up in the happy mood and was pleasantly surprised to realize she could actually follow along without too much difficulty.

When the singing ended, the young people paired off, and the games began. Laura was breathless by the time she and Eli finished playing several rounds of six-handed reel, which to her way of thinking was similar to square dancing.

"Would you like a glass of lemonade and some cookies?" Eli asked as he led Laura over to one of the wooden benches along the wall.

She nodded. "That sounds wunderbaar."

Eli disappeared into the crowd around the refreshment table, and Laura leaned her head against the wooden plank behind her. She caught a glimpse of Pauline Hostetler sitting across the room with her arms folded. She appeared to be watching her, and not with a joyful expression.

It was obvious to Laura that Pauline wasn't fond of her. In the months since Laura had been part of the Amish community, Pauline hadn't spoken one word to her. *I'm sure she's jealous because Eli chose me and not her, and I guess I can't really blame her.*

"Here you go." Eli handed Laura a glass of cold lemonade. "I was going to get us some cookies, but the plate was empty. I didn't want to wait around 'til one of the Beachy girls went to get more."

"That's okay. I ate a few too many of your sister's peanut butter cookies earlier this week, and I don't want to gain any weight."

Eli frowned. "I think you could use a few extra pounds."

Do you want me to end up looking like your slightly plump mother? Laura didn't vocalize her thoughts. Instead, she quietly sipped her lemonade. They would be going home soon, and she didn't want to say anything that might irritate Eli or provoke another argument.

CHAPTER 17

"If you're ready to go home now, I'll get the horse and buggy," Eli told Laura after they had finished their refreshments.

She smiled up at him. "I'm more than ready."

"I won't be long. Come outside when you see my horse pull up in front of the barn. There's no point in us both getting bit up by all the swarming insects tonight." He strolled out the door, leaving Laura alone by the refreshment table. She caught sight of Pauline, who had exited the barn only moments after Eli.

"I hope she's not going after him," Laura muttered under her breath.

"What was that?"

Laura whirled around and was greeted with a friendly smile from a young woman about her age, whom she'd seen before but had never personally met.

"I was talking to myself," Laura admitted, feeling the heat of a blush creep up the back of her neck.

The other woman nodded. "I do that sometimes." Her smile widened. "My name's Anna Beachy, and you're Laura, right?"

Laura nodded. "I'm staying with Martha Rose Zook and her family."

"I know. Martha Rose and I are friends. Have been since we were kinner, but I don't see her so much now that she's married and raising a family." Anna's green eyes gleamed in the light of the gas lamps hanging from the barn rafters. "Our moms were friends when they were growing up, too."

Laura kept on nodding, although it was a mechanical gesture. While this was interesting trivia, and Anna seemed like a nice person, she was most anxious to get outside and see if Eli had the buggy ready. What was taking him so long, anyway?

"Our families have been linked together for quite a spell," Anna continued. "Martha Rose's mamm, Mary Ellen, is the stepdaughter of Miriam Hilty. The dear woman's gone to heaven now, but Miriam, who everyone called 'Mim,' was a good friend of Sarah Stoltzfus, Rebekah Beachy's mamm. Rebekah's my mamm, and she's partially paralyzed. She either uses a wheelchair or metal leg braces in order to get around. Has since she was a young girl, I'm told." Anna paused a moment, but before Laura could comment, she rushed on. "Now, Grandma Sarah is living with my aunt Nadine, and—"

Laura tapped her foot impatiently, wondering how she could politely excuse herself. "I see," she said in the brief seconds Anna came up for air. "It does sound like you have a close-knit family." She cleared her throat a few times. "It's been nice chatting with you, Anna, but Eli's outside getting his horse and buggy ready to take me home. I'd better not keep him waiting."

"Jah, okay. Tell Eli I said hello, and let him know he should inform his big sister that she owes me a visit real soon."

"Since I'm staying with Martha Rose, I'll be sure she gets the message." Laura hurried away before Anna could say anything more.

Once outside, she headed for the long line of buggies parked alongside the Beachys' barn. She stopped short when she saw Eli talking to Pauline.

When Pauline reached out and touched Eli's arm, he took a step back, bumping against his buggy. What was going on here? This didn't set well with him. Didn't Pauline know he was courting Laura?

"That English woman will never make you happy," Pauline murmured. "Take me home tonight, and let her find another way."

Eli brushed Pauline's hand aside. "I can't do that. I brought Laura to the singing, and I'll see that she gets home." He sniffed. "Besides, I love her, and as soon as she and I join the church, I'm planning to ask her to be my wife."

Pauline's pinched lips made her face look like a dried-up prune. "You're not thinking straight, Eli. You haven't been right in the head since that fancy woman came sashaying into your life."

"You have no right to say anything about Laura," Eli defended. "You don't even know her."

"I know her well enough to know she's not right for you."

Eli glanced toward the barn and spotted Laura heading out the door. "I need to go. Laura's waiting for me to give her a ride home."

Tears pooled in Pauline's eyes, and her chin trembled. "I—I thought there was something special between us. I thought—" She choked on a sob and fell into his arms.

Eli just stood there, not knowing what to do, but before he could think of anything, Laura showed up, and he knew right away that she was hopping mad.

"What's going on here?"

Pauline pivoted toward Laura. "What's it look like? Eli was hugging me."

Eli's face heated up. "Pauline, that isn't so, and you know it." He could see Laura's face in the moonlight, and it was nearly as red as his felt. How could he make her understand what had really happened? He knew she was a bit insecure in their relationship, and he was sure that seeing Pauline with her arms around him hadn't helped any.

"I should have known you were chasing after Eli when I saw you leave the barn." Laura's voice shook as she stood toe-to-toe with Pauline.

Pauline didn't flinch, nor did she back down. "All I did was say a few words to Eli, and it's not my fault he decided to give me a hug."

Eli touched Pauline's arm, and she whirled back around to face him. "I know you're not happy about me and Laura, but lying isn't going to help."

Pauline shrugged his hand away. "You'll be sorry you chose her and not me. Just wait and see if you're not." She wrinkled her nose and stalked off.

Laura was fit to be tied. Did Eli really make the first move, or had Pauline deliberately hugged him just to stir up trouble? Even if it broke her heart, she needed to know what had transpired. She had to know the truth.

"Are you ready to go home?" Eli gave her a sheepish look.

"I was ready half an hour ago. And don't go thinking you can soft-soap me with that cute, little-boy look of yours, either."

"You remind me of *en wiedicher hund*," Eli said with a chuckle. "You've got quite a temper, but seeing how you acted when you saw me and Pauline together lets me know how much you really love me."

Laura folded her arms and scowled at him. "I'm beginning to know a lot more of your Pennsylvania Dutch language, and I'll have you know, Eli Yoder, I do not look like a mad dog."

He tickled her under the chin. "You do love me though, right?"

"You know I do. That's why it always makes me angry whenever I see that woman with you." She leaned a bit closer to him. "Tell me the truth, Eli. Did she hug you, or was it the other way around?"

Eli pursed his lips. "She hugged me. Honest."

"Did you encourage her in any way?"

He shook his head. "She knows I love you, Laura, and she's jealous, so she wants to make you think there's something going on with us." He helped Laura into the buggy. "Think about it. Who's the woman I've been courtin' all summer?"

"As far as I know, only me."

Eli went around and took his own seat, then picked up the reins and got the horse moving. "Let's stop by the lake on the way home."

Laura gazed up at the night sky. It was a beautiful evening, and the grass was lit by hundreds of twinkling fireflies. The buggy ride should have been magical for both of them. Instead, Pauline had thrown a damper on things.

Laura knew she was probably being paranoid where Pauline was concerned, but she couldn't seem to help herself. "I'm not much in the mood for love or romance right now, so I think it would be good if we just head straight to your sister's house."

Eli moaned. "Maybe our next date will go better."

"Jah, let's hope so."

Laura felt closer to Eli's sister than she did the rest of his family. Martha Rose had patiently taught her to use the treadle sewing machine; bake shoofly pies; and given her lessons in milking, gathering eggs, and slopping pigs. It was none of those things that made Martha Rose seem special, however. It was her friendly attitude and the way she had accepted a complete stranger into her home. Laura wasn't sure if it was Martha Rose's hospitable nature or if she was only doing it to please her brother, but living with this young woman and her family for the past few months had helped Laura understand the true meaning of friendship.

Having been raised as an only child in a home where she lacked nothing, Laura knew she was spoiled. The Amish lived such a simple life, yet they seemed happy and content. It was a mystery she couldn't explain. Even more surprising was the fact that on days like today, she almost felt one with the Plain People. Their slow-paced, quiet lifestyle held a certain measure of appeal. Although Laura still missed some modern conveniences and the freedom to dress as she pleased, she also enjoyed many things about being Amish.

Little Ben was one of the things she enjoyed most. He often followed her around, asking questions and pointing out things she had never noticed before. He was doing it now, out in his mother's herb garden.

"Guck emol datt!" the child said, pointing to a clump of mint.

Laura nodded, knowing Ben had said, "Just look at that." She plucked off a leaf and rubbed it between her fingers, the way she'd seen Martha Rose do on several occasions.

Ben sniffed deeply and grinned. *"Appeditlich!"*

"Jah, delicious," Laura said with a chuckle. She was amazed at the little boy's appreciation for herbs, flowers, and all the simple things found on the farm. Most of the English children she knew needed TV, video games, and electronic toys to keep them entertained.

In spite of Laura's fascination with little Ben, she had no desire to have any children of her own. If she ever were to get pregnant, she would lose her shapely figure and might never regain it. If she had children, she might not be a good mother.

The baptismal ceremony and introduction of new members was scheduled for early September. Laura kept reminding herself that she needed to be ready by then, since most Amish weddings in this area were held in late November or early December after the harvest was done. If she wasn't able to join the church before then, it would probably be another year before she and Eli could be married. Of course, he hadn't actually proposed yet, but she was hopeful it would be soon.

For that matter, Eli still hadn't kissed her. She worried he might have lost interest in her. Maybe he was in love with Pauline and just wouldn't admit it. If only she could be sure.

Laura saw more of Eli's sister than she did him these days. His job at the furniture store kept him busy enough, but now he was also helping his father and brothers in the fields. Over the last month, she'd only seen him twice, and that was on bi-weekly church days.

"So much for courting," Laura complained as she trudged wearily toward the chicken coop. "If I weren't so afraid of losing Eli to Pauline, I'd put my foot down and give Eli an ultimatum. I'd tell him either he'd better come see me at least once a week, or I'm going home to Minnesota."

There was just one problem. Laura didn't want to go home. She loved Eli and wanted to be with him, no matter what hardships she had to face.

The day finally arrived for Laura and Eli, as well as several other young people, to be baptized and join the church.

Laura was nervous as a cat about to have kittens. She paced back and forth across the kitchen floor, waiting for Amon to pull the buggy out front.

Little Ben jerked on his mother's apron while she stood at the sink, finishing with the dishes. *"Boppli,"* he said, pointing to her stomach.

Laura stopped pacing and whirled around to face Martha Rose. "Boppli? Are you pregnant, Martha Rose?"

Martha Rose nodded. "I found out for sure a few days ago."

"How is it that Ben knew and I didn't?"

"He was there when I told Amon. I planned to tell you soon."

"Oh," was all Laura could manage. Maybe she wasn't as much a part of this family as she had believed.

Amon stuck his head through the open doorway and grinned at them. A thatch of blond hair hung across his forehead, and his brown eyes seemed so sincere. "All set?"

"Jah." Martha Rose smiled at Laura. "Let's be off then, for we sure wouldn't want to be late for Laura's and Eli's baptisms."

* * *

Eli paced nervously across the front porch of their farmhouse. Today's preaching service would be held at their home, and he could hardly wait. This was the day Laura would become one of them. This was the day they would both be baptized and join the church. He was sure that, even before he'd met Laura, she was the reason he'd held off joining the church, because they were meant to be together.

The sight of Amon Zook's buggy pulling into the yard halted Eli's thoughts. He skirted around a wooden bench and leaped off the porch, skipping over all four steps.

Laura offered him a tentative-looking smile as she stepped down from the buggy. He took her hand and gave it a squeeze. "This is the day we've both been waiting for, Laura."

She nodded, and he noticed there were tears in her eyes.

"What's wrong? You aren't having second thoughts, I hope."

"No, I'm just a bit nervous. What if I don't say or do the right things today? What if—"

He hushed her words by placing two fingers against her lips. "You went through the six weeks of biweekly instructions just fine. Today's only a formality. Say and do whatever the bishop asks. Everything will be okay; you'll see."

"I hope so," she whispered.

The service started a few minutes after Eli and Laura entered the house. He took his seat on the men's side, and she sat with the women.

The song leader led the congregation in several hymns, all sung in the usual singsong fashion, and the baptismal rite followed two sermons.

When Bishop Wagler called the candidates for baptism to step forward, Laura's legs shook so hard she feared she might not be able to walk. The deacons provided a small pail of water and a cup, and the bishop told the twenty young people to get on their knees. He then asked them a question. "Are you willing, by the help and grace of God, to renounce the world, the devil, your own flesh and blood, and be obedient only to God and His church?"

Laura cringed. If she were to answer that question truthfully, she would have to say that she wasn't sure. But she couldn't let anyone know how weak her faith was or that she had no real understanding of God's grace, so along with the others, she answered, "Jah."

"Are you willing to walk with Christ and His church, and to remain faithful through life and until death?"

"Jah."

"Can you confess that Jesus Christ is the Son of God?"

Numbly, as though her lips had a mind of their

own, Laura repeated along with the others, "I confess that Jesus Christ is the Son of God."

The congregation then stood for prayer, while Laura and the others remained on their knees. Bishop Wagler placed his hands on the first applicant's head, while Deacon Shemly poured water into the bishop's cupped hands and dripped it onto the candidate's head.

Laura awaited her turn, apprehensive because she wasn't sure she believed the things she had said, and trembling with joy at the prospect of hopefully receiving a marriage proposal from Eli soon. As water from the bishop's hands trickled onto Laura's head and down her forehead, she nearly broke down in tears. She would have plenty of time to think about her relationship with God. Right now, all she wanted was to be with Eli. Her love for him was all that mattered.

CHAPTER 18

When the service was over, Laura felt relief as she stepped outside into the crisp fall air. It was official. She was no longer a fancy English woman. For as long as she chose to remain Amish, she would be Plain.

Most of the women were busy getting the noon

meal set out, but Laura didn't care about helping. All she wanted to do was find Eli. It didn't take her long to spot him, talking with Deacon Shemly over near the barn.

Are they talking about me? Is Eli asking the deacon if he thinks I'm sincere? Laura grabbed the porch railing and gripped it until her knuckles turned white. *What if one of the deacons or Bishop Wagler suspects that I'm not a true believer? What if he's counseling Eli to break up with me?*

"We could use another pair of hands in the kitchen," Martha Rose said as she stepped up behind Laura. "The menfolk are waiting to eat."

Laura spun around to face her. "Why don't the menfolk fix the meal and wait on us women once in a while?"

Martha Rose poked Laura's arm. "You're such a kidder. Everyone knows it's a woman's duty to serve the men."

Laura opened her mouth, fully intending to argue the point, but she stopped herself in time. She had just joined the Amish church. It wouldn't be good to say or do anything that might get her in trouble. Especially not with Eli out there talking to Deacon Shemly. She might be reprimanded if she messed up now.

"What do you need help with?" Laura asked, stepping into the house and offering Martha Rose a smile.

"Why don't you pour coffee?" Martha Rose motioned to a table nearby. "The pitchers are over there."

Laura shrugged and started across the room. "Jah, okay."

As Pauline began to serve the men their meal, she tried to keep her mind focused on what she was doing and not on the terrible pain chipping away at her heart. She didn't know how she had made it through the baptismal service. It was so hard to see the joyful look on Laura's face when she was greeted with a holy kiss and welcomed into the church by Alma, the bishop's wife.

Pauline knew full well that the ritual of baptism placed Laura into full fellowship, with the rights and responsibilities of adult church membership. From this day on, she would have the right to partake of the elements during the Communion services held twice a year. She would be free to marry Eli, too, and Pauline was fairly certain he would propose to Laura as soon as possible now that they were both part of the Amish church.

She glanced across the room and spotted Laura serving the table where Eli sat. She could barely stand to see the happy expression on Eli's face, not to mention Laura's smug look. She knew it was wrong to harbor such bitterness, and it had been wrong to lie about Eli hugging her after the singing, but she couldn't seem to help herself. *Why can't Eli love me? Why can't he see how much better I would be for him than Laura?*

She squeezed her eyes shut. *Oh, God, please help me learn to deal with this.*

Lunch was finally over, and everyone had eaten until they were full. Laura was just finishing with the cleanup when she saw Eli heading her way.

"Come with me for a walk," he whispered, taking Laura's hand and leading her away from the house.

"Where are we going?"

"You'll see."

A few minutes later, they stood under a huge weeping willow tree out behind the house, away from curious stares. Eli's fingers touched Laura's chin, tipping her head back until they were staring into each other's eyes. "You're truly one of us now," he murmured.

She nodded, feeling as though her head might explode from the anticipation of what she felt certain was coming. "We're both officially Amish."

Eli bent his head, and his lips touched hers in a light, feathery kiss. She moaned softly as the kiss deepened.

When Eli pulled away, she leaned against him for support, feeling as if her breath had been snatched away. It seemed as though she had waited all her life to be kissed like that. Not a kiss of passion, the way Dean had done, but a kiss with deep emotion. Eli loved her with all his heart; she was sure of it now.

"I can finally speak the words that have been in my heart all these months," Eli said, gazing deeply into her eyes. "I love you, Laura, and I want you to be my wife."

Tears welled in her eyes and spilled over onto her cheeks. "Oh, Eli, I love you, too." She hugged him tightly. "Jah . . . I will marry you."

"I just spoke with Deacon Shemly," Eli said. "If it's all right with you, we can be married on the third Thursday in November."

"It's more than all right." Laura blinked away another set of tears. "I can't wait to call my parents and give them the news."

Eli thought his heart would burst from the sheer joy of knowing Laura would soon be Mrs. Eli Yoder. She loved him; he was sure of it. Why else would she have given up her old life and agreed to become Plain? He wanted to shout to the world that he was the luckiest man alive and had found a most special woman to share the rest of his life with.

While he wasn't able to shout it to the world, Eli knew he could share his news with the family. Grabbing Laura by the hand, he started to run.

"Where are we going?"

"To tell my folks our good news."

Laura skidded to a halt. "Do you think that's such a good idea? I mean, can't you wait and tell them later . . . after you go home?"

Eli grimaced. "Now why would I want to wait that long? The family deserves to hear our news now, when we're together."

"They may not want you marrying a foreigner," Laura argued. "Your mother doesn't like me, and—"

Eli held up his hand to stop her words. "You're not a foreigner anymore, and I'm sure Mom likes you just fine."

Laura drew in a deep breath and released it with a moan. "Okay. Let's get this over with then."

Eli spotted his folks sitting in chairs on the porch, visiting with Martha Rose and Amon. Little Ben played at their feet, dragging a piece of yarn in front of an orange-colored barn cat's nose.

Eli led Laura up the steps and motioned her to take a seat in one of the empty chairs. He pulled out another one for himself and sat beside her.

"Today's baptism was good." Mom smiled at Eli. "We're glad you finally decided to join the church."

He grinned. "And Laura, too. She's a baptized member now, same as me."

Mom nodded and looked over at Laura. "We welcome you into our church."

"Jah, you're one of us now," Pop agreed.

"Danki." Laura offered them a smile, but it appeared to be forced.

In an attempt to reassure her, Eli took her hand. "Laura's agreed to become my wife. We'd like to be married the third Thursday of November."

Mom and Pop exchanged glances, and Eli was afraid they might say something negative about his plans. Much to his relief, Mom gave a nod in Laura's direction. "We hope you'll be happy being Amish, Laura, and we hope you will make our son happy, as well."

"Eli's a fine man with much love to give," Pop put in. "He'll make a good husband and father; just you wait and see."

Martha Rose left her seat and bent down to give Laura a hug. "Congratulations. Soon we'll be like sisters."

Amon thumped Eli on the back and then added his well-wishes.

Eli grinned. "I think Laura was a bit naerfich about telling you, but I knew you would all share in our joy."

Laura shot him an exasperated look, and he wondered if he'd said too much. Maybe he shouldn't have mentioned that she felt nervous.

He was trying to think up something to say

that might make her feel better, when Pop spoke again. "Say, Eli, if you're gonna marry this little gal, then don't ya think you should try to fatten her up some?"

Eli looked at Laura, then back at his father, but before he could open his mouth to reply, she said, "Why would Eli want to fatten me up?"

"I've seen you at some of our meals, and you don't hardly eat a thing. Why, you'll waste away to nothing if you don't start eatin' more."

Laura stood so quickly, she nearly knocked over her chair. "I have no intention of becoming fat, Mr. Yoder!"

Pop tipped his head back and howled. "She's a feisty one, now, isn't she, Eli?" When he finally quit laughing, he looked at Laura and said, "If you're gonna marry my son, then don't ya think you should start callin' me Johnny? Mr. Yoder makes me feel like an old man." He glanced over at Mom and gave her knee a few pats. "I'm not old yet, am I, Mary Ellen?"

Mary Ellen grunted as she pushed his hand aside. "Go on with you, now, Johnny. You've always been a silly boy, and I guess you always will be."

Mom and Pop both laughed, and soon Martha Rose and Amon were chuckling pretty good, too.

Laura tapped her foot against the porch floor, and Eli figured it was time to end it all before she said or did something that might embarrass them both.

He stood and grabbed her hand. "I think Laura and I should take a walk down to the creek. She needs to get cooled off, and I need to figure out how I ended up with such a laughable family."

Two weeks before the wedding, Laura's and Eli's names were officially published at the close of the preaching service, which was held in the Zook home.

Laura's heart bubbled with joy as she helped her future sister-in-law and several other women get lunch served after church had let out. Everyone had a job to do, even Anna Beachy's mother, Rebekah, who sat at the table in her wheelchair, buttering a stack of bread.

Martha Rose handed Laura a jar of pickled beets. "Would you mind opening these?"

Laura glanced at the other four women, but they all seemed focused on their job of making ham-and-cheese sandwiches. She shrugged and took the jar over to the cupboard, wondering why no one had said anything about her upcoming marriage. Were they displeased with Eli's choice for a wife? Would they have rather heard Pauline's name published with Eli's?

She held her breath as she forked out the beet slices and placed them in a bowl. She disliked the smell of pickled beets. If she lived to be a hundred, she would never figure out what anyone saw in those disgusting, pungent things. She had just finished putting the last one in the bowl, when Pauline entered the kitchen.

"The tables are set up in the barn." Pauline glanced over at Martha Rose. "Do you have anything ready for me to carry out there?"

"You can take this plate of sandwiches." Mary Ellen held up a tray, and Pauline took it from her, never once looking Laura's way or acknowledging her presence.

Pauline was almost to the door when Martha Rose spoke. "Laura, why don't you go with Pauline? You can take the beets, then stay to help pour beverages."

Laura drew in a deep breath and let it out in a rush. The last thing she needed was another close encounter with her rival. She didn't wish to make a scene, however, so she followed Pauline out of the room without a word of protest.

They had no more than stepped onto the porch when Pauline whirled around and faced Laura. "You think you've won Eli's heart, don't you? Well, you're not married yet, so there's still some hope for me. You may have fooled Eli, but I can see right through you."

Laura took a few steps back, wanting to get away from Pauline, and wondering if the young woman really did know she wasn't being completely honest with Eli. Sure, she loved him and wanted to get married. She had become Amish, too. But deep down inside, she didn't think she needed God and was sure she could do everything in her own strength.

"I'm sure Eli will come to his senses soon," Pauline continued to rant. "He's blinded by romantic notions right now, but one of these days he'll realize you're not really one of us and can't be trusted." She gazed into Laura's eyes, making her feel like a child who had done something wrong.

Laura's mind whirled as she tried to figure out some kind of appropriate comeback. All she could think to do was run—far away from Pauline's piercing gaze. She practically flew into the barn, dropped the bowl of beets onto the nearest table, and sprinted off toward the creek.

When Eli looked up from the table where he sat with his brothers and saw Laura dash out of the barn, he knew something wasn't right. He was about to go after her, but Pauline stepped between him and the barn door. "Let her go, Eli. I'm sure she just needs to be alone."

Eli's forehead wrinkled. "What's going on, Pauline? Did you and Laura have words?"

Pauline placed the plate of sandwiches on one of the tables and motioned him to follow her out of the barn. When they were out of earshot and away from scrutinizing eyes, she stopped and placed both hands on Eli's shoulders.

He shrugged them away. "What's this all about?"

"That English woman will never make you happy. She's an outsider and always will be. She doesn't belong here, so you'd better think twice about marrying her."

Eli's face heated up. "I love Laura, and she's not an outsider. She's a member of our church now and has agreed to abide by our Ordnung."

Pauline squinted. "You're blinded by her beautiful face and smooth-talking words, but I know what's in her heart."

"What gives you the right to try and read someone else's mind?"

"I didn't say *mind,* Eli. I said *heart.* I have a sixth sense about things, and my senses are telling me—"

"I don't care what your senses are telling you." Eli drew in a deep breath to steady his nerves and tried to offer her a smile. "Look, Pauline, I'm sorry things didn't work out between us, but if you'll search your own heart instead of trying to see what's in other people's hearts, I'm sure you'll realize that we could never have been anything more than friends."

Pauline's blue eyes flashed angrily. "We could have been more than friends if she hadn't come along and filled your head with all sorts of fancy English ideas."

Eli was trying hard to be civil, but he'd had as much of Pauline's meddling as he could stand. He had to get away from her. He needed to be with Laura.

"I never meant to hurt you," he said sincerely, "but I love Laura, and she loves me. She gave up being English so we could be together, and nothing you say is going to change my mind about her."

Pauline's eyes filled with tears, making Eli feel like a heel. He was sorry for hurting her, but it didn't change anything. He didn't love her now and never had. Even when they'd been courting, he'd only seen her as a friend.

Eli gently touched her arm. "I pray you'll find someone else to love." He walked away quickly, hoping she wouldn't follow. His life was with Laura, and she needed him now.

Laura sank to the ground and leaned heavily against the trunk of a tree as she gazed at the bubbling creek. *Maybe I made a mistake thinking I could become part of a world so plain and simple. Maybe Eli should have chosen Pauline.*

She sucked in her bottom lip, and a fresh set of tears coursed down her cheeks. Could Pauline really see through her? Did the accusing young woman know Laura was only pretending to be a follower of God?

But how could she know? No one knew what was in Laura's heart or mind. She'd taken her biblical training classes, studied the Amish language, and learned how to cook, sew, and keep house. She wore plain clothes and no makeup and had learned to live without electricity or many other modern conveniences. What more was there? Why would Pauline think she couldn't be trusted?

"Because you can't," a voice in her head seemed to taunt. *"You're lying to Eli, and you're lying to yourself."*

Laura dropped to the ground and sobbed. She knew what she wanted out of life—Eli Yoder. She wanted him more than anything. If she had to pretend to have a relationship with God in order to join the Amish faith so she and Eli could be married, what harm had been done?

Laura jerked her head when someone touched her shoulder. She looked up and saw the face of the man she loved staring down at her.

"What's wrong? Why are you crying?" he asked, helping Laura to her feet.

"I—I had an encounter with your ex-girlfriend." She sniffed and reached up to wipe the tears from her face. "Pauline doesn't like me, and she's trying to come between us."

"No, she's not. I just spoke with Pauline, and I put her in her place but good."

"You did?"

He pulled her into his arms. "I told Pauline it's you I love, and nothing she says will ever change my mind."

"You mean it?"

"Jah, I do. Pauline and I have never been anything more than friends, and she knows it. I don't understand why she's bent on making trouble, but don't worry, because I'll never stop loving you, Laura." Eli bent to kiss her, and Laura felt like she was drowning in his love. Everything would be all right now. It had to be.

CHAPTER 19

Laura was excited about the wedding and pleased that her parents would be coming soon. She was anxious for them to meet Eli. Her friend Shannon wouldn't be coming, because she had gone to California to visit her grandmother who was dying of cancer. Darla wouldn't be coming, either, because she had to work. But that was all right with Laura. She knew Darla didn't approve of her becoming Amish. The last letter she'd received from Darla had said that she'd finished school and was working in Philadelphia, designing windows for one of the big department stores.

Laura had asked Anna Beachy and Nancy Frey, the schoolteacher, to be her attendants, and the ceremony would be held at Amon and Martha Rose's house, since Laura lived with them.

"When are your parents arriving?" Martha Rose asked as she and Laura sat at the table, putting the finishing touches on Laura's wedding dress.

Laura snipped a piece of thread and smiled. "Their plane was supposed to get into Harrisburg late last night, and they were going to rent a car and drive out here as soon as they'd had some breakfast this morning, so I expect they should be showing up soon."

"They're more than welcome to stay with us. We have plenty of room."

"I know you do, and it's a kind offer, but Mom and Dad are hotel kind of people. I don't think they would last five minutes without TV or a microwave."

Martha Rose pursed her lips. "You're managing."

"Jah." Laura smiled. "I'm anxious for them to get to know all of you before the wedding on Thursday."

"It will be nice to meet them, as well."

"Since tomorrow will be such a busy day for

us, what with getting things ready for the wedding and all, I figured it would be best if they weren't in the way."

Martha Rose's eyebrows lifted in question. "Why would they be in the way? If they'd like to help, I'm sure we can find plenty for them to do."

"The Amish lifestyle is quite different from what they're used to, and Mom's idea of work is a full day of shopping or traipsing around town trying to drum up donations for one of her many charity functions." Laura sighed. "I just hope they don't try to talk me out of marrying Eli."

"Why would they do that? I'm sure you've told them how much you love my brother."

"Oh, yes, and Dad said if I was happy, then he was, too. I think it gives him pleasure to see me get what I want."

"Having one's way is not always of the Lord," Martha Rose admonished. "We're taught to be selfless, not self-centered. Surely you learned that from your religious training prior to baptism."

"Certainly. I just meant when I was younger and didn't know much about religious things, I was rather spoiled." She shrugged. "Dad still thinks of me as his little girl, but I know he and Mom both want my happiness."

"So, you're happy being Amish?"

"Of course. Why wouldn't I be?"

Martha Rose opened her mouth as if to answer, but their conversation was interrupted when a car came up the graveled driveway, causing their two farm dogs to carry on.

Laura jumped up and darted to the back door. "It's them! My folks are here!" She jerked the door open and ran down the steps.

Her father was the first to step from their car, and the bundle of fur in his hands brought a squeal of delight from Laura's lips. "Foosie!" Her arms went around Dad's waist, and she gave him a hug.

"Your mother and I thought you might like to have your cat, now that you're about to be married and will soon have your own home."

Mom stepped out of the car and embraced Laura. "It's good to see you." She frowned and took a few steps back. "Oh, dear, you've changed, and you look so tired. What happened to our beautiful, vibrant daughter, and why are you dressed in such plain clothes?"

Laura had expected some reservations on her parents' part, but her mother's comment took her by surprise. If she wasn't beautiful anymore, did that mean she was ugly?

"Laura is still beautiful . . . in a plain sort of way, and you should know enough about the Amish to understand why she's dressed that way." Dad raised his eyebrows at Mom, then handed the cat over to Laura. "Here you go, sweetie."

Laura rubbed her nose against Foosie's soft fur and sniffed deeply. "I—I don't think I can keep her."

"Why not?" Mom asked.

"Eli and I will be living with his parents until our own house is complete." Laura stroked Foosie's head. "Since it will be several months before it's done, Eli's folks might not appreciate having an inside cat invade their home."

"But I thought Amish people liked animals." Dad gazed around the farmyard and pointed to the cows in the field. "See, there's a bunch of animals."

"Don't forget about those dreadful dogs that barked at us when we pulled in," Mom added.

Laura shook her head. "Those are farm animals. They're not pampered pets."

"Be that as it may, I would think your husband would want you to be happy," Mom said as she fluffed the sides of her windblown hair.

Before Laura could respond, Martha Rose was at her side, offering Laura's parents a wide smile. "I'm Martha Rose Zook. And you must be Laura's folks."

Mom nodded, and Dad extended his hand. "I'm Wesley Meade. This is my wife, Irene."

"I'm glad to meet you," Martha Rose said, shaking his hand.

"This is a nice place you've got here. I've always had a fondness for the country life," Dad said in a wistful tone.

Martha Rose motioned toward the house. "Won't you please come inside? It's kind of nippy out here in the wind, and I've got some hot coffee and freshly baked brownies waiting."

"Sounds good to me." Dad's wide grin brought a smile to Laura's lips. He looked like an enthusiastic child on Christmas morning.

Everyone followed Martha Rose to the house. When they stepped onto the back porch, Laura halted. "Uh, what would you like me to do with my cat?"

Martha Rose blinked. "Ach! I didn't realize you were holding a cat. Where'd it come from?"

"We brought it from Minnesota," Dad answered. "Foosie is Laura's house pet."

Laura rocked back and forth on her heels. What if Martha Rose made her put Foosie out in the barn? She knew the cat would never get along with the farm cats. Besides, she might get fleas.

"Bring the cat inside," Martha Rose said, opening the door. "I'm sure Ben would love to play with her awhile."

Once Laura's parents were seated at the kitchen table, Laura placed Foosie on the floor beside Ben. He squealed with delight and hugged the cat around the neck.

"Now don't *dricke* too hard," Martha Rose admonished her son. She quickly poured mugs of steaming coffee, and Laura passed around the plate of brownies.

"What's a dricke?" Mom asked.

"It means 'squeeze,' " Laura explained.

"Schee bussli," Ben said, as Foosie licked his nose.

"Ben thinks Foosie is a nice kitten," Laura said, before either of her parents could raise the question.

Martha Rose handed Laura's father a mug. "Laura says you plan on staying at a hotel in Paradise while you're here."

He nodded. "That's right. We made our reservations as soon as Laura phoned and told us about the wedding, and that's where we stayed last night when we got in."

"You're more than welcome to stay here. We have plenty of room."

Dad's eyes brightened. "Really? You wouldn't mind?"

Mom shook her head while smiling sweetly. "That's kind of you, Martha Rose, but I think it would be less hectic if we stay at the hotel."

Dad shrugged, but Laura didn't miss the look of disappointment on his face. "Whatever you think best, dear," he mumbled.

"I made my own wedding dress." Laura held up the pale blue dress she'd been hemming earlier.

Mom's mouth dropped open. "Oh, my! It doesn't look anything like a traditional wedding gown."

"It's a traditional Amish dress," Martha Rose stated.

"I see."

Laura could see by the pinched look on her mother's face that she was anything but happy about this Plain wedding. For that matter, she was probably upset about Laura marrying an Amish man. Mom most likely thought her only daughter had lost her mind.

Laura turned to look at her dad. He was grinning like a Cheshire cat and obviously enjoying the homemade brownies, for he'd already eaten three.

"Eli and his parents are coming over for supper," Laura said, changing the subject. "I'm anxious for you to meet him."

Martha Rose nodded. "Eli's excited about meeting your folks, too."

Eli opened the Zooks' back door and stepped inside, along with his folks and two brothers. Laura, who had been standing near the kitchen sink, rushed to his side. "My parents are here, and I'm so glad you came!"

Eli grinned and squeezed her hand. "I'm glad, too."

Introductions were soon made, and Eli knew

233

right away that he was going to like Laura's father. He wasn't so sure about her mother, though. Irene seemed to be scrutinizing everything in the room, and she had said very little to either Eli or his family.

Soon everyone took their seats at the table. Laura and Martha Rose had made a scrumptious-looking supper of ham, bread stuffing, mashed potatoes, green beans, coleslaw, and homemade bread.

All heads bowed in silent prayer, and Eli noticed that Laura looked relieved when her parents followed suit.

"Laura tells me you work in a law office," Eli said as he passed Laura's dad the platter of ham.

"Sure do. In fact, I have several other lawyers working for me." Wesley grinned and forked two huge pieces of meat onto his plate. "Umm . . . this sure looks tasty."

"Pop raises some hogs," Lewis spoke up. "He's always got plenty of meat to share with Martha Rose and Amon."

Eli's father nodded and spooned himself a sizable helping of bread stuffing. "I'm not braggin' now, but I think I've got some of the finest hogs in Lancaster County."

Mom reached over and patted Pop's portly stomach. "Jah, and some pretty good milking cows, too."

Laura moved the fork slowly around her plate, and Eli noticed that she hadn't taken more than a few bites of food since they'd sat down.

Pop glanced over at Laura's father and frowned. "Say, I'm wonderin' just how much influence you have on that daughter of yours."

Wesley gulped down some milk before he answered. "I'm not altogether sure. Why do you ask?"

Pop pointed a finger at Laura's plate. "She eats like a bird. Just look at her plate. Hardly a thing on it!"

Laura's face blanched, then turned red as a cherry. "I eat enough to sustain myself. I just don't think one needs to become chubby in order to prove one's worth."

The room became deathly quiet, and Eli could almost feel her embarrassment. It wasn't like Laura to blurt something out like that, and he had to wonder what had gotten into her. Was she nervous because her fancy English parents were here? Did she feel embarrassed for them to be sitting at the same table with a bunch of Plain folks?

"I . . . um . . . meant to say, I prefer to watch my weight," Laura quickly amended. "If others choose to overeat, that's their right."

"Laura, what are you saying?" Eli whispered. "Are you trying to make some kind of trouble here tonight?"

She shook her head. "I—I'm sorry. I don't know what came over me."

"I think our daughter might be a bit nervous." Irene offered a pleasant smile as she patted Laura's arm. "It isn't every day she introduces her father and me to her future husband and in-laws."

Martha Rose nodded. "Laura's been jittery as a dragonfly all day. Haven't you, Laura?"

Laura's only reply was a quick shrug.

"In fact, Laura did most of the work today, just to keep her hands busy," Martha Rose added.

"I did work pretty hard, but that's because I wanted Martha Rose to rest." Laura glanced over at her mother. "Martha Rose is in a family way."

Irene's eyebrows furrowed. "Family way?"

"She's pregnant, hon." Wesley chuckled. "I haven't heard that expression since I was a boy growing up on the farm, but I sure can remember what 'being in a family way' means."

"Your folks were farmers?" The question came from Pop, who leaned his elbows on the table as he scrutinized Laura's father.

Wesley nodded. "My parents farmed a huge spread out in Montana, but my father sold the farm several years ago since none of us boys wanted to follow in his footsteps." His forehead wrinkled. "Sometimes I wonder if I made the wrong choice, becoming a fancy city lawyer instead of an old cowhand."

Little Ben, who up until this moment had been busy playing with the bread stuffing on his plate, spoke up for the first time. *"Maus!"* He pointed to the floor, disrupting the conversation.

"Maus? Where is it?" Martha Rose was immediately on her feet.

"Schpringe, bussli!" Ben bounced up and down in his chair.

"What on earth is going on?" Irene's high-pitched voice held a note of concern.

"Aw, it's just a little mouse, and Ben's tellin' the kitty to run," Jonas said with a chuckle. "I'll bet that fluffy white cat will take 'em in a hurry."

"Fluffy white cat?" Mom's eyes were wide. "When did you get an indoor cat, Martha Rose?"

Martha Rose gave no reply, just held a broom in her hand and ran around the kitchen, swinging it this way and that. It was a comical sight, and Eli laughed, right along with the rest of the men.

Foosie dodged the broom and leaped into the air, as the tiny, gray field mouse scooted across the floor at lightning speed. By now, everyone at the table was either laughing or shouting orders at Martha Rose.

"Open the door!" Amon hollered. "Maybe it'll run outside."

Laura jumped up and raced for the door. "No, don't open that door! Foosie might get out, and

I'd never be able to catch her once the dogs discovered she was on the loose."

Foosie was almost on top of the mouse, but just as her paw came down, the critter darted for a hole under the cupboard, leaving a very confused-looking cat sitting in front of the hole, meowing for all it was worth.

Laura's father was laughing so hard that tears rolled down his cheeks. "Well, if that doesn't beat all. In all the years we've had that cat, I don't believe I've ever seen her move so fast." He wiped his eyes with a napkin and started howling again.

Laura planted both hands on her hips. "I don't see what's so funny, Dad. Poor Foosie has never seen a mouse before. She could have had a heart attack, tearing around the kitchen like that."

Another round of laughter filled the room. Even Martha Rose, who moments ago had been chasing the mouse with her broom, was back in her seat, holding her sides and chuckling as hard as everyone else.

Eli stood and moved to Laura's side. "I think you were nervous for nothing. The cat and mouse game got everyone in a happy mood."

"So what did you think of Eli and his family?" Wesley asked his wife as they drove back to their hotel in Paradise later that evening.

She shrugged, a small sigh escaping her lips.

238

"They seemed like nice enough people, but I don't understand how our daughter thinks she can ever fit in with them."

He drummed his fingers along the edge of the steering wheel. "She's already one of them, Irene. Laura has joined the Amish church and is about to marry an Amish man."

"I know that, Wesley, but Laura is used to nice things—modern conveniences, pretty clothes, makeup, and pampering. It doesn't seem right to see her dressed so plainly or watch her washing dishes over a sink full of hot water the way she did tonight after we ate dinner."

"Have you heard her complain?"

"Not in so many words, but you saw how tired she looked, and I sensed her unhappiness." She paused and released another sigh. "And what of that comment she made tonight about not wanting to get fat?"

"She was feeling nervous about us meeting Eli and his folks. You mentioned that yourself."

"Maybe so, but I've got a feeling our daughter will be making a mistake by marrying Eli, and I'm afraid she won't realize it until it's too late." She glanced over at him and shook her head. "The Amish don't believe in divorce, you know. Laura mentioned that in one of her letters."

He shrugged. "I think you worry too much. It was obvious to me by the way Laura and Eli looked at each other that they're very much in love. If our daughter loves a man so much that she can give up her fancy way of life and become Plain, then I say more power to her."

She clicked her tongue noisily. "If I didn't know better, I would think *you* had a desire to join the Amish faith."

Wesley shook his head. "You needn't worry about that. I like my favorite TV shows too much." He grinned over at her. "It would be nice to live our lives at a little slower pace, though, don't you think?"

Irene leaned her head against the seat and closed her eyes. "Dream on, dear. Dream on."

CHAPTER 20

"Today's the big day," Martha Rose said when Laura entered the kitchen bright and early Thursday morning. "Did you sleep well last night?"

Laura yawned, reached into the cupboard for a mug, and poured herself some coffee from the pot sitting at the back of the stove. "Actually, I hardly slept a wink. I was too nervous about today."

Martha Rose pulled out a chair and motioned for Laura to take a seat. "I understand how you feel. I was a ball of nerves on my wedding day, too."

"Really? Except for that incident with the mouse the other night, I've never seen you act nervous or upset about anything."

"I wasn't really nervous about the mouse. Just wanted to get it out of my kitchen." Martha Rose got another chair and seated herself beside Laura. "I think all brides feel a bit anxious when they're about to get married."

Laura took a long, slow drink from her cup. "I hope I can make Eli happy."

"You love him, don't you?"

"Of course I do."

"Then just do your best to please him. Always trust God to help you, and your marriage will go fine; you'll see."

Laura nodded, but she wasn't sure it would be as easy as Martha Rose made it seem. Especially since she didn't have any idea how she was going to put her trust in God.

When Pauline heard a knock on her bedroom door, she pulled the pillow over her head. A few seconds later, the door opened, and her mother called, "What are you still doing in bed? We'll be late for Eli and Laura's wedding if we don't get a move on."

"I'm not going."

"Not going?"

Pauline pushed the pillow aside and groaned. "I'm not feeling so well."

Mom took a seat on the edge of the bed and placed her hand on Pauline's forehead. "You don't have a fever."

"Maybe not, but my head is sure pounding. It feels like it's going to split wide open."

"Maybe once you've had some breakfast you'll feel better."

"I'm feeling kind of *iwwel,* too. In fact, I'm so nauseated I doubt I could keep anything down."

"Are you sure you're not just looking for an excuse to stay home from the wedding because you don't want to see Eli marry someone else?"

Unbidden tears rolled down Pauline's cheeks, and she swiped at them with the back of her hand. "I can't go to that wedding, Mom. I just can't deal with it."

Mom offered Pauline a look of understanding as she patted her arm. "Jah, all right then. You stay here and rest in bed." She slipped quietly from the room.

Pauline rolled over so she was facing the wall and let the tears flow. She knew she had to find the strength to deal with this somehow, but if she stayed in Lancaster County, where she would see Eli and Laura so often, she didn't think her broken heart would ever mend. Maybe she would consider going to visit Aunt Irma in Ohio for a while. She might even stay there indefinitely.

* * *

The wedding began at eight thirty, with the bride and groom and their wedding party already sitting in the front row. The ministers then took their places, followed by the parents of the bride and groom, the groom's grandparents, other relatives, and friends. The men and women sat in separate sections, just as they did at regular church services.

When everyone was seated, Eli's brother-in-law, Amon, announced a hymn from the *Ausbund*. On the third line of the song, all the ministers in attendance rose to their feet and made their way up the stairs to the room that had been prepared for them on the second floor. Eli and Laura followed them to the council room.

Laura drew in a deep breath as she glanced down at her light blue wedding dress, which was covered with a white organdy apron. *Am I really doing the right thing? Will Eli and I always be as happy as we are right now? I've given up so many things to become Amish, but can I be content to do without worldly things for the rest of my life?*

She glanced over at her groom standing straight and tall and looking as happy as a child with a new toy. He was so handsome, dressed in a pair of black trousers, a matching vest, and a collarless, dark jacket. Accentuating Eli's white cotton shirt was a black bow tie, making him look every bit as distinguished as any of the lawyers who worked at her father's law firm.

Once they had entered the council room upstairs, Laura and Eli were instructed to be seated in two straight-backed chairs, where they received encouragement and words of advice from the ministers. Then Bishop Wagler asked if Eli and Laura had remained pure. With a solemn expression, Laura was glad she could answer affirmatively, along with Eli.

The bride and groom were then dismissed, while the ministers remained for council among themselves. This would be the time when they would decide who would take the different parts of the wedding ceremony.

Eli and Laura were met at the bottom of the stairs by their attendants. When they returned to the main room with the young men leading the women, the congregation sang the third verse of *"Lob Lied,"* the second hymn sung at most Amish church services. The wedding party came to the six chairs reserved for them and sat in unison, the three women facing the three men.

As the congregation finished "Lob Lied," the ministers reentered the room and took their respective seats. Deacon Shemly delivered a sermon, alluding to several Bible verses related to marriage. When the sermon was over, they offered a silent prayer. All those present turned and knelt, facing the bench on which they had been sitting. Laura was relieved to see that her parents did the same.

When the prayer was over, the congregation stood, and the deacon read a passage of scripture from Matthew 19, verses 1–12. When he was done, everyone returned to their seats.

Next, Bishop Wagler stepped forward and delivered the main sermon, which included several more biblical references to marriage. Then, looking at the congregation, he said, "If any here has objection to this marriage, he now has the opportunity to declare it."

There was a long pause, and Laura glanced around the room, half expecting Pauline to jump up and announce that she was in love with Eli and would make him a better wife than Laura ever could. However, there was no sign of Pauline, and for that, Laura felt hugely relieved. Maybe Pauline had stayed home today, unable to deal with seeing Eli marry someone other than herself. Laura couldn't blame the woman. She would feel the same way if she were in Pauline's place.

"You may now come forth in the name of the Lord," the bishop said, motioning for Eli and Laura to join him at the front of the room. Laura felt the touch of Eli's arm against hers, and it gave her added courage. This was it. This was the moment she had been waiting for all these months.

There was no exchange of rings, but when the bishop asked Eli if he would accept Laura as his wife and not leave her until death separated them, Laura felt as if the tie that bound them together was just as strong as if they had exchanged circular gold bands. As Laura answered a similar question from the bishop, she couldn't help but notice that her groom's eyes were brimming with tears, and the smile he wore stretched from ear to ear. She knew without question that he really did love her, and she hoped they would be this happy for years to come.

When the wedding ceremony was over, Eli and Laura moved outside to the front lawn, while the benches were moved aside and tables were set up for the meal. Even though there was a chill in the air, the sun shone brightly, and the sky looked as clear and blue as the small pond behind his parents' home. It was a perfect day for their wedding, and Eli was content in the knowledge that Laura was now his wife.

Many who had stepped outside came over to offer Eli and Laura their congratulations, including Laura's parents. When Wesley and Irene hugged their daughter, Eli noticed the tears in their eyes, and he felt a pang of guilt. He knew he was the cause of Laura leaving her fancy life and becoming one of the Plain People. Because of her love for him, she wouldn't see her own family so much, and he wondered if she had any regrets about giving up all the modern things her wealthy father could offer and Eli couldn't.

When Wesley shook Eli's hand, Eli smiled and said, "I'll take good care of your daughter. I hope you know that."

Wesley nodded. "I believe you're an honest man, and I can see how much you love Laura."

"Jah, I do."

"Please, let her keep Foosie," Irene put in. "Our daughter needs a touch from home."

Eli grinned. "I'll speak to Mom and Pop about the cat. I'm sure they won't mind having a pet inside as long as it's housebroke."

"Oh, she is." Laura reached for Eli's hand. "Foosie's never made a mess in the house. Not even when she was a kitten."

Eli's sister stepped up to them, along with Amon and little Ben. Martha Rose hugged Eli and Laura, then excused herself to go help in the kitchen. Laura bent down and scooped Ben into her arms, and he kissed her on the cheek. It was obvious that the child was enamored with her, and she seemed to like him equally well.

She'll make a good mudder, Eli mused. *Lord willing, maybe we'll have a whole house full of kinner.*

247

The wedding meal was a veritable feast. Wesley had never seen so much food in one place. Long tables had been set up in the living room and adjoining room, and the benches that had been used during the ceremony were placed at the tables. Eli's parents invited Wesley and Irene to sit at a table with them, while Laura and Eli took their place at a corner table Laura had referred to as the *eck*. They were served roasted chicken, mashed potatoes, bread filling, creamed celery, coleslaw, applesauce, fruit salad, bread, butter, jelly, and coffee. Then there were the cakes—three large ones in all.

"After eating so much food, I probably won't sleep a wink tonight," Wesley said, nudging his wife with his elbow.

She grimaced. "Can't you restrain yourself and practice moderation?"

Johnny reached for another piece of chicken and snickered. "No man can practice moderation when there's food involved."

"Our two children do look happy, don't they?" Irene said, leaning close to Eli's mother, who sat on her left.

Mary Ellen nodded. "For a while, I wasn't sure things would work out between the two of them, but now that Laura's joined the church and has proven herself, I've come to believe things will turn out okay."

Johnny thumped Wesley on the back. "I'll bet in another year or so, you two will be makin' a trip back here to see your first grandchild."

As Laura and Eli sat at their corner table, eating and visiting with their guests, Eli eyed Laura's plate and noticed that she hadn't eaten much at all.

"Eat hearty, *fraa*." Eli needled her in the ribs with his elbow. "Today's our wedding day, and this is no time to diet."

She turned to face him. "If I eat too much today, I might have to go without food for the rest of the week."

He snickered. "Jah, right."

Laura glanced across the room and nodded at her parents, sitting at a table with Eli's folks. "Mom and Dad seem to be having a good time, despite the fact they hardly know anyone."

Eli nodded. "Want to sneak away with me for a bit?"

"Sneak away? As in leave this place?"

"Jah. I think it's time for us to get a little fresh air."

They pushed away from the table and slipped out the back door.

"I'll race you to the creek," Eli said, once they were on the porch.

"You're on!"

Laura was panting for air by the time they

reached the water, and so was Eli. She collapsed on the grass, ignoring the chill, and Eli dropped down beside her, laughing and tickling Laura until she finally called a truce.

"So, it's peace you're wanting, huh?" Eli teased. "All right, but you'll have to pay a price for it."

Laura squirmed beneath his hands. "Oh, yeah? What kind of payment must I offer the likes of you, Eli Yoder?"

"This," he murmured against her ear. "And this." He nuzzled her neck with his cold nose. "Also this." His lips trailed a brigade of soft kisses along her chin, up her cheek, and finally came to rest on her lips. As the kiss deepened, Laura snuggled closer to Eli.

When he finally pulled away, she gazed deeply into his dazzling blue eyes. "I love you, Eli, and I always will."

"And I love you, my *seelich,* blessed gift."

Laura and Eli spent their first night as husband and wife at Martha Rose and Amon's house so they could help with the cleanup the following morning. Then they would live with Eli's parents until their own place was finished, hopefully by spring. The thought of living with her in-laws caused Laura some concern. Would Mary Ellen scrutinize her every move? Would Laura be expected to do even more work than she had while living with the Zooks?

Forcing her anxiety aside, Laura stepped into Martha Rose's kitchen. Eli had kissed her good-bye some time ago and left with his brothers to take the benches that had been used yesterday back over to the Hiltys' place, where church would be held next week. Laura knew her folks would be here soon to say their good-byes, and she hoped Eli would be here in time.

Martha Rose was busy baking bread, but she looked up and smiled when Laura entered the room. "Did you sleep well?"

Laura shuffled across the kitchen, still feeling the effects of sleep. She nodded and yawned. "I'm sorry I overslept. After Eli left to take the benches back, I must have dozed off again."

"Guess you needed the rest. Yesterday was a pretty big day."

"Yes, it was." Laura reached for the pot of coffee on the stove.

"There are still some scrambled eggs left." Martha Rose gestured with her head toward the frying pan at the back of the stove. "Help yourself."

Laura moaned. "After all I ate yesterday, I don't think I need any breakfast."

"Breakfast is the most important meal of the day, and now that you're a married woman, you'll need to keep up your strength."

Laura dropped into a chair at the table. "What's that supposed to mean?"

"Just that you'll soon be busy setting up your own house."

"Not really. Eli and I will be living with your folks, remember?"

Martha Rose nodded. "Jah, but not for long. If I know my brother, he'll be working long hours on your future home." She winked at Laura. "He's a man in love, and I think he'd like to have you all to himself."

Laura felt the heat of a blush stain her face. "I—I'd like that, too."

"So, dish up plenty of eggs now."

Laura opened her mouth to offer a rebuttal, but the sound of a car pulling into the yard drew her to the window. "It's my parents. They've come to say good-bye." She jerked open the door and ran down the stairs. If she was going to get all teary-eyed, she'd rather not do it in front of Eli's sister.

As soon as Mom and Dad stepped from the car, the three of them shared a group hug.

"I'll miss you," Laura said tearfully.

"Be happy," her mother whispered.

"If you ever need anything—anything at all —please don't hesitate to call." Dad grinned at her. "I know you Amish don't have phones in your houses, but you can always call from a payphone or from one of your English neighbors' like you did before."

Laura nodded as a lump formed in her throat.

She didn't know why saying good-bye to her folks was so hard; she'd been away from them for some time already. Maybe it was the reality that she was a married woman now—an Amish woman, to be exact. There could be no quick plane trips home whenever she felt the need, and it wasn't likely that Mom and Dad would come here to visit that often, either.

"We should really go inside and say good-bye to your new sister-in-law," Mom said as she started for the house.

"Where's Eli?" Dad asked. "We do get to tell our son-in-law good-bye, I hope."

"Eli went with his brothers to return the benches we used at the wedding," Laura explained. "He's not back yet."

Mom's mouth dropped open. "The day after your wedding?"

Laura nodded.

Dad glanced at his watch. "We should leave soon if we're going to make our plane."

"I'm sure Eli will be here shortly, but if you can't wait, I'll tell him—" Laura's words were halted by a piercing scream. At least she thought it was a scream. She turned toward the sound coming from the front porch and saw Foosie clinging to one of the support beams, hissing and screeching, with Amon's two dogs yapping and jumping after her.

"Foosie must have slipped out the doorway

253

behind me." Laura turned back to face her parents. "I'd better go rescue her, and you two had better get to the airport. You don't want to miss your flight."

Mom gave Laura a quick peck on the cheek, then climbed into their rental car. Dad embraced Laura one final time, and just before he took his seat on the driver's side, he said, "Don't forget to call if you need us."

Laura nodded and blinked back tears. She offered one final wave, then raced toward the house.

CHAPTER 21

Laura had visited Eli's parents' home several times, but she'd never had occasion to use the rest room. It wasn't until she and Eli moved her things to his house and were settled into their room that Laura was hit with a sickening reality. Despite the fact that most Amish homes in the area had indoor bathrooms, the Yoders still used an outhouse.

"I'll never be able to use that smelly facility," she complained to Eli as they prepared for bed that night.

He flopped onto the bed with a groan. "I can't do anything about it tonight, but I promise as soon as our own home is done, it will have a bathroom."

"That will be fine for when the time comes that we get to move, but what about now? I'll need a *real* bathroom here, too, Eli."

"I'll see about turning one of the upstairs closets into a bathroom when I can find the time."

"Why can't your father or brothers build the bathroom?"

"They're busy with other things, too, and to tell you the truth, I don't think having an inside bathroom is all that important to any of 'em."

Laura paced back and forth in front of their bedroom window. "So while I'm waiting for you to find the time, how am I supposed to bathe?"

"We have a large galvanized tub in the washroom for that. You'll heat water on the stove, and—"

"What?" Laura whirled around to face him. "I can hardly believe you would expect me to live under such primitive conditions!"

Eli looked at her as if she'd taken leave of her senses. "Calm down. You'll wake up the whole house, shouting that way." He left the bed and joined her at the window. "You've gotten used to living without other modern things, so I would think you could manage this little inconvenience. After all, it's really not such a *baremlich* thing."

She squinted. "It's a terrible thing to me. And this is not a 'little' inconvenience. It's a catastrophe!"

"Such resentment I see on your face." He brushed her cheek with the back of his thumb. "You've done well adjusting to being Amish, and I'm proud of you."

How could she stay mad with him looking at her that way? His enchanting blue eyes shone like the moonlight, and his chin dimple looked even more pronounced with his charming smile.

Laura leaned against Eli's chest and sighed. "Promise me you'll build us a decent bathroom as soon as you can."

"I promise."

The next few weeks flew by as Laura settled into her in-laws' home. There wasn't as much privacy as Laura would have liked, but she knew the situation would only be temporary.

One evening as she and Eli were in their room looking at some of the wedding gifts they had received, Laura commented that her favorite gift was the oval braided rug in rich autumn hues that Martha Rose had made. With a smile of satisfaction, she placed it on the wooden floor at the foot of their bed. "Look how well it goes with the quilt I purchased at the farmers' market that first day we met." She motioned toward the lovely covering on their bed. "These two items can be the focal points in our room."

Eli raised his eyebrows. "I don't know anything about focal points, but the rug does looks good." He pulled Laura to his chest and rubbed his face against her cheek. "Almost as good as my beautiful wife."

"Eli, you're hurting me. Your face is so scratchy!"

He stepped back, holding her at arm's length. "It'll be better once my beard grows in fully."

She stared up at him. "I know Amish men are expected to grow a beard once they're married, but I'm going to miss that little chin dimple of yours."

Eli grinned. "It'll still be there; you'll just have to hunt for it."

Laura giggled. "You're such a tease."

He tickled her under the chin. "And that's why you love me so much, jah?"

She nodded and gave him another hug. "I surely do."

Eli knew Laura wasn't happy living with his folks, and the absence of an indoor bathroom was only part of the problem. Almost every day when he came home from work, she greeted him with some complaint about his mother. He wasn't sure if the problem was Mom's fault or Laura's, but he hoped it would work itself out.

257

One Saturday, Eli decided to take Laura out for lunch at the Bird-in-Hand Family Restaurant, which had always been one of his favorite places to eat.

"This is such a nice surprise," Laura said, as the two of them were seated at a table inside the restaurant. "It's been so long since we did anything fun, I'd forgotten what it was like."

Eli snickered. "I think you're exaggerating some, but I'm glad you're enjoying yourself."

Laura glanced at the buffet counter behind them. "I might not be enjoying myself so much after I count up the calories I'll be consuming here today."

Eli's forehead wrinkled. "You worry way too much about your weight, Laura. What are you gonna do when you're in a family way?"

Laura opened her mouth as if to respond, but Selma and Elmer Hostetler stepped up to their table just then.

"Did I hear that someone's expecting a boppli?" Selma asked with a curious expression.

Laura's face turned red, and Eli shook his head. "Not us, but my sister is."

"So I heard." Selma smiled. "How many kinner are you two hoping to have?"

"Oh, as many as the good Lord allows," Eli replied.

Laura's mouth dropped open like a broken window hinge. "Huh?"

Elmer nudged his wife on the arm. "What kind of question is that for you to be askin' these newlyweds? You're worse than our outspoken daughter, and now you've embarrassed Laura."

Selma's face had reddened, too, and Eli felt the need to change the subject. "Speaking of Pauline . . . is she here with you today?"

"Nope. She moved to Kidron, Ohio, last week."

"Kidron? What's she doing there?"

"Went to be with her aunt."

Selma shifted her weight from one foot to the other as she cleared her throat. "I . . . uh . . . think she needed a change of scenery in order to get over her breakup with you. I'm sure she'll be back when she feels ready."

Eli couldn't help but feel a little guilty for being the cause of Pauline leaving her family, but what should he have done—married the girl just to make her happy?

"We ought to get ourselves some food and get back to our seats, don't ya think?" Elmer nudged Selma again.

"Jah, sure. Enjoy your meal," she said, nodding at Eli and then Laura.

When the Hostetlers moved away, Eli stood. "Guess we'd better get some food now, too."

Laura made no reply; just pushed away from the table and moved over to the buffet counter with a disgruntled expression. When they returned to the table a short time later, Eli felt a

259

sense of concern seeing how little food she had put on her plate.

"Aren't you hungry?"

"I was until Pauline's folks showed up."

"Why would them stopping by our table make you lose your appetite?"

Laura took a drink from her glass of iced tea before she spoke. "Well, let me see now . . . First, Selma embarrassed me by asking if I was pregnant; then she asked how many children we planned to have. As if that wasn't enough, she made sure you knew why Pauline has moved to Ohio." She grimaced. "Didn't that make you feel uncomfortable, Eli?"

"Jah, a bit, but Selma's right about Pauline needing a change of scenery, and I'm sure it is my fault that she decided to go."

"How can it be your fault? You told me there was nothing but friendship between you and Pauline. I never understood why she thought there was more."

Eli shrugged. "I guess she wanted there to be, and when I started seeing her again after you and I decided it would be best if we went our separate ways—"

Laura held up her hand. "Just a minute. It was you who decided that, not me."

He nodded. "You're right, but that was before you'd made the decision to become Amish."

She leaned forward, staring hard at him. "So if I hadn't made that decision, would you have married Pauline?"

Eli took a sip of his water, hoping it would help cool him down. What he'd wanted to be a pleasant afternoon for the two of them was turning into a most uncomfortable situation, and if he didn't do something soon, they might end up in an argument.

"Well, Eli . . . are you going to answer my question or not?"

He set his glass on the table. "I can't rightly say, but I don't think I would have married her."

"You don't *think* so? If you never loved her, then marrying her shouldn't have been an option." Laura's voice had risen so high, Eli feared those sitting nearby would hear. "I'll bet you would have married her if I hadn't agreed to become Amish, wouldn't you?"

He put a finger to his lips. "Let's talk about something else, okay?"

"Let's just eat our food and forget about conversation."

"That suits me fine." Eli bowed his head for silent prayer, and when he lifted it, he noticed that Laura had already begun to eat. He didn't know if she had joined him in prayer or not, but he decided it was best not to ask. They could finish this discussion later.

* * *

On the buggy ride home, Laura kept her eyes shut, hoping Eli would think she was asleep and wouldn't try to make conversation. The last thing she wanted was another argument, and she was pretty sure they would quarrel if she told him all the things that were going on in her mind.

When Laura felt the buggy turn sharply and heard the wheels crunch through some gravel, she figured they had pulled into the Yoders' driveway, so she opened her eyes.

Before they got to the yard, Eli pulled back on the reins and guided the horse and buggy to the edge of the driveway.

"What are you doing? Why are we stopping?"

"So we can talk."

"There's nothing to talk about."

"I think there is."

She drew in a deep breath and released it with a weary sigh. "What do you think we need to talk about?"

"This business with you thinking I would have married Pauline, for one thing. If I've told you once, I've told you a hundred times, Pauline and I were never more than friends."

"She wanted it to be more." Laura balled her hands into fists. "I think your mother did, too."

"Mom? What's Mom got to do with this?"

Laura pursed her lips as she squinted. "Oh, Eli, don't look so wide-eyed and innocent. We've

262

been living with your folks several weeks now. Surely you can feel the tension between me and your mother."

He merely shrugged in response.

"She's mentioned Pauline a few times, too. I think she believes Pauline would have made you a better wife."

A vein on the side of Eli's neck began to bulge, and Laura wondered if she had hit a nerve.

"Your mom is always criticizing me," she continued. "I can never do anything right where she's concerned."

"I don't believe that."

"Are you calling me a liar?"

"No, but I think I know Mom pretty well."

"You don't know her as well as you think. She scrutinizes my work, and she—"

"Enough! I don't want to hear another word against my mamm!"

As the days moved on, Laura became more frustrated. Nothing seemed to be going right. Their house still wasn't done; Eli wasn't nearly so cheerful and fun-loving anymore; Foosie was an irritant to Eli's mother; Laura dreaded the extra chores she was expected to do; and worst of all, she couldn't stand that smelly outhouse! She was on her way there now and none too happy about it.

On previous trips to the privy, she'd encountered several disgusting spiders, a yellow jackets' nest, and a couple of field mice. She was a city girl and hated bugs. She shouldn't have to be subjected to this kind of torture.

Laura opened the wooden door and held it with one hand as she lifted her kerosene lantern and peered cautiously inside. Nothing lurking on the floor. She held the lamp higher and was about to step inside when the shaft of light fell on something dark and furry. It was sitting over the hole.

Laura let out a piercing scream and slammed the door. She sprinted toward the house and ran straight into Eli, coming from the barn.

"Laura, what's wrong? I heard you hollering and thought one of Pop's pigs had gotten loose again."

Laura clung to Eli's jacket. "It's the outhouse . . . there's some kind of monstrous animal in there!"

Eli grinned at her. "*Kumme*—come now. It was probably just a little old *maus*."

"It was not a mouse. It was dark and furry . . . and huge!"

Eli slipped his hand in the crook of her arm. "Let's go have a look-see."

"I'm not going in there."

He chuckled. "You don't have to. I'll do the checking."

Laura held her breath as Eli entered the out-house. "Be careful."

She heard a thud, followed by a loud *whoop*. Suddenly, the door flew open and Eli bolted out of the privy, chased by the hairy creature Laura had seen a few moments ago. It was a comical sight, but she was almost too frightened to see the full humor in it.

"What was that?" she asked Eli, as the two of them stood watching the critter dash into the field.

"I think it was a hedgehog," Eli said breathlessly. "The crazy thing tried to attack me, but I kicked him with the toe of my boot, right before I walked out of the outhouse."

Laura giggled as her fear dissipated. "Don't you mean, '*ran* out of the outhouse'?"

Eli's face turned pink, and he chuckled. "Guess I was movin' pretty fast."

The two of them stood for a few seconds, gazing into each other's eyes. Then they both started laughing. They laughed so hard, tears streamed down their faces, and Laura had to set the lantern on the ground for fear it would fall out of her hand. It felt good to laugh. It was something neither of them did much anymore.

When they finally got control of their emotions, Eli reached for her hand. "I'll see about indoor plumbing as soon as spring comes; I promise."

CHAPTER 22

Wesley sat on the couch, staring at the Christmas tree. The little white lights blinked off and on, and the red bows hung from the evergreen branches in perfect order—but this Christmas would be anything but perfect.

He glanced at the unlit fireplace. A garland of fake holly had been strung across the mantel, but there was no Foosie lying on the rug by the hearth.

The Christmas cards they had received were stacked neatly in a red basket on the coffee table, but the only card that mattered to him was the one they'd gotten from Laura and Eli. It had included an invitation to come there for Christmas, and Laura had even suggested they stay there with them. Wesley had wanted to go, and he'd even been willing to adjust his work schedule so they could, but Irene wouldn't hear of it. She had insisted that she couldn't leave town during the holidays because she had too many commitments.

"Yeah, right," he mumbled. "She just doesn't want to give up all the modern conveniences she's convinced she can't do without."

"Who are you talking to, Wesley?"

He glanced at the doorway and was surprised to see Irene standing there holding a large poinsettia plant in her hands.

"I didn't hear you come in. Did you just get home?"

She nodded and placed the plant on the end table near the couch. "I've been out shopping."

"That figures."

"What was that?"

"Nothing."

Irene slipped off her coat and laid it neatly on one end of the couch. Then she took a seat in her recliner and picked up the remote. "How come you're not watching television? Isn't it about time for your favorite show?"

"I get tired of watching TV."

"Since when?"

"Since I came to the conclusion that there are better things I can do with my time."

"You mean like sitting here staring at the tree?"

"Christmas is just a few days away. It seemed like the thing to do."

She wrinkled her nose. "Are you being sarcastic?"

"I wouldn't dream of it."

"Wesley, are you still pouting because we can't go to Pennsylvania for Christmas?"

"What do you mean, 'We can't go to Pennsylvania'?" He stood and began to pace. "We could have gone if you weren't so busy with *things*."

"Those *things* are important, and I—"

He stopped pacing and whirled around to face her. "Don't you miss our daughter? Wouldn't you rather spend Christmas with her than go to some silly ball?"

"Of course I'd like to be with Laura, but I've been planning this gala affair for several months." She released a sigh. "How would it look if the person in charge of the Christmas ball wasn't there to see that everything went according to plan?"

He grunted and started across the room.

"Where are you going?"

"Upstairs to bed. I'll need to get my beauty rest if I'm going to escort Princess Irene to the ball on Christmas Eve."

Laura stood in front of the living-room window, staring out at the blanket of pristine snow covering the ground and every tree in the Yoders' yard. It looked like a picture postcard, and despite the fact that Laura missed her parents, she felt happier today than she had in weeks.

She moved away from the window and took a seat in the wooden rocker by the fireplace. Even though there was no Christmas tree inside the house or colored lights decorating the outside of the house, a few candles were spaced around the room, along with several Christmas cards from family and friends. *Guess I did end up with an Early-American look after all. It's just a little plainer than I had expected it to be.*

Laura spotted the Christmas card they had received from her parents, along with a substantial check, and her heart clenched. *I do miss Mom and Dad, and I wish Eli and I could have gone there for Christmas or that they would have come here. But Mom was involved with a Christmas ball she'd planned at the country club, and even though Dad sounded like he wanted to come, he never seems to get his way where Mom's concerned. Maybe he should take lessons from Eli and his father. They don't have much trouble making a decision, even if it goes against what their wives might want.*

Eli had been looking forward to Christmas. He'd made Laura a special gift, and this afternoon, his sister and her family would be joining them for Mom's traditional holiday feast.

"Life couldn't be any better," he said to the horse he was grooming. "Maybe later we'll hitch you up to the sleigh, and I'll take my beautiful wife for a ride."

The horse whinnied as if in response, and Eli chuckled. "You kind of like that idea, don't you, old boy?"

Eli entered the house a short time later, holding Laura's gift under his jacket. "Where's my fraa?" he asked Mom, who was scurrying around the kitchen.

She nodded toward the living room. "Your wife's in there. I guess she thinks I don't need any help getting dinner on."

Eli merely shrugged and left the kitchen. No point getting Mom more riled than she already seemed to be. He found Laura sitting in the rocking chair, gazing at the fireplace. *"En hallicher Grischtdaag!"*

She looked up and smiled. "A merry Christmas to you, too."

Eli bent down and kissed the top of her head. "I have something for you."

"You do? What is it?"

Eli held his jacket shut. "Guess."

She wrinkled her nose. "I have no idea. Tell me . . . please."

He chuckled and withdrew an ornate birdhouse, painted blue with white trim.

"Oh, Eli, it's just like the one you showed me at the farmers' market the day we first met."

He smiled. "And now you will have a place for it, come spring."

She accepted the gift, and tears welled in her eyes. "Thank you so much. It's beautiful."

"Does my pretty fraa have anything for her hardworking husband?" Eli asked in a teasing tone.

"I do, but I'm afraid it's not finished."

270

"You made me something?"

She nodded. "I've been sewing you a new shirt, but your mom's kept me so busy, I haven't had time to get it hemmed and wrapped."

Eli took the birdhouse from Laura and placed it on the small table by her chair. He pulled her toward him in a tender embrace. "It's okay. You'll get the shirt finished soon, and I'll appreciate it every bit as much then as I would if you'd given it to me now."

Laura rested her head against his shoulder. "I love you, Eli. Thanks for being so understanding."

Silent prayer had been said, and everyone sat around the table with expectant, hungry looks on their faces. Mary Ellen had outdone herself. Huge platters were laden with succulent roast beef and mouthwatering ham. Bowls were filled with buttery mashed potatoes, candied yams, canned green beans, and coleslaw. Sweet cucumber pickles, black olives, dilled green beans, and red-beet eggs were also included in the feast, as well as buttermilk biscuits and cornmeal muffins.

Everyone ate heartily. Everyone except for Laura and little Ben. Their plates were still half full when Mary Ellen brought out three pies—two pumpkin and one mincemeat—along with a tray of chocolate doughnuts.

Ben squealed with delight. *"Fettkuche!"*

"No doughnuts until you eat everything on your plate," Martha Rose scolded.

Ben's lower lip began to quiver, and his eyes filled with tears.

"Being a crybaby won't help you get your way," Amon admonished.

"He's only a child." Laura pulled one of the pumpkin pies close and helped herself to a piece. "Surely he can have one little doughnut."

All eyes seemed to be focused on Laura, and Ben, who had moments ago been fighting tears, let loose with a howl that sent Laura's cat flying into the air.

"Now look what you've done." Amon shook his finger at Ben. "You've scared that poor bussli half to death."

Foosie ran around the table, meowing and swishing her tail. Laura bent down and scooped her up, but the pinched expression on Mary Ellen's face was enough to let her know that in this house, cats didn't belong at the table. Laura mumbled an apology and deposited Foosie back on the floor.

"You're not settin' a very good example for the boy, Laura." This reprimand came from Eli's father. "If you're not gonna eat all your food, then I don't think you should take any pie." Johnny looked pointedly at Eli. "What do you think, son? Should your fraa be allowed to pick

272

like a bird, then eat pie in front of Ben, who's just been told he can't have any fettkuche 'til he cleans his plate?"

Laura squirmed uneasily as she waited to see how Eli would respond. She felt his hand under the table, and her fingers squeezed his in response.

"Don't you think maybe you should eat everything else first, then have some pie?" Eli's voice was tight, and the muscle in his jaw quivered. Was he upset with her or only trying to please his father?

"I'm watching my weight, and the only way I can keep within my calorie count is to leave some food on my plate."

"You could pass up the pie," Mary Ellen suggested.

Laura grimaced. Why was everything she did always under scrutiny? Why did she have to make excuses for her behavior all the time? She pushed away from the table. "I'm not really hungry enough for pie, anyway." She gave Eli a quick glance, then rushed out of the room.

CHAPTER 23

Spring came early, and the building of Eli and Laura's home resumed as soon as the snow had melted. It couldn't be finished soon enough as far as Mary Ellen was concerned. Ever since Eli had married Laura, she had tried to be a good mother-in-law, but it wasn't easy when Laura seemed so distant and often touchy. Here of late, she'd been acting moodier than ever, and Mary Ellen wondered if *she* might be the cause of Laura's discontent.

"Why don't the two of us do some baking today?" she suggested to Laura one morning after breakfast. "We can make a couple of brown sugar sponge rolls. How's that sound?"

Laura groaned. "Do we have to? I'm really tired this morning, and I thought it would be nice to sit out on the back porch and watch the men work on my house."

Mary Ellen's forehead wrinkled. "Are you feeling poorly?"

"I'm fine. Just tired."

"Maybe a good spring tonic is what you need." She opened the cupboard near Laura and plucked out a box of cream of tartar, some sulfur, and a container of Epsom salts. "All you

274

have to do is mix a little of each of these in a jar of water. Then take two or three swallows each morning for a few days, and you'll feel like your old self in no time at all."

Laura's face paled, and she coughed like she was about to gag. "I'm fine, really. Just didn't sleep well last night. A few cups of coffee, and I'll be good to go."

Mary Ellen shrugged and stepped aside. "Suit yourself, but remember the spring tonic in case you're still not up to par come morning."

"Danki. I'll keep it in mind."

As they rode home from church one Sunday afternoon, Eli worried. Laura had seemed so pensive lately. Had someone said or done something to upset her? He offered her a smile. "Sure was a good day, wasn't it?"

"Uh-huh."

"Is there something troubling you? You seem kind of down in the dumps today."

She shrugged. "I'm just getting tired of going to other people's houses and seeing that they have indoor plumbing, while we still have none."

"I said I'd build one in our new home, and I'm still planning to put one in Mom and Pop's house as soon as I find the time."

"You've been saying that for months, Eli, and it's taking a lot longer than I thought it would." She grunted. "I can't stand that smelly outhouse!"

Eli glanced over at her and squinted. "I'm working every free moment I have, and so are Pop and my brothers. Can't you learn to be patient?"

Laura sat staring straight ahead with her lips pursed and said nothing.

"The Bible says, 'The trying of your faith worketh patience.' It's in the book of James."

"My faith in things getting better has definitely been tried, and so has my patience," she mumbled.

Eli blinked. Was there no pleasing this woman? He'd said he would install indoor plumbing in their new home. That ought to be good enough.

"Eli, could I ask you a question?"

He blew out his breath. "Not if it's about indoor plumbing."

"It's not."

"Okay, ask the question then."

She reached across the seat and touched his arm. "Do you think Pauline Hostetler would have made you a better wife?"

Eli lifted one eyebrow and glanced over at Laura. "Pauline? What's she got to do with anything?"

"I just want to know if you think—"

"I can't believe you would bring that up again, Laura. You should know by now how much I love you."

Her eyes filled with tears and she sniffed.

"What's wrong? Why are you crying?"

"Your mother and I were doing some baking the other day, and she brought up the subject of Pauline."

"Oh? What'd she say?"

"Just that Pauline is a good cook and likes to bake." Laura's voice rose a notch. "I'm sure she thinks Pauline would have made you a better wife than me."

Eli pulled sharply on the reins, steered the buggy to the side of the road, and gathered her into his arms. "I love you, Laura. Only you."

"I'm glad to hear that." Laura snuggled against his jacket. "But that doesn't take care of things with your mother. Do you have any idea what I can say or do to make her realize that I'm a better wife for you than Pauline could ever have been?"

Eli touched her chin lightly with his thumb. "You'd best leave that up to me."

When Eli and Laura entered the house a short time later, Laura went up to their room, saying she was tired and needed a nap.

Eli found his mother sitting in the living room on the sofa, reading a book. Apparently his folks had gotten home from church quite a bit ahead of them. He decided this might be a good time to speak with her about the conversation she'd

277

had with Laura the other day. "Mom, can I talk to you for a minute?"

She looked up and smiled. "Jah, sure. What's on your mind?"

He took a seat in the rocking chair across from her. "It's about Laura."

"Is she feeling all right? The other day she mentioned that she was really tired, and I suggested she take a spring tonic."

Eli winced at the remembrance of drinking his mother's sour-tasting tonics when he was a boy. "I don't think a spring tonic will take care of what ails my fraa."

"Is she still fretting over your house not being done? She's mentioned several times that she can't wait until it's finished." Mom's forehead wrinkled. "I think she's anxious to have her own place to run, and to tell you the truth, I'm looking forward to having my space, too."

"Jah, it will be good for both of you when the house is done." Eli sat there a few minutes, trying to formulate the right words to say what was on his mind.

"You're looking kind of pensive, son. Is there something more you wanted to say?"

He nodded. "Laura thinks you would have been happier if I'd married Pauline instead of her. When you mentioned how well Pauline can cook the other day, it really hurt Laura's feelings."

"I think Laura's too sensitive for her own good." Mom clicked her tongue. "I meant nothing by what I said."

"Are you sure about that?"

Mom stared at the book she held in her hands. "I—I suppose I was kind of hoping you would choose Pauline, but once your decision was made, I accepted it."

"Then why did you bring Pauline up to Laura, and why does Laura feel as if you don't approve of her?"

"As I said before . . . she tends to be rather sensitive."

Eli nodded. Laura was touchy about some of the things he said, too—especially in recent weeks.

"I'll apologize to her and try to be more careful with what I say," Mom promised.

"Danki. I appreciate that."

"I'm not feeling well. I think I'll stay home from church today," Laura mumbled when Eli tried to coax her out of bed two Sundays later.

"You were feeling all right last night."

"That was then. This is now."

"You should get up and help Mom with breakfast," Eli murmured against her ear.

She groaned. "I don't feel like helping today."

Eli touched her forehead. "You're not running a fever."

"I'm not sick . . . just terribly tired."

"Maybe you should consider taking Mom's spring tonic. It does put a spring in your step; I promise."

"I'm not taking any tonic. I would feel fine if I could get a little more rest."

Eli pulled back the covers, hopped out of bed, and stepped into his trousers. He walked across the room to where the water pitcher and bowl sat on top of the dresser. After splashing a handful of water on his face and drying it with a towel, he grabbed his shirt off the wall peg and started for the door. "See you downstairs in five minutes."

When the door clicked shut, Laura grabbed her pillow and threw it across the room. "Maybe I should go home to my parents for a while. I wonder how you'd like that, Eli Yoder!"

Laura was quiet on the buggy ride to preaching, and during the service she didn't sing. Not only was she still tired, but she felt irritation with Eli for not having any understanding and insisting that she get up and help his mother with breakfast this morning. He should have had a little sympathy and agreed that she could stay home and rest.

Laura's attention was drawn to the front of the room as Bishop Wagler began his sermon, using Mark 11:25 as his text. "In Jesus' own words, we

280

are told: 'And when ye stand praying, forgive, if ye have ought against any: that your Father also which is in heaven may forgive you your trespasses.' "

Laura frowned. *That verse doesn't make any sense to me. How can I forgive Mary Ellen for her comments about Pauline the other day when she didn't even say she was sorry? And Eli never said he was sorry for the way he talked to me this morning, either.*

She glanced over at Martha Rose, who sat on the bench beside her. She wore a smile on her face and looked almost angelic. But then, Eli's sister always seemed to be happy, even when she had a bout of morning sickness or things weren't going so well. *Maybe it's because she doesn't have to share her home with her mother-in-law!*

"I thought Bishop Wagler's sermon was good, didn't you?" Eli asked as he glanced over at Laura on their trip home from church later that day.

She merely shrugged in response.

"If we don't forgive others, we can't expect God to forgive us."

Still no reply.

"I forgive you for throwing that pillow at me this morning."

Her mouth dropped open. "You knew?"

He nodded. "Heard it hit the door."

"I wasn't really throwing it at you," she said, as a smile tugged at the corners of her mouth. "Just venting was all."

"Because I asked you to get out of bed and help my mamm?"

"Jah."

Holding the reins with one hand, he reached his free hand over and took hold of Laura's hand. "Didn't mean to sound so bossy. Will you forgive me?"

She nodded and slid closer to him. "Of course I forgive you."

His eyebrows raised. "Is that all you've got to say?"

She sat silently for several seconds; then a light seemed to dawn. "I'm sorry, too."

He grinned and gave her fingers a gentle squeeze. "You're forgiven."

Laura leaned her head on his shoulder and sighed. "I'm glad we got that cleared up. Now if I could just get your mother to apologize for what she said to me about Pauline."

Eli's eyebrows raised. "She hasn't apologized yet? She said she was going to."

Laura shook her head.

"She probably got busy and forgot. Want me to have another talk with her?"

"No, just forget it. We'll move into our house soon; then things should be better."

CHAPTER 24

Eli and Laura's house was finally ready, and Eli had included a small bathroom, just as he'd promised. He and his father had also put one in their house, so Laura knew she would have that convenience handy whenever they visited his folks. Eli and Laura's new home had five bedrooms, a roomy kitchen, a nice-sized living room, and of course, the small bathroom.

Mary Ellen had given Eli and Laura some furniture, and Laura was glad to finally have a home she could call her own. It would be a welcome relief not to have Eli's mother analyzing everything she said and did. As far as Laura was concerned, the completion of her house was the best thing that had happened since she'd moved onto the Yoders' farm.

On the first morning in her new home, Laura got up late. When she entered the kitchen, she realized Eli was already outside doing his chores. She hurried to start breakfast and was just setting the table when he came inside.

"Your cereal is almost ready," she said with a smile.

He nodded. "Is my lunch packed? I have to leave for work in five minutes."

"Oh, I forgot. I'm running late this morning. Usually your mother gets breakfast going while I make your lunch."

"It's okay. I'll just take a few pieces of fruit and some cookies." Eli opened his lunch pail and placed two apples, an orange, a handful of peanut butter cookies, and a thermos of milk inside. He took a seat at the table, bowed his head for silent prayer, and dug into the hot oatmeal Laura handed him.

"Can you stop by the store and pick up a loaf of bread on your way home tonight?" Laura asked, taking the seat beside him.

Eli gave her a questioning look.

"I won't have time to do any baking today. I have clothes to wash, and I want to spend most of the day organizing the house and setting out some of our wedding gifts."

Eli gulped down the last of his milk and stood. "Jah, okay. I know it's important for you to set things up the way you want them." He leaned over and kissed her cheek.

"Ouch! You're prickly!"

"Sorry." Eli grabbed his lunch pail and headed for the door.

"Wait! Can't you visit with me awhile this morning? You've been working such long hours lately, and it seems like we never get to talk anymore."

"We'll talk later. I've got to go now, or I'll be late for work."

Laura waved at his retreating form. When she shut the door, she sighed deeply and surveyed her kitchen. "This house is so big. Where should I begin?"

As Laura stood at the kitchen sink doing the breakfast dishes, she began to fret. Eli had changed since their marriage. He not only looked different, what with his scratchy beard, but he never seemed to have time for her anymore.

"Work, work, work, that's all he ever thinks about," she muttered. "If Eli cared about me the way he does his job, I'd be a lot happier. Whatever happened to romance and long buggy rides to the lake?"

A single tear rolled down her cheek, and she wiped it away with a soapy hand. "Life is so unfair. I gave up a lot to become Eli's wife, and now he won't even listen to me." Laura glanced down at Foosie, who lay curled at her feet. "Too bad Mom and Dad can't come for a visit." She sniffed deeply. "No . . . they're too busy, just like Eli. Dad has his law practice, and Mom runs around like a chicken hunting bugs, trying to meet all of her social obligations."

The cat purred contentedly, seemingly unaware of her frustrations.

"You've got life made, you know that?"

A knock at the back door drew Laura's attention away from Foosie. *Oh, no. I hope that's not Mary Ellen.*

She dried her hands on her apron and dabbed the corners of her eyes with a handkerchief, then went to answer the door.

To her surprise, Martha Rose and little Ben stood on the porch, each holding a basket. Martha Rose's basket held freshly baked apple muffins, and Ben's was full of ginger cookies.

Laura smiled. She was always glad to see her sister-in-law and that adorable little boy. "Come in. Would you like a cup of tea?"

Martha Rose, her stomach now bulging, lowered herself into a chair. "That sounds good. We can have some of the muffins I brought, too."

Ben spotted Foosie, and he darted over to play with her.

"What brings you by so early?" Laura asked as she pulled out a chair for herself.

"We're on our way to town to do some shopping, but we wanted to stop and see you first," Martha Rose answered. "We have an invitation for you and Eli."

Laura's interest was piqued. "What kind of invitation?"

"Since tomorrow's Saturday and the weather's so nice, Amon and I have decided to take Ben to the lake for a picnic supper. We were wondering if you and Eli would like to come along."

Laura dropped a couple of tea bags into the pot she'd taken from the stove before she sat down. "Would we ever! At least, I would. If Eli can tear himself away from work long enough, I'm sure he'd have a good time, too."

Martha Rose nodded. "We'll meet you there around four o'clock. That'll give everyone time enough to do all their chores." She waved her hand. "Speaking of chores—you look awfully tired. Are you working too hard?"

Laura pushed a stray hair under her head covering and sighed. "I have been feeling a little drained lately. I'll be fine once I get this house organized."

Martha Rose opened her mouth to say something, but Laura cut her off. "What should I bring to the picnic?"

"I thought I'd fix fried chicken, two different salads, and maybe some pickled-beet eggs. Why don't you bring the dessert and some kind of beverage?"

"That sounds fine," Laura answered, feeling suddenly lighthearted. They were going on a picnic, and she could hardly wait.

"How was your day?" Eli asked, as he stepped into the kitchen that evening and found Laura sitting at the table, tearing lettuce leaves into a bowl.

"It was okay. How about yours?"

"Busy. We got several new orders at the store today, and my boss said we might have to put in more overtime in order to get them done."

She groaned. "I hope not. You work too much as it is."

He placed his lunch pail on the counter and joined her at the table. He was too tired to argue, and it seemed like he never won an argument with Laura anyway, so what was the use?

"Your sister and little Ben came by today." Laura looked over at him and smiled. "She invited us to join their family on a picnic at the lake tomorrow."

"What time?"

"She said for supper, and that they'd be there by four."

"That might be okay. I'll need to work in my shop awhile, and I promised Pop I'd help him do a couple of chores, too."

"What time will you be done?"

"Probably by four, I would imagine."

"Then we can go on the picnic?" Laura's expression was so hopeful, there was no way Eli could say no.

He leaned over and kissed her cheek. "Jah, tomorrow we'll join my sister and her family for a picnic."

The lake was beautiful, and Laura drank in the

peacefulness until she felt as if her heart would burst.

Martha Rose was busy setting out her picnic foods, and the men were playing ball with little Ben. Laura brought out the brownies and iced mint tea she had made, and soon the plywood table they'd brought from home was brimming with food.

Everyone gathered for silent prayer, and then the men heaped their plates full. Laura was the last to dish up, but she only took small helpings of everything. When she came to the tray of pickled-beet eggs, a surge of nausea rolled through her stomach like angry ocean waves. Pickled eggs were sickening—little purple land mines, waiting to destroy her insides.

Laura dropped her plate of food and dashed for the woods. Eli ran after her, but he waited until she had emptied her stomach before saying anything.

"You okay?" he asked with obvious concern.

Laura stood on wobbly legs. "I'm fine. It was the sight of those pickled eggs. They're disgusting! How can anyone eat those awful things?"

Eli slipped his arm around her waist. "Maybe you've got the flu."

She shook her head. "It was just the eggs. Let's go back to the picnic. I'm fine now, honest."

The rest of the day went well enough, and

Laura felt a bit better after drinking some of her cold mint tea. She even joined a friendly game of tag, but she did notice the looks of concern Eli and his sister exchanged. At least nobody had said anything about her getting sick, and for that, she was glad.

A few days later while Laura was outside gathering eggs from the henhouse, she had another attack of nausea. She hadn't eaten any breakfast, so she figured that was the reason. Besides, the acrid odor of chicken manure was enough to make anyone sick.

On her way back to the house, she spotted Eli's mother hanging laundry on the line. Mary Ellen waved and called to Laura, but Laura only nodded in return and hurried on. She was in no mood for a confrontation with her mother-in-law this morning, and she certainly didn't want to get sick in front of her.

"I'm almost finished here," Mary Ellen called. "Come have a cup of coffee."

Laura's stomach lurched at the mention of coffee, and she wondered how she could graciously get out of the invitation.

Mary Ellen called to her again. "I know you're busy, but surely you can take a few minutes for a little chat."

Laura inhaled deeply and released a sigh. "All right. I'll set this basket of eggs inside, then be right over." *May as well give in, or Mary Ellen will probably report to Eli that his wife is unsociable.*

Laura entered the house and deposited the eggs in the refrigerator. Then she took a glass from the cupboard and went to the sink for a cool drink of water. She drank it slowly and took several deep breaths, which seemed to help settle her stomach some.

She opened the back door. "Well, here goes nothing."

When she stepped into the Yoders' kitchen a few minutes later, she found Mary Ellen seated at the table. Two cups were sitting there, and the strong aroma of coffee permeated the air.

Laura's stomach did a little flip-flop as she took a seat. "Uh, would you mind if I had mint tea instead of coffee?"

Mary Ellen pushed her chair aside and stood. "If that's what you prefer." She went to the cupboard and retrieved a box of tea bags, then poured boiling water from the teapot on the stove into a clean mug and added one bag. "You're looking kind of peaked this morning." she said, handing Laura the tea.

"I think I might have a touch of the flu."

"You could be in a family way. Have you thought about that?"

Laura shook her head. "It's the flu. Nothing to worry about."

"Would you like some shoofly pie or a butter-milk biscuit?"

"I might try a biscuit."

Mary Ellen passed Laura a basket of warm biscuits. "So, tell me, how long has this flu thing been going on?"

"Just a few days."

"If it continues, maybe you'd better see the doctor."

There she goes again, telling me what to do. Laura reached for the small pitcher on the table and poured some milk into the tea, stirring it vigorously. With a splash, some of the hot liquid splattered onto her hand, and she grimaced. "I'll see the doctor if I don't feel better soon."

Mary Ellen moved her chair a little closer to Laura's. "I . . . uh . . . have been meaning to apologize for bringing Pauline up to you a few weeks ago. I shouldn't have said anything about the woman's cooking skills."

"Apology accepted." Laura took a sip of tea. "Have you heard anything about Pauline since she moved to Ohio?"

"Just that she got there safely and seems to like it well enough."

"Any idea how long she'll be staying?"

Mary Ellen shrugged. "Guess it all depends."

Laura drummed her fingernails along the edge

of the tablecloth. "On how soon she gets over Eli? Is that what you mean?"

"Jah."

"Eli has told me several times that he and Pauline were never more than friends, but I guess she was hoping for more."

Mary Ellen wasn't sure how to respond, because the truth was she'd been hoping for more, too. She had always liked Pauline and had thought she would have made Eli a good wife. *Maybe if Eli hadn't played around during his rumpschpringe years so long and had settled down and joined the church sooner, he would have married Pauline. Probably wouldn't have met Laura, either.*

"Are you about finished with your tea? Would you like another cup?" she asked, hoping the change of subject might clear the air between them.

"I am almost done, but I'm feeling kind of tired all of a sudden, so I think I'll head home and rest awhile."

Mary Ellen studied Laura. Dark circles showed under her eyes, and her face looked pale and drawn. Either she'd been working too hard setting up her new household, or there was something physically wrong. She figured it would be best not to make an issue of it, though. No point in setting herself up to say something wrong and then need to apologize again. So she merely smiled and said, "Guess I'd better get busy making some pickled-beet eggs I promised Johnny he could have. Have a good rest of the day, Laura."

Laura nodded, pushed her chair aside, and dashed from the room.

Mary Ellen shook her head. "Something tells me there's a lot more going on with Eli's wife than she's willing to admit."

CHAPTER 25

Laura's nausea and fatigue continued all that week, but she did her best to hide it from Eli. She didn't want him pressuring her to see the doctor, or worse yet, asking a bunch of questions the way his mother had.

One morning, Laura decided to go into town for some supplies. She asked Eli to hitch the horse to the buggy before he left for work, as she still didn't feel comfortable doing that on her own. As soon as her morning chores were done, she set her dark bonnet in place over her white *kapp* and climbed into the waiting buggy.

When Laura arrived in town, her first stop was the pharmacy. She scanned the shelves until she found exactly what she was looking for. She brought the item to the checkout counter and waited for the middle-aged clerk to ring it up. He gave her a strange look as he placed the small box inside a paper sack. Laura wondered if she was the first Amish woman who had ever purchased a home pregnancy kit.

The test couldn't be taken until early the next morning, so when she got home later in the day, Laura found a safe place to hide it. The last thing she needed was for Eli to discover it and jump to the wrong conclusions. He would surely think she was pregnant, and she was equally sure she wasn't. She couldn't be. Of course, she had missed her monthly, but that wasn't too uncommon for her. Then what about the fatigue and nausea? Those were definite signs of pregnancy; even she knew that much.

Laura waited until Eli left for work the following morning before going to her sewing basket, retrieving the test kit, and rushing to the bathroom.

Moments later, Laura's hands trembled as she held the strip up for examination. It was bright pink. The blood drained from her face, and she sank to the floor, steadying herself against the unyielding wall. "Oh, no! This just can't be!"

She studied it longer, just to be sure she hadn't read it wrong. It was still pink. "I can't be pregnant. What will it do to my figure?"

Some time later when Laura emerged from the bathroom, her eyes felt sore and swollen from crying. She went straight to the kitchen sink and splashed cold water on her face.

I can't tell Eli or even my folks about this yet. I need time to adjust to the idea first.

"How long can I keep a secret like this?" she moaned. After some quick calculations, she figured she must be about eight weeks along. In another four to six weeks, she might be starting to show. Besides, if she kept getting sick every day, Eli would either suspect she was pregnant or decide she was definitely sick and take her to the doctor.

"What am I going to do?" she wailed, looking down at Foosie, asleep at her feet.

No response. Just some gentle purring from the contented-looking cat.

Laura glanced out the window and saw the mail truck pull up to the box by the road. "Guess I'll walk out and get the mail while I think about this situation some more."

Laura found a stack of letters in the box and was surprised to see one from Darla. She hadn't heard anything from her friend from school in several months, and she'd figured Darla had probably forgotten her by now.

Back in the kitchen, Laura took a seat at the table and opened Darla's letter. It didn't say much except that she had a few days off from her job in Philadelphia and wondered if Laura would like to meet her for lunch at a restaurant near Strasburg on Friday of next week.

Laura figured there was plenty of time to get a letter sent back to Darla before Friday, so she moved over to the desk on the other side of the room and took out a piece of paper and a pen. Having lunch with Darla wouldn't solve her immediate problem, but at least it would be a nice outing and was something to look forward to.

Before Laura left the house the following Friday, she wrote Eli a note telling him where she was going and that she would try to be back in time to get supper going before he got home. Then she hitched one of their most docile mares to the buggy and headed out.

When Laura pulled into the restaurant parking lot some time later, she was pleased to see Darla's little sports car parked there. She climbed down from the buggy, secured the horse to the hitching rail, and headed into the restaurant.

She spotted Darla sitting at a table near the window and hurried over to her. "Hey, it's good to see you," she said, taking a seat on the other side of the table. "Thanks for inviting me to join you."

Darla smiled at first, but then her forehead wrinkled as she frowned. "I barely recognized you in those Amish clothes. You sure have changed."

Laura nodded and held out her hands. "Just look at my nails."

Darla shook her head and grunted. "Every one of them is broken." She stared at Laura, making her feel suddenly uncomfortable. "You look tired. What do you do, work all day and never sleep?"

Laura reached for the glass of water the young waitress had just brought and took a sip. "I do work hard, but my fatigue doesn't come from just that."

"What then? Did you jog all the way here or something?"

Laura would have laughed if she hadn't felt so crummy. She wished there were some soda crackers on the table, because she needed something to help calm her nausea.

"You're looking kind of pasty there, kiddo. Are you feeling sick?"

Laura nodded, and tears welled in her eyes. "I—I'm pregnant."

Darla's eyebrows lifted high on her forehead. "I knew marrying that Amish guy would bring you nothing but trouble."

"I don't need any lectures," Laura snapped. "Besides, I could have gotten pregnant no matter who I'd married."

"So what are you going to do about it?"

"Do?"

"Yeah. It's obvious to me by the look on your

face that you're anything but happy about being pregnant."

Laura sighed. "I enjoy being around Eli's nephew, and I would like to have a baby of my own sometime. I just hadn't expected it would be this soon or that I would feel so rotten." She looked down at her still-flat stomach. "I wonder how long it will be before I lose my shape."

"Probably won't take too long at all. How far along are you?"

"A little over eight weeks, according to my calculations."

"Good. Then it's not too late to have an abortion."

"A what?" Laura nearly choked on the water she'd put in her mouth.

"You don't want to be pregnant; am I right?"

"Well, no, but—"

"There's a clinic in Philly, and I can make the appointment for you if you'd like." Darla leaned across the table. "No one but you and me would ever have to know, and I'm sure you would feel better once this was all behind you."

Laura shook her head. "Oh, no, I couldn't. . . ."

"If money's a problem, I could float you a loan."

"This is not about money." Laura's voice rose to a high pitch, and her hands trembled so badly, she had to set her glass down to keep from spilling the water.

"If you've got enough money, then what's the problem?"

"The problem's with the abortion, Darla. I could never do anything like that."

"Why not?"

"It—it's against the Amish beliefs to take the life of an unborn baby." The tears Laura had been fighting to keep at bay spilled over and dripped onto her cheeks. "And I would never dream of doing such a thing." She placed her hand against her stomach. "This baby is part of me and Eli, and even though I'm not looking forward to being fat and unattractive, I want to make him happy. I want to do what's right."

Darla's gaze went to the ceiling. "Not only have you changed in appearance, but I can see that you've gotten all self-righteous and sappy now, too."

Laura gripped the handles of her black purse and pushed away from the table. "This was a mistake," she said through clenched teeth. "I should never have agreed to meet you for lunch."

"Where are you going?"

"Home. To tell Eli I'm going to have his baby."

Laura lifted the teakettle from the back of the stove and poured herself a cup of raspberry tea. This afternoon she felt better than she had in many days, and the reason was because she had put Darla in her place and decided to come home and wait for Eli so she could give him the news of her pregnancy.

She thought about little Ben—always playful and curious, so full of love, all cute and cuddly. Laura had never cared much for children until she met Ben. She loved that little boy and was sure she would love her own child even more.

If Laura had listened to Darla, it not only would have ended her baby's life but it would also have ruined things between her and Eli. She was sure she would have been excommunicated from the Amish church, too.

Did Darla really think Laura could take the life of her unborn child and go on as though nothing had ever happened? While Laura might not understand all the biblical implications of the Amish beliefs, she did want to be a good wife to her husband, and she was sure that having Eli's child would only strengthen their marriage. She would just have to work twice as hard at counting calories once the baby came so she could get her figure back as quickly as possible.

The screen door creaked open, pulling Laura out of her musings. Eli hung his straw hat on a wall peg and went to wash up at the sink. "I hope supper's about ready, because I'm hungry as a mule!"

"There's a chicken in the oven, and it should be done soon." Laura turned to him and smiled. "I was wondering if we could talk before we eat, though."

He shrugged. "Sure, what's up?"

She motioned him to sit down, then poured him a cup of tea. "How do you really feel about children, Eli?" she asked, keeping her eyes focused on the cup.

"I've told you before, someday I hope to fill our house with kinner."

"Would November be soon enough to start?"

His forehead wrinkled.

"I'm pregnant, Eli. You're going to be a father soon."

Eli stared at her with a look of disbelief. "A boppli?"

She nodded.

He jumped up, circled the table, pulled Laura to her feet, and kissed her so soundly, it took her breath away. "The Lord has answered my prayers!" He grinned and pulled away, then started for the back door.

"Where are you going?"

"Over to my folks'. I've got to share this good news with them. Have you told your parents yet?"

She shook her head. "I wanted to tell you first."

"Guess you should go over to the neighbors' after supper and use their phone. I'm sure your folks will be as happy about this news as I know mine will be."

Laura swallowed around the lump in her throat. She hoped they would all be happy.

Laura hung the last towel on the line and wiped her damp forehead with her apron. It was a hot, humid June morning, and she was four months pregnant. She placed one hand on her slightly swollen belly and smiled. A tiny flutter caused her to tremble. "There really is a boppli in there," she murmured.

She bent down to pick up her empty basket, but an approaching buggy caught her attention. It was coming up the driveway at an unusually fast speed. When it stopped in front of the house, Amon jumped out, his face all red and sweaty, his eyes huge as saucers. "Where's Eli's mamm?" he panted.

Laura pointed to Mary Ellen's house. "Is something wrong?"

"It's Martha Rose. Her labor's begun, and she wants her mamm to deliver this baby, just like she did Ben."

Laura followed as Amon ran toward the Yoders'. They found Mary Ellen in the kitchen, kneading bread dough. She looked up and smiled. "Ah, so the smell of bread in the making drew the two of you inside."

Amon shook his head. "Martha Rose's time

has come, and she sent me to get you."

Mary Ellen calmly set the dough aside and wiped her hands on a towel. "Laura, would you please finish this bread?"

"I thought I'd go along. Martha Rose is my friend, and—"

"There's no point wasting good bread dough," Mary Ellen said, as though the matter was settled.

Amon stood by the back door, shifting his weight from one foot to the other. Laura could see he was anxious to get home. "Oh, all right," she finally agreed. "I'll do the bread, but I'm coming over as soon as it's out of the oven."

When Laura arrived at the Zooks' some time later, she found Amon pacing back and forth in the kitchen. Ben was at the table, coloring a picture. "Boppli," he said, grinning up at her.

Laura nodded. "Jah, soon it will come." She glanced over at Amon. "It's not born yet, is it?"

He shook his head. "Don't know what's takin' so long. She was real fast with Ben."

"How come you're not up there with her?"

Amon shrugged. "Mary Ellen said it would be best if I waited down here with the boy."

"Want me to go check?"

"I'd be obliged."

Laura hurried up the stairs. The door to Martha Rose and Amon's room was open a crack, so she walked right in.

Mary Ellen looked up from her position near

the foot of the bed. "It's getting close. I can see the head now. Push, Martha Rose . . . push!"

Laura's heart began to pound, and her legs felt like two sticks of rubber. She leaned against the dresser to steady herself.

A few minutes later, the lusty cry of a newborn babe filled the room. Tears stung the backs of Laura's eyes. This was the miracle of birth. She had never imagined it could be so beautiful.

"Daughter, you've got yourself a mighty fine girl," Mary Ellen announced. "Let me clean her up a bit; then I'll hand her right over."

Martha Rose started to cry, but Laura knew they were tears of joy. She slipped quietly from the room, leaving mother, daughter, and grandmother alone to share the moment of pleasure.

Laura had seen Dr. Wilson several times, and other than a bit of anemia, she was pronounced to be in good condition. The doctor prescribed iron tablets to take with her prenatal vitamins, but she still tired easily, and Eli felt concern.

"I'm gonna ask Mom to come over and help out today," he said as he prepared to leave for work one morning.

Laura shuffled across the kitchen floor toward him. "Please don't. Your mom's got her hands full helping Martha Rose with the new baby. She doesn't need one more thing to worry about."

Eli shrugged. "Suit yourself, but if you need anything, don't think twice about calling on her, you hear?"

She nodded and lifted her face for his good-bye kiss. "Have a good day."

Eli left the house and headed straight for his folks' house. Laura might think she didn't need Mom's help, but he could see how tired she was. Dark circles under her eyes and swollen feet at the end of the day were telltale signs that she needed more rest.

He found Mom in the kitchen, doing the breakfast dishes. "Shouldn't you be heading for work?" she asked.

He nodded. "I wanted to talk with you first."

"Anything wrong?"

He shrugged and ran his fingers through the back of his hair. "Laura's been working too hard, and I think she could use some help."

"Want me to see to it, or are you thinking of hiring a *maad*?"

"I'd rather it be you, instead of a maid, if you can find the time."

She smiled. "I think I can manage."

"Danki." Eli grasped the doorknob, but when another thought popped into his head, he pivoted back around. "Do you think Laura's happy, Mom?"

She lifted an eyebrow in question. "Why wouldn't she be? She's married to you, after all."

He shrugged. "I ain't no prize." His eyebrows drew together. "Do you think she's really content being Amish?"

Mom dried her hands on a towel and moved toward him. "Laura chose to become Amish. You didn't force her, remember?"

"I know, but sometimes she looks so sad."

"Ah, it's just being in a family way. Many women get kind of melancholy during that time. She'll be fine once the boppli comes."

Eli gave her a hug. "You're probably right. I'm most likely worried for nothing."

CHAPTER 26

A few days before Eli and Laura's first anniversary, Eli arrived home from work one afternoon and found Laura lying on the sofa, holding her stomach and writhing in pain.

Alarm rose in his chest as he rushed to her side. "What is it, Laura?"

"I—I think the baby's coming."

He knelt in front of the sofa and grasped her hand. "When did the pains start?"

"Around noon."

"What does my mamm have to say?"

"She doesn't know."

"What?" Eli couldn't believe Laura hadn't

called his mother. She'd delivered many babies and would know if it was time.

"I wasn't sure it was labor at first," Laura said tearfully. "But then my water broke, and—"

Eli jumped up and dashed across the room.

"Wh–where are you going?"

"To get Mom!"

Laura leaned her head against the sofa pillow and stiffened when another contraction came. "Oh, God, please help me!" It was the first real prayer Laura had ever uttered, and now she wasn't even sure God was listening. Why would He care about her when she'd never really cared about Him? She had only been pretending to be a Christian. Was this her punishment for lying to Eli, his family, and even herself?

Moments later, Eli bounded into the room, followed by his mother.

"How far apart are the pains?" Mary Ellen asked as she approached the couch.

"I—I don't know for sure. About two or three minutes, I think," Laura answered tearfully. "Oh, it hurts so much! I think Eli should take me to the hospital."

Mary Ellen did a quick examination, and when she was done, she shook her head. "You waited too long for that. The boppli's coming now."

Eli started for the kitchen. "I'll get some towels and warm water."

"Don't leave me, Eli!"

"Calm down," Mary Ellen chided. "He'll be right back. In the meantime, I want you to do exactly as I say."

Laura's first reaction was to fight the pain, but Mary Ellen was a good coach, and soon Laura began to cooperate. Eli stood nearby, holding her hand and offering soothing words.

"One final push and the boppli should be here," Mary Ellen finally said.

Laura did as she was instructed, and moments later, the babe's first cry filled the room.

"It's a boy! You have a son," Mary Ellen announced.

Laura lifted her head from the pillow. "Let me see him. I want to make sure he has ten fingers and ten toes."

"In a minute. Let Eli clean him up a bit," Mary Ellen instructed. "I need to finish up with you."

"Mom, could you come over here?" Eli called from across the room. His voice sounded strained, and a wave of fear washed over Laura like a drenching rain.

"What is it? Is something wrong with our son?"

"Just a minute, Laura. I want Mom to take a look at him first."

Laura rolled onto her side, trying to see what was happening. Eli and Mary Ellen were bent over the small bundle wrapped in a towel, lying on top of an end table. She heard whispering but couldn't make out their words.

"What's going on? Tell me now, or I'll come see for myself."

Eli rushed to her side. "Stay put. You might start bleeding real heavy if you get up too soon."

Laura drew in a deep breath and grabbed hold of Eli's shirtsleeve. "What's wrong?"

"The child's breathing seems a bit irregular," Mary Ellen said. "I think we should take him to the hospital."

"I'd like Laura to be seen, too," Eli said with a nod.

Laura had only gotten a glimpse of her son before they rushed him into the hospital nursery, but what she'd seen concerned her greatly. The baby wasn't breathing right. He looked kind of funny, too. He had a good crop of auburn hair, just like Laura's, but there was something else . . . something she couldn't put her finger on.

"Relax and try to rest," Eli said as he took a seat in the chair next to Laura's hospital bed. "The doctor's looking at little David right now, and—"

"David?" Laura repeated. "You named our son without asking me?"

Eli's face flamed. "I . . . uh . . . thought we'd talked about naming the baby David if it was a boy."

She nodded slowly. "I guess we did. I just thought—"

Laura's words were interrupted when Dr. Wilson and another man entered the room. The second man's expression told her all she needed to know. Something was wrong.

"This is Dr. Hayes," Dr. Wilson said. "He's a pediatrician and has just finished examining your son."

Eli jumped to his feet. "Tell us . . . is there something wrong with David?"

Dr. Hayes put a hand on Eli's shoulder. "Please sit down."

Eli complied, but Laura could see the strain on his face. She felt equally uncomfortable.

"We still need to run a few more tests," the doctor said, "but we're fairly sure your boy has Down syndrome."

"Are you saying he–he's going to be handicapped?" Eli's voice squeaked, and his face blanched.

"Quite possibly. The baby has an accumulation of fluid in his lungs. It's fairly common with Down syndrome. We can clear it out, but he will no doubt be prone to bronchial infections—especially while he's young."

Laura was too stunned to say anything at first. This had to be a dream—a terrible nightmare. This couldn't be happening to her and Eli.

"Once we get the lungs cleared and he's

breathing well on his own, you should be able to take the baby home," Dr. Hayes continued.

"Take him home?" Laura pulled herself to a sitting position. "Did you say, 'Take him home'?"

The doctor nodded, and Eli reached for her hand. "Laura, we can get through this. We—"

She jerked her hand away. "We've just been told that our son probably has Down syndrome, and you're saying, 'We can get through this'?" She shook her head slowly. "The baby isn't normal, Eli. He doesn't belong with us."

Eli studied Laura a few seconds. "Who does he belong with?"

"If he's handicapped, he belongs in a home for handicapped children."

Eli looked at her as if she had lost her mind. "That's not our way, Laura. We take care of our own—even the handicapped children."

"But I don't know how."

"You'll learn, same as other parents with handicapped children have done."

Laura turned her head toward the wall. "Leave me alone, Eli. I need to sleep."

He bent to kiss her forehead. "I'll be back tomorrow, and we can talk about this then."

As soon as Eli left the room, Laura reached for the phone by the side of her bed. It was time to call Mom and Dad.

* * *

"Meade Residence, this is Wesley speaking."

"Dad, it's me."

"Laura, it's good to hear your voice. Your mother and I were just talking about you. We were wondering how you're doing and—"

"Is Mom there?"

"Yes, she's out in the kitchen."

"You'd better put her on the phone. I have something important to tell both of you." Laura's voice trembled, and he felt immediate concern.

"Irene, pick up the phone in there," Wesley hollered. "Laura's on the line."

A few seconds later, his wife came on the phone. "Hello, Laura. How are you, dear?"

Laura sniffed and sucked in her breath, like she was choking on a sob. "N–not so good, Mom. The baby's here, and—"

"You've had the baby? Oh, that's wonderful. What did you have?"

Wesley shifted the phone to his other ear while he waited for Laura's response. If she was only calling to tell them that the baby had been born, would she sound so upset?

"The doctors have some more tests to run, but they think David—our son—might have Down syndrome."

Wesley winced as he heard his wife's sharp intake of breath. "Laura, could you repeat that?"

"The baby was born this evening, and his breathing is irregular. He's got auburn hair like mine, but he doesn't look right, Dad." There was a pause. "The doctors told us awhile ago that they suspect Down syndrome, and Eli expects—" Laura's voice broke on a sob.

"Eli expects what, Laura?" Wesley prompted.

"He expects me to take care of the baby, even if he is handicapped."

"What? He's got to be kidding!" Irene's voice came through the line so shrill that Wesley had to hold the phone away from his ear. "Laura, if the baby is handicapped, he should be put in a home."

"That's what I said, too, but Eli said it's not the thing to do, and—" Laura coughed and sniffed. "I know nothing about caring for a disabled child, Mom. I'm not even sure I can take care of a *normal* baby."

Wesley's forehead beaded with sweat, and he reached up to wipe it away. "Do you want us to come there, Laura? I can see about getting some plane tickets right away."

"Oh, but Wesley, I have a hectic schedule with that benefit dinner I'm planning for the hospital guild this week. It would be hard for me to find someone to fill in for me at this late date."

He gritted his teeth. How could Irene think of a benefit dinner at a time like this? Didn't she realize how much Laura needed them right now? "If your mother's too busy, I'll fly out there myself."

Laura drew in a shuddering sigh. "Could you wait a few days—until we get the test results back on David, and Eli and I have had time to figure out what we're going to do?"

"Sure, I can do that. Maybe by then your mother will be free to come with me."

No comment from Irene. What was that woman thinking, anyhow?

"I'd better go," Laura said. "A nurse just came into the room to check my vitals."

"Okay, honey. Call us as soon as you have some news."

"I will. Bye."

As soon as Wesley hung up the phone, he headed straight for the kitchen. If nothing else got resolved tonight, he was going to give his wife a piece of his mind!

CHAPTER 27

The baby was brought to Laura the following day, and she could barely look at him. The nurse held David up and showed her that he had ten fingers and ten toes.

Fingers that are short and stubby, Laura thought bitterly. She noticed the infant's forehead. It sloped slightly, and his skull looked broad and short. The distinguishing marks of Down syndrome were definitely there. The doctor had been in earlier and explained that David might also be likely to have heart problems, hearing loss, or poor vision. He'd said that Down syndrome was a genetic disorder, resulting from extra chromosomes.

How could this have happened? Laura screamed inwardly as tears rolled down her cheeks. She looked away and told the nurse to take the baby back to the nursery.

Laura was still crying when Eli entered the room, carrying a potted plant. "I got you an African violet from the Beachys' greenhouse, and—" He dropped it onto the nightstand and moved quickly to the bed. "What's wrong? Is it something about David?"

She hiccupped loudly and pulled herself to a sitting position. "I just saw the baby and was told earlier that he does have Down syndrome."

Eli sank to the chair beside her bed and groaned. "I was afraid of that."

"I called my parents last night."

"What'd they say?"

"Mom said David should be put in a home."

"No."

"I think she's right, Eli. A disabled child would take a lot of work."

He nodded. "Jah, I know, but David has just

as much right to live a normal life as any other child."

"But he's not normal, and I—I don't know how to care for him."

"Mom will be there to help whenever you need her."

Laura shook her head as another set of tears streamed down her cheeks. "I can't do this, Eli. Please don't ask it of me."

Eli rubbed his thumb gently back and forth across her knuckles. "God gave us David so He must have had a reason for choosing us as his parents. Now we'll love him . . . cherish him . . . protect him . . ."

Laura's eyes widened. "God was cruel to allow such a thing!"

"God knows what's best for each of us. The book of Romans tells us that all things work together for good to them that love God," Eli said softly. He pointed to the African violet. "Just like this plant needs to be nourished, so does our son. God will give us the strength and love we need to raise him."

Laura closed her eyes and turned her head away from Eli. Was she somehow responsible for this horrible nightmare?

Laura went home from the hospital the following morning, but the baby would have to stay a few more days. The doctors said he might be ready to take home next week, so this gave Laura a short reprieve. She needed some time to decide what to do about the problem.

Eli had taken time off from work to hire a driver and pick her up at the hospital, but soon after the driver dropped them off at home and Eli had seen that Laura was settled in, he left for work. It was better that way. She wanted to be alone, and if he'd stayed home with her, they would have argued about Eli expecting her to care for David.

Laura poured herself a cup of chamomile tea and curled up on the living-room couch. Reliving her dialogue with Eli at the hospital, her heart sank to the pit of her stomach.

She closed her eyes and tried to shut out the voice in her head. *God is punishing me for pretending to be religious. I tricked Eli into marrying me by making him think I had accepted his beliefs and his way of life.*

Laura's eyes snapped open when she heard a distant clap of thunder. She stared out the window. Dark clouds hung in the sky like a shroud encircling the entire house.

"The sky looks like I feel," she moaned. "My life is such a mess. I wish I had never met Eli Yoder. We should never have gotten married. I should not have gotten pregnant."

The realization of what she'd said hit Laura with such intensity, she thought she had been struck with a lightning bolt. "Oh, no! Dear Lord, no!" she sobbed. "You're punishing me for not wanting to be pregnant, not just for lying to Eli about my religious convictions." She clenched her fists so tightly that her nails bit into her skin as she grappled with the reality of the moment. "That's why David was born with Down syndrome—because God is punishing me." Laura fell back on the sofa pillows and sobbed until no more tears would come.

When the wave of grief finally subsided, she sat up, dried her eyes, and stood. She knew what she had to do. She scrawled a quick note to Eli, placed it on the kitchen table, and went upstairs.

"Laura, I'm home!" Eli set his lunch pail on the cupboard. No sign of Laura in the kitchen. He moved through the rest of the downstairs, calling her name. She wasn't in any of the rooms.

She must be upstairs resting. She's been through a lot this week, so I'd better let her sleep awhile.

Eli went back to the kitchen. He would fix himself a little snack, then go outside and get started on the evening chores.

There was an apple-crumb pie in the refrigerator, which Mom had brought over last night. He grabbed a piece, along with a jug of milk, and placed them on the table. Not until he took a seat did Eli see the note lying on the table. He picked it up and read it:

Dear Eli,

It pains me to write this letter, even more than the physical pain I endured in child-birth. I know you don't understand this, but I can't take care of David. I just don't have what it takes to raise a handicapped child.

I have a confession to make. I'm not who you think I am—I'm not really a believer. I only pretended to be one so you would marry me. I tried to be a good wife, but I could never seem to measure up.

Pauline was right when she said she would be better for you. It would have saved us all a lot of heartache if you had married her instead of me.

I hope you'll forgive me for leaving you in the lurch, but I've decided to go home to my parents. I know I'm not deserving of your forgiveness, but please know that I do love you. I've always loved you.

Always,
Laura

The words on the paper blurred. Eli couldn't react. Couldn't think. Could hardly breathe. He let the note slip from his fingers as a deep sense of loss gnawed at his insides. *Laura wouldn't pack up and leave without speaking with me first, without trying to work things out.*

When the reality of the situation fully registered, he propped his elbows on the table and cradled his head in his hands. "Oh, Laura . . . I just didn't know."

During her first few days at home, Laura slept late, picked at her food, and tried to get used to all the modern conveniences she had previously taken for granted. Nothing seemed to satisfy her. She was exhausted, crabby, and more depressed than she'd ever been in her life. Things had changed at home. Maybe it was she who had changed, for she now felt like a misfit.

Today was her and Eli's first anniversary, and she was miserable. As she sat at the kitchen table, toying with the scrambled eggs on her plate, Laura thought about their wedding day. She could still hear Bishop Wagler quoting scriptures about marriage. She could almost feel the warmth of Eli's hand as they repeated their vows. She had promised to be loyal to Eli, to care for him and live with him until death separated them, but she'd failed miserably. A painful lump lodged in her throat. She deserved whatever punishment God handed down.

Mom entered the kitchen just then, interrupting Laura's thoughts. "This came in the mail," she said, handing Laura a letter. "It's postmarked 'Lancaster, Pennsylvania.' "

Laura's fingers shook as she tore open the envelope, then began to read:

Dear Laura,

I knew you were upset about the baby, and I'm trying to understand. What I don't get is how you could up and leave like that without even talking to me first. Don't you realize how much David and I need you? Don't you know how much I miss you?

David's breathing better now, and the doctors let him come home. Mom watches him when I'm at work, but it's you he's needing. Won't you please come home?

Love,
Eli

Tears welled in Laura's eyes and spilled onto the front of her blouse. Eli didn't seem angry. In fact, he wanted her to come home. He hadn't even mentioned her lies. Had he forgiven her? Did Eli really love her in spite of all she'd done?

Maybe he doesn't believe me. He might think I made everything up because I couldn't deal with our baby being born handicapped. He might want me back just so I can care for his child.

Laura swallowed hard and nearly choked on a

sob. No matter how much she loved Eli and wanted to be with him, she knew she couldn't go back. She was a disgrace to the Amish faith, and she had ruined Eli's life.

The days dragged by, and Laura thought she would die of boredom. The weather was dreary and cold, and even though Mom tried to encourage her to get out and socialize, Laura stayed to herself most of the time. She thought modern conveniences would bring happiness, but they hadn't. Instead of watching TV or playing computer games, she preferred to sit in front of the fire and knit or read a book. There was something about the Amish way of life she couldn't quite explain. At times when she'd been living with Eli, she had felt a sense of peace and tranquillity that had calmed her soul like nothing else she'd ever known.

It was strange, but Laura missed the familiar farm smells—fresh-mown hay stacked neatly in the barn, the horses' warm breath on a cold winter day, and even the wiggly, grunting piglets always squealing for more food. Laura was reminded of something Eli had once said, for much to her surprise, she even missed the pre-dictable wake-up call of the rooster each morning. She missed her plain clothes, too, and felt out of place wearing blue jeans again.

By the middle of December, Laura felt stronger

physically, but emotionally she was still a mess. Would she ever be able to pick up the pieces of her life and go on without Eli? Could she forgive herself for bringing such misery into their lives?

If God was punishing her, why did Eli have to suffer, as well? He was a kind, Christian man who deserved a normal, healthy baby. He had done nothing to warrant this kind of pain. How could the Amish refer to God as "a God of love"?

Laura sat on the sofa in the living room, staring at the Christmas tree, yet not really seeing it. *What's Eli doing right now? Does he miss me, like he said in his letter? No doubt he and the baby will be spending the holidays with his parents. If I could turn back the hands of time and make everything right between me and Eli again, I'd even learn how to fix the pickled beets he likes so well.*

Laura glanced at her parents. They sat in their respective recliners: Dad reading the newspaper, Mom working on Christmas cards. They didn't seem to have a care in the world. Didn't they know how much she was hurting? Did they think this was just another typical Christmas?

A sudden knock at the front door drew Laura out of her musings. She looked over at the mantel clock. Who would be coming by at nine o'clock at night, and who would knock rather than use the doorbell?

Dad stood. "I'll get it."

Laura strained to hear the voices coming from the hall. She couldn't be sure who Dad was talking to, but it sounded like a woman. *Probably one of Mom's lady friends or someone from Dad's office.* She leaned against the sofa pillows and tried not to eavesdrop.

"Laura, someone is here to see you," Dad said as he entered the living room with a woman.

Laura's mouth dropped open, and she leaped from the couch. "Martha Rose! What are you doing here? Is Eli with you?" She stared at the doorway, half expecting, half hoping Eli might step into the room.

Martha Rose shook her head. "I've come alone. Only Amon knows I'm here. I left him plenty of my breast milk, and he agreed to care for baby Amanda and little Ben so I could make the trip to see you." She smiled. "The bus ride took a little over twenty-seven hours, and Amon knows I won't be gone long. Besides, if he runs into any kind of problem with the kinner, he can always call on Mom."

Laura's heart began to pound as she tried to digest all that Martha Rose had said. "What's wrong? Has someone been hurt? Is it Eli?"

Martha Rose held up her hand. "Eli's fine . . . at least physically." She glanced at Laura's

325

folks, then back at Laura. "Could we talk in private?"

Laura looked at Mom and Dad. They both shrugged and turned to go. "We'll be upstairs if you need us," Dad said.

"Thanks," Laura mumbled. Her brain felt like it was in a fog. Why had Martha Rose traveled all the way from Pennsylvania to Minnesota if there was nothing wrong at home? Home— was that how she thought of the house she and Eli had shared? Wasn't this her home—here with Mom and Dad? She studied her surroundings. Everything looked the same, yet it felt so different. It was like trying to fit into a pair of shoes that were too small.

When Wesley and Irene entered their room, Irene took a seat on the end of their bed and released a sigh. "I wonder what Martha Rose wants. I hope she's not here to try and talk Laura into going back to Pennsylvania with her."

"If she is, it's none of our business." Wesley leaned on the dresser and stared at her.

"You don't have to sound so snippy. I only want what's best for our daughter."

His defenses rose, and he marched across the room. "And you think I don't?"

"Calm down, Wesley. It's not like you to shout like that."

"I'm not shouting. I'm speaking my mind, which is something I should have done a long time ago."

Irene's chin trembled, and tears shimmered in her green eyes. The old Wesley would have succumbed to that pathetic look, but not anymore. He was tired of saying things just because they were what she wanted to hear. It was high time he stood up to her and said what was on his mind.

He took a seat on the bed beside her. "I love you, Irene, and I have ever since we met in college."

"I—I love you, too."

"But just because I love you doesn't mean I always agree with you or will do things your way."

"What are you trying to say?"

He tucked his thumb under her chin and tipped her head back so she was looking into his eyes. "I'm saying that I don't agree with you where Laura's concerned."

"What do you mean?"

"I think Laura's place is with her husband and baby."

Her eyes widened. "You can't mean that, Wesley. Laura's baby is handicapped, and he will need special care."

He nodded. "I think Laura is capable of giving David whatever help he needs."

"But she doesn't want to care for him; she's said so many times."

"That's because she thinks she can't, but I believe she can."

"What makes you so sure?"

He smiled and reached for her hand. "She's her mother's daughter—full of courage, determination, and strength she doesn't even know she has."

"You–you think that about me?"

"Sure do."

She leaned her head against his shoulder. "That's the nicest thing you've ever said to me, dear."

He kissed the top of her head. "Laura's place is with Eli, just as much as your place is with me."

"Laura, are you okay?" Martha Rose asked, placing a hand on Laura's trembling shoulder.

"I . . . uh . . . sure didn't expect to see you tonight." Laura motioned to the sofa. "Please, have a seat. Let me take your coat. Would you like some tea or hot chocolate?" She was rambling but couldn't seem to help herself.

Martha Rose took off her coat and draped it over the back of the couch. Then she sat down. "Maybe something to drink, but after we talk."

Laura sat beside her. "What's so important that you would come all this way by bus?"

"My brother has been so upset since you left. He told me he wrote a letter asking you to come home."

"Did he also tell you that I've been lying to him all these months?"

"About being a believer?"

Laura nodded.

"Jah, he mentioned that, too."

Laura swallowed hard. "Then you understand why I can't go back."

Martha Rose reached inside her coat pocket and pulled out a small Bible. She opened it and began reading. " 'If any brother hath a wife that believeth not, and she be pleased to dwell with him, let him not put her away.' " She smiled. "That's found in the book of 1 Corinthians."

Laura's eyes widened. "Are you saying Eli could choose to stay with me even though I'm not a believer?"

Martha Rose nodded. "It doesn't have to be that way, though."

"What do you mean?"

"You could give your heart to Jesus, Laura. He wants you to accept His death as forgiveness for your sins. 1 John 3:23 says, 'And this is his commandment, that we should believe on the name of his Son Jesus Christ, and love one another, as he gave us commandment.' "

As Martha Rose continued to read from the Bible, Laura was finally convinced of the truth in God's Word, and soon tears began streaming down her face. "Oh, Martha Rose, you have no idea how much I've sinned. I did a terrible thing, and now God is punishing me. How can I ever believe He would forgive me?"

"Romans 3:23 says, 'For all have sinned, and come short of the glory of God.' If we ask, God will forgive any sin." Martha Rose clasped Laura's hand.

"When I first found out I was pregnant, I—I didn't even want our baby."

"Why, Laura?"

"I was afraid of having a child. I know it's a vain thing to say, but I wanted to keep my trim figure." She gulped. "Even more than that, I wanted Eli all to myself." Laura closed her eyes and drew in a shuddering breath. "God's punishment for my selfish thoughts was David. I believe that's why He gave us a disabled child."

Martha Rose shook her head. "God doesn't work that way. He loves you, just as He loves the special child He gave you and Eli. God wants you to ask His forgiveness and surrender your life to Him."

"I—I want to change, but I don't know if I have enough faith to believe."

"All you need to do is take that first little step by accepting Jesus as your Savior. Then, through studying His Word and praying, your faith will be strengthened. Would you like to pray right now and ask Jesus into your heart?"

Laura nodded and bowed her head. After surrendering her will to God and asking His forgiveness for her sins, the peace she so desperately sought flooded her soul. When she went to bed that night, a strange warmth crept through her body. She felt God's presence for the very first time and knew without reservation that she was a new person because of His Son, Jesus. Martha Rose slept in the guest room across the hall, and Laura thanked God that her special friend had come.

CHAPTER 28

Laura clung tightly to Martha Rose's hand as they stepped down from the bus. She was almost home, and even though she still had some doubts about her ability to care for a disabled child, it was comforting to know she would have God to help her. She scanned the faces of those waiting to pick up passengers. There was no sign of Eli or Amon.

"Are you sure they knew we were coming?" Laura asked Martha Rose, feeling a sense of panic rise in her throat.

"I talked to Eli at the furniture shop where he works, so I'm certain they'll be here." Martha

Rose led Laura toward the bus station. "Let's get out of the cold and wait for them inside."

The women had no more than taken seats when Amon walked up. He was alone.

Laura felt like someone had punched her in the stomach. "Where's Eli? Didn't he come with you?" *Maybe he's changed his mind about wanting me back.*

"Eli's at the hospital," Amon said, placing a hand on Laura's shoulder.

Her stomach churned like whipping cream about to become butter. "The hospital? Is it the baby? Is David worse?"

Amon shook his head. "There was an accident today."

"An accident? What happened?" Martha Rose's face registered the concern Laura felt.

"Eli cut his hand at work, on one of those fancy electric saws."

Laura covered her mouth with her hand. "How bad?"

"He lost part of one finger, but the doctor said he should still be able to use the hand once everything heals."

"Oh, my dear, sweet Eli," Laura cried. "Hasn't he already been through enough? If only I hadn't run away. If only—"

Martha Rose held up her hand. "No, Laura. You can't go blaming yourself. Just as David's birth defect is no one's fault, this was an accident, plain and simple. In time, Eli will heal and be back at work."

Laura looked down at her clasped hands, feeling like a small child learning to walk. "Guess my faith is still pretty weak. I'd better pray about it, huh?"

Martha Rose nodded. "Prayer is always the best way."

Eli lay in his hospital bed, fighting the weight of heavy eyelids. Against his wishes, the nurse had given him a shot for pain, and now he felt so sleepy he could hardly stay awake. Amon had left for the bus station over an hour ago. What was taking so long? Maybe Laura had changed her mind and stayed in Minneapolis. Maybe . . .

"Eli? Eli?" A gentle voice filled his senses. Was he dreaming, or was it just wishful thinking?

He felt someone touch his arm, and his eyes snapped open. "Laura?"

She nodded, her eyes full of tears. "Oh, Eli, I'm so sorry!" She rested her head on his chest and sobbed. "Can you ever forgive me for running away . . . for lying about my relationship with God . . . for wanting you to change when it was really me who needed changing?"

Eli stroked the top of her head, noting with joy that she was wearing her covering. "I've already forgiven you, but I must ask your forgiveness, too."

She raised her head and stared into his eyes. "For what? You've done nothing."

He swallowed against the lump in his throat. "For not being understanding enough." He touched her chin with his uninjured hand. "I think I expected too much, and sometimes I spoke harshly instead of trying to see things from your point of view. If I'd been a better husband, maybe you would have found your way to God sooner."

Laura shook her head. "It wasn't your fault. I was stubborn and selfish. That's what kept me from turning to God. I believed I could do everything in my own strength. I thought I could have whatever I wanted, and it didn't matter who I hurt in the process." She sniffed deeply. "When I finally found forgiveness for my sins, I became a new creature." She leaned closer, so their lips were almost touching. "I love you, Eli."

He smiled. "And I love you. Christmas is only a few days away, and I'm convinced that it's going to be our best Christmas ever." He sealed his promise with a tender kiss.

Epilogue

Laura stood at the kitchen counter, about to open the jar of pickled beets she would serve with the stew they'd be having for supper. She gazed out the window at Eli and their two-year-old son as they romped in the snow. David was doing so well, and she thanked God for him every day. He was such an agreeable, loving child. How could she have ever not wanted him? Eli had been right all along. David was special—a wonderful gift from God.

A soft *meow* drew Laura's attention from the window. She turned toward the sound, and her lips formed a smile. Foosie ran across the kitchen floor, and their nine-month-old daughter, Barbara, followed in fast pursuit.

Laura chuckled at the sight of her perfect little girl, up on her knees, chasing that poor cat and pulling on its tail. No wonder Foosie preferred to be outdoors these days.

"Life couldn't be any better," Laura whispered. Not only had she made peace with God, but her parents had also moved to Lancaster County, where her father practiced law at a small firm during the week and tinkered in his garden every weekend. Laura had finally come to realize that Eli's folks really did care about her, and she'd even made things right with Pauline, who had written her a letter not long ago, apologizing for her bad behavior.

As Laura poured the beets from the glass canning jar into a bowl, she looked up. "Lord, I thank You for the two wunderbaar children and the husband You gave to me, and I especially thank You for turning a fancy, spoiled English woman like me into a plain Amish wife who loves You so much. You have truly blessed me, and I ask for Your blessings on each one in our extended families."

Recipe for Laura's Pickled Beets

Ingredients:
- 3 quarts small beets
- 3 cups cider vinegar
- 2 tablespoons salt
- 4 cups sugar
- 1½ cups water
- 2 cinnamon sticks

Cook the beets in a large pan until tender and put into clean, hot canning jars. Combine the rest of the ingredients in a separate pan and boil until it becomes a syrup. Pour the boiling syrup over the beets, then seal. Cold pack them for 10 to 15 minutes.

About the Author

Wanda E. Brunstetter enjoys writing about the Amish because they live a peaceful, simple life. Wanda's interest in the Amish and other Plain communities began when she married her husband, Richard, who grew up in a Mennonite church in Pennsylvania. Wanda has made numerous trips to Lancaster County and has several friends and family members living near that area. She and her husband have also traveled to other parts of the country, meeting various Amish families and getting to know them personally. She hopes her readers will learn to love the wonderful Amish people as much as she does.

Wanda and her husband, Richard, have been married forty-three years. They have two grown children and six grandchildren. In her spare time, Wanda enjoys reading, ventriloquism, gardening, stamping, and having fun with her family.

Wanda has written 25 novels, as well as several stories, articles, poems, puppet scripts, gift books, and a devotional book.

To learn more about Wanda, visit her Web site at www.wandabrunstetter.com and feel free to e-mail her at wanda@wandabrunstetter.com.

Center Point Publishing
600 Brooks Road • PO Box 1
Thorndike ME 04986-0001 USA

(207) 568-3717

US & Canada:
1 800 929-9108
www.centerpointlargeprint.com

M. K.

ep

To all those who have inspired, challenged, prodded, and pushed me over the years, but most of all to my wonderful wife, Stephanie, for her encouragement and patience, and for bringing Alex Michael into the world.

MY FIRST
100 MARATHONS

Skyhorse Publishing books may be purchased in bulk at special discounts for sales promotion, corporate gifts, fund-raising, or educational purposes. Special editions can also be created to specifications. For details, contact the Special Sales Department, Skyhorse Publishing, 555 Eighth Avenue, Suite 903, New York, NY 10018 or info@skyhorsepublishing.com.

www.skyhorsepublishing.com

10 9 8 7 6 5 4 3 2 1

Library of Congress Cataloging-in-Publication Data
Horowitz, Jeffrey.
My first 100 marathons : 2,620 miles with an obsessive runner / Jeffrey Horowitz.
p. cm.
ISBN 978-1-60239-318-9 (hardcover : alk. paper)
1. Marathon running—United States. 2. Marathon running—Training—United States. 3. Long-distance runners—United States—Anecdotes. 4. Horowitz, Jeffrey. I. Title. II. Title: My first hundred marathons. III. Title: My first one hundred marathons.
GV1065.2.H67 2008
796.42'520973—dc22
2008028945

Printed in the United States of America

My First
100 Marathons
2,620 Miles with an Obsessive Runner

Jeff Horowitz

Skyhorse Publishing

CONTENTS

Out the Door and Around the Block

There is an old proverb that says a journey of a thousand miles begins with a single step. Sometimes, though, a quick trip to the emergency room begins that way, too.

That was my story. It was 1985. Ronald Reagan was president, New Wave was on the radio, and I had just moved away from home for the first time. I had come down to Washington, D.C., from New York City, for law school. After a rocky start, I found a good roommate, settled in, and acquired a love for my new hometown. I had always been overweight—"husky" was the euphemism the clothing stores seemed to like—but now I had added some new padding around my middle, and I was determined to do something about it. A new body for my new life. Except that as a grad student, I was barely getting by on my meager savings and student loans, living on spaghetti and tuna fish, and using furniture I'd built from of cinder blocks and boards. There wasn't much spare cash for a health club, personal trainer, chef, or a masseuse. But running fit the bill. I already had sneakers and shorts, so all I needed to do was head out the door and begin. Simplicity itself.

I started off with a few slow laps around the block where I lived in Arlington, Virginia. As out of shape as I was, I still immediately recognized how right it felt. I'd played sports as a kid growing up in Queens, New York, but I never excelled; I wasn't what anyone would call a naturally gifted athlete. But I was persistent, which was a trait that cut me out to be a good distance runner. Soon, my runs lengthened into laps around a small park, and then out-and-back runs down the street toward the Potomac River. Reaching my turnaround point, I gazed across the water at the spires of Georgetown University.

In those moments, I was filled with a sense of possibility. Running cleared the day's cobwebs from my mind and focused my thinking, and gave me time and space to sort out anything that was bothering me, or to detach and think of nothing at all. It had also started to reshape my body. Those new extra pounds fell away, taking some of the older, more stubborn fat along with them. Running also made me more aware of my body's needs; I quickly realized that I could only be as good as the fuel I took in, so I started to avoid all of the greasy and sugary foods that had found their way into my diet.

As the months passed, I realized that, little by little, I was actually turning into a real runner. I had never run any races, and I hadn't been on any track teams, but now I felt that I was not just some guy trying to stay in shape. I was an athlete.

If I was going to do this, then, I had to do it right. It was time for me to shelve those ratty old Pro-Keds I'd been running in and upgrade to some real running gear, which is what led me one day to a local sporting-goods store, where I eyed the shoes displayed on the back wall and tried to make sense out of the little information cards that fell out of them. Judging the technology diagrammed on those cards, you would have thought that the shoes had been to the moon and back.

I ended up taking home a pair of gray hi-tech marvels, my first true running shoes. They set me back $69, which seemed wildly extravagant.

As soon as I got home, I laced them up and went out for a run, hoping that I hadn't foolishly wasted my month's eating budget. I didn't expect miracles; all I wanted was that they at least would feel, well, *different.* And they did. Oh, how they did! Suddenly I had spring in my step, and I felt like I could run forever.

Armed with my fancy new shoes, I ran down the street toward the river, but this time I didn't stop. I crossed Key Bridge into D.C., and then followed the river south. I passed the Watergate Hotel and the Kennedy Center for the Performing Arts—a fancy building on the site of an old brewery—and crossed back into Virginia at the next bridge, completing a five-mile loop.

I was hooked. As my runs took me farther, I started wondering what I could do with my newfound love of running. I'd always been the kind of person who hated half steps; once I found a passion for something, I wanted to dive into the deep end of it. It wasn't that I ever needed to prove anything; I just wanted to fully and completely experience whatever it was that intrigued me. And now, that thing was running. I'd have to pursue that passion wherever it led me.

In hindsight, it's also obvious to me now that running provided the perfect counterpoint to sitting at a desk studying law. The mind-numbing tedium of studying left my body aching for some outlet. I didn't understand it at the time, but our bodies need attention and encouragement as much as our minds. They are not meant to be kept quiet, preserved like a specimen in a jar. We are meant to *move.* When we forget that we are not just intellectual, emotional, and spiritual beings, but also animals, we do so at our peril.

As a dedicated runner, then, the obvious next step would be to enter a road race. The idea of having a number pinned to my shirt—a very public declaration that I was a runner, an athlete—was thrilling. But which race? Most new runners start out with a 5K or 10K, but those races were shorter than my training runs. They just couldn't capture my imagination, couldn't give me that intoxicating mix of fear and excitement that I craved. I needed something big.

I knew the answer, of course: the marathon. Growing up, I lived in the shadow of the New York City Marathon. Even though I had never run more than a few miles at a time back then—and even then just barely—I felt that someday I would run that distance. Now, all these years later, the time had come to run a marathon. I would be David, throwing myself against the Goliath of running. If I came out victorious, I would truly understand what it meant to be a runner.

Luckily, one of the best marathons in the country was in my backyard—the Marine Corps Marathon, held the last weekend of every October. It starts at the Iwo Jima Memorial in Arlington, taking runners on a grand tour of D.C. and northern Virginia, circling the Pentagon, the Capitol, the Smithsonian, and the Jefferson and Lincoln Memorials before returning to the Iwo Jima Memorial for the finish. Since its course included some of my new training routes, it was easy for me to imagine running the race. I was nervous, but the more I thought about it, the more reasonable this crazy idea seemed to be.

The mailing of an application is itself a very symbolic and important act. As I wrote the check, sealed the envelope, and dropped it in the mailbox, I felt the solemnity of the moment, and a new seriousness of purpose. *I'm in for it now*, I thought. Even now, decades later, when online registration has mostly replaced the mailing of applications, I pause before clicking the final button that will commit me to a race. *Are you sure you want to do this?* But I knew then—have always known, in those kinds of situations—what I was getting myself into. I wasn't worried about it. It was simply time to get to work.

I began by increasing my weekly mileage, with the goal of building up to a 21-mile run three weeks before the race. In 1986, there wasn't the flood of training advice that runners today have to wade through; there was really very little good information available at all. There was

Jim Fixx's book on running, a few other training books, and a couple of running magazines. I read as much as I could, and more or less sorted my way through it by trial and error.

Sometimes this involved more error than I liked to admit. Once, after a good 15-mile run, I decided to run 15 miles every day, on the reasonable—though entirely wrong—assumption that if a little is good, more must be better. After a week of this, my muscles ached and I was tired to the bone. Obviously, my 15-mile-a-day plan wasn't a good idea.

Despite my blunders and setbacks, my training advanced, and finally I completed my last long run. I had met my training goal. I was ready for the marathon! Elated, I went on a short celebration run the next day with my roommate. We followed a horse trail into the woods—not my usual route—and early into the run I rolled my foot on a rock. I felt a sharp pain in my ankle, and I knew instantly that I had sprained it badly. I considered stopping, but I thought that managing pain was part of being a marathoner, so I decided to keep running.

Bad idea. There's often a very fine line between bravery and stupidity and on that Sunday morning in October 1986, I crossed it. After running 6 more miles, I made it back to my room, slumped in an easy chair, gently removed my running shoes, and inspected the damage. My ankle had turned as dark as thunderclouds, and was quickly swelling up to double its normal size. I phoned my girlfriend Kathleen and quietly, humbly, asked if she could drive me to the emergency room. Kathleen had no love of running, but she knew from the sound of my voice that this was serious. She came right over.

My short little celebration run had landed me on crutches. I was out of the marathon. I had thrown all my hard work out the window. I had blown my once-in-a-lifetime opportunity. I was devastated.

The death of a dream is a sad and painful thing. Eventually, I reconciled myself to my loss, and focused on just returning to a regular running routine. Once again, though, I demonstrated my capacity for stupidity by rushing my recovery and reinjuring my ankle. Once. Twice. Three times. Little by little, I managed to parlay a simple sprain into a six-month layoff.

Finally, showing a glimmer of wisdom, I left my ankle alone until it felt completely healed, and then left it alone some more. Eventually, I was able to return to a regular, pain-free, modest running routine.

As the weeks went by, though, I found myself thinking again about the marathon. It was like an old lover you swore you'd never call again, but whose number you kept. I began increasing my weekly mileage, waiting for the pain to come, but it never did. Finally, one day I wrote another check and sealed another envelope. I was going back to the Marine Corps Marathon.

In the final weeks before the race I was cautious to a fault, refusing to run off-road, step on cracks, or walk under ladders. I was rewarded by making it to the race day healthy and whole. Before the race even started, I had already accomplished my goal.

There were things that I still had left to learn, however. As I walked to the starting line near the Iwo Jima Memorial, I saw a woman standing just a few feet from the roadway, near a tree. She was carefully holding back her shorts to one side as she crouched slightly in the direction of the tree. It took me a moment to realize what she was doing. She was peeing. Right there, in front of 13,000 runners and their families and friends. Even more startling, though, was the fact that no one around her seemed the least bit surprised. She could have been blowing her nose for all they cared.

It was a revelation. I wasn't yet familiar with running culture, with the fact that runners are endlessly fascinated with their bodies—how they work, how they look, what goes into them, and most importantly, what comes out and when. And they were not the least bit shy about discussing all these issues with anyone at any time. Remember: I had done most of my training alone at that point, so I was like a feral child, a Tarzan among socialized runners.

Then the starting cannon roared—a Marine Corp Marathon tradition—and I had no more time to think about such things. The crowd surged forward. We began to run, and then suddenly, inexplicably, came to a full stop. Bodies crashed into one another. After a few moments of awkward shuffling, the crowd moved forward again, and we were able to settle into a regular running pace.

I was confused. What had just happened? There was open road in front of us. Why the sudden traffic jam? I didn't know it at the time, but that stop-and-go phenomenon happens in almost every big race. And I still don't know why. But I've learned not to let it bother me.

I ran cautiously, hoping to save enough energy to get me through the final few miles. We ran south to the Pentagon before returning north and crossing Key Bridge into D.C. We ran past the historic row houses and shops of Georgetown, and along the riverfront to the Lincoln Memorial, where we turned eastward toward the Smithsonian museums and the Capitol. I thought about how this route must seem for the out-of-town runners; even as a resident, I often have moments—as I did during the race—where I'm startled by how beautiful D.C. is.

I passed the halfway point at the U.S. Capitol feeling surprisingly strong. With 13 miles behind me, I decided to take a calculated risk—I picked up the pace. Streaking downhill past the Smithsonian museums, I passed the Jefferson Memorial and turned south toward lonely Hains Point, a pointy spit of land—landfill, actually—that juts out into the Potomac River.

This would be the make-or-break point for many runners. Hains Point brought with it miles 19 and 20 of the race, where the dreaded Wall lurked. If a runner had not properly prepared his or her body during training to burn fat, then it would be somewhere around this point where the supplies of blood sugar in the body—glycogen—would be used up. When that happens, a runner feels like someone just cut his or her power cord. Even well-trained runners who don't face this problem still find this stretch of road difficult because so many miles have been conquered, but there are still so many miles yet to come. This is the point where mental toughness weighs in. It's no wonder that veteran runners say the marathon is really two races: the first 20 miles, and the last 6.2.

I didn't know all of this at the time, which was probably a good thing, since I couldn't worry about something I wasn't expecting. But as I approached the turnaround at the tip of Hains Point, I felt my energy wane and my willpower slip. I was suddenly so tired of running.

Then I saw him. Or rather, heard him. A lone fan, standing beside his open car trunk at the tip of Hains Point, was blasting the theme from *Rocky* on his car stereo. Suddenly, adrenaline surged through my veins, and I felt new life in my tired legs as I followed the course back north for the final few miles to the finish line.

Before I could claim my finisher's medal, however, there was the 14th Street Bridge, a long, wide, rolling overpass that would take us from D.C. to Virginia. I later learned to call this stretch the Anvil of God, since, on a warm day, the sun can pour heat down on a runner along this stretch with unrivaled cruelty.

On this day, though, I had come too far to be denied, and I conquered that last obstacle and then raced the final few miles toward the finish line at the Iwo Jima Memorial. I passed the final mile marker— Mile 26!—and followed the course up a short, steep incline toward the memorial. Spectators massed along the retaining fence cheered as I followed the course as it circled the memorial, eager for a glimpse of that glorious finish line.

But where was it? Those final two-tenths of a mile seemed to stretch on forever. But finally, there it was: the finish line. I crossed it, and turned toward one of the marines to accept my finisher's medal. "Outstanding," he said. And I had to admit, it was.

I had run the second half 15 minutes faster than the first half, an impressive negative split, as I later learned to call it. I felt both brilliantly alive and bone tired, something I'd never before experienced, but that I completely enjoyed. I even liked the soreness that overtook my legs over the next few days. My friends were horrified watching me hobble downstairs backward, but I knew that every ache meant that I had faced my fear and doubt and won. I had run a marathon.

Having reached that milestone, I turned toward a few others that were on my calendar. In 1988, I graduated from law school, passed the bar exam, and began working as an attorney with the federal government. Instead of making D.C. a quick stopover, I was settling down as a permanent resident. And instead of being a distraction from my studies, running became my lifestyle. Perhaps if I spent less time in front of a computer, I wouldn't have become so devoted to it. Or maybe I was genetically predisposed to run. Either way, I found myself figuring out how to fit my running into my new work schedule. I woke up before dawn to run, brought my gear to the office for a quick lunchtime workout, and ran on weekends. Whatever it took, I made it work.

Three years later, I ran the Marine Corps Marathon again, no longer burdened with a fear of the unknown, but instead looking for another hit of that exhilarated/exhausted feeling. After another successful run, I turned homeward, toward New York City. I was finally ready to check off that boyhood goal.

On race morning, I stood shoulder to shoulder with 20,000 other runners in Staten Island, at the foot of the Verrazano Bridge. The gun went off, and we all surged up the mile-long climb to the apex of the bridge, jostling for a little elbow room along the way. After cresting, I found myself warmed up and energized for the mile-long descent. It was the fastest mile I'd ever run. And I still had 24 more miles to go. I quickly realized how monumentally stupid I'd just been, and how I'd pay dearly for it later in the race.

I settled down into a slower pace and made my way through Brooklyn and Queens, and then climbed the Queensboro Bridge to Manhattan. As I descended on the far side—at a comfortable pace, this time!—I began to hear a mysterious low roar. I was almost on the Manhattan side, but I still couldn't see where the noise was coming from. Then I saw it: a solid mass of people, five or six deep, straining the barricades, screaming like they had lost their minds. I was dumbstruck.

The party continued up First Avenue, as people lined the streets, hung out windows, crowded onto balconies, and stood on rooftops, all cheering like mad. I felt like an astronaut in a parade. It shot a bolt of lightning into me. I ran effortlessly up toward Harlem.

That's where my earlier foolishness hit me. This time I was the one who felt as though someone had cut my power cord. I was reduced to walking. Suddenly, a huge man jumped out of the crowd and rushed toward me. I braced myself, but he just yelled, "I didn't come out here to see you walk!" Believe me, I was back to running in no time flat!

From there, it was on to the Bronx, into neighborhoods that I had never seen in all my years living in New York. Then it was time for the homestretch down Fifth Avenue and into Central Park. My mother and younger sister were waiting for me near the finish line, and had talked other bystanders into cheering for me as I came into view, but I was so focused on the finish line that I never heard a thing. No matter. Just knowing they were there, watching for me and cheering me onward, gave me the extra strength I needed.

Finishing that race meant a lot to me. It taught me that I could overcome adversity during a race, and also that I had a lot yet to learn about running this thing.

In March of 1993, I ran my fourth marathon, in Virginia Beach. After the race, in the hotel corridor, I met an older runner who told me that he had just run his thirty-fifth marathon. I was astonished.

The number seemed impossible, like Joe DiMaggio's consecutive-game hitting streak. I was sure that this guy was a different breed of runner.

I expected to feel tired after the Virginia Beach marathon, but instead, I craved more. There was something about the marathon that called to me, that captured my imagination, that left me feeling a sense of accomplishment like I'd experienced nowhere else. I wasn't sure if it was a good idea to run another marathon so soon—I hadn't heard of anyone else doing something like that—but I felt fresh and strong, and was certainly motivated, so I ran the Pittsburgh Marathon two months later, where the scorching heat reduced me to walking most of the last few miles. My suffering there was alleviated by the sight of one late-night reveler in leather pants and boots, who, after stumbling out his door and squinting at the bright daylight, looked at all the runners streaming past and asked someone, "Where are they all going?"

I ran two more marathons that same year, still electrified by the experience. Like a child who's discovered how to walk, I was amazed at what my body could now do. It was as if I'd walked through a doorway into a brand-new, beautiful room that I hadn't known was there. I even began to earn a reputation at work as being an avid marathoner; I became known as *that running guy*.

The marathons then came in bunches, like a blizzard following a few errant snowflakes. I ran six in 1994, including one in Philadelphia, where I found myself desperate at one point to relieve myself, but without a Porta-Jon or bush in sight. Spectators lined the streets, but I had little choice but to use a light post as my bathroom stall. Looking over to my left, I saw a policeman. He just looked the other way. This road racing was a funny business.

By 1995 people had begun calling me "obsessed," but I thought of myself as just being enthusiastic, and I continued running and racing. I traveled back and forth across the continent, and overseas as well. In 1998, in Madison, Wisconsin, I reached marathon number 35, and I realized that I was now like the older runner I had met a few years earlier in Virginia Beach. Like him, I was now a different breed of runner.

But what kind of runner was I now? I had proven beyond any doubt that I could run a marathon, and yet the marathon distance still intrigued me. Rather than slaking my thirst for racing, each marathon left me wanting more. I knew that I could simply keep running and racing, but that alone wouldn't be enough. I had entered my first marathon because I needed a goal to focus my training. Now I needed a similar goal to focus my racing. I had proven to myself that although I might not be the fastest runner in the field, I was one of the most durable. So my challenge would be to find out exactly how durable I was. If thirty-five marathons once amazed me, what would be a suitable goal now?

100 marathons. As soon as I thought of it, I knew that I had the right answer. Even if it was an arbitrary number, it was beautiful. It seemed complete. Ninety-nine marathons cried out for one more; 101 marathons seemed a stop on the way toward another goal. But 100 was perfect. It was also a number that would, in its audacity, seem insane even to other athletes. Totaled up in miles, it described a course heading west from my home in Washington, D.C., all the way to Carson City, Nevada. It was a feat of running that most people couldn't imagine, but it was something that I really felt that I could do. The thought of it also scared and exhilarated me, which meant, of course, that it was just the kind of challenge I was looking for.

In fact, as I discovered, I wasn't the first person to take on and beat such a challenge. Still, the club of people who have run 100 marathons is a pretty select one, and even if that weren't true—even if hundreds of thousands of other runners across the globe had done it—it was not something *I* had done. And that was the point. Ultimately, it was going to be a challenge not of the human spirit and body, but of *my* spirit and body. And so I committed myself to it.

Then, seemingly way too soon, it happened. It actually took eighteen years, but it happened. One hundred marathons. 2,620 miles of racing. Finished.

Here are the memories and lessons of those eighteen years of marathon racing. My first 100 marathons. Compressed within these pages are the joys and agonies of all those long miles, and, I hope, some of the knowledge that came from making a habit of pushing myself beyond pain and fear and doubt.

When I talk about my marathons, I feel like a child who can't wait to show his birthday gift to his friends. "See this? Isn't it the coolest thing you've ever seen?" After almost two decades, I think it still is, and by the time you've reached the end of this journey, I hope you'll see why.

Running Tip #1

Getting Started

- *Get proper gear.* Buy shoes in a proper running store, where they can identify your particular needs. And avoid cotton clothing; cotton stays wet and makes you colder if you're cold and hotter if you're hot.
- *Warm up.* Start each run with a 5-minute walk or slow jog. Running too hard too soon will only make for a miserable run.
- *Breathe smoothly.* Find a pace that allows you to talk while running. Runners who run out of breath don't run very long.
- *Stay relaxed.* Keep your shoulders low, and swing your arms smoothly, with your hands near your upper hip.
- *Don't overstride.* Your foot should land directly under your body.
- *Don't be too ambitious!* Keep your mileage increases to no more than 10 percent from week to week.

Why Run the Marathon? First Lap

Looking back, I could see that once I put on my first pair of running shoes and set out down the street, it was probably inevitable that I would want to run a marathon. Like a Little League baseball player dreaming of the major leagues, distance runners dream of the marathon.

It didn't necessarily have to be that way—I'm told that there are runners out there who are content to do their training and never pin on a race number. Regular training, as opposed to racing, brings all the proven benefits of weight control, cardiovascular health, and improved emotional outlook, and all with as little work as three sessions of 20–30 minutes a week. And many runners who choose to race are often content to just run 5Ks and 10Ks. But that wasn't good enough for me, or for almost a half-million other people in the United States every year who are drawn to the marathon. Why? At some level, it isn't good enough to just say that it seemed like a good challenge, that it felt right, that it was hard but fun.

It's a simple question, really, so there should be a simple answer: Why run the marathon?

Perhaps the answer is in our desire to be part of something bigger than ourselves, to connect with history and become a part of it. The marathon, after all, is the most famous and storied of all footraces. Here's the original story, in a thumbnail sketch, taken straight from Herodotus (more or less): Sometime around 490 BC, Darius the Great of Persia amassed a huge army and moved to conquer each of the Greek city-states, which had not yet united into a single power. The cities fell one by one, and soon only Athens and Sparta remained independent.

Darius landed some 30,000 soldiers at the plains of Marathon and prepared to attack Athens. Athens gathered a force of 10,000 soldiers to meet them under the leadership of Athenian general Miltiades, who immediately sent a runner named Phidippides to Sparta, some 150 miles distant, to ask for help. The Spartans were celebrating a religious holiday, and would only send warriors once the festival ended five days later. Phidippides raced back and relayed the news to Miltiades, who decided to strike alone before the Persians became fully prepared. The Athenians flanked the Persians and then encircled them, hacking their way through toward the Persian center. Once the carnage had ended, Darius's army had suffered some 6,400 casualties, while Miltiades had lost a scant 192 men. More or less.

News of the victory was delivered by a *hemerodromoi*— an "all-day runner." And that was the end of that. Except that centuries later, in the retelling, it was Phidippides who raced the 25 miles from the battlefield to Athens, shouted *"Nenikékamen!"*— we are victorious!"—and then dropped dead.

More or less.

Well, the battle certainly happened, as a large burial mound on the modern plains of Marathon silently confirms. And runners were certainly used as messengers. As for the rest, well, we'll never know for sure.

Now flash forward: the modern Olympic Games were being held in 1896 in Athens, and among the events planned was a 25-mile footrace called a marathon, held in commemoration of Phidippides's legendary run. The race ended with a dramatic and rousing victory for the Greek runner Spiridon Louis. Witnessing the first Olympic Games was a young Bostonian who was so enamored of the marathon that upon returning home, he convinced his athletic club to host a similar marathon race. Thus was born the Boston Marathon, the oldest annually held marathon in the world. But the marathon race wasn't yet a set distance; it wasn't yet the race we know today.

By 1908, the Olympic movement was firmly established, and the Games were being held in London. The royal family, apparently impressed by the fortitude of the distance runners, wanted to witness the race finish from the royal box. Accommodating their wishes added another mile and 385 yards to the 25-mile race distance. And that's how we ended up with the strange total of 26.2 miles for the marathon race.

The marathon, as an established race, is now over a century old. We have seen barefoot champions and computer chips in racers' shoes, and the erosion of racial and gender biases. We have also seen record times drop to seemingly inhuman levels, with the current world's best mark at 2 hours, 4 minutes, 26 seconds for men and 2 hours, 15 minutes, 25 seconds for women.[1]

---

1 These records were set by Haile Gebrsellasie of Ethiopia in the 2007 Berlin Marathon and Paula Radcliffe of Great Britain in the 2003 London Marathon.

Amazing stories. Captivating figures. Triumph, elation, tears, and disappointment. It's all there. Perhaps, then, we marathoners race to become part of this great tradition, to become part of an unbroken line of history stretching back to those brave Athenians, to share in the glory.

Perhaps, except that most modern marathoners probably don't know all of this history when they toe the line on race day, and in truth, it would have little impact on their choice to race a marathon even if they did. And glory? No. Except for the lucky few elite runners, modern marathoners do not race for fame or fortune. We toil in obscurity, part of the mass of bobbing heads that fill a city's streets on a Sunday morning once a year. Our friends and family will tire of congratulating us after several days have gone, and our names and finishing times will eventually be lost to history.

So, again, why run the marathon?

Maybe the answer is not in the history of the race, but in the moment, in the here and now of conquering the racecourse. Few of us ever find ourselves enjoying the adulation of the crowds, and having thousands of people screaming encouragement and calling your name is an adrenaline rush of the first magnitude. That would certainly get most people out of bed in the morning.

Some people misunderstand the attraction of cheering, though. An administrative assistant in my office once decided to write a short piece about my running for our newsletter. I started by explaining to him the thrill of Boston and New York. During everyday life, I told him, you rarely know exactly where you stand. You might be doing great at work and in your relationship, or you might be doing badly, but most often it's hard to tell. Life is filled with mixed signals, and anything can change in a second, often with little explanation, and no one cheers you on if you do the right thing. But when you run a marathon, life is wonderfully and beautifully simple. You run 26.2 miles as fast as you can, and you get a medal if you finish. Along the way you have hundreds or thousands of people telling you what a great job you're doing and how great you look. What's not to love about that?

My interviewer nodded appreciatively and diligently took notes. When he left my office, I felt like an evangelist who had just brought someone new into the flock. *He gets it,* I thought.

Then the newsletter came out, and I quickly turned to his article. "Jeff is going to run the Boston Marathon this month," it began. "He said he does it for the attention." Ugh.

But while the cheers of the crowd are a good motivation for a great many people, a few hours of cheering hardly seems a good return on the months of sacrifice and effort that preceded it. Cheers also cannot fully explain my own marathon odyssey, because few of my marathons attract runners by the tens of thousands. Some of them cannot attract even 100 racers. Instead of being cheered by hundreds of thousands of spectators and fans at these races, I'm often only quietly observed only by a few hardy volunteers shivering by their refreshment tables. On those days, far from the boisterous crowds, the question remains: Why the marathon?

Why Run the Marathon? First Lap

The failure to be able to explain my running passion became a problem for me. The more I was asked the question, the more I realized that I needed an answer, if only for my own peace of mind. I came to fear that perhaps I wasn't running *toward* something, so much as I was running *away* from something. One day I watched a report on television about a man who overcame his addiction to drugs and alcohol by running a marathon every weekend. The interviewer marveled at the amazing transformation, but I wasn't so impressed. It sounded to me only that the man had traded one set of addictions for another. I had seen people like that, and the results were never good. Eventually, the wheels would come off, and some debilitating injury would end their marathon streak. Usually the person would then lurch off in another direction, and become addicted to something else. I felt that my own enthusiasm was much different, but how could I be sure?

What I needed were some tests, some indicators that I had not wandered off onto dangerous ground. I found one while racing in St. Louis in 1997. During the course of 26.2 miles, you tend to notice the other runners around you. It's not uncommon for strangers to congratulate one another at the finish line, or to strike up a conversation and offer encouragement during the race to pass the time. In St. Louis, I realized that the man next to me had matched me stride for stride over several miles.

"Nice pace," I told him. "You're looking strong."

"Thanks," he replied. "I need to be fast. I told my wife that I wouldn't do this anymore. She thinks I'm out getting the newspaper."

I'm no marriage counselor, but even I could see trouble there.

From that exchange, I spotted a potential test: I would simply ask whether I had ever tried to hide my running. Although the answer wouldn't say much about why I was running, it would, hopefully, prove that whatever the reason was, it wasn't a bad one.

I probed my memory, and found my answer: I hadn't lied about my racing.

I then asked myself a second question: had I ever forced myself to run? Sure, there were some days where it was a bit tough getting out the door, but I generally looked forward to my runs, and enjoyed them. There was a moment in just about every run where I felt strong and eternal; not exactly the mythical "runner's high," but a comforting sense of well-being that made all the difficult parts of the run worthwhile. Skeptics say it's simply the result of an endorphin and adrenaline cocktail that my body concocts for me, but that seemed such a spiteful way of describing it, like describing love as a product of certain glandular secretions. When I feel it, it feels great, and that's good enough for me. Of all of life's great pleasures—sex, a great meal, a glorious sunset— a good run has to be near the top.

Such pleasure hardly ever comes without a price, however. If the pleasure of running is truly chemical, it's possible to become addicted to those chemicals. Evidence of such addiction isn't hard to find; many runners insist on hitting the roads despite aching joints and strained muscles. It seems like they had somehow lost sight of the fact that running is supposed to make them feel better, not worse. It's important to be dedicated enough to train hard. However, as I learned—the hard way—it's even more important to be dedicated enough to know when to stop.

I discovered the next test in my third attempt at the Marine Corps Marathon. After finding success in 1987, I decided to try again the following year. I had a difficult training cycle, though, and had dramatically cut back on my running in order to relieve an ache in my knees. My injury disappeared, but as I stood at the starting line before the race, I was nervous that my sacrifice left me unprepared for the race.

I flew through the early miles in the race, and I began to think that I had worried needlessly. But the first lesson of the marathon is not to put too much stock in how you feel at any one moment, since there is plenty of time for things to change. Sure enough, an hour later I was struggling badly. Like a car that has run out of gas, but is still rolling, I shuffled onward toward the finish. Doubt crept into my thinking for the first time, and I began to realize that I would soon have to make a tough decision.

At mile 17 I looked down at my feet, and saw that they were hardly moving, with 9 miles still left to go. I was exhausted, and I suddenly knew that the time had come. I dropped out of the race. I stepped over to the curb and just stopped. It was an odd sensation. Just stepping off the course is a temptation that nips at the heels of every runner who finds himself or herself in distress, but the desire to stay on the course is so great that most of us would rather risk a complete breakdown and injury than take those few steps to the side. But when I did it, it felt as though I no longer even had a choice. I was through, and I knew it. To confirm that point, my muscles stiffened and cramped as soon as I hit the grass.

I should have been upset about my failure, but I wasn't. I knew I had fought as valiantly as I could, but that it was simply not my day. Elite runners drop out of races all the time to save their bodies from unnecessary punishment. But even as I was heading home, I began to analyze why it had happened. Being at peace with my decision to drop out didn't mean that I ever wanted to repeat that experience.

In the years since that day, I have looked back on that DNF (Did Not Finish) as a benchmark of sorts. It was proof that I knew when it was time to quit. Since then, every time I pass mile 17 in a race, I think of that failure, and remind myself that I would always struggle to run the best race that I could, but that in the end, I would not push myself into the danger zone out of sheer stubbornness. I knew that as much as I wanted to finish every race that I entered, I would never be unmindful of the cost. After overcoming injuries and setbacks, I would not sell my running future for a fleeting moment of personal glory on race day. I would not force myself to run.

Still, simply refraining from lying about my racing and avoiding injuries hardly sounds like a ringing endorsement for a lifestyle choice. I was hoping for something that would be a little more useful, that would get to the heart of my running. Ultimately, I found it, and it was a simple thing.

Crossing the finish line, as I had explained to countless people, was a wonderful, life-changing experience, and its glory is never diminished by the number of times I've done it. If anything, my earlier DNF only made each marathon finish that much more precious to me, since I had been forced to realize how much could go wrong in preparing for and racing a marathon. I came to realize that if ever I should cross a finish line and feel disappointed over my time and my performance, the marathon would no longer be a transcendent event for me. It would have lost its meaning, and devolved into drudgery and work. When that happened, I knew that it would be time for me to quit.

So far, though, that day had not yet come, and each marathon finish was a life-affirming event for me, whether I ran my best times or my worst, because in each marathon I did my best, and that was cause enough for celebration.

With those thoughts in mind, I gave myself a clean bill of mental health, reassured that I was not running for the wrong reasons. But still, I had not really answered the question why. But why does anyone do anything? Why do painters paint and singers sing? I realized that I would not be able to answer this question all at once, so I put it away to ponder another time, and went out for a run.

A New Quest

B_y the end of 1995, I had run eighteen marathons, but my life had changed quite a bit. As an attorney with the National Labor Relations Board, I protected employees' rights to act together to improve their working conditions. It was an interesting job, exposing me to stories from a great number of people from all walks of life, and giving me an opportunity to help people who had been treated unfairly. But as much satisfaction as I got from that job, I was still enthralled by my running. At work, it was frustrating to see how many people I couldn't help—or couldn't help enough—and there were days when I wondered how much I had really accomplished.

With running, however, my achievements were clear, and the joy I took in my running wasn't tempered by any misgivings or compromises. Little by little, running spilled over into all the corners of my life; even the drawers in my office were filled with energy bars and running clothes.

And I had still not yet become bored of the marathon. I had braved an arctic cold front in Delaware that brought windchill temperatures below zero and froze sweat into icicles hanging from runners' headbands and caps. I had completed marathons in eleven different states, from Virginia to Nevada, plus D.C. It occurred to me that with a little organization, I could run a marathon in every state. The thought quickly settled comfortably in my mind. It was an elegantly simple and daunting challenge. Fifty states, fifty marathons. An added bonus to my goal of running 100 marathons, there for the taking.

As it turned out, just as with my 100-marathon goal, I hadn't been the first person to imagine this quest, either. There was actually an informal club of runners who had set this goal for themselves, and some of them were even working on their second tally. Rather than feeling diminished by this fact, however, I felt comforted. Nothing confirms our sanity more than finding out that there are people out there crazier than ourselves. Membership in the club was open to runners who had completed marathons in ten different states. I was eligible, so I joined the club. I was now an official marathon lunatic.

During the six years that I'd been racing, I also had seen my best time, my Personal Record time, drop from 3 hours, 45 minutes in my first marathon, to 3 hours, 35 minutes. Ten minutes may not sound like much, but it felt like a monumental achievement to me.

My dream for the marathon, my fantasy goal, was to qualify for the Holy Grail of road racing, the Boston Marathon. Boston was special to me not only for its storied history, but also for its elitism; it was the only marathon in the country for which you had to prequalify. There are no slow, novice racers in Boston, at least not officially, because having a race number itself means that you have already finished a marathon in qualifying time. The required times vary according to age and gender, as explained on the race Web site. I was in the most challenging group: men under 35 years of age. To toe the line in Boston, I would have to run a marathon in 3 hours 10 minutes or less. That was 25 minutes faster than I had run a marathon in six years of racing. Impossible. Or so I thought.

Qualifying is not actually the only way to the start line for the Boston Marathon. The Boston Athletic Association donates a certain number of race numbers to designated charities, which give them to runners who have met a designated fundraising goal. I was so sure that I would never qualify for the race that I managed to get a number this way. So I ran Boston, but I did not have the "Boston Marathon experience." I hadn't qualified, and I didn't have the kind of speed or toughness to run Boston the way it deserved to be run. Rather than a race, my marathon there felt more like a long training run. It just didn't feel right. I swore to myself that if I ever lined up at the start of another Boston Marathon, it would be because I had earned it, and deserved to be there. Until that happened, in my mind, I had never really run the race.

I kept running, and my times did improve. I posted 3:21:28 in Chicago in October 1995, and then 3:19:41 in the Mayor's Midnight Marathon in Anchorage Alaska in June 1996. That race wasn't held at midnight, as its name promised, but it might as well have been. There really isn't any darkness in Alaska in June. There is daylight, twilight, then daylight again. It was a confusing place for someone from "the Lower 48." There were none of the telltale signs of gathering evening. At one point I realized that it was late evening only because all of the stores had closed. Apart from that, it looked like high noon.

I couldn't help having a bit of fun with this; I called my mother and told her that I was calling from a pay phone in a park in the dead of night. Being a native New Yorker, Mom feared the worst. "Get out of there!" she told me, her voice rising. "Don't worry, Mom. I'm just watching a softball game right now, under clear blue skies."

I returned from Alaska still nine minutes from qualifying for Boston. It might as well have been nine hours for all it mattered. I was sure that I had pushed my body to its limit; it had gone about as fast as it would ever go.

Then I discovered track workouts. I had always trained alone, but I knew that running didn't have to be that way. I found out about a running club in D.C. that held track workouts every Wednesday at Georgetown University, and one day after work I showed up at the track, curious and eager. By the time it was over, I felt like I had stepped from the black-and-white world of Kansas into the splendor of Oz. I had discovered speed work.

Speed work, also called interval training, conditions the body to run faster by alternating hard repeats of shorter distances with slower recovery laps. Done correctly, it avoids the injuries that come with added stress from hard running, while making the most of the beneficial adaptations caused by hard running. It was as different from running long miles as riding a supercharged motorcycle is from taking a leisurely drive in the country.

I loved it. On the first day I showed up for training, I was near the back of the pack during the workout, but in the following weeks I slowly moved up toward the front. We ran different workouts every week—quarter-mile intervals, half miles, miles. Each one was an adventure. Ironically, the trick was not running too hard, since sprinting improves short distance speed, but doesn't prepare the body to run faster for longer distances. It took wisdom and experience to know how fast to run, and little by little, I learned.

The coach who called out our weekly workouts assured us that speed work would not only improve our race times but also familiarize us with pacing, as we learned to associate given effort levels with particular clock times. If I had any doubts about this claim, they were dispelled when I ran with a woman who told me her exact goal for each repeat, and then proceeded to run each interval within a second or two of her goal, without ever looking at her watch. She did it by feel alone.

I was impressed. That was the kind of runner I wanted to be.

I met other runners as well at the track: men and women, old and young, fast and, well, less fast. I joined them for food and beer after the workouts, and met them for long Sunday morning runs. There was Camilla, Yvonne, Stewart, Darryl, and two Beths, both of whom were fast runners. I was discovering that running didn't have to be a solitary sport; there was a running *community*.

One day on the track, I tried to block out the discomfort of hard running by thinking about West Virginia. A marathon was being held there that coming Sunday, and I was debating whether I wanted to drive out there to run it. In addition to adding to my overall marathon total, racing in West Virginia would also add to my total of states, since I hadn't entered a marathon there yet. That was the positive side. I would have to drive out there alone to do it, though. That was the negative.

By the time the workout was over, I still hadn't decided what to do. As I stretched and gathered up my gear, another runner told me in passing that he was debating running a marathon that weekend himself. It was June, when few marathons are held because of the heat. Could he be thinking about West Virginia? He was. Would he be interested in going out there together and splitting the driving? He was. That's how I met Dave Harrell.

Dave was more than twenty years older than me. He had come to marathoning later in life, but like me, had taken to it with a passion. He had run a dozen or so marathons, all over the mid-Atlantic and Northeast. He ran with an easy, gliding style, an economy of effort that enabled him to win or place in his age group in many of the races in which he competed.

Dave, however, differed from me in one important respect: his racing strategy. Not one for subtlety, Dave started each race with the intent to run as fast as he could for as long as he could. While most runners start off conservatively and then try to maintain or even increase their speed over the miles, Dave liked to jump out in front early, which he usually paid for with great suffering in the final few miles. It was an unorthodox style, strange to see and difficult to match, uncommon in a runner with Dave's experience. But that was how Dave liked to run, and he wasn't going to change.

The race in West Virginia was called the Ridge Runner, and true to its name, it started with two daunting climbs in the first mile up a ridge, with another long ascent late in the race, and a fast, painful descent at the end. At the crack of the starter's gun, I was surprised to see Dave take off like a bat out of hell. I had thought we might run together, at least for a while, but upon seeing the road rise up in front of me, I decided to let him go, and concentrated on hauling myself up to the top of the ridge. As the race wore on, I found myself feeling stronger, as I usually did at some point midway through my races, and I picked up my pace. It was a beautiful course, and I enjoyed the views all the way through to the end. I flew down the final descent and crossed the finish line, and finally found Dave, who had already crossed the line before me. As I soon learned, he had only crossed it some 41 seconds before I did.

Dave and I didn't know each other well at this point, but that didn't stop us from talking trash. I thought it was obvious that if I had known that he was less than a minute in front of me, I would have sped up and caught him. Unbelievably, Dave insisted that if he knew I was right behind him, he would have sped up and left me in the dust. By the time we made it back to our hotel, we had decided that there was only one way to resolve our dispute: a 40-yard dash. Never mind that we just ran a difficult marathon. Our competitive fires were lit, and there was no other way to douse them.

So, still wearing our race clothing, now whitened with a salt residue from our sweat, we marked out the course in front of the hotel: from here to that second streetlight. *Go!* I ran as fast as I could, but I was horrified to see Dave pull a step in front of me. Laughing and yelling, I lunged forward and grabbed at his singlet, but he evaded me and made it to the finish first. Again. Grrrrr! No hard feelings, though; it had all been in fun, and we went into our hotel to clean up and check out.

On the ride home, and later at the track, Dave and I talked about our race goals. I suggested to Dave that given his past marathoning experience, and his ambitious plans for the future, all it would take for him to also complete the fifty states would be a bit of organization and planning. With his volume of racing, if we timed it right, Dave and I might also reach 100 marathons together. Dave rolled it around in his mind for a moment, then grinned. I had found a racing partner.

I don't know what drove Dave to run with such dedication. It wasn't something we ever spoke about. Sometimes those kinds of questions are the hardest to answer; I still wasn't even exactly sure why I took to long-distance running like I had. At the least, it was a good balance to the hours I spent at a desk. I've heard it said that running is like meditation, since the rhythm of the legs and the breathing can lull one into a quiet, thought-free state. I've experienced that, but I've also experienced moments of deep, focused thought, where I worked through problems and issues that have arisen in my life. Perhaps my love of running came from one of these things, or perhaps it came from them all. Or, perhaps, it came from something else entirely. I couldn't exactly say.

I don't know if Dave wondered about these things. If he did, he never told me. We did most of our communication with our legs, over hundreds and hundreds of miles. We both knew, without ever saying it aloud, that each of us had recognized that there was something perfect about the marathon, something that made it one of the most important things in our lives. We understood this about each other. There was nothing more that needed to be said. Any other questions that I had, I would have to answer on my own.

Running Tip #2

Ten-Week Speed Program

It's been said that there are as many running programs as there are coaches. Here's mine. Give it a chance, and remember to do a 1-mile warm-up and cooldown.

- Week 1—4 X 880m (half-mile) @ 10K race pace/moderately hard (15–20 seconds faster than marathon race pace), with a 440m slow recovery between each repeat
- Week 2—6 X 880m @ 10K race pace/moderately hard, with a 440m recovery
- Week 3—440m (quarter mile), 880m, 1320m (3-quarter mile), 880m, 440m @ 10K race pace/moderately hard, with a 440m recovery
- Week 4—8 X 880m @10K race pace/moderately hard, with a 440m recovery
- Week 5—10 X 440m @ 5K race pace/hard, with a 220m recovery
- Week 6—3 X 1760m (1 mile) @ 10K race pace/moderately hard, with a 440m recovery
- Week 7—2 X 2 miles @ 10K race pace/moderately hard, with a 440m recovery
- Week 8—1 X 1760m, 1 X 2 mile, 1 X 1760m @ 10K pace/ moderately hard, with a 440m recovery
- Week 9—10 X 880m (half mile) @ 10K pace/moderately hard, with a 440m recovery, 5 minute rest after repeat number 5
- Week 10—4 X 1760m @ 10K race pace/moderately hard, with a 440m recovery

The Magical Year

By 1996, I had worked in the same office for eight years. I enjoyed working for the Labor Board and wanted to stay there, but I also wanted to do something different. So I became an appellate litigator for my agency, defending its decisions before the U.S. Courts of Appeal. The first time I stood up at the podium to argue a case was a nerve-racking moment. The courtroom seemed huge, and was subtly designed to impart an aura of importance to the proceedings, as well as intimidate all who entered. As I looked up at the three judges who would hear my case, my heart felt like it was about to rip through my body. And then I began to speak. "May it please the Court, my name is Jeff Horowitz, and I represent the National Labor Relations Board."

Suddenly, calmness came over me, and I felt completely at ease as I laid out the facts and the law for the judges, answering their questions and deflecting any criticism. It only lasted 10 minutes—average for an appellate argument—but when it was over, I felt an incredible sense of power and release. I loved it. Some attorneys in my office loved the grind of writing the briefs we had to submit, and dreaded oral argument, but I was the opposite. I liked the immediacy and danger of appearing in court.

It was almost as good as finishing a marathon. Almost. But compared to the adrenaline rush of the marathon finish line, it was no contest. Racing was my drug of choice.

Still, I had a lot to learn. In May, I flew to Cleveland for the old Revco Marathon. Having already run twenty-one marathons, I thought myself invincible, so I went out for Chinese food the night before the big race. Spicy eggplant. It turned on me at about mile 14 of the course the next day. Of course, there were no portable toilets anywhere in sight just then, and as I snuck down a dark alleyway, clutching the biggest leaves I could find, I swore that I would never take any chances again.

So, I was not invincible. Lesson learned.

Even with all my mistakes, I was still doing an awful lot right, and I had my breakthrough year in 1997. I had been doing speed work regularly, and was doing my long weekend runs with a fast bunch of guys. I felt quick and strong, and as the 1997 racing season, I felt an upsurge of confidence. I knew with great certainty that I would set a personal record every time I raced.

I was right. I ran a 5K in under 20 minutes, a 10-mile race in 62 minutes, and a half-marathon in 1:27. In late September, I ran marathon number 30 in East Lyme, Connecticut, in 3:12:57. Only 3 minutes separated me from the Boston Marathon. I began to believe it was possible.

I was scheduled to run my next marathon three weeks later in Detroit. It was a well-organized race with potential: a fast, flat course, not too big a field. I drove out there with my running buddies, who were also racing, and patiently waited for the race. We went to a University of Michigan football game, toured the city, ate, and rested. Finally, it was time to run.

The Detroit Marathon actually started in Canada, and boasted the only underground mile in marathoning, as runners were herded through a tunnel back to the United States. As with every marathon, the air seemed to crackle with energy as we waited for the race to start. My friends and I began as a pack, hoping to run together for as long as possible. As we ran, I happened to notice one woman in particular, running directly in front of me. My eyes traced down her long blond hair to her blue running tights, stretched taut over her lean body. Her stride was beautiful, and utterly mesmerizing. After a few seconds that seemed like an eternity, I sheepishly looked away. Glancing left and right, I saw that a row of five or six guys, including my friends, all had their eyes glued to the same spot. As if on cue, we all looked up, noticed each other, and broke into embarrassed laughter.

The early miles flew by. I separated from my friends and surged forward, settling into my target pace. As I moved into the second half of the race, I felt strong and was running well. I suddenly understood the pressure of having an ambitious time goal; every mile marker brought a quick recalculation of pace and split times. I counted down miles and counted seconds, and I knew that I had none to spare. In my previous thirty marathons, I was able to run relaxed, losing myself in the joy of the moment and in my thoughts, but not in Detroit. I spent precious energy trying to concentrate on the task at hand, to keep focused for mile after mile, hour after hour. It was excruciating. I used to daydream about being an elite runner, trading my desk for a schedule of full-time training and racing. It used to sound like heaven, but not any more; I realized that being a professional runner must be hard work.

With a mile to go, I was still on pace to qualify for Boston. I was tired and my muscles ached, but I knew that I only had minutes of pain left, and a lifetime to recover. *I could do this*, I thought. Being a marathoner meant that you were the kind of person who kept running when other people would quit. I was a marathoner. I would not quit. I pushed as hard as I could, my mind focused only on the rhythm of my running. Finally the finish line was in view. Flying across, I checked my time. 3:08:59. I had done it! A new personal best, and a qualifying time. I was going to return to Boston, and no one could say that I didn't deserve to be there.

But my big year wasn't over yet. I decided to risk mailing in an application for a race I wasn't sure I could even finish: the JFK 50 Mile. The name alone scared me. I had never before run an ultramarathon, and the thought of nearly doubling my longest race distance seemed insane. That, of course, is exactly what drew me to it. As intoxicating as it is to finish a marathon, something irretrievable is lost when that goal is first achieved: the fear that you cannot do it. The excitement that goes with that uncertainty is gone forever. After the finish line is crossed, the only question that remains for the future is whether you can do it again, or do it faster. Usually that's a good thing, but I found myself missing the unknown, missing the fear. When I mailed in my 50-miler race application, I felt a deep nervousness that I hadn't felt in years. After returning from Detroit, I gave myself a little recovery time, and then committed to myself to training with a fresh sense of urgency.

I did have several factors in my favor. First, I was already an accomplished marathoner, which meant that my body had become adept at relying on fat to fuel my running, instead of just glycogen. I had covered enough miles to make this adaptation, so I was confident that I would have an easier time transitioning to an ultramarathon than a beginning recreational runner would have transitioning to a regular marathon.

The second factor that calmed me was my realization that the longer the race distance, the less important it was to cover the target distance in training. This was reassuring; I wouldn't have to do a 50-mile training run in order to prepare for a 50-mile race. From everything I had read, the consensus seemed to be that a 35-mile run would give me a sufficient endurance base to conquer the JFK. Running 35 miles sounded much easier than running 50, which made this whole enterprise seem much more possible.

Still, 35 miles is still a long way to run by yourself. I would have to plan a way to get access to the supplies I would need. One option would be to just carry the food and drink I'd require, but that didn't sound too appealing, since I was looking at a 5-hour session. Another option would be to map out a route and stash food and drink on the course, but that didn't seem like a great idea either, since I couldn't be sure that the stuff I'd left out in plain view hours earlier would still be there when I really needed it. What I really needed, I thought, was to have refreshment stops, manned by volunteers, just like they have in the marathon. That's when the obvious solution hit me: I would use a full marathon as a training run, making full use of the course support throughout, and simply add another 9 miles of running at the end. Brilliant.

The race I chose was the Vulcan Marathon in Birmingham, Alabama, which was scheduled just three weeks after the Detroit Marathon, and just three weeks before the JFK. In addition to the perfect symmetry of this timetable, racing in Birmingham would add Alabama to the list of states I had run. I talked Dave into joining me—getting him to agree to run a marathon was like talking a kid into eating candy—and we flew down to Birmingham together.

Being from the Northeast, I thought sophistication ended at the Mason-Dixon line, but I discovered that Birmingham had beautiful neighborhoods, golf courses, and thriving shopping districts nestled within the city's boundaries. It was a good lesson to learn: there was a lot about this country that I knew nothing about.

On race day, Dave and I decided to abandon our all-out approach to marathoning, and instead committed ourselves to finishing the race together—no small accomplishment with pedal-to-the-metal Dave!—with a goal finish time of 3:30. I knew this meant that we'd both have to show restraint at different times, but as the race unfolded, I knew that we were doing the right thing. Not only was I reserving enough energy to continue running after I crossed the finish line, I was also enjoying having Dave as my companion throughout the race. Our shared racing goals had created a special bond, and the Vulcan Marathon seemed a fitting celebration of our brotherhood.

When the finish line came within view, we tried our best to cross the line at exactly the same time—3:31, within one minute of our goal. The official race Web site ended up awarding Dave the win by a few seconds, which led to endless ribbing. But that was later. After crossing the finish line, I still had work to do. I collected my medal and set out back on a street parallel to the course.

I was feeling surprisingly spry, and after running about 4.5 miles, I reversed course and dove back into the crowd of marathoners heading toward the finish line. It was a strange experience for me, since I was surrounded by runners who I never really got to see before: the back-of-the-pack runners who usually finished in 5 or 6 hours. As I weaved though them, I got more than one confused look from people who must have been wondering how I could be running so hard and still be so far back. I got more puzzled looks and comments from the aid station volunteers who recognized me from my first pass. I just shrugged and smiled and raced onward. When I got to the finish line, I veered off the course, and fought off the well-meaning and urgent directions of volunteers who tried to guide me into the finisher's chutes. I pulled out my medal and smiled. I had finished another marathon, but more importantly, I believed that I was ready for the JFK.

The JFK 50 Miler is legendary among ultramarathoners. It was inaugurated in 1963, after President Kennedy challenged his military staffers to complete a 50-mile hike in a single day. The race quickly grew into one of the largest ultramarathons in the country, with a starting field of 700–1,000 runners. That's a lot of crazy people in one place.

They would have to be fast, too; the JFK has a finishing cutoff time of 14 hours, with several checkpoints. Runners who failed to reach the checkpoints within the cutoff times would be removed from the course.

But for those who completed the race, there would be glory and bragging rights: according to the race Web site, less than one-tenth of 1 percent of Americans have completed a 50-mile race. Elite company indeed.

I thought about this as I lay down the night before the race. I kept thinking about the number 50. Suddenly, I just couldn't see any way that I could possibly finish the race. It was just too long. I'd been fooling myself; I'd never make it. Then I thought of something my mother had once told me: gambling is wrong, she said, but if I wanted to bet on something, I should bet on myself. Something clicked for me when I thought of that. I would take a chance on me. With that, I drifted off to sleep.

The JFK 50 Miler is held in Hagerstown, Maryland, conveniently located just a few hours from where I lived. On race day I woke up well before dawn and drove to the start, where I found a large group of mostly older, often heavier runners milling about at the local school, which served as the race day headquarters. It was a different sort of racing crowd than I expected. I thought everyone would look lean and sinewy, their bodies worn down to just the essentials. Instead, I saw some a lot of portly runners who looked to me like they might not even be able to make it around the block. We filed over to the race start in the darkness, and at the blast of the starter's gun we began our journey.

The race began on city streets, and as we ran, I eavesdropped on the conversations around me. These runners, even the heavier ones, talked about having run the JFK numerous times, and other ultras as well. These were experienced guys. At that moment I decided to stop judging them by their shape, and instead credit their accomplishments and try to follow their lead. When they began to walk on the upgrades, I followed suit, and when they paused at aid stations and ate the sandwiches and soup that were offered, I did that, too. This wouldn't guarantee me success, but it would put the odds in my favor.

The race soon led us onto the Appalachian Trail. I wasn't an experienced trail runner, but I thought that the trail portions chosen for the race would surely be the easiest available. Oh, was I wrong. The trail meandered up and down on rough, uneven paths, over rocks, boulders and exposed branches. I was soon acquainted with the agony of stubbed toes and sore ankles. I became so focused on my foot placement that I failed to see a thick, low-lying branch in my path. I ran smack into it headfirst. Everything flashed bright white, and I could hear a distant voice asking if I was okay. I mumbled "yes," and hoped it was true.

Eventually, we left the trail, and ran onto the C&O canal towpath. I was familiar with the canal from the portion of it that ends in D.C. While I had never been this far out on it, I knew that it would be a flat, hard-pack dirt path. We were to run 26 miles on it, almost a full marathon. I was already sore and tired, and doubted if I would be able to finish the race, but I was determined not to drop out unless things got much worse. They would have to pull me off the course for failing to hit the cutoff times. Otherwise, I'd keep moving forward.

The race became an exercise in myopia; I tried to forget how much road lay before me, and concentrated only on getting to the next mile marker, and the next aid station. At each station I swallowed down as much food as I could handle, and then shuffled forward. My pace dropped to little more than a fast walk, but I was not alone. Others around me were in the same condition, or worse. One runner was so disoriented that he failed to notice a hip-level barrier that we had to circle. He hit it full-stride and flipped over onto his back. Undeterred and uncomplaining, he slowly arose and resumed running, mechanically but relentlessly.

The mile markers came and went, conveying impossible-sounding information. Mile 30, mile 31, mile 32. At mile 35, a strange thing happened; I began to feel better. I stopped taking walk breaks, and picked up the pace. By the time I exited the canal for a final 8 miles on the roads, I had sped up to a respectable 8:30-per-mile pace. Darkness descended as I raced those final miles, and when the finish line loomed before me, in front of a local high school, I looked up at the clock and smiled in disbelief. Nine hours 24 minutes. I had run all day, from predawn to nightfall. Even as I collected my medal, I couldn't believe I had done it. There was still the long drive home, though, and the fact of my race set in firmly as my legs ached and my muscles sagged. I had never felt so tired and sore, not even after my very first marathon. I would need weeks to fully recover physically, and almost as long to recover my desire to race.

So what to make of this? What was I to do with an ultramarathon finish? Could I add it to my list of marathons? After all, it was *at least* a marathon. That seemed fair enough. But even as I wrote it down, I knew it couldn't stay on the list. I was committed to running marathons, and that's a precise distance. I was free to run any other distance also, but they could not be included on the list. I could not add four 10Ks together and call them a marathon, and neither could I divide my marathons into eight separate 5K-plus finishes. My totals would be precise and beyond question; I had officially run thirty-two marathons and one *ultra*marathon.

The JFK 50 brought an end to my 1997 racing campaign. There were still adventures to be had in my future, exotic journeys and great races, but there would never again be a year for me quite like 1997.

Running Tip #3

Form Drills

Drills break down the running motion into distinct movements and improve running efficiency, form, and speed. Once a week, find a 50-meter stretch of road or track. Warm up and do each of these drills 2–4 times, taking a 30-second recovery between each repeat.

- *Butt kicks.* Take short steps while kicking your heels up as high as you can. This drill strengthens the hamstrings, a primary muscle group used in running.
- *High steps.* Take short steps as you pick your knees up as high as they can go. This drill strengthens the calves and hip flexors, which is the area where the bottom of your abdomen meets your leg—a muscle group that's crucial to the running motion, and emphasizes proper running posture and the lift-off phase of running.
- *High Skips.* Swing your arms strongly and skip as high as you can. This drill helps build explosive power in your running stride to improve hill-running and a strong finishing kick in your racing.
- *Stiff-legged Running.* Also called "soccer kicks." Run on your toes, keeping your legs locked out as straight as possible the entire time. This drill will also strengthen the hip flexors.
- *Strides.* Don't sprint; run hard but in control, with an emphasis on monitoring your form. This drill gives you a chance to work on any inefficiency in your form, and prepares your body for the next phase of your workout—your actual distance run—by lengthening your stride.

Pain, Fear, and Faith

As my marathon total climbed, I found that people weren't asking me why I ran out of admiration now so much as with concern. Many of them had seemed to become suspicious about my running. They began calling me obsessed, in that "I'm joking but you should really think about this" kind of way, and seemed to assume that my running enabled me to avoid dealing with some deeper, darker issues. They said that I must be running away from something.

I didn't think that was true. Running wasn't an escape; if anything, it was a lantern in the dark, a mirror showing me things about myself that I had to face. I could no sooner run away from my problems than I could run away from my own body; when I ran, there was only the road, my thoughts, and time. Eventually, inevitably, I would have to think about anything troubling me. Perhaps it was the rhythm of my footsteps that calmed me down and sharpened my thinking, or perhaps I just reacted well to the rush of endorphins, but whatever the reason, when I ran I saw things more clearly, and could see answers to questions that seemed insolvable only hours before.

Do you remember that poem, "Footprints in the Sand"? Sure you do. You've seen it on automobile air fresheners and on cheesy plaques at every truck stop you've ever wandered into. It goes like this: A man looked back on the path he'd traveled all his life and saw that although the Lord often walked by his side, during the most difficult times, there was only one set of footprints in the sand. The man turned to the Lord and asked, "Why did you abandon me when I needed you the most?" The Lord answered, "Oh, my son, it was then that I carried you."

I hate that story. Not just because it's the worst kind of corny, dime-store religious palaver, although that's exactly what it is; I hate it because it turns me to mush. Every time I read it, my heart rises into my throat and my eyes begin to moisten. Good god, that's actually happening to me right now. I just can't help it, and it's infuriating.

My running reminds me of that story. During the hardest times of my life—when I lost loved ones, when my heart was broken, when I was studying for the bar exam, and whenever I felt alone in the world—running was there for me, providing some relief from my troubles, putting things in perspective and letting me see that the road always continued onward. My running carried me and sustained me.

I've always thought that everyone should have some activity in their lives in which they can become so immersed that they lose track of time. When that happens, when there is no past or future, but only the present, you can find a little bit of that most rare commodity: a little peace of mind. When I relax on a long run, I can get to that place, and in that relaxed state, I can see answers to the problems in my life, and put things in perspective.

This is especially true on my longest runs. During a shorter run of six to eight miles, I know that I'll be finished within an hour, give or take a few minutes. That run becomes a small part of the day's plan, and during the run, I find myself looking ahead to what I need to take care of next when the workout is over, and sometimes I get impatient to be finished so I can get on with the day's chores. But on an 18- to 20-mile run, I know that I'll be on the road for hours, and when I'm finished, I'll be in no mood to rush off to tackle other projects and run errands. The long run becomes the 500-pound gorilla sitting in the middle of a room, completely impossible to ignore. On those days, I give in to the gorilla, and settle into a comfortable pace, knowing that there is nothing else that I need to concern myself with other than putting one foot in front of the other. Any impatience that I might have had during shorter runs disappears. On the long days, there's just me, the road, and endless time.

Not that running is always a pleasure. Running, especially marathon racing, also brings pain. During the last miles of a marathon, my quadriceps muscles are often aching, my hamstrings might be complaining, my calves are possibly cramping, and even my shoulders are fatigued. None of this surprises me; in fact, all of it is entirely expected. I think of these aches and pains as old friends come to visit. I even welcome them, since they signal to me that I'm back in familiar territory, and that the end of the race must be near.

I don't usually talk about these aches and pains with nonrunners, though, because I don't think they'll understand. It's not that marathon runners are masochists—at least not in the traditional sense, and certainly not most of them. It's just that pain means something else to us than it means to most other people. To a runner, pain is a sign of achievement; it's proof that we've expended the maximum effort. When our sides ache from oxygen debt and our legs burn with lactic acid build-up, or when we spend the days after a hard race hobbling pitifully up and down stairs, we know that we had run as hard as we possibly could. The pain, then, is not a cause for concern; it's a cause for celebration. And when we feel perfectly fine after finishing a race, we hear a little voice inside asking us whether it might be true that we could have run faster than we did. In fact, one of my running fantasies is to collapse immediately after finishing a marathon, having used my very last measure of energy to throw myself across the finish line for a new personal best. That would be a perfect race.

But I don't actually enjoy the pain. It's not fun to cool down after a race and discover that your body has stiffened up so much that you could no longer easily or painlessly step down from the curb to the street. Nor is there easy rest for a weary body when every toss and turn in the middle of the night brings complaints from sore muscles, and every attempt to stand up from a chair takes minutes rather than seconds. This kind of pain is humbling; it's disruptive not only to a regular workout routine, but to any kind of normal life. It's a deep-to-the-bone kind of soreness that I would never have known if I had never run a marathon.

The memory of these aches leads me to look down at my legs with pity at every starting line, since they don't know yet what hell I'm about to put them through. But after an hour or two of running, they'll figure it out, and brace themselves for the familiar challenge. If they could speak, perhaps they would tell me not to worry. They understand that this pain is fleeting; we have weathered it before, and we can weather it again. Just get on with it, they would say.

Actual injuries are an entirely different story. There is no long-time runner who hasn't experienced their share of sprains, strains, fractures, and tears. Get a group of runners together, and before long they'll start talking about their injury histories, like war veterans comparing battle scars. During those moments, it might be easy to believe that runners don't mind being injured, but that's dead wrong. If the storytellers are smiling, it's only because the injuries are healed, or because they're trying not to let their frustration show. Dealing with an injury is often a greater test of a runner's resolve than any grueling workout or race.

Once I began to run marathons on a regular basis, many of my friends predicted that my bones would turn to dust, and I'd be crippled within just a few years. Some doctors said much the same thing.

The injuries that I sometimes struggled with only seemed to confirm their predictions. After overcoming that bad ankle sprain in 1986, I suffered a sequence of regular setbacks over the next few years. At one point I had terrible back spasms and had to undergo physical therapy, and another time I developed pain in my knees due to tightness in the muscle and connective tissue that runs along the outside of our legs, called the ilio-tibial band. On a less serious but no less painful side, I also developed awful-looking blisters during my early races. I tried to prevent them by slathering my feet with petroleum jelly, or wrapping each toe with medical tape. In desperation, I once both wrapped and jellied my feet. Not a good idea. By race's end, I was left with a slippery mass of balled up tape jammed in the front of my shoes.

Another time, I felt a blister developing on my right pinky toe early in a race. Being an old pro by this point, I pulled over to an aid station and wrapped tape around the toe. Problem solved. I jumped back in the race and ran smoothly for the next 19 miles, but after crossing the 26 mile marker, with the finish line within sight just up ahead, I suddenly felt a very painful pop in my right foot. I was quickly reduced to a hobble, and I was sure that I had torn a ligament in that pinky toe. After pulling myself across the finish line, I staggered straight to the medical tent, where I sat down and pulled of my right shoe. The end of my sock was covered in blood. I pulled off the sock, and then had a medical technician carefully cut the tape along the length of my toe. I slowly pulled the tape back, and gazed at what I saw underneath. The toe was a raw stick of meat. Stuck on the tape was my skin and toenail. Slowly, it dawned on me what had happened. I had developed a blister underneath the toenail, and finally, at mile 26, it popped violently, unhinging both the nail and the surrounding skin. Luckily, it didn't feel as bad as it looked, but whenever I want to make someone cringe, I pull that story out from my bag of tales.

Eventually, I found the right combination of treatments to get my feet safely through my races, and eventually they seemed to just toughen up and blister less frequently. My other injuries also healed and disappeared, leaving me wiser. I began to see my body as a kind of mine-field which I could traverse only by stepping carefully around the spots where I knew explosives lay. *Not there! You'll get a sore knee if you do that. And that will hurt your back!*

Despite all of those training and racing woes, however, I came to realize over the years that I was actually a very durable runner. I had a stable stride an unusually large vastus medialis—the muscle above the kneecap that helps hold the kneecap in place. Like most other runners, I still had to work on my flexibility and strengthen the muscles in my back and abdominal areas, but I had come to realize that while I might not be the fastest runner in the field, I was built to keep running.

Still, if I have a different relationship to pain than most nonrunners, I also have a different collection of fears. Preparing for and running the JFK 50 Mile led me to consider again the role of fear in running, since, for the first time in a very long while, I had ventured outside of my com-fort zone into unknown territory. By that time I was very confident that I could run a marathon. After all, I had already run thirty-two of them. But I was very worried about the JFK 50. I felt a fear of failure that I had not felt in years. It was a feeling that was unsettling and disturbing, though not entirely unpleasant.

Fear, like any stress, is a double-edged sword. Unhealthy and par-alyzing in large doses, it's also essential for achievement, and leads to the cathartic hormonal release that we all find so pleasurable. This is the fear that we seek out and pay for with every horror movie and roller-coaster ride we experience. But runners live with a more common brand of fear, cousin more to insecurity than to terror. This is the fear that whis-pers in our ear that past achievement matters little because our bodies are no longer in the condition they were in a few months or even weeks ago. This is the fear that gains traction with every disappointing workout and slow training run we endure. It is the fear that undermines our confidence day by day, replacing it with gnawing doubt.

Runners, like many other people, seek to conquer our fears by clinging to ritual. We have our lucky socks and hats, our favorite old shirts and shoes. We swear by our food choices, our race-morning routines, and our prerace warm-up. Some of these rituals are rooted in experimentation that would make a scientist proud, while others are shrouded in superstition and faith. For example, I personally would never wear a race's shirt before finishing that race. It's a *finisher's* shirt, after all, and wearing it before you cross the finish line could result in a powerful jinx. It just makes sense. Or, at least, it does to me. But however established, these rituals and superstitions hang on with the tenacity of a pit bull, because to a runner, preparation is everything, and if we repeat the exact details that led to past success, then that success can be replicated. We convince ourselves that there will be no failure, no shame, no heartbreak on this day, because we have done everything right. With all the necessaries attended to, success should follow, as surely as night follows day. Fear is conquered.

In a larger sense, though, our fear is not about a single training session, or a particular race. It is about our mortality; it is about our knowledge that there is a limit to our improvement. We know that eventually, inevitably, age, the swiftest runner, will catch us and hang on our backs. Our legs will slow, our finishing times will climb like the temperature on a sweltering day, and we'll realize that we're one mile closer to the end of our life's race. We run every workout and race under this cloud. Just as running fulfills the promise of life, it contains within it the seeds of decline.

But we need not give into this fear. With every strong workout, every fast lap, every personal best, we push the darkness back. To do so requires determination, and yes, pain. Speed workouts hurt, racing hard hurts, but we do it. We do it to push away the fear, to hold onto the illusion of immortality one more moment. To live fully, completely.

With experience, we can learn not to despair with every slow run, secure in the knowledge that a great workout will likely soon follow. Even an occasional bad race won't be the harbinger of doom. Eventually, we know, decline will set in. But not today, not here, not now. I will muzzle this fear, and cover the Earth in great hungry strides, cheating time and decay with every step for as long as I can.

As I pondered these thoughts, I began to see the human body as something of a divine instrument, and running itself as an expression of faith and an affirmation of the wonder of life. This was my private belief, though, and I wasn't eager to make a public declaration of it. Religion was, I felt, a private matter, and I wasn't interested in expressing my views to anyone who might not be interested in hearing about them.

Not everyone else agreed. I once heard about Catherine Ndereba, the great four-time Boston Marathon champion and 2004 Olympic silver medalist, when she graciously spoke to a small crowd of runners before the Barbados Marathon in 2003. She was open and warm, and everything you could hope for in a celebrity.

But Catherine began her talk by thanking God for her accomplishments, and referred again and again to her faith as the source of her power. I shifted uneasily, and I thought I saw others do the same. We weren't interested in talking about religion; we wanted to talk about running, and questions from the crowd steered her away from religion by asking her instead about her training schedule and her views on her competitors. I respect Catherine's beliefs, and admire her great ability, determination, and courage, but I didn't much like being preached to.

I came to feel uncomfortable with another expression of faith in the running community as well: those runners who literally wear their beliefs of their sleeves. I began seeing slogans like "With God All Things Are Possible" splashed across their shirts, followed in short order by others bearing biblical quotes and psalms. Not what I would do, but it really wasn't any of my business. But then one day I passed a runner with a shirt declaring "Jesus is my coach." Really? What speed work does Jesus recommend for marathoners? Does Jesus believe in effort-based training, or does He use a stopwatch? Does Jesus recommend supplements? Of course, I said none of those things to him; I didn't want be rude or offensive. But flip declarations of faith are, in my view, little more than advertising slogans, and I don't like them.

There is a role for faith in running, as in all of life. All runners have faith, of one kind or another; it's what enables us to try going beyond the limits that we once thought would stop us. But all runners know, too, that faith is only the safety net; real achievement comes from our own sweat, from our conscious choice to sacrifice and work hard. Making choices is the foundation for all morality, and rather than relying on faith to guide us in our actions, we should fashion our actions to reflect our faith. Running, to me, is what the cathedral was to the masses in the Middle Ages: a visible declaration of the wonder of creation. For me, running is the best expression of a runner's faith. Through pain and injury, and success, we are who we are, and become who we want to be.

My quest continued.

Running Tip #4

Dealing with Injuries

Injuries happen. The trick is not just to avoid injury, but to respond intelligently when you feel one coming on. If you respond quickly and correctly when you develop a problem, you'll be back running at 100 percent in almost no time at all. Generally, cutting back on training, and stretching, strengthening, and icing the area will help. Thinking that you could just bully your body into submission, however, will *not* work. Trust me, I know.

Here's a short list of the most common training ailments, with suggested treatments. As with any injury, if symptoms persist for more than a week or two, worsen, or if the pain feels sharp rather than dull, you should see a doctor.

- *Black toe.* The toenail turns black, and sometimes falls off. This is a sign that your shoes are too small, and the toe is jamming against the front of the shoe, resulting in bruising of the nail bed. The fix? Buy shoes that are at least a half size or more larger than your dress shoes.
- *Knee pain—on the front.* This is probably patella tendonitis, and is caused by excessive movement of the knee cap over the knee joint. Insufficient muscle strength in the front of the upper leg—the quadriceps muscles, particularly on the inner side—is usually to blame. Do leg strengthening exercises such as squats, leg presses, or lunges.

- *Knee pain—on the outside.* Called iliotibial band syndrome, this is an inflammation of the muscle and connective tissue running from the upper front hip bone (ilium) down along the outside of the leg, over the outside of the knee, down to the kneecap and calf (tibia bone). Tightness causes the IT band to rub against the outside of the knee, causing pain. Treat with ice and self-massage, and stretch until you feel tightness in your hip and backside.
- *Knee pain—on the back of the knee.* This is often caused by tightness in the hamstrings. Stretch your hamstrings and do self-massage.
- *Pain on the heel or arch.* This is likely plantar fasciitis, an inflammation of the connective tissue in that area. A common indicator of plantar fasciitis is pain in the arch first thing in the morning. Treat with gentle stretching and icing.
- *Pain on the front of the lower leg/shin.* Likely shin splints, a result of training too intensely too soon, especially on hard surfaces. Ice by massaging the area with a frozen cup of water, holding the open end on the affected area. Strengthen the area by doing "duckwalks"—walking once a day back and forth across a room on your heels with your toes up in the air for 5–10 minutes.

Mountain Madness

In the summer of 1998, I was just over a third of the way to my 100-marathon goal—close enough to claim to know what I was doing, but far enough to still not be able to imagine actually achieving it. When I sat down and thought about all the miles and races before me, I felt farther away from my goal than ever. I realized that the only way to keep on my path was to ignore that I was on it; by refusing to acknowledge how far I had to go, I would be able to keep putting one foot in front of the other. It was the same strategy that I used in each race I ran. As I told people, I never imagined running 26.2 miles at a time—I saw myself as running a single mile twenty-six times in a row. Somehow, it that made all the difference. But now, to reach the ultimate finish line, I would have to extend this trick to years, not just hours.

Some runners seem to maintain their motivation through familiarity, returning to the same races year after year, like salmon returning to their spawning grounds. They find comfort in running familiar ground, and take pride in not missing a single edition of their favorite races. Or perhaps they discover new, subtle things about the course every time they run them, like a Shakespearean scholar who finds new meaning and artistry with every reading of *Macbeth*.

That's not me. I have run certain marathons multiple times—Boston, New York, and the Marine Corps Marathon—but by and large I want to see something new and different every time I race. For me, there's no greater way to experience a new place than on the run, and there's no better way to distract myself from pain and fatigue than by running down unfamiliar roads. That's really why I began to travel to run in the first place.

Of course, not all races are created equal; some are more exotic and challenging than others. And then there are some that some races that are so far off the beaten path that it seems misleading to simply call them marathons. The Pikes Peak Marathon is one such race.

Pikes Peak is a 14,110-foot-high granite mountain in central Colorado, thrusting skyward from the city of Colorado Springs, with the smaller town of Manitou Springs hugging its eastern flank. The fledgling United States gained title over the mountain in the Louisiana Purchase, and it was named for Zebulon Pike, the man President Jefferson sent to survey the southwestern border of the new territory in 1806. Pike tried to scale the mountain, but was turned back by a blizzard. The summit was finally conquered in 1820, but the surrounding area wasn't settled for another fifty years. In 1873, the U.S. Army built a weather station on the summit, and by 1888 a toll road had been built to the top. A cog railroad was soon added, and by 1901 the first automobile climbed the peak. In 1918, a hiking trail to the top was completed, named the Barr Trail, for the father and son team who constructed it.

Once it became possible to reach the top, human nature being what it is, people began to challenge each other to race to the summit. An auto race was held in 1916, and then, on Sunday, June 28, 1936, twenty-five men and two women lined up for the first Pikes Peak footrace. Nineteen made it to the top. Twenty years would pass before another such race was attempted.

On Friday, August 10, 1956, fourteen runners lined up to race once more to the top, this time in honor of the 150th anniversary of Zebulon Pike's mission. According to legend, the race was the result of a bet between smokers and nonsmokers. As it turned out, no one fared especially well, as only four people made it to the summit. But the race had touched something in people's imagination, and this time it would not die. It was held again the following year, and then again, until it became an established event. Slowly the field of participants grew from a handful of lunatics the first several years, to several hundred lunatics by the 1970s, and then to several thousand lunatics by the 1990s. It turned out that there was a bottomless supply of lunatics who wanted to throw themselves at the mountain, but because the Barr Trail was too narrow to allow a large field of runners, most of these would-be ascenders had to be turned away. Despite the difficulty of getting into the race, or perhaps because of it, enthusiasm for the event grew. The Pikes Peak Marathon had become an institution.

I wasn't aware of any of this history in 1998 when I mailed off my application to Colorado. I just wanted this race to be my thirty-seventh marathon. Lady Luck must have smiled on my application, though, because soon I received a confirmation of entry, along with a twenty-page information booklet. I was a bit mystified. Usually prerace instructions aren't longer than a page or two. But this booklet had twenty pages of instructions and warnings. *Twenty pages!* What had I gotten myself into?

I kicked off my shoes, threw myself onto my couch, and began to read. What surprised me about the race was the sheer volume of things to worry about. First, of course, was the climb. While most marathons have a significant hill or two, this one was nothing *but* hill; runners climb 7,815 feet up, and then race 7,815 feet down. The toll on the legs would be staggering, as muscles and joints would be tested in every possible way.

But that's not even the worst of it. The race *starts* at 6,295 feet above sea level, and climbs above the timberline where no tree can grow, into the thin air above 14,000 feet. At those heights, breathing becomes difficult, and running becomes almost unthinkable. The booklet recommended that participants train themselves in the technique of forced breathing, in which the diaphragm is repeatedly pushed to take in more air without exhausting the chest wall muscles.

But that wasn't even the worst of it. Apart from the climb and the altitude, there was the volatility of the summer weather on Pikes Peak to worry about. It was said to be utterly and dangerously unpredictable. "Pikes Peak can have rapid and extreme weather changes several times each day," the booklet warned. "Chilling rain, snow and sleet showers, high winds and dramatic temperature changes can occur [on race day] in August." The temperatures could drop by as much as fifty degrees from the starting line in Manitou Springs to the mountain peak. But that wasn't the real problem, the booklet insisted. The greatest danger to runners actually comes from sudden lightning storms above the tree line.

I put the booklet down and looked at the ceiling, pondering what I had just read. The contents of the booklet sounded frightening, and the chances for a flawless marathon looked slim. In fact, from the look of things, I would be lucky just to make it back alive and in one piece.

I smiled.

After conquering the challenge of simply getting into the race, I had to decide how to adjust my training to handle the unusual demands that the race would make on my body. The race organizers suggested arriving in Colorado two weeks before the event in order to begin acclimatizing to the altitude. Much as I would like to have done that, my boss, Uncle Sam, seemed to have other priorities, and I just couldn't take the time off. Other than constructing a hyperbaric tent over my bed to mimic high altitude—which I did consider for a hot second—my plan was just to fly out there the day before the race and hope for the best.

Training for the climb itself was also a matter of hope. I spent long hours laboring on the stepper machine and running hills, betting that would prepare me for the mountain. As for the dealing with the weather, I planned to bring enough gear to be prepared for any contingency. I packed layers and throwaway clothes—enough, really, for a week's worth of racing.

Finally, there was nothing left to do but rest and fly out to Colorado. I arrived in Manitou Springs in the early afternoon the day before the race, and spent some time walking around town before picking up my race packet. On the outskirts of town was the beautiful and aptly named Garden of the Gods, where a walking path snaked around pale red monoliths and rock outcrops. Manitou Springs itself looks like it had gracefully made the transition from mining town to tourist attraction, but without being infected with too much gaudiness. The streets were lined with small shops and restaurants nestled in century-old buildings. You had the feeling it wouldn't be all that unnatural to see a stagecoach rumble past. All this was interesting enough, but my thoughts were elsewhere. I wanted to get my race number and focus on the task at hand.

Usually, race organizers set up shop in a conference room of the host hotel, which is where you expect to go to pick up your race packet. Not so at Pikes Peak. Organizers set up their tables in a park, giving would-be racers a chance to look up at the Peak before they accepted their race number. Rather than filling runners with dread, however, the sight of the Peak seemed to inspire excitement in the race crowd. Newcomers and veterans alike seemed like so many greyhounds in the slip, waiting for the bell to ring. I tried to ignore it. I wanted to be calm, and save all my energy for the race.

The following morning I found myself shoulder to shoulder with other runners in Manitou Springs, near the park I had visited the day before. It was a cool morning, and I could see the breath of the runners around me as they stretched, pawed at the ground with their feet, and looked skyward toward our goal. This is the most difficult time for a runner—the twilight between preparing for a race and actually running.

There is nothing left to do but worry about things that had gone wrong in training, and there is not yet the reassurance that comes with actual racing, when the body tells you that everything will be okay. This is just the waiting, and it can seem endless.

That time passed, though, as it always does, and the blast of the starter's gun released us. We raced through town, past the storefronts and homes, seeking out the entrance to the Barr Trail. Soon we found it. We plunged into the woods and started to climb in earnest. Runners jockeyed for position on the narrow trail, eager to spend their nervous energy. I held my position, but I didn't worry too much about skipping ahead. Passing people was not going to be my concern this day; I just wanted to make it up and back in one piece.

The air was clean and fresh, and the leaves around me were a vivid green as I settled into a smooth rhythm. The climbs were mixed with flat stretches, where our footfalls were muffled by soft dirt. Eventually, I realized that the forest was thinning, and that the soaring trees were shrinking. Soon, they gave way to large bushes, and then they, too, disappeared, replaced by pale yellow and orange rock. We had reached the tree line, the point at which the forest had to turn back from the altitude and climate of the mountain. Now things would get interesting.

The sun shone brightly now as I made my way up the rocky incline. The gentleness of the forest floor had disappeared with the trees, and now I had to make my way over loose rock and sharp boulders. Looking up the distant cliff-side in front of me, I could see a line of tiny runners zigzagging the switchbacks, looking like ants on a foraging mission. To my left stretched out the vastness of the southwest and an endless blue sky. It was a beautiful sight, but like the siren's call, it could lead me to disaster if gazing at it caused me to stumble and fall on the rocks underfoot. This was not the time for long, admiring gazes toward distant peaks.

I came across Barr Camp, a little oasis on the trail where volunteers waited with water and snacks. Their enthusiasm was infectious, and I threw myself back on the trail with renewed energy. Soon, though, my breathing became labored, and I realized that it wasn't caused just by the steady climb; the air was getting thinner. Everyone around me was moving slowly, and I joined them in walking the steepest sections of trail. My head started throbbing, and I leaned back on a boulder to rest. I tried to breathe down into my stomach, drawing as much precious air into my lungs as possible. From my rocky perch, I could see runners dotting the trail below me, forming a jagged seam on the mountainside. Wisps of clouds appeared overhead, and I wondered what the temperature was at the peak. I recalled that the race materials said that the typical time up to the half-way point at the top was the same as an entire flatland marathon, plus one half hour. I was starting to believe it.

I took another deep breath and pushed myself off the rock, reclaiming a spot in the line of runners inching their way to the top. I looked up, trying to gauge how much more there was to climb, but every spot I had been sure was the top instead turned out to be only a bend in the trail. I knew I was getting close, though, because the lead runners passed me on their way back down. I marveled at how fresh they looked; while I was struggling to walk, they flew downhill. I couldn't imagine having that kind of energy. For that matter, I could hardly imagine running the 13 miles back down to the finish line, but I refused to let myself think about that. I concentrated on simply putting one foot in front of the other, and blocked out all other thoughts.

The air became cooler, but there weren't any of the dramatic weather changes that we had been warned about. I moved mechanically, gulping air, wondering if there was actually a top to this mountain. And then suddenly, there it was. I had made it up to 14,110 feet, the top floor. There was a visitor center at the top, and plenty of spectators to cheer us on, but there was no time to celebrate. The top of the trail led us through a narrow defile through the rock, where volunteers unceremoniously spun us around and pointed us back downhill.

I pivoted and began to move forward, and then discovered an amazing thing: I could run! And more than that, I could run fast. It was as if I was being sucked into a vortex, and I felt better with every step. I slid on the gravel and hopped over rocks and boulders, spinning on the switchbacks like a car burning rubber on a wild turn. I couldn't believe how great I felt. It was nothing short of miraculous.

I had read that the difference between suffering altitude sickness and feeling fine can be as little as several dozen feet. I don't know if that's true, but I can tell you that each step down restored my strength and confidence. I was having fun. I ate up great chunks of trail with each stride, offering encouragement to the runners still moving toward the top. Like watching a movie in reverse, I saw the bits of brush appear between the orange and yellow rock, followed by small bushes and stunted trees. Soon, I was back in the woods again, below the tree line.

I was still flying, but my legs had started to protest. As much fun as downhill running can be, it's still hell on the quads, which have to work overtime to keep their fool owner from toppling forward and doing a face-plant. Not a problem, though: I had learned long ago how to ignore my screaming legs. I was more concerned about the footing. Downhill running on trail and broken rock is usually a recipe for disaster, but so far I had no problem handling the challenge.

No sooner had that thought entered my mind, hanging in the air like a thought balloon in a comic strip, than I found myself sprawled on the ground with my ankle screaming in pain. I pulled myself upright and took a tentative step. More screaming from below. I had twisted my ankle badly, that much was obvious. But standing alone in the woods, with runners off in the distance in front and behind me, and help—in the form of a rest stop—miles farther down the road, I had no choice but to keep moving. I took a few more easy steps. Not as bad as I first thought, really, once I got moving. I tried an easy jog. That seemed manageable. As I continued running, the pain subsided. Perhaps the adrenaline coursing through my body had blocked it out, or perhaps my body had responded by releasing a good dose of cortisol, a natural anti-inflammatory. Whatever it was, I was grateful for it, and promised to reward my body with a stop at the next aid station to have my ankle wrapped.

With the toughest part of the course behind me, I knew I wouldn't drop out unless I had no choice. I quickly constructed a cost-benefit test: how much of a layoff would I be willing to accept to complete the race? A week? Certainly. A month? Sure. Several months. Well … I guess so. Permanent injury? No, of course not. But how could I tell which of these fates lay in my future if I kept running?

I decided to turn the question around: rather than worry about what might happen, I would look only for clues as to what would certainly happen. Unless permanent injury became obviously inevitable, I would keep running for as long as I could. At the next aid station a volunteer wrapped my ankle tightly, and I was off again, rolling downhill, betting on my ankle against the mountain.

The miles flew by, and soon I was reached the end of the trail. After so many hours of running on dirt and rock, it was strange to be on asphalt again. From there I only had a short piece of running through town to the finish line, and it was mostly downhill. Usually that would be welcome relief, but not now. My quads were screaming at me, and my toes jammed painfully into the front of my shoes with each step. I groaned out loud and rolled my eyes in agony; I didn't think I could stand much more. Finally, there was only one more corner to turn, and there it was: the finish line. The clock read 6 hours 58 minutes.

I collected my medal and sat down in a folding chair in the tent just past the finish line. I had been tested, but I had not broken. My ankle would recover, my toes would heal, and my legs would eventually forgive me, but this moment would never be forgotten.

Looking around me, though, I saw that my injuries paled in comparison to those sustained by other runners. The tent looked like an army triage center. There were bloody elbows and knees, as well as cut and bruised faces. There had obviously been a lot of falling up on the mountain. Despite all the blood and bruises, though, I didn't see any sad faces. We had all survived, and better still, had triumphed. The bloody bandage became a badge of honor, a sign of how close to the edge each of us had pushed ourselves.

Later that night, I laid my still-wrapped ankle on a pillow and slung a bag of ice over it. It was classic RICE therapy: Rest, Ice, Compression, and Elevation. I knew that was the proper way to treat a sprain, and I thought just this once I would play it by the book. I didn't have high expectations.

The next morning, I was surprised to find that the swelling of my ankle had gone down, and that the pain was mostly gone as well. This RICE thing actually worked. Who woulda thunk it? I was back running within just a few days, good as new. Better than new, actually, because I had conquered Pikes Peak, America's toughest marathon. I felt that victory in my 100-marathon quest was now assured. But if I thought that there would be no more challenges, I was greatly mistaken, as I would soon find out.

Running Tip #5

Race Recovery

- *Eat something 15–30 minutes after training or racing.* This will kick-start refueling of your muscles and repair of any cellular damage.
- *Take a cold bath, massage your legs, grab some couch time.* All of these will help move blood and waste products out of your legs.
- *Take the long view.* Plan on needing one day of rest or easy training for every hard mile you raced.
- *Get back to it slowly.* Run no longer than an hour at a time for the first few weeks after a hard marathon.
- *Beware the sniffles.* Your immune system takes a battering on race day, so get plenty of sleep, drink lots of fluids, eat well, wash your hands frequently, and avoid touching your eyes and nose.

The question would not go away. I would go days and weeks without thinking about it, but sooner or later I would figuratively reach into my pocket, pull it out, sit it on a table, and look at it. Why run the marathon? I couldn't seem to find a good, complete answer to that question.

In the years following my first marathon, I had pursued my growing passion for fitness and became a certified personal trainer and running coach, filling my early morning and evening hours with sessions in a local gym, and my weekends coaching charity fund-raising marathon teams. I became a fitness evangelist, preaching and living the healthy life. I did not want to induce any delusions of immortality, though. I told my clients at our first session that our goal was to improve where we could, maintain as best we're able, and extend the quality of our life; nothing less, but nothing more.

This sounded right to me, but it opened a door onto bigger questions. I thought about something I once read former New York Mets and Philadelphia Phillies relief pitcher Tug McGraw had said. After blowing a game, he would ponder something he called the Ice Ball Theory, which went something like this: some day, many millions of years from now, our sun will become a supernova, scorch the earth, and then flame out into nothingness. After that, our planet will wander eternity in a dark void, a giant ice ball hurtling through space. At that point, no one will be around to care that on a sunny afternoon Tug McGraw once served up a home run pitch to lose a baseball game. Tug found it much easier to sleep at night after running that scenario through his mind.

The problem with the Ice Ball Theory, as I soon realized, was that it proved too much. Instead of just showing how little any one mistake matters in the scheme of things, it showed how *nothing* really matters. Not a very comforting idea after all. The question for me, then, became not just why run the marathon, but instead, if all achievement and failure eventually fade into the void equally, why bother doing anything at all?

These philosophical musings suddenly took on an unexpected urgency. One of my new clients, Burt, told me that he was HIV positive, and that he was also undergoing chemotherapy. He seemed uncomfortable talking about his health, and I didn't press for details beyond what I needed to know as his trainer, but I did tell him that I was proud of him for taking control of his life and for trying to improve himself. It was the type of life-affirming act that brought me into training in the first place.

Burt had more body fat than he should have been carrying, and he wasn't as strong as he wanted to be. His self-esteem had also taken a battering from the disease. I knew that training him would be a challenge for both of us. We began slowly, getting him comfortable with the exercises, discovering his limits, and gently pushing them to new levels. As time went by, Burt was amazed to see his strength improving. Soon, he told me, his friends noticed as well, and commented on his changed appearance. Burt also experienced a change of attitude: instead of being the victim of his disease, he began to show confidence and a new enthusiasm for life. I was accustomed to helping people get results, but this was something new for me. Something special was happening.

One day I called Burt to set up another appointment. He sounded scared and very upset. He was feeling very ill, and he told me that a friend was about to take him to the hospital. I told him not to jump to any conclusions, since he had been feeling so good for so long. We would just keep an open mind and wait to hear what the doctors had to say. He promised to call me as soon as he felt up to it.

I was very busy at the time, and several weeks passed before I realized how long it had been since I'd spoken with him. I was filled with dread as I punched his phone number, made infinitely worse when I was patched through into another employee's voice mail. I left several messages at his home number that I hoped sounded calm and upbeat, but that urged him to call me.

Finally he called. It turned out that he had had a bad reaction to the various medications that he was taking. His doctors had given him a transfusion and kept him in the hospital for a week. He had lost a lot of weight and strength, but what was worse, he had also lost his confidence and sense of purpose, and was depressed about the big step backward that he had taken in his fitness program. He said that he doubted that he could get back to where he was before his illness. Not to worry, I told him. As my father used to say when my sisters or I had a setback, this was only a stumble, not a fall. I instructed him to use the weight machines for a week without worrying about how much weight he was lifting, just to get reacquainted with the movements. After that, I would put together another training program for him, and we would set about the task of rebuilding him.

Despite my confidence, Burt was still discouraged. He was sure that we couldn't possibly get back to where we had left off earlier. But I explained to him that as long as the laws of physics, chemistry, and anatomy still apply in our universe, we were sure to climb right back up the fitness ladder. It was just a matter of time. That's the wonder of the human body: give it a reasonable challenge, and it will rise to the occasion.

Burt took my advice, and we resumed our training. Soon, his strength and muscle mass started to return. It was only later that he told me how much my encouragement had helped him through his dark times. Instead of spiraling downward in free fall, he was able to once again take control of his life by having a plan to follow. Fitness wasn't just restoring his body; it was restoring his hope and his faith.

Burt continued to regain his strength, but his battle with his disease also continued. He moved to Boston to be closer to his family. We kept in touch, but then, suddenly, I stopped hearing from him. I found out that Burt had died from his illness. I'm usually very positive and upbeat about life, but I was suddenly filled with a sense of futility. What had it mattered that we had improved his strength 30 percent last year? What was the point of all that hard work?

I began then to think of my high school biochemistry lessons, about the energy bonds that held the electrons of our molecules in their orbits. The solidity of our bodies, of the entire physical world, really, was just an illusion; at the atomic level, there was more empty space than matter. I began to imagine my body—all of our bodies—not as whole organisms, but rather as collections of molecules bound together by only by these energy bonds. What if these molecules suddenly decided to disperse? What if the only thing keeping our atoms from flying apart was our own willpower, our stubborn refusal to cease to exist? How long could any of us be expected to hold these millions of molecules together before we tired and failed?

I began to think of the endless upkeep all of our bodies require to stay in proper trim. Every day, the body needs to be fed, to be trained, to be stretched and washed. The heart beats, the blood flows, and waste is eliminated. Sleep provides some respite, but then the cycle begins again, every day, until we cease to exist.

It was an exhausting thought. I began to imagine an escape from the tyranny of this routine, of a time and place without decay, where there is no struggle to improve and maintain one's collection of molecules. A place where there is no injury, no need to train, no need to run. A place where there is stillness.

I had reached the bottom, a place beyond the marathon, beyond running, beyond wondering about the active life. I had peered into a dark hole where existence itself is questioned. From the Big Bang through the thousands of millennia of existence, to the end of time and a return to the stillness from which it all was born, I saw that nothing truly endured but the stillness itself.

I shook off these dark thoughts, recoiling like a child touching a hot oven. Down that hole is a place where existence denies itself. A place without change is a place without the possibility of improvement, without challenge. Because it has neither success nor failure, it is a place without meaning. A place of such stillness is a place of death.

I decided to imagine my body differently. Instead of seeing it on the verge of pulling apart, I see my molecules spinning tightly in their orbits, strengthened and nourished by their numbers and their energy bonds. Every movement strengthens them further, and they shine brighter in the flexing and stretching of my muscles. I returned to solid ground, within the sphere of my experience. This was now familiar to me, because I knew the peaceful fatigue that I felt when I lived the active life; I knew that the joy of exertion conquers the stillness.

My body spoke in one voice, and made its choice. It chose movement, it chose running, it chose the marathon. It chose life. That was enough for now.

To the End of the Earth

When January 1999 rang in, I had been racing for twelve years, and had run a total of 39 marathons. I had run up and down a mountain, and I had qualified for the Boston Marathon. In short, I felt that I was quite experienced. I had become something of a marathon connoisseur; while some people collected art or fine wine, I collected marathons. My collection had a serious flaw, however; I had yet to race away from American soil. That had to change. But I wanted my first race off American soil to be memorable. True to my nature, I wanted it to be *inspiring*. And I found it. After running my 40th marathon in Houston, I picked a jaw-dropping race for my 41st. In fact, I wasn't going to simply run a marathon; I was going to undertake an honest-to-goodness *expedition*. I had signed on for a race at the end of the world. I was going to run the Antarctica Marathon.

To be honest, the idea of running a marathon in Antarctica hadn't been burning in my thoughts. In fact, the idea never even occurred to me until I received a phone call from my friend Ginny Turner, a fellow marathoner who was also pursuing the fifty-state Holy Grail. I had met Ginny in South Bend, Indiana—at a marathon, of course. Standing inside Notre Dame's stadium after crossing the finish line, I explained to her the legendary "Touchdown Jesus," the image of Christ painted larger than life on the side of a building that can be seen from inside the stadium, beyond the goalposts. Some nameless smart-aleck many years ago had noticed how the figure's upraised arms resembled an umpire's signal for a score, and so a legend was born. Ginny and I became fast friends after that, and kept in touch over the following months, comparing marathon notes and schedules. So I wasn't at all surprised when she called me one day to tell me that she was planning to run another marathon. But I never expected to hear that it would be in Antarctica.

Ginny wanted me to join her on the expedition. I was interested, of course, but skeptical. I had been working as an attorney for a decade, but as a government employee, my salary was still low, and I was still saddled with massive student loans to repay. This would be an expensive adventure, and I just didn't think I could manage the cost. But as I opened my mouth to explain to Ginny why I couldn't go, she hit me with her final sales pitch: when she returned later and told me all about the journey, I would realize that I should have gone with her, and would forever regret not going. That stopped me cold. She was absolutely right. I found myself saying yes to her, even as my mind scrambled to figure out a way to pay for it. I got off the phone and signed up for the expedition that was to take place the following month.

Having committed to the race, I thought it would be a good idea to find out exactly what I'd gotten myself into. Once I received the race materials, I settled back for a nice read. The Antarctic Marathon—also called The Last Marathon, because that's the last place a sane person would think of running a race—is held in February, at the height of the austral summer. It was organized by a travel company that catered to marathoners, a reflection of the financial clout of the burgeoning marathon culture. Our group was comprised of over 160 runners from around the world, led by a team of naturalists who would handle technical matters and shore landings, and who would explain this vast wasteland to us.

My journey began with a 10½-hour overnight flight from New York's JFK airport to Buenos Aires. As if that wasn't challenging enough, I managed to arrive at the gate only 15 minutes before departure. This brand of reckless tardiness was, unfortunately, bred in my bones; the rest of my family treats deadlines no more respectfully than I do. Upon my arrival at the gate, the airline staff was both relieved and annoyed to see me, knowing that a member of a large group on the flight was unaccounted for just moments before the doors were to close. In their haste to get me on board, they assigned me to the first available seat they could find. It was in first class. Not really a good incentive for me to correct my errant behavior. Of course, this occurred in the years before the post-9/11 security clampdown, when such last-minute adventures were possible.

After arriving in Buenos Aires and meeting other members of the team, I joined a few of them for a little walk around the city, to shake off the kinks and to get the lay of the land. Getting around Buenos Aires turned out to be easy; it's really a walkers' city, crisscrossed with broad, beautiful boulevards, and filled with beautiful European architecture. Avenida 9 de Julio, at some 600 feet across, is one of the broadest thoroughfares in the world, while Florida and Lavale avenues are open pedestrian malls. We saw tango dancers whirling among street musicians, vendors in the flea market of San Telmo, and one of the copies of Rodin's *Thinker* pondering ceaselessly in front of the Congreso Nacional. Nearby was the beautiful opera house, the Teatro Colón, where Toscanini and Caruso had performed. And, of course, we made our pilgrimage to Eva Perón's tomb in the Recoleta cemetery. The site itself is unremarkable, but the cemetery as a whole is fascinating. It's a virtual city of the dead, filled entirely with mausoleums, each vying to be the most ostentatious.

Being a native New Yorker, however, I also insisted on descending belowground to check out the subway system. I discovered that the stations were like underground cities, containing dozens of small shops and eateries. The platforms were lined with beautiful ceramic murals, and the trains were wood-paneled antiques.

Making our way back to our hotel, we strolled along Puerto Madero, where a canal lined with fine restaurants opens into the Río de la Plata. Couples strolled the promenade, sharing ice cream cones and whispered conversations. When we finally made it back to our hotel room, I fell into my bed and, as my grandmother would have said, slept like the dead.

By the following morning, I was recovered and ready to run. I found the Parqué Natural y Zonade Reserva Ecológica Costanera Sur, just east of Puerto Madero, where I did laps on a popular running and cycling circuit: an 8-kilometer hardpack dirt and gravel road that encircled the park. Later, I joined the full team and the travel company staff for a debriefing. In addition to other warnings, the hotel staff cautioned us about a tourist scam that involved one conspirator spraying mustard on an unsuspecting victim, while another conspirator suddenly appears and offers to help clean off the mustard. That's when bandits suddenly appear from nowhere to snatch bags and cameras from the distracted victim, and run off in different directions. This must be a joke, I said, but I was assured that it was true.

As if to prove the point, Ginny and I later got mustarded while wandering around near the Teatro Colon opera house. Although we didn't see who had surreptitiously sprayed us with mustard, we knew what to expect once we saw that we'd suffered a condiment attack, so we ignored offers of "help" from a nearby elderly woman, and quickly walked off before any bandits appeared. I was indignant; I didn't grow up on the streets of Manhattan to get mugged in Buenos Aires!

Finally, it was time to begin the next leg of our journey: a 4½-hour flight south to Patagonia, at the tip of South America. On the way down, strong winds buffeted our plane, and the pilot made an emergency landing to wait out the squalls. We stayed in our seats as the jet shuddered on the tarmac, silently exchanging worried glances among ourselves. Finally, the winds died down, and we returned to the air. As far as I was concerned, this is when the expedition officially began.

Eventually we arrived in a small but beautiful airport, topped with a latticework of timber and glass. We were in Ushuaia, in Argentinean Tierra del Fuego, the land of fire, named for the burning torches along the shore that were spotted by passing sailors. It was an apt name, because it was a dramatic place. The wind blew, the rain fell, clouds drifted in and out, and sometimes the sun even shone—often all within half an hour. The turbulence of the weather was echoed in the forbidding look of the cragged peaks surrounding the city. I had heard the place described as the City at the End of the World, and that seemed appropriate, too. Despite the human footprint on the land, it still appeared primordial.

Ushuaia is small, but it still offered some interesting sights, like the old prison, now open for nonconvict visitors. There was also a large nature preserve, and, most interesting to me, little houses mounted on sleds. As I learned, real estate ownership had been a loose concept at the tip of the world. When a dispute over land occurred, local residents traditionally solved the problem by simply moving their houses across the road. There weren't many of these sled-houses left, though; in Ushuaia, as in so many northern cities, open land was becoming a less and less readily available commodity.

With our time in Ushuaia concluded, our group met on the dock to board one of two chartered Russian research ships for the two-and-a-half day journey south through the treacherous Drake Passage. I had signed on with the smaller ship, which carried forty-six passengers. At this point we met our full expedition staff, led by Shane Evoy, a large, bearded, garrulous man who seemed perfectly suited to his work. The staff seemed to be a fun and enthusiastic bunch. One crew member confided to me that they had been looking forward to seeing us for weeks, since our ultra-fit group was a nice change from the often sedentary, elderly tourists that they usually escort to the Southern Continent.

Along with the expedition staff was the Russian crew who manned the vessel. Not many of them spoke English, but they proved themselves to be very hard-working, prompting me to learn at least one word of Russian: *spaciba*, meaning thank you. We were allowed to go up to the bridge and watch them in action, as long as we kept out of their way. The kitchen staff was equally good, providing three great meals a day, plus snacks. As a bachelor living alone back in the States, I found myself eating better aboard the ship than I did at home.

The ship itself was comfortable, but utilitarian. There was no lido deck or pool, but there was a bar—well-used on our trip—a lecture room, a small library, and even a sauna. Bathrooms and shower stalls were shared, with plenty of hot water available. The cabins were wood-paneled, each with two closets and a desk. Bunks had reading lights and curtains for privacy. Laundry service was available on the ship as well, though that seemed to be the kind of extra frill this group wouldn't go for. We thought ourselves hardier stock than that.

As part of the prerace package, I received an informational guidebook, which I devoured along with a score of other books on the history and environment of the White Continent. Once on the ship, I watched films and attended lectures offered by the expedition's naturalists. Surprisingly it wasn't hard to get a feel for the place. Antarctica, I learned, had no indigenous people, and was populated only by whales, penguins, seals, a few species of birds, and the shrimplike krill on which many of the other animals fed. Not much of anything, really.

Still, Antarctica proved fascinating in the way a simple, pure color on canvas can be captivating. But I couldn't help viewing all of the information I came across through the eyes of a runner, so when I read about air avalanches, called *katabatic winds*, I felt myself gritting my teeth. While most wind is caused by differences in air pressure, these winds are caused instead by gravity. Just as hot air rises, cold air can fall, and in Antarctica, cold air sometimes falls so rapidly that it can blow at 40 mph or more. I knew that if this occurred during my race, there wouldn't be much I could do about it other than lean in and fight like hell. As I read about those winds, I suddenly realized that nothing I had done before—including Pikes Peak—had really prepared me for what I might find down here on race day.

No Antarctic education is complete, of course, without learning the story of exploration. The tales of courage, suffering and vanity left me awestruck. Especially memorable was the Shackleton expedition. Ernest Shackleton set out in 1914 on the aptly named *Endurance* to become the first man to traverse the Antarctic continent, the South Pole having already been won. Before he even managed to reach land, however, his ship became ice-locked. All efforts to free the ship failed, and by late 1915, the shifting mass of ice had crushed his ship, leaving the crew to live on the ice with three lifeboats and whatever supplies they were able to salvage from the *Endurance* before it went under. Eventually, the ice broke up, and the crew took to the lifeboats and made their way through rough seas and freezing weather to a spit of rock called Elephant Island.

Their new home was well outside any established shipping lanes, and realizing that their chances for rescue were slim—and recognizing, too, that a steady diet of nothing but penguin meat was taking a terrible toll on his crew—Shackleton set out with a few handpicked men in one of the lifeboats to find help. In what has been hailed as one of the all-time greatest feats of seamanship, Shackleton managed to steer his 22-foot open boat 800 nautical miles through wild and freezing seas to King George Island, where there was a whaling station. But the currents had forced Shackleton to land on the far side of the island, and now he and his crew had to scale uncharted mountains to reach the station. Once again, Shackleton accomplished the impossible, and after they stumbled into town, the station's captain could scarcely believe the tale that the ragged, unshaven, exhausted band of men told him. By August 1916, Shackleton managed to secure a ship and rescue his crew. All hands made it back home alive.

Lying back in my warm and comfortable bunk, I could scarcely believe such a thing had ever happened. But there was a postscript to the story. When Shackleton returned to England, he expected to be hailed as a hero, but in his absence all of Europe had been embroiled in the bloodbath known as the Great War. Faced with the story of men who risked their lives for adventure and glory, and who lived to tell the tale, a weary and grief-stricken public gave a collective shrug. Shackleton's agonies paled in comparison to the tragedies *they* had endured.

Somehow, I felt an odd kinship with Shackleton. He set out to face suffering—perhaps not as much as he bargained for, but guaranteed suffering nonetheless—when it would have been just as easy and acceptable to stay home. Although his aim was clearly fame and fortune, I felt that there must have been something more to make the deprivation worthwhile: a desire, a need, to test his own limits. That much resonated with me. I knew that I, too, valued suffering for its own sake, though mostly just in 26.2-mile doses.

Our ship made its way from Ushuaia through the Beagle Channel into open water, escorted by Magellanic penguins swimming below, and albatross soaring above. After rounding Cape Horn, we entered the dreaded Drake Passage, where the Atlantic and the Pacific oceans converge to create the roughest seas on Earth. Waves routinely crest there at 25 to 30 feet, and often higher. For me, surviving the Drake was the biggest challenge of the trip. I never had what you would call a strong stomach, and I was well aware of the irony of my being on a ship on high seas after a lifetime of enduring queasiness on ferries and carnival rides.

I hadn't come unarmed. I'd prepared for the "Drake Shake" with every antinausea treatment known to science, and a few others besides. My doctor provided me with antinausea scopolamine patches, my pharmacist provided me with acupressure wristbands and old-fashioned Dramamine, and an herbalist sold me ginger candies to settle my stomach. I also knew that gazing at a stable point on the distant horizon while breathing deep gulps of fresh air would be helpful. With all these remedies in my bag of tricks, I felt as ready as I could possibly be.

I was surprised, then, and even a bit disappointed, to find that the seas were calm. Instead of the Drake Shake, we got the Drake Lake. All that worrying for nothing. With such calm waters, I was even able to get in a workout, ducking though portholes and sliding around the corners of the deck as I ran for 45 minutes. Several team members joined in, and we quickly dubbed our workout the Drake 5K. Much to our delight, we were told by the expedition staff that the Russian crew thought we were crazy.

After two-and-a-half days of listening to lectures, socializing at the bar, and gazing out at the horizon, we finally saw a few bits of sea ice. Then we had our first glimpse of land. We were out of the Drake Passage and were approaching the South Shetland Islands, just off the Antarctic Peninsula. It was summer in Antarctica, but the temperature was still in the 20s and low 30s, with gusting winds bringing it down into the teens. We all dug out our waterproof gear as the expedition staff prepared for our first landing. There weren't any docks or piers to welcome us, so all landings were wet. After scampering down a gangway, we climbed ten at a time into inflated, motorized boats called Zodiacs, which were driven as far up onto the rocky beach as possible. One by one, we swung our legs over the side and charged the surf like soldiers at Normandy. After experiencing this landing, I understood why we had each been required to acknowledge in writing that we were not guaranteed a marathon; if bad weather made a wet landing hazardous, there would be no race.[2]

When I first signed up for the expedition, the tour company director told me that although I was coming down to Antarctica for the marathon, it would slip into lesser significance when compared to everything else I would see down there. He was right. Our first stop was a visit to the Polish scientific base camp, followed by a landing at a penguin rookery, where thousands of Chinstrap and Gentoo penguins mingled about, molting and nesting. Following the staff's directions, we sat very still, and soon the cute, impossibly clumsy little guys came right up to us, climbing onto our laps and nibbling on our pant legs. I captured their cooing and braying on a micro tape recorder, which I thought would provide a perfect soundtrack for slide shows back home. All of this was wonderful, but one thing was not: the smell. These were wild animals, after all, and when they crowd together in one place by the thousands, there were bound to be repercussions.

Not so different from runners at a starting line, actually.

After making several other Zodiac landings, including one to the ruins of a former whaling station at Deception Island, we finally made our way to King George Island, where the staff laid out our marathon course. It was to be a double figure-8 loop, and it was every bit as difficult as we imagined it would be. The first loop of the figure 8 (which would also be the third loop as I made my way around the course for the second time), was a 1½-mile run across a rocky beach, up the side of a glacier, and back. We would then run along rough dirt roads and across a frigid stream past several scientific bases.

---

2 In fact, in the very next Antarctic Marathon expedition, held two years later, a landing was not possible. Nonetheless, in a feat that could be described as either monumentally determined or frighteningly compulsive, a marathon was held onboard the ship, consisting of 420 laps around the deck. Let's just say that I'm glad that I didn't have to consider that option.

This island, and indeed, this entire frozen continent, is governed by the Antarctic Treaty system, which provides that while no country may claim sovereignty over these lands or engage in commercial exploitation of its natural resources, countries may establish scientific bases to conduct research. A human presence is especially evident on King George Island, where seven nations built small villages. Our group was hosted by the Uruguayans, and their base would mark the start and finish of the race.

On race day, we awoke early and ate breakfast. The waters were calm, so we were able to land without incident. We were allowed into the small dining hall in the Uruguayan base to prepare ourselves for the race, but because their living space was modest, we weren't allowed to keep any of our bags inside the building. It was a small inconvenience, and no one seemed to mind. We also had to provide our own water bottles, which the staff placed out on the course for us.

As we lined up for the start of the race, I saw that several of the local residents had taken up the tour leader's offer to join us for the race. Most striking was an older, plump Russian woman who wore running shorts, a T-shirt, and oven mitts instead of the tights, long sleeve shirts, jackets and running gloves that the rest of us wore. Clearly, improvisation is a crucial skill down there.

The starting signal was given—a horn blare from a megaphone—and we dashed across the broken rock toward the glacier. I had expected that its surface would be a slippery sheet of ice, but instead I found it to more like an ice chip mountain. That made it not only more treacherous than I was expecting, but also prone to suddenly giving way, leaving a runner knee-deep in a previously hidden hole. Cracks in the ice only compounded the problem, making for very slow going.

After reaching the turnaround point on top of the glacier, and smiling for the official race cameraman, I carefully made my way back down past the Uruguayan base, and then continued along rough dirt roads, over steep hills, and past a small lake, toward the Chilean base and on to the Chinese and the Russian bases that lay beyond. I later learned that one member of our team stopped into the Chinese base, where he bartered for a watch and was treated to a warm drink.

Not being as creative, I just focused on the race. A spot of warm weather created mud fields for us to slog through, as curious penguins watched closely. There was something eerily magnetic about the penguins; I saw more than one runner veer off course toward them, as if hypnotized. A few shouts brought them back to their senses and to the racecourse. More perilous, though, were the skuas: big, darkly colored birds that were reported to be fiercely protective of their nests. If we wandered too close to one of their nests, we were told, a skua would swoop down and attack us. The problem, though, was that their nests weren't always in plain view. At one point on the course several of us apparently came too close, because a skua took wing and made repeated dives at us, which we warded off by wildly swinging our arms.

After more than five hours of sliding, mucking, hiking, and even running across the Antarctic tundra, I finally crossed the finish line. Marathon number 41 was in the books. I was neither the first nor the last runner to finish. Since the fancy new trail shoes I had brought had given me some nasty blisters, I was perfectly happy to have just made it through the whole way. We returned to our ship to clean up, nap, and fill our bellies, and then were transported to the larger ship for an onboard awards presentation.

The following day, we set off for another highlight: our dramatic landing on the Antarctic mainland itself. We boarded the Zodiac boats again, and made out way to a landing on the Antarctic Peninsula. It was similar to the other landings we had made, but somehow, it felt different. Gazing at the rock and ice around us, I think we all felt that we were finally, truly, at the bottom of the world, at one of the last unspoiled expanses left on Earth. I wondered whether our brand of ecotourism was helping to build political support to preserve it, or whether, despite our precautions and good intentions, we were the beginning of a flood of tourists who would unwittingly destroy it.[3] Our usually rambunctious group had fallen into silence; I supposed that they were all wondering the same thing.

And then it was back through the Drake. This time the seas were not so friendly, as the ship pitched and rolled through 35- and 40-foot waves. We were banned from the outside deck, as well as the bridge. Digging deep into my bag of tricks, I managed to keep my insides inside and my stomach quiet, provided that I stayed prone in my bed. Strangely enough, the same corkscrewing, rolling action that slammed me from wall to wall and turned my stomach when I tried walking felt comforting once I lay down. I decided not to fight it; I buried myself under my covers, and drifted off to sleep, rocked by the southern ocean like a baby in a crib.

Two days later we landed in Ushuaia, and few days after that I was standing in a terminal at JFK airport in New York City. It was snowing, and the temperature was near zero—colder, in fact, than it was just then in Antarctica. I stood for a few minutes off to the side of the arrival gate, trying to adjust to the sudden noise and bustle. I had never before felt so different from everyone else.

---

3 My fears were, unfortunately, well-founded. In November 2007, the cruise ship *MS Explorer* sank in Antarctica. While all 154 passengers and crew were rescued, the ship left behind a mile-long oil spill that could not be immediately cleaned up because of bad weather. As scientists worried about the effect of the spill on the 2,500 penguins who were about to pass that area, the Argentinean government announced that it was considering limiting the level of ecotourism to the area.

Running Tip #6

Preparing for Antarctica

- *Don't bother with speed work.* The Antarctic Marathon isn't for PRs, so instead, concentrate training on hills and trails.
- *Bring the right clothing.* Dress in layers: running tights, a long sleeve wicking top, and lightweight running gloves to keep warm, covered by wind pants, a lightweight water-resistant running jacket, and lightweight water-resistant gauntlet mittens over your gloves. Shed clothing cautiously, since the wind could suddenly pick up and the temperature drop.
- *Bring the right gear.* Use trail shoes, gaiters (short, protective ankle sleeves that help keep out dirt and water), and mini-crampons (rubber outsoles with short, plastic spikes for better traction on ice).
- *Bring a disposable, panoramic camera.* After all, this is a once-in-a-lifetime kind of race.

Finally: Boston!

After returning home from Antarctica, I felt oddly depressed. For the first time as a runner, I felt unmotivated. I realized that Antarctica was to blame. I had harbored so much anticipation for the race that once it was over, I felt let down. The Boston Marathon was coming up in just two months, and I couldn't afford a training slump. To properly prepare for Boston, I needed another marathon to restore my motivation and keep me in prime condition. That's how I came to run the 1999 Los Angeles Marathon.

Signing up for the race was the easy part, but I was a bit sloppy on figuring out the logistics. I had traveled alone to run the race, and ended up staying in a hotel about 8 miles or so from the race start. I took a taxi to the race packet pick-up the day before the marathon, which was located near the race start, and was surprised to see how expensive the cab ride would be. Not wanting to blow my budget on transportation, I researched bus routes, and discovered that one bus would drop me off right next to the start. Perfect. The following morning I got up early and waited at the stop next to my hotel. I had given myself plenty of time—unusual for me, but I didn't want to take any chances. Finally, the bus came, and I settled back for a relaxing ride. Everything was under control.

And then, suddenly, there was chaos. The bus pulled over and the driver announced that this was as far as the bus would go, due to street closings caused by the marathon. How could I not have realized this would happen? Anger and frustration boiled up inside me, stoked by the realization that we were still about six miles from the race start, with precious little time to spare before the gun.

No need to panic, yet; I just had to hail a cab, and everything would be okay. I began walking down the street in search of a taxi. I quickly realized, though, that the streets were deserted due to the street closings. All I saw were traffic cones and occasional police cruisers. Checking my watch, I saw that there were just 5 minutes until the race start. It was time to panic. I broke into a run, scouring each street that I passed for signs of life. I picked up the pace, and went into top gear. I knew this wasn't the way to warm up for a marathon, but I had little choice.

Finally, I saw a cab, and was able to flag it down. I explained my situation to him, and he zipped off to the freeway, promising to get me to the race. We had just a few scant minutes, and six miles to go. I anxiously counted the passing seconds as we weaved through traffic. With my eyes glued to my watch, I saw the official starting time come and go. We were still on the highway. I was heartbroken. My driver reassured me that we were close, and as we neared the start downtown, I told him to just pull over. I threw money toward the front seat and leapt out of the cab, scrambled up the embankment, and hurtled over the guardrail. In front of me was the starting area, now bereft of all runners. The race was already 10 minutes old. People were milling about, and workers had started taking down the starting sign. This race was not turning out to be a good motivator for running Boston the following month!

"Runner coming through!" I yelled, dodging and weaving through the crowd. Up ahead, an electronic mat straddled the street, activated by a chip containing a transponder that each runner fixed to his or her shoe. Most big races use these to track runners and record each runner's finishing time. As I crossed the starting line, the very last person to do so in a field of more than 10,000 runners, I heard a reassuring beep. I was officially in the race.

Starting dead last has its benefits, as I soon learned. Usually the ranks of runners in a big race are shoulder to shoulder for the first mile or so, until they begin to spread out. It's only then that you can settle into your own target race pace. Not so for the last-place runner, however. From my vantage point, I could see that the field had already spread, and I was able to run as fast as I wanted from the very start. I began to wonder if this might not be a good way to intentionally start my races, but I quickly put that thought out of my head. Like a dog ordered to sit still while a juicy steak was inches from its nose, I knew that I wouldn't be able to fight off the urge to run once the gun goes off in a race and everyone surges forward. I was disciplined enough to run the marathon, but not disciplined enough to not run it, even for ten minutes.

I soon discovered another great benefit to starting in the back; you get to pass people. You get to pass *a lot* of them, and that's a good feeling. But more than that, you get to really see the race; I saw people who would usually be invisible to me, buried in sea of humanity far behind me. Among these faces in Los Angeles were several runners I knew from other races, people I didn't even know were planning to run L.A. If I hadn't started in the back of the pack, I never would have seen them, and never would have had a chance to say hello. It was a rare and welcome treat.

When all was said and done, I crossed the finish line in L.A. with a good time, and a story to boot. Marathon number 42 was history. And better still, I had restored my desire to race. I was like a lion pacing in a cage, and Boston was the meat laid in front of me.

Boston had always seemed like a dream to me, like a Camelot for runners, more myth than reality. I had run it once before as a charity fund-raiser, but that didn't feel right to me. Not to take anything away from all those dedicated and caring runners who race as fund-raisers—many of whom I coached myself—getting my Boston race number without running a qualifying time was hollow for me because I hadn't *earned it.* But in April 1999, I had earned my spot officially. From the barren wasteland of Antarctica to the famous starting line of the Boston Marathon in the outlying town of Hopkinton, I was on quite a roll.

From the moment I arrived in town, I couldn't help but get swept up in the excitement. While other cities sometimes ignore or tolerate their marathons, Boston is absolutely in love with theirs, and it showed. Banners and signs advertising the race were everywhere. Stores offered marathon merchandise—and not just the running stores—and seemingly everyone I met asked if I was running the race. Strangers smiled and wished me luck. Suddenly, marathoning wasn't a fringe sport, it was front-page news.

The runners themselves flooded the streets, shops, and restaurants like locusts. There was an audible buzz in the air, made up of dozens of simultaneous conversations about training, about the racecourse, and about qualifying races. The Boston Marathon began to feel like it was something more than a race; it began to feel like a mass movement.

And that, of course, is what it is. Any doubts were dispelled at packet pickup at the cavernous convention center, where thousands of people lined up to get their race numbers and to check out the expo. At most races, packet pickup is often little more than a quick, prerace chore, but here it's an *event*, a celebration of life and of running. Just making it into Boston is an achievement, and being part of the race said something about a person's work ethic and lifestyle.

Even the official Boston Marathon shirt made a statement. It was devoid of any splashy multi-color race emblem, and it lacked the tangle of corporate sponsor logos that covered most other race shirts. In Boston, you always get a long-sleeved shirt with a small Boston Athletic Association logo on the breast and *Boston Marathon* written down one arm. The color of the shirt varies from year to year, but the design never changes. It's quiet and dignified, and there's no other running shirt like it.

After picking up my race packet, I wandered around the expo. The energy was unbelievable. There was a palpable excitement in the air, heightened by the presence of so many of the world's greatest runners, past and present, signing autographs and talking with fans. In contrast to many professional athletes in other sports, these pros were friendly and accessible, swapping stories, training tips, and race strategies with anyone they met. I wondered whether this easy rapport stemmed from the fact that on race day, we would all face the same challenge. While even the most rabid Red Sox fan would likely never dig in at the plate at Fenway Park, any runner of any ability can go head-to-head against the best runners in the world by simply entering a race. Even Boston, with its qualifying times, provides a place where runners of modest ability can mix with the elite. And on race day, we have a shared experience: we all have to handle the weather, the course, and the challenge of covering the miles as fast as we can. It's a leveling experience.

Perhaps, too, the difference between running and other sports lies in the basis for excellence. While all top athletes train and practice, runners rely mostly on the relentless grind of their training, and not on any superior hand-eye coordination, as baseball and basketball players do. Elite runners are genetically gifted, sure, but without intense training, those gifts are wasted. Their training creates a strong work ethic that leaves humility in its wake. There are no short cuts in marathoning, so anyone who is a marathoner has worked hard. It's a lesson no one forgets.

After a few hours, I had had enough of the expo, and staggered out with a bag of promos, giveaways, premiums, and samples. I ate an early prerace meal, and spent the next few hours lying sleeplessly in bed. Finally, it was race day. Not Sunday morning, though, as it would be with most races, but Monday, the state holiday known as Patriot's Day. In Boston, that means a day off, a Red Sox game, and the Marathon.

Getting to the marathon was an adventure in itself. The Boston Marathon, like marathons in New York City, Las Vegas, and numerous other places, uses a point-to-point course. This turns the marathon into a true journey, as runners pass from town to town, along country roads, over train tracks, into the heart of the city. The problem, though, is that unlike loop or out-and-back courses, runners don't return to where they started. This creates a logistical challenge: thousands of runners have to be transported from downtown Boston out to the start line, where water, shelter, and bathrooms are provided for them as they wait several hours for the last of the participants to arrive. I'm sure race morning is a mad scramble for the race staff, but for the runners, it's an exercise in rushing to do nothing, and it can be quite frustrating.

Most point-to-point races require a predawn lineup for bus transport. In Boston, the race doesn't begin until noon, and the wait at the high school in Hopkinton—transformed into the Athletes' Village on race day—can be three hours or more.[4] This is my least favorite part of the marathon experience. I've learned to deal with it, and I've even found some ways to make the process a bit more tolerable. At the New York City Marathon one year, instead of waiting on line with other runners for the bus to starting area in Staten Island, some friends of mine and I rented a limo to drop us off at the starting line. It felt decadent, but split between us, it really wasn't too expensive at all, and not only did we avoid the predawn bus lines and were able to sleep a little bit later, but we were able to enjoy the envious and curious stares from other runners as we emerged from our ride.

In Boston, though, I wasn't so lucky or creative. I waited on one of the many long lines at Boston Commons as the fleet of yellow school

---

4 In 2007, years of tradition were abandoned as the race was moved up to 10 A.M. to avoid the worst of the midday heat that had plagued runners in the preceding few years.

buses made their circuit to the race start and back. Eventually, I boarded one of the buses, and settled into a window seat. As the bus droned and rocked, I fell into a drowsy stupor. Finally we arrived at our base camp. Rows of Porta-Jons and several big tents had been set up on the school grounds, along with a stage where various speakers and musicians provided information, advice, and entertainment. My drowsiness quickly disappeared, both from a sudden adrenaline rush and from the shock of cold air. April is a tricky time in Massachusetts; it could be scorching hot or icy cold, but no matter which it is, the chances are that at some point you'll be uncomfortable on race day. That year, it was cold, which made waiting for the race to begin an awful ordeal.

Well, not entirely awful. There was one special marathon tradition that I witnessed and would never forget: the moment marathon legend Johnny Kelley took the stage. Kelley first ran the Boston Marathon in 1928, and won the race in 1935 and 1945. He finished in second place seven times, and was in the top ten eighteen times. He also competed in the 1936 Olympic Games, but he was perhaps more famous for holding the record for the number of times he'd entered the Boston Marathon (sixty-one), and the number of times he finished it (fifty-eight). He was also immortalized in the 1936 race, when eventual winner Tarzan Brown (and how's that for a name!) passed him on the last of three brutal hills in the town of Newton, a moment, the press reported, that broke Kelley's heart. That hill would forevermore be known as Heartbreak Hill, and would eventually be the site of a statue depicting a young Johnny Kelley running hand in hand with an older version of himself.

As I stood before the stage in Hopkinton that morning, Kelley looked thin and frail, a vestige of the great athlete that he once was. Then he spoke. He told us to enjoy the day, to be careful on the course, and to enjoy ourselves. Finding a reserve of strength, as he must have done all those times on Heartbreak Hill, Kelley asked if we'd like him to sing for us. We all clapped and cheered, and Kelley broke into his signature song,

"Young At Heart." The crowd went crazy, laughing and applauding, as cameras clicked all around me. Everyone seemed to recognize that this was one of those special moments, one we would carry with us and share with others for many years to come.[5]

After several hours, we were called away from the school and out onto the street, where corrals had been roped off to separate runners according to their expected finishing times. Standing around for hours drinking water, coffee, and sports drink—as nasty a combination as I could think of—had taken its toll on many of the runners, but the good folks of Hopkinton didn't seem very sympathetic to our plight. Many homeowners patrolled their bushes like guard dogs, shouting away any runners who tried to take care of business surreptitiously. Rather unfriendly, I thought, but what did I know? I lived in a condo, and knew zilch about gardening. For all I knew, the cumulative effects of 18,000 or so overly hydrated, nervous runners could lead to permanent deforestation, so I tried to be sensitive to the concerns of the local community.

The excitement grew as noon approached. Then finally, after years of dreaming, months of planning, hours of waiting, we were off. The Boston Marathon had begun!

The cheering at the starting line was incredible, as the runners passed through a gauntlet of spectators and tried to settle down into their pace. The Boston Marathon is really a tour through a series of towns, which the marathon fanatics can recite in order: *Hopkinton—Ashland—Natick—Wellesley—Newton—Brookline—Boston.* Strategically, this presents some interesting possibilities. Most people focus on the big hills of Newton, stacked one after another between miles 17 and 21, where runners have just started feeling deep fatigue and doubt. What most people don't really consider, however, is that the Boston Marathon is actually a

---

5 Johnny Kelley last ran the Boston Marathon in 1992, when he was eighty-four. He died on October 6, 2004, at the age of ninety-seven.

very fast course, dropping 413 feet over the first 17 miles. Over the next 4 miles, in Newton, runners must climb back up 187 feet, but then the course drops another 127 feet from Newton to the finish line. Apart from those difficult hills in Newton, then, the Boston Marathon is mostly a downhill course.

So, what to do? Conventional wisdom is to run the first 17 downhill miles conservatively and save energy for Newton. Once those big hills are conquered, it would be time to turn on the gas and fly through the final 5 miles to the finish. That was the way Boston was supposed to be run.

Naturally, I decided to do something different. My problem with the conventional wisdom was that the miles before Newton represented two-thirds of the whole race. If I ran that part conservatively, then even if I felt great in the last 5 miles and ran that section hard, I wouldn't be able to make up for all those mediocre early miles, and I would wind up with a mediocre finishing time. On the other hand, if I ran those first 17 miles hard, and struggled through the hills of Newton, I would have only 5 miles between myself and the finish line. I would no doubt be dog tired at that point, but if I could just muster up a little more courage and manage to hold onto my pace, I could wind up with a great finishing time.

Or, I could blow up, and find my body in full revolt in Newton, leaving me sprawled on the grass on the side of the road, exhausted and broken.

Those were basically my options as I saw them. Dare greatly and risk dropping out, or run conservative toward a good, if not glorious, finish.

I thought back to the words of the late Steve Prefontaine, probably the greatest middle-distance runner the United States has ever produced. Pre would often flout conventional wisdom by running out front instead of biding his time for a strong finish. In the 1972 Olympic Games, he pushed the pace in the 5K, running a courageous race but ultimately finishing fourth. "A lot of people run a race to see who's the fastest," he said. "I run to see who has the most guts." That's how I wanted to run. I couldn't win in Boston, of course, but I would run as courageously as anyone there.

With that settled, I streaked through Hopkinton, weaving my way through the runners and enjoying the loud encouragement of the fans packing the roadsides. My legs felt fresh and strong, with lots of pop. In the words of the old Irish toast—appropriate in Boston—it felt as though the road were rising up to greet me. I recognized Darryl, a fellow runner from my track group in D.C. I shouted hello as I flew past. I was running well, and enjoying myself.

The sights of the marathon came and went. I flew past the clock tower in Ashland, the old train station in Framingham, and approached Wellesley. I had heard other runners joking about the enthusiastic co-eds there, but I wasn't prepared for the sheer bedlam of it all. Row upon row of women screamed out to us, offering us encouragement along with offers of kisses. Some guys grinningly took them up on their offers and received a peck, but I was too shy even for that. And, of course, I still had my race to run.

Next up was fabled Newton, and I knew this was where my race would truly begin. If I could make it through the three hills of Newton without breaking, I would have a chance at a great finish.

I hit the first hill, and rode it as the course turned onto broad Commonwealth Avenue. The climb was over a mile long, but I kept my legs churning, and finally I crested the top. The next mile was a gentle downhill, giving all of us a chance to recover our strength and determination for the next challenge ahead. The runners around me were silent, their faces held tight. They seemed like fishermen sailing into a squall, determined not to break. We rode the next hill the same way.

And then Heartbreak Hill was upon us like a storm. Runners swung their arms and fought to hold their pace, grunting and breathing heavily. The crowds were thick along the street and in the broad, grassy median, screaming and waving banners and signs. They knew that this was the most dramatic part of the race, because it was here that the race was usually won and lost; the finish was only for the coronation. And it was here, too, that the humanity and courage of the runners was most evident. We spoke to each another, offering encouragement, trying to share our energy, hoping that together we could bring everyone to the top. A stranger looked over at me and said, "Run with me. We can do this. Run with me."

I pushed to keep up with him, repeating the mantra, "We're almost there, we're almost there, we're almost there." I saw the hilltop just up ahead, and I lowered my eyes. It was so far away, and the road was so steep. I counted off ten seconds before I looked up again. The top of the hill still seemed so distant. I looked back down. Finally, I was there, at the top. I had conquered Heartbreak Hill. I had slowed, but not by very much, and now I just had to pick up the pace and race to the finish in Copley Square.

But did I have anything left in my legs?

I took a moment's breather, and then tried to accelerate. There was that moment's gap, that briefest moment between the command my mind gave, and the response of my legs. I lived a lifetime in that moment, fearful that my legs would refuse to answer my call. But they did. They had not abandoned me. I streaked down the back side of the hill, with renewed strength and hope.

Soon, the excitement of Newton faded behind me, and with it, the adrenaline rush that conquering the hills had given me. There were still 5 miles left to go, and that was a very long way to run on tired legs. I tried to focus only on the patch of road in front of me, and concentrated on maintaining my pace.

I streaked down Commonwealth Avenue, along the train line, and looked up for the massive neon Citgo gas sign in Kenmore Square that would tell me that the finish line was only a mile away. Seeing the sign would be like spotting a lighthouse in a storm at sea; it was the promise of safety, of release from pain and fatigue.

Suddenly, someone jumped in from the crowd and began to match me, stride for stride. It was Lynn, a teammate from my Antarctica adventure. We had kept in touch, and since she lived nearby, she said she'd come to Boston and try to run me in to the finish line. Now there she was, when I needed her most. She didn't have to say much as she ran with me, but I drew energy from her, taking strength from her companionship. I ran like a machine now, thinking only about keeping my legs moving, pushing, pushing, pushing, concentrating on nothing but running.

Finally, the course veered away from Commonwealth Avenue and turned right onto Hereford Street for a couple of blocks, and then left onto Boylston Street. The finish line was just up ahead now. I could see it. It was just a few blocks away. I only had a minute of running left, I told myself. After all these hours, just one single minute. I told myself that I could endure any kind of pain for just one minute. I pushed as hard as I could, sprinting toward the finish line. Lynn matched me, and then drifted away as I flew through the finish line.

I had run the Boston Marathon in 3 hours, 9 minutes, just a single heartbeat slower than my personal best. In the process, I also requalified to run the Boston Marathon the following year. Most importantly, though, I had run courageously, and I felt like I truly belonged at Boston. In this, my 43rd marathon, near the halfway point to reaching my 100-marathon quest, I finally felt like a marathoner.

There was another thing about Boston that was auspicious. I hadn't kept in touch with too many of my old high school friends, but I'd heard through the grapevine, such as it was, that one of our classmates, Stephanie Kay, was teaching art at Boston University. Stephanie and I had been friends in school. We were not very close friends, but I always thought that we got along well. I liked her, but I thought that she was perhaps a little out of my league. She was very pretty, and being an artist, she hung out with the cool crowd. But we were adults now, and I was curious about what she looked like and how she was doing. I left her a message through her office, just letting her know that I was coming into town for the race and would love to catch up with her. I didn't hear back. Well, that was all right. It had been well over a decade since we'd last seen each other, and my message had come out of the blue, so I couldn't blame her for tossing it aside. I guessed that she just wasn't interested.

It would be a while until I found out how wrong I was.

Running Tip #7

Massage

Nonrunners assume that it's better to run downhill than up, but that's not always true. Downhill is *faster*, but it's far more brutal than uphill. After crossing the finish line in Boston, my joints stiffened and my muscles began to ache from all the pounding my body had absorbed. The quadriceps muscles on the front of my legs, which had kept me from falling right on my face, were totally shot. A few days' rest didn't bring much relief. I needed help. I was ready for a massage.

Hard training and racing causes micro-tears and the accumulation of waste products in muscle cells. Adhesions also can occur, in which muscles cells stick together, limiting flexibility and healing. Massage forces waste out of the muscle tissue and breaks up adhesions, resulting in reduced recovery time, improved range of motion, and a lower occurrence of injury.

It can take a while for the benefits of massage to become fully apparent, although the results could sometimes be very dramatic. Once, a massage therapist was working deeply (and painfully!) on a spot in my upper back where I'd been feeling pain, when I suddenly broke out in a drenching sweat. The therapist said it was common for stressed bodies to release their tension that way, and it really did feel as though a clenched fist had suddenly opened up. I felt better immediately.

But don't get massage only when you're injured; aim to get a massage monthly, or even biweekly or weekly if you can afford it. Or try self-massage: knead and rub your target muscles deeply, stroking toward your heart, using massage oil to reduce friction. There are also products available to facilitate self-massage, such as a rolling-pin like device that works especially well on hamstrings and quads.

Across the Pond and Around
the World

After conquering Antarctica, traveling abroad for a marathon didn't seem to be such a far-fetched idea. Following Boston, I ran the Salt Lake City Marathon in Utah. Even though I had raced to the top of Pikes Peak, I had never run an entire race at altitude before, and it seemed to have an effect on me that I hadn't anticipated: I suddenly developed an endless need to pull over to the bushes. I had never experienced anything like it before, and I don't know why it happened, but the result was that I was alternately passing and getting passed by the same handful of runners. Finally, one of them had had enough, and as I emerged from the woods for what must have been the tenth time, he yelled out "stop passing me!" All I could do was sheepishly apologize.

Next was an uneventful marathon in Tupelo, Mississippi—uneventful for me, though not for Dave, who joined me for that race. While I flew down for the race, Dave opted to minimize costs by taking an overnight bus down. At one rest stop, he lost track of time, and watched in alarm as his bus pulled out without him on board, but with all his racing gear sitting neatly on his window seat. He hopped the next bus and gave chase. Luckily, this new bus was an express, and he overtook his gear at the next major stop. After all that, running the race was easy for him. Once the race was over, Dave and I decided to go have lunch and celebrate with a few beers. The lunch was easy to find, but not the beer; we couldn't find any place to serve us alcohol on a Sunday. Tough lesson for a city boy like me to learn!

Following Mississippi, I set my sights on Berlin for marathon number 46. Berlin was a city in transition, ground zero for the collapse of communism and the birth of a new Europe. I read about how the city was rebuilding itself and was bristling with energy and excitement. The racecourse was supposed to be a very flat and fast course—several marathon world records had been set there. It seemed like the perfect marathon adventure.

I managed to talk two of my running friends into going with me. Our flights went smoothly, and we checked into our hotel without a problem. We also made it to the packet pickup easily enough; the Berlin Marathon is a huge race, with 20,000 or so participants, so all we had to do was get close to the race headquarters and look for people in running shoes toting their race packets and the goodie bags. We made our way to the great hall and collected our paperwork, only to discover that the race instructions were written only in German.

It's my conceit as an American that no matter where I go, I expect the locals to speak English, and that all instructions will be translated for my convenience. Apparently, the Germans had different ideas on the subject. I scanned the runner instructions. Some of the words bore a passing resemblance to English, but others were just a maze of letters. I was baffled by the German propensity to take lots of small words and mash them together into mammoth tongue twisters. Luckily, the materials had a similar layout to American race instructions, so we were able to more or less figure things out.

However odd and unsettling packet pickup had felt, race morning seemed as familiar and comfortable as an old shirt. Runners gathered at the starting line and did what runners everywhere do; they ate energy bars, drank water, stretched, napped, talked, paced, worried, and relaxed. Eventually, they huddled close together behind the starting line, and then exploded forward en masse at the blast of the starting gun. I found myself part of a teeming, sweating mass pouring through the Brandenburg Gate. It was unforgettable. I was surprised, though, to see mile markers popping up more often than I expected. I checked my last split time—the pace in which I'd run my last mile. My watch read 3:44. That would put me right about at the world record for the mile. *That can't be right*, I thought. Then it dawned on me. *Kilometers.* Those markers measure *kilometers*, not miles. The world record was safe, and worse yet, I would have to pass another 41 of those markers before I was through.

I immediately understood the downside of measuring a marathon course in kilometers—when I see a sign that reads "26," my body knows, like one of Pavlov's dogs, that it has only another minute and a half or so of running, and then it's quitting time. Not so in a European marathon. Marker 26 only tells me that I have another 16 kilometers to go. It's a definite downer.

On the other hand, kilometer markers fly past quicker than mile markers, which gives the feeling of progress being made. It's also an ego boost to pass numbers that get so staggeringly high: 35, 36, 37! On a practical level, having such a profusion of markers also provides runners with more opportunities to check their pace and make any necessary adjustments.

I also discovered anew that a marathon is a splendid way to tour a city. Anyone can lay out a 5K or 10K race course to avoid the seamier sides of a city, but a marathon exposes all there really is to see, the warts along with the beauty. In Berlin, we snaked our way over to the former East Germany, and what I saw there startled me. I had grown up during the Cold War, and had imagined East Germany as the formidable industrial muscle of the Soviet bloc, churning out weapons and superior athletes.

What I saw was no mighty enemy; the buildings all seemed shoddy and in disrepair. If ever this had been a place bustling with energy, that time had long since passed. I felt like I had peeked behind the curtain looking for the Wizard of Oz, only to find a little tired old man.

There *was* bustling energy in Berlin while we were there, but it was coming from the West. As we ran, we could see dozens of construction cranes dominating the city skyline like mythic giants. Berlin was a city in transition, and as I ran the course, I thought it would be interesting to come back and race the city again in a few years to see what it would grow to be.

Everything about the Berlin Marathon was as I expected it to be, but after crossing the finish line, I encountered one of the oddest sights I'd yet seen at a race: race volunteers carrying large bundles of cash for on-the-spot deposit refunds for race chips. I couldn't imagine anyone flashing wads of cash like that in Central Park in New York City, not even on marathon day with mounted police nearby. Fuhgeddaboutit.

After Berlin, I ran the Marine Corps and New York marathons again—a personal tradition at this point—and then ended 1999 by adding Washington State and Florida to my list of completed states. That made it eleven marathons in 1999, which was a new record for me, and I had reached marathon number fifty, the halfway point in my quest. But I didn't stop to ponder it, because I was busy running marathons in South Carolina, Maryland, Boston again, and Maine. Next up: joining a running group to head to Beijing for marathon number 55.

Beijing, like Berlin, was another city in transition. Its biggest changes would not come until years later, when it began building up in earnest for 2008 Olympic Games, but even in October 2000 there were signs of the coming transformation. There were more cars than I expected to see, and the clothes and bicycles of the younger Chinese were flashier and more colorful than the dour, drab designs sported by their elders.

Our tour guide helped minimize communication problems, but there was still opportunity for misadventure. One day, with no group activity scheduled, another team member and I climbed into a taxi, aiming to visit a local temple. We showed a photo of our intended destination to the driver, then sat back in the cab. Before long, the driver turned onto a highway, and as the miles and minutes ticked by, my friend and I exchanged nervous glances. After a 45-minute odyssey, the cab pulled up in front of a marketplace. We had no idea where we were, but we knew one thing: if we let that cab drive away, we might never find our way back. Having had the foresight to bring a book of matches from our hotel, we showed it to the driver and pointed at the address. He shrugged, and set off to return us to where we started. We never did make it to that temple, but things could have turned out much worse.

On race day, my traveling companions and I gathered with the other runners in Tiananmen Square. As we waited for the start, I looked around and tried to imagine the confrontation a decade earlier between government troops and the mass of protesters who had camped there. Our group had talked about it, but it was a topic that none of the local Chinese seemed willing or able to discuss with us. On race day, there was no dissent visible among those gathered; we were all runners. Crossing the cultural divide, I bartered my American running jacket for a Chinese Olympic team jacket, a deal consummated wordlessly with a Chinese runner, using rough pantomime to transcend our language barrier. It's a marathon treasure that's as meaningful to me as many of the medals I've earned.

Finally, we all gathered at the start line, and the familiar crack of the starter's gun sent us out on a loop of the square, under the larger-than-life gaze of Chairman Mao. His stern image was everywhere—not only on official posters but also on clock faces, shirts, mugs, and souvenir trinkets. He seemed to be making a transition himself, from revered leader to high camp. Ironic comeuppance for a despot.

After exiting Tiananmen Square and racing through the city, we were herded out onto one of the city's surrounding highways, where we tallied most of the miles in our race. The few spectators we passed stood in hushed observance, offering support with only an occasional clap or shout. After the spectacular start, the rest of the race was, to be honest, a very boring slog.

We finished our race on the highway, an appropriate end to a mostly disappointing race. I was still glad to have to have made the journey, though, especially after visiting an unrestored section of the Great Wall in an area well outside of Beijing. Still, the race itself seemed like a missed opportunity for the Chinese. A marathon should be used as a forum to showcase a city, to give visitors a glimpse into its natural and architectural beauty, its history, and its culture. Beijing had so much to offer, and yet the race did so little with it.

In addition to running on foreign soil, I undertook another challenge that year; in addition to my regular job, I became a marathon coach for a charity fundraising team in my spare time. I had jumped from being a marathoner to being a marathon evangelist. In 2000, I signed on with the Arthritis Foundation's Joints in Motion program, and the following year also signed up to coach the American Diabetes Association's Team Diabetes. Coaching forced me to articulate many of my beliefs about marathoning, and also to reconsider the elements of my training regimen. It was a great way to share my passion for marathoning, and I grew to love it. Also, as the old Navy recruiting posters used to say, it was a great way to see the world. I traveled with these teams to Dublin, Rome, Athens, and Amsterdam, and in each of these places, I ran along with them. I was as happy as an obsessed runner could be; I was helping charities and sharing my love for the marathon as I experienced races all around the world.

The trade-off, however, was my commitment to never running a marathon all-out if I was with a team. I didn't want to be in a position where I might be unavailable to help my team, whether from injury or mental and physical fatigue. I wanted to be able to not only finish the marathon with the runners I was pacing, but to also run back and see after our other, slower participants.

Still, it was an enormously rewarding experience. Many of our team members had never considered themselves athletes, and by the end of our time together, they had discovered a strength and resolve they never knew they possessed. This realization was a powerful thing, and I was thrilled to be part of it for so many people.

My first trip abroad with a charity team was for the Dublin Marathon, in October 2000, just two weeks after Beijing. Conditions in Ireland were brutal that year, as race day greeted us with driving rain and high winds. During the race, I tried ducking behind larger runners to lessen the impact of the wind, like a cyclist drafting another rider. Nothing helped, though. It was just one of those days.

The Irish fans seemed undisturbed by bad weather, however. They lined the roads and shouted "Well done, lads!" to the runners flying past. One spectator in particular remains in my memory: at mile 11, a golden-haired girl, no more than seven or eight years old, looked up hopefully as we ran past and squealed, "Give us a smile!" Those of us within earshot of this little sprite couldn't help but comply.

One unexpected feature of the race was that rather than hand out cups of water like they do in the States, the race volunteers in Dublin handed out full bottles. Not a bad idea, except that few runners drank the entire bottle, or even carried it for very long. The result: for the block or two after each water stop, half-filled water bottles flew through the air like hand grenades.

At the finish line, exhausted, shivering runners were treated to coffee and chocolate—not the bananas and bagels found at most races, but still very welcome. It had been a grueling day. I felt worst for the first-time runners, who perhaps didn't know that a marathon didn't have to be this hard. They had conquered more than the usual marathon challenge, and I tried to help them realize that. They were finally convinced by the front page of *The Irish Times* the following morning, which ran the headline "Runners Defy Wind and Rain in Marathon of Suffering." I kept that page, and have it somewhere still, buried in a stack of race memorabilia.

One month later, I found myself flying out to Hawaii with a different charity team for the Honolulu Marathon. Although we were still technically in the United States, Hawaii felt exotic. Perhaps that was because Hawaii is the only state with an historic palace, and because so many Japanese runners had entered the marathon. At one store, I actually wondered for a moment if they accepted dollars, proving true the old saying, better to be silent and thought a fool, rather than speak and remove all doubt.

In most marathons, my plan is to start out comfortably and slowly ease into my goal race pace, saving enough energy in reserve for a fast finish. But in Honolulu, with the threat of a hot sun weighing heavily on me, I decided to flip my strategy; I would start out fast and try to get as many miles as possible under my belt before the heat set in. It was a risky strategy, especially since I was committed to keeping some energy in reserve to use helping my team afterward, but I felt sure the best strategy would be to do what I could to avoid running more than necessary in the hot tropical sun.

We were in the Christmas holiday season, but the weather was warm as we lined up with 20,000 other runners in the predawn darkness in Waikiki, awaiting the traditional fireworks show that accompanied the race start. After looping Waikiki, we were sent out for two loops around Diamondhead, the volcano that dominated the Honolulu waterfront skyline. Despite my attempts to avoid spending too much time in the sun, I still found myself feeling dehydrated and depleted by the time

I made it to the finish line in Kapiolani Park 3 hours and 25 minutes after having started the race. Luckily, I recovered quickly, and was able to head out back on the course to run with my team and make sure they were all having the experience they had trained so faithfully for. And as for me, marathon number 57 was in the books, and Hawaii was on my list of states.

Running Tip #8

Avoid Dehydration

Your body uses water, in the form of sweat, to shed heat. This water comes mostly from blood plasma, and unless you replace it, your heart won't be able to pump the resulting sludge to your working muscles. As little as a 2 percent loss in body fluid can seriously affect exercise performance. Loss of blood plasma also makes it harder for your heart to send blood to the skin to cool off your core. When this happens, you risk heat exhaustion, and even heat stroke, which can be fatal.[6]

Signs of dehydration

- *Dry skin*
- *Cold or clammy skin*
- *Nausea*
- *Disorientation*

---

6 There's been some research, especially by Dr. Timothy Noakes of the University of Cape Town—who himself has run more than seventy marathons and ultramarathons—suggesting that dehydration isn't really dangerous at all. Instead, he argues, it actually helped early man hunt game across the open plains by reducing his body weight. Rising core temperatures and reduced speed are not caused by dehydration, he says, but instead by overexertion. While these are certainly intriguing ideas, and might very well be true, I'd recommend caution here, and stick for the time being with the conservative viewpoint until more research is done in this area.

Your plan of attack

- *Drink regularly.* Water is the old standby, but a sports drink also replaces essential minerals and provides some simple sugars for fuel. Drinking is the key; what you drink is up to you.
- *Weigh yourself.* Comparing your weight before and after exercise will tell you how much fluid you need to replace under various conditions.
- *If in doubt, act.* Slow down and take in more fluids. Slurp water from a garden hose, or knock on someone's door and explain your problem. Pour cool water on your wrists, arms and head. Sit down in a shady area. If you don't feel better quickly, call 911. Don't be brave; this is a potentially dangerous situation.

Island Running

As the jet descended toward the runway, it wasn't hard for me to remember why I had decided to come to Bermuda. Looking out the window, I saw palm trees. It was the middle of January, 2001, and here I was, looking at *palm trees*. Back home in Washington, D.C., I wouldn't see green outdoors for another two months or so. The temperature, as promised in the Department of Tourism brochures, was in the mid-60s, with cloudy skies. A little warm for running, perhaps, but I knew what to do about that, right?

Often thought of as one of the Caribbean islands, Bermuda actually lies far to the north, some 570 miles east of the North Carolina coast. Although it's commonly considered a single island, it is actually a collection of some 150 separate islands, many of them no more than a speck of rock peeking above the bright blue waters. They are the tips of long-dormant volcanoes, together forming a long, fishhook-shaped archipelago, inhabited by some 61,000 people. Because these islands are swept by the friendly Gulf Stream winds, the temperature in Bermuda stays moderate all year long, with temperatures ranging from a low in the upper 60 degrees F, to a high in the mid-to-upper 70 degrees F.

In the middle of this fishhook is the city of Hamilton, established in 1790 as a convenient meeting place for all of Bermuda's scattered residents. Now the capital of Bermuda, its streets are filled with pubs, restaurants, and little shops. The main thoroughfare here is Front Street, which runs parallel to the harbor, and which features a roofed sentry box affectionately called "the birdcage," from which a police officer directs traffic.

Near the birdcage on Front Street is the Number 1 Passenger Terminal, site of the race packet pick-up. When I arrived to get my number, I found that the field would be, well, an *intimate* gathering of runners. There were only 392 runners registered for the full marathon, and 313 registered for the half. This was a far cry from the huge crowds at the marathons in New York, Boston, and Chicago, but small races do have their charm.

I spent the rest of the day doing a little sightseeing and a little eating, but mostly just resting and waiting. Rain was predicted, and sure enough, I heard the tapping of rain splashing against the window in the middle of the night. By the time I got up and went out the door, though, the rain had tapered off, leaving a cool, overcast morning. Perfect.

By 8 A.M., I was back on Front Street for the start of the race. The course is a double loop, with the half-marathoners pulling over to the side in Hamilton as the marathoners forge ahead for another lap.

I always have mixed feeling about that kind of format. It's nice to muster the entire running crowd together for as long as possible, especially in small races, but it's also quite a letdown to head toward the half-marathoner finish line with a pack of runners, and emerge alone on the other side.

As the starter's gun went off and we surged up Front Street, I thought about The Hill. When I first began to consider running the Bermuda Marathon, my first question was, where's the hill? In a marathon, there's almost *always* a hill. Sure enough, it's there: a nearly 40-meter climb at 3½ miles called McGall's Hill, revisited at 16½ miles.

The first mile flashed by in a blur of storefronts and adrenaline, and then we slipped out of the city center, onto a beautiful country road heading east. The road wasn't crowded, but neither was it empty; there were runners everywhere. We rolled over a few small rises, and then we were upon The Hill. It looked impressive, but it was early in the race, and we collectively ate it up.

Green. I'd noticed it upon arriving, but now I saw it everywhere. Lush green, bright green. The island doesn't have a soil base deep and rich enough to support large-scale agriculture, but its native plants thrive tenaciously, lining the marathon course with color. And there were other colors as well: houses splashed with blues and yellows and pinks, with bright white rooftops, kept clean so rainwater falling from their sides may be captured in underground cisterns for later use.

I noticed something else, too. Something that was *not* there. Garbage. I didn't see any trash along the streets, not in Hamilton, not on the country roads, not anywhere. So far, it was a runners' paradise.

We turned north onto the wonderfully-named Devil's Hole Road, and soon, at mile five, we were treated to a spectacular view of Harrington Sound. From there we turned toward Flatts Village, a former smugglers' haven that served as the site for the execution of witches in the mid-1600s. Today, the village is a benign and friendly haven for sailboats and fishermen, and true to its name, it was flat. The crowds had been sparse so far, but now there were several small groups of spectators. They seemed interested and supportive, though more reserved than the usual marathon crowd. That didn't surprise me. Bermuda, as a British possession, retains some Old World mannerisms that were brought across the Pond, including a tradition of high tea. Bermudans don't scream and yell along the course, but they are quick to return a polite "hello" or "good morning."

After Flatts Village, we turned onto North Shore Road. It was here, at mile 8, that I was rewarded with the first ocean view of the race, and it was breathtaking. Jagged dark volcanic rock met glorious blue water in a spray of white foam. It was almost enough to make me stop to enjoy the moment, but I knew I'd be back to see it again on my second loop.

The road settled into a pattern of rolling hills, and I noticed that the porous limestone, used widely as a building material, left structures appearing weathered and ancient. A stone archway overhead looked absolutely medieval. I also noticed the salty breeze blowing in off the ocean— another welcome distraction. On the left were signs for the Railway Trail, a running path made up of segments from Bermuda's old narrow gauge railway line, completed in 1931 and abandoned in 1947. It looked full of beauty and adventure, carved through rock and draped in foliage. I fought the urge to veer off and explore it. At mile 11 we turned south, back toward Hamilton. An old man sitting in a folding chair by the side of the road called out, "Once you pass me, it's easy to the finish!" I called back, "See you again soon!" I hoped I would.

The last 2 miles into Hamilton were downhill and fast. The sun fought its way through the clouds and scattered them, and the foliage retreated. The temperature climbed as the halfway point loomed ahead and the half-marathoners put on a burst of speed. I joined them and flew through the finish line, but my race was only half over, and my legs suddenly seemed to lose their bounce. McGall's Hill, redux, was just 3 miles away. As I tried to regain my focus and marshal my reserves, a man on a scooter passed by and offered me a candy. "I'll be with you guys all the way!" he promised as he sped ahead to the next runner. An older Japanese man passed me and called out "I'm faster than last year!" "Good for you!" I yelled back, and felt energized by his enthusiasm. I threw an invisible lasso around him, and let him pull me along for a few miles. Before long, I found my stride again, and settled into a groove.

And just in time, too. McGall's Hill loomed ahead, and it seemed to have grown since I'd last seen it. That leaden feeling crept back into my legs, and I concentrated on just moving ahead, putting one foot in front of the next. Looking off to my left I saw rolling green fields. Sitting there on the hillside was a woman with long brown hair, with her dog by her side. She smiled and waved, and I waved back.

And then I was at the top of the hill. This time, I noticed that there was a church on the hilltop, and, to its right, a cemetery. I was glad I didn't notice it earlier; it would have seemed too ominous. But not now; McGall's Hill was history.

Now I relaxed, remembering the flat miles that lay ahead. The heat was taking its toll, however, and I worried that soon I would start slowing down. As I re-entered Flatts Village, I tried to put a confident face on my running, for myself as well as for the spectators. I heard someone call out "You're seventeenth!" Me? Really? I've never had someone yell out my place during a race before. One more benefit of a small race field. It was enough to give me a boost over the next few miles.

I realized that the crowds, sparse though they were, were as determined as the runners to see the race through. They remembered me from my first lap, and called out as I passed by. The children waved and the women smiled. "You're looking good!" the old women said. "You too!" I replied, and they laughed and laughed. The old man I saw on the first loop, still sitting in his chair, waved to me like he's known me for years, and up ahead I saw Runner Number 16. It seemed that he wasn't that far ahead.

The street signs read "4 kilometers to Hamilton," and I tried to accelerate. The scooter-man pulled alongside again. No thanks, no candy for me, but thank you, thank you. More people lined the path now, and I started counting down the minutes I thought I had left to run. Mile 25 was downhill, and I wondered whether the extra speed I gained from the descent was worth the pain in my legs and lungs. But there was Mr. 16, and I was near to him, very near, then next to him. He smiled and said hello. I smiled back, and surged onward. Up ahead was Front Street again, and the finish line, meant for me this time. I crossed it, relieved and grateful for having completed another marathon, to have another medal. I turned around, and there was Mr. 16th, though now he was 17th. We smiled, less competitors now than comrades-in-arms.

I stepped inside the terminal, and went upstairs where there was the promise of food and drink. I took in fluids during the race, but it was so hot, and now I was so thirsty. Race Secretary Pam Shailer told me that it actually *hailed* during race weekend the previous year, and I was happy to have been spared any rain or ice. There were pastries, fruit, hot chocolate, and soup laid out for us, and soon I felt revived. Downstairs, there were two massage therapists ministering to the runners, and I got in line. When it was my turn, the therapist introduced himself—his name was John Ford, and he seemed to know just about everyone there. More importantly, his fingers were magic, and brought welcome relief to my tired body.

Marathon number 58 was in the books.

Running Tip #9

Avoid Hyponatremia

Hyponatremia is the opposite of dehydration; it's a dilution of sodium and other electrolytes caused by drinking too much water, which is most common among athletes who are on the marathon course for more than 4½ hours. It can be deadlier than dehydration, and in extreme cases, can lead to coma or even death.

Because its symptoms are similar to those of dehydration, hyponatremia is often misdiagnosed. The first question to ask a runner in distress is how much water have they been drinking? That will tell you what their problem likely is.

Over-the-counter nonsteroidal anti-inflammatory drugs ("NSAIDs"), such as aspirin, naproxen sodium (Aleve), and ibuprofen (Advil and Motrin), seem to increase the risk, perhaps because they inhibit the body's ability to excrete water. Women might also be at higher risk because they're smaller than men and can more easily overload on water.

Symptoms

- *fatigue*
- *cramping*
- *dizziness, nausea and vomiting*
- *bloating and puffiness in the face and fingers*
- *headache, confusion, and fainting*

Prevention

- *Use sports drinks that contain sodium.*

- *Add salt to your food in hot weather, unless you're on a salt-restricted diet.*

- *If you feel symptoms of hyponatremia while running, eat some salty food, like pretzels.*

- *Don't take any NSAIDs immediately before or during your race; if you must take a pain reliever, take acetaminophen (Tylenol).*

Running Here, Running There, Running Everywhere!

In March 2001, I traveled with an American Diabetes Association fund-raising team to Italy for the Rome Marathon. With the ancient Coliseum as a backdrop, the race start was as impressive a sight as one could ever hope to find. As I stood shoulder to shoulder with the mass of other runners, I realized that I'd never before encountered such a stink from a race crowd, particularly before the event even started. Did no one here ever use deodorant?

Self-preservation led me to work my way out of the crush in search of fresh air. I wriggled to the outside, and wandered forward, where the elite runners waited in secure corrals. I saw the Africans, loose and smiling and confident. And there was an Italian team, laughing, standing around ... and smoking. I blinked in disbelief. Yep, there they were, sneaking in a last butt before the gun went off. *Only in Italy*, I thought.

With the race start just minutes away, I gulped in a lungful of fresh air and dove back into the crowd. Suddenly the mass surged forward. I assumed that the race staff had opened up the corrals, and that the crowd was pressing forward toward the starting line. I expected that our advance would soon grind to a halt, but somehow the crowd kept pressing forward. Soon there was enough room for us to break into an easy run. I couldn't understand what was going on.

Slowly it dawned on me that the race had begun. There had been no announcement, no starting gun, and no countdown. The race utilized an electronic chip system, to track each runner, but still, it was a very unsettling way to start a race. A friend with more European racing experience than I had later told me that this was typical of races abroad; if the runners get impatient, the officials just send them, like a mother telling her whining kids, *Fine, you want to go out and play so badly, well, go!*

Organization continued to be a problem after the race was under way. The first water stop wasn't ready for us by the time we came streaking by. Since Rome, like many European marathons, provide water and sports drinks every 5 kilometers—3.1 miles to us Americans—rather than the traditional mile or two in the United States, that meant that many runners went without any water for the first 6 miles of the race. It was already shaping up to be a hot, sunny day, so I knew that dehydration would be a problem. I began forcing down extra fluids as soon as drinks were available, and I told the runners I was pacing to do the same.

Not everyone was thinking ahead, though. I spotted a runner from the Canadian Diabetes Association, who was wearing an outrageous sunburst team singlet, in contrast to the solid red shirt that my Team Diabetes runners wore. I introduced myself. His name was Geoff, and he was running his first marathon. I was pacing several of my teammates already, and we all decided to run together. Geoff was running very well, but he hadn't been taking in enough fluids, and as the miles wore on he began to cramp. My teammates and I made sure he drank more, helped him stretch, and even rubbed his aching calves. Geoff urged us to go on, but I told him that if I surged ahead to the finish line, this would be just another race for me, neither the best nor the worst of my finishing times. But if I stayed with him and made sure he finished, it would make the race much more meaningful. The other runners in our little group agreed, and we decided to finish the race together.

We continued past the Vatican and the Circus Maximus, down cobblestone streets and narrow alleys. The cobblestones turned out to be more foe than friend, as they robbed our legs of their bounce and left them sore and aching. Spectators yelled out *forza!* (strength). At one point I overheard a spectator yell out *bocca al lupo!* as we passed, to which one of my runners yelled back *crepi il lupo!* I asked the runner what all that ruckus was about.

"Ah," he said, "that's just something people say in Italy during races. He yelled, 'you're in the mouth of the wolf!' and I called back the traditional response, 'may the wolf die!' It's how they wish you good luck." Like almost everything Italian, it was more dramatic than how things are done back home.

As we ran, we picked up a few more Team Diabetes runners who were happy to share in the team spirit. Finally, the Coliseum, and the finish line, loomed up ahead. We crossed the finish line and celebrated like it was New Year's Eve. It was as happy a finish as I've ever seen, and Geoff thanked me by giving me his team singlet—more appreciated once I'd laundered it!—as well as buying me several beers at our team get-together that evening. The friendship we forged proved to be lasting; Geoff and I kept in touch after we returned home, updating each other on our lives and running, keeping alive the hope that we'll be able to meet up for another marathon someday.

After returning from Rome, I ran Boston again—I was becoming a regular, though I never took it for granted—and then I met up with Dave in Austria for the Vienna Marathon in May. He was there for work, and the timing seemed too good to pass up. We raced along the Danube, passing beautiful parks and buildings, as the Viennese called out "*Hopp hopp!*" meaning, "jump faster!" I felt like I was where I was supposed to be, doing what I was supposed to be doing. I was flying around the world, meeting wonderful people, running marathons, and also feeling like I was making a difference in people's lives. It all felt like an amazing dream. Everything was perfect.

It was May of 2001. It was the last season of our national innocence, before everything would change forever.

Running Tip #10

Travel Like a Runner

Before you go

- *Be willing to go it alone.* It's more fun to travel with friends, but you can make new friends easily during a race.
- *Clip your toenails before you leave home.* That's one less thing to worry about, and one less piece of equipment to risk getting confiscated by security.
- *Bring only carry-on baggage.* You'll be able to safeguard your racing gear, and you can more easily switch flights if there are any delays, or take advantage of requests for volunteers to give up their seats in exchange for free-flight vouchers.
- *Make a list of the essentials, and pack before the day of departure.* But don't panic if you forget something; unless you're traveling to a remote locale, you can still buy what you need when you arrive.

Be prepared for the flight

- *Drink plenty of water and bring your own healthy snacks.* Bring your own bottle and ask flight attendants to fill it.
- *Flex your legs or move around often.* The risk of developing potentially life-threatening blood clots during a long flight is higher among runners, perhaps because of our lower heart rate and blood pressure. Wearing compression socks might also help.

Have a plan

- *Deal with time zone changes.* Plan on one day of adjustment for every hour you lost or gained, although sometimes not adjusting works better if you're traveling east to west and you have a very early race start.
- *Scout around.* Become familiar with the course and the city. If you're racing in a high altitude, arrive in town a week early, or add 30 seconds per mile to your expected race pace.

Speed Dreams

It was a conundrum. I loved marathons so much that I wanted to run them as often as possible, yet the more I ran them, the harder it would be for me to reach my potential as a marathoner. Running a marathon just about every month relieved me of the need to do long training runs, since my races *were* my long training runs. But I sacrificed intense training between races, since I was usually either recovering from one race or tapering for the next. I knew that I was also preventing my body from fully recovering from each of my marathon efforts. This hadn't resulted in injury, but I wasn't priming my body for one supreme effort, the one that would get me to my next goal in running: a sub-three hour marathon.

Finally, in the summer of 2001, I decided to take up the challenge. I had run six marathons in the first half of the year, but I committed to making my next one—number 64—"The One." I took a month off from hard running to let my body fully rest, then picked the Steamtown Marathon in Scranton, Pennsylvania, in October as my target race. My work colleague and running buddy Jim was planning on doing it, and had been talking up its virtues. It was known as a fast race, mostly downhill, with a net drop of 955 feet. Eventually I was won over, and signed up, hoping that as long as I could keep my feet moving, I could count on gravity to bring me home in record time

That summer, Jim and I trained ferociously. Although I had done speed work with my running friends and run marathons with them, I had never before focused on a single race with any of them. Jim and I developed a unique camaraderie, stopping by each other's office with updates on our workouts and pace calculations. Our lunchtime tempo sessions, run faster than race pace, were epic. I loved them, and began to keep a journal to record my thoughts.

It's Thursday afternoon, and Jim is waiting for me. Today is our tempo run, a 10-mile loop that is supposed to leave us breathless and exhilarated. Last week Jim ran strong, and opened a half-block lead over me with two miles left. I forced my leaden legs to give just a little bit more, and Jim slowed just a bit to let me pull even. Afterward, I was exhausted. And now Jim is waiting for me again.

We start out easy, weaving through crowds and traffic. The D.C. parks insinuate themselves through the city like vines wrapping around a tree. Our loop takes us from the downtown business district to Georgetown, and from there onto a 3-mile wooded trail. We would emerge at the northern edge of the city and run down Connecticut Avenue, back to our starting point. It's a beautiful route, about 10 miles long, but it's also our proving ground. These weekly runs are an important part of my plan to build speed for Steamtown. If I can just keep up with Jim.

We work our way through Georgetown, and enter the woods. We're running well, but shorter on breath than either of us would like. Our conversation dwindles down to a few short words, and then just the sound of our heavy breathing. As we jump logs and hop over streambeds, I imagine that I'm an early settler, chasing game for the family dinner. Or perhaps an escaped convict, with the howl of bloodhounds getting ever louder behind me. Leaves brush past my face, and I feel a surge of energy. I pick up the pace.

We leave the woods, and I glance down at my watch. We're ahead of our usual pace, but the toughest part lies ahead. The downhill must be run hard if it is to be run honestly. It's a 4-mile stretch that should leave my lungs burning and my thoughts muddled. Less effort than that makes it just another easy run, and puts Jim a half block ahead of me.

We sweep down the avenue and overtake a bus picking up passengers. I consider the traffic lights ahead, and the scheduled stops the bus has to make. We'll run along the bus route for the next three miles, and if we run hard, I think to myself, we can beat it. Again, I pick up the pace.

Now we're flying, our bodies moving smoothly, feet barely touching the ground. We've raced the bus a full mile, and it still hasn't gotten the better of us. It pulls close, flirts with us, but then brakes to pick up passengers, or is halted by a red light. I become accustomed to the ebb and flow of its loud, droning engine. And then the National Zoo appears, its entrance gate enveloped by a swarm of tourists. We step out toward the street, and collect the open-mouthed stares of children. I pick up the pace.

Ahead is the bridge over Rock Creek Park. This is where I watched Jim surge ahead last week and was unable to match his strength. Today, my lungs are burning, but I feel strong. Jim falls a few strides behind, surges to make up lost ground, then falls back and surges again. He will not gain a half block on me today. The bus is behind us now for good, vanquished. We have less than two miles to go. I pick up the pace.

Now we make a left onto broad Massachusetts Avenue for the last few blocks of our run. We are running without thinking, like machines, just trying to hold on. "Almost there, just a little bit more," I intone, as much for myself as for Jim. And then we are just one block away. I am tired, but I am in love with the effort, and I tell Jim I will sprint the last block. He joins me, and we tear down the street, mad for speed and adrenaline.

And then the workout is over. We shuffle, letting our heartbeats slow and our breathing return to normal. I look at my watch. Six minutes faster than

*last week. "Great run," Jim says breathlessly. "Great run. My best 10-miler
ever." I smile and nod, happy and alive.*

*We take turns, Jim and I, pulling and pushing each other through our
training runs, tearing through the woods and racing buses, chasing after our
marathon dreams. We are athletes in the greatest, craziest, most competitive,
most supportive, most elegant, most brutal sport in the world. And next week,
with any luck, Jim will be waiting for me again, ready to hit the trails.*

That was my summer: sweat and effort and dirty running clothes.
The days shortened, and a chill crept into the air, and summer faded
behind us.

It was September, 2001.

When I was growing up, my parents and my older relatives would
sometimes recall exactly where they were and what they were doing when
President Kennedy had been shot. It seemed so odd to me for so many
people to have such a personal memory of such a famous moment.

Not any more.

I recall exactly where I was and what I was doing on the morning of
September 11th. I was in a neighborhood local gym where I trained, making
my way through a cardio session on some of the cross-training machines.
I distracted myself by looking up at the overhead TVs, catching the morning news. Little by little, reports came in about an errant plane that had
struck one of the World Trade Center towers. Like everyone else, I thought
it must have been an accident, similar to when a plane struck the Empire
State Building decades before. But of course, it was nothing like that, and
as the events of that morning unfolded, I stayed glued to my LifeCycle,
extending my workout from one hour, to two, to three. I couldn't leave my
seat, and almost compulsively, maniacally, I kept pedaling.

Reports of the second plane hitting a tower came in, and the footage
was horrible and mesmerizing. At one point, as the commentators talked
on about what was happening in Manhattan, I realized the footage of a

smoking building being shown on TV wasn't the World Trade Center; it was the Pentagon, right here in my city's backyard. Obviously, something had happened there as well, but hadn't yet been reported. I climbed down from the exercise bike. Everything seemed unreal as I made my way downstairs. By the time I got there, a staff member at the front desk told me that one of the towers had collapsed. The second one followed shortly after.

I called my office and spoke to one of my friends there. He told me that everyone who was there was preparing to leave, and that I shouldn't bother coming in. I cleaned up and went over to visit a friend who lived on the top floor of an apartment building. He had a beautiful view of the city, facing south to the Potomac River. Toward the Pentagon.

When I arrived there, I found that several others had come as well. We stared at the horizon, where a smoke cloud hung in the air. It was the first tangible proof that something terrible had happened. We sat most of the day with our eyes glued to the television, taking in the reports and trying to make sense of it all.

The next meeting of my charity marathon training group was somber. Instead of being upbeat and boisterous as usual, they were quiet and apprehensive. We had been training for a return trip to the Dublin Marathon, but with our departure only a month and a half away, there was little chance that we would see a return to normalcy before we were scheduled to depart. This was what we had to deal with.

We started off by talking about the toll that the recent events had taken on all of us. I said that I planned to continue training the group and would go to Dublin, as I hoped all of them would also do. Some people said that they no longer felt comfortable leaving the country. I wanted to tell them that everything would be okay and that they should still go, but how could anyone be sure?

Most of the runners opted to continue with the program. We would continue training, and go to Dublin. I hoped that I had not just put all of their lives at risk.

Meanwhile, Jim and I made it through our own training program, and drove out to Scranton on October 6, the day before the Steamtown Marathon. Scranton is an old locomotive town, and though its glory years are long gone, it honors its past with a museum and, of course, the race. I had calculated that I needed to run at a 6:51-per-mile pace to get my sub-3-hour time. 6:51. Just thinking about those numbers made me nervous.

On race day I felt good. The skies were clear, and there was a slight chill in the air. I did a light warm-up, and waited for the starter's gun, shaking my legs, looking for clues as to how they felt. Did they feel strong? Did they have pop? Was I hungry? Stuffed? Thirsty? Bloated? I considered it all, and decided everything was right. I was ready to go.

The race started, and we ran through the city streets, immediately lurching downhill. I was breathing cleanly, strongly. We twisted and turned on the city streets, and soon left them behind, heading out toward quieter roads. I felt great. I pulled ahead of Jim and weaved through the small crowd, feeling like I was hardly touching the ground. As we ran past tall trees bathed in green leaves, I struck up a conversation with a man next to me, and then passed him behind. I had never felt so good before so early in a race. I pitied all the other animals in nature for their slowness. I looked down at my watch. I was running 20–30 seconds faster than my goal pace. I should have been worried; energy is like a bank account, and if you spend it in one place, particularly early in a race, it won't be there later when you really need it. I was blowing my reserves with wild abandon, but I felt confident that I was fine. I had trained hard, and this was the pace that felt comfortable. Perhaps my energy account had accrued interest, I thought. I would not slow down. I would run hard and hold on to the finish line. It would be like Boston, but better.

It wouldn't take long for me to realize how wrong I was. I had carefully drawn up a training plan and spent months following it, but then I threw all that hard work away on race day. It was a rookie mistake, and there's a price to be paid for such recklessness. By mile 16, I knew that I would have to ante up. I hadn't yet slowed, but that intoxicating energy was ebbing, and I realized that I wouldn't be able to sustain the pace I had set. If I could just keep running well, though, I told myself, I still could make my sub-3-hour goal.

Over the next few miles, I slowly began to accept the reality of my situation. The hard downhill running had taken a toll on my quadriceps. I began to consider fallback goals as my sub-3-hour dream began to slip away. By mile 20 I was running on a beautiful bicycle path through the woods, but I couldn't enjoy it. I was in trouble, and like a beaten fighter looking for a place to fall down, I began to consider when I would start walking.

Walk breaks are an accepted part of racing for many people, especially first-time marathoners, and I recommend them to my teams. When you take a walk break, you give your running muscles a moment's rest, and you also give your mind a manageable goal to work with: just run reasonably hard for another mile, and then you can have another walk break. Breaking the race up into segments like that makes it seem much easier to handle. As I've told my teams, the marathon is just too big to swallow in one gulp.

In Steamtown, though, my walk breaks during the last 6 miles of the race were not strategic. They were acts of desperation. My legs ached with fatigue, and they demanded that I stop running. As soon as I started walking, the race I had trained for was effectively over. I managed to talk my legs into running again for a few minutes at a time over the final few miles, but as the minutes ticked by, I saw even my various fallback goals slip away. First, my dream of a sub-3 hour finish vanished, followed shortly by my hopes for a new personal record. Eventually, I realized that I would not even achieve a Boston qualifying time. Finally, I reached the last stop on my descent: I just wanted to finish the race. When it was finally, mercifully, over, my official time was 3:20:14. Not bad, really: it was the eighth best time of the sixty-four marathons I had run, but that was a deceiving statistic. The Steamtown Marathon had broken me.

As I gathered myself and waited for Jim, I thought about a story a childhood friend recently told me. Supposedly, a new guy had recently walked into a gym back in New York where we used to train and started boasting about how much he could lift. "It's all mind over matter," he said. "If I can believe it, my body can achieve it." With that, he loaded 300 pounds onto the bench press, laid down on the bench, lifted the bar off the support, and ... crashed it down onto his face, knocking out three teeth.

The lesson, of course, is that mind over matter works *as long as you're in the ballpark.* I could believe with all my heart and soul that I could fly, but if I jump out of a top floor window, I'm still going to go splat on the sidewalk.

That's how I felt about my performance in Steamtown. I went splat. There was nothing in my training to justify the early pace I had set for myself. My training hadn't put me in the ballpark for the race I was running. It was a difficult lesson to learn, especially at this late date, when I already had a dozen years of marathoning experience behind me and should have known better. As much as I tried to put on a happy face, it was hard for me to hide my sadness and anger. I had wasted a good opportunity to achieve something special.

Once, long ago, I swore to myself that if ever I crossed a marathon finish line and was disappointed, I would hang up my running shoes. Was it now time for me to quit? I thought things over during the long drive home. By the time I reached my apartment, I had reconciled myself to what had happened. I decided that whatever my original goal had been, finishing the race was still a wonderful achievement, especially given how badly I felt during those last few miles. I could have quit, but didn't, and that was still something to be proud of.

I wasn't ready to hang up those shoes just yet.

Running Tip #11

Training Food

People exercising for 90 minutes should take in 4 calories per minute to maintain performance—that's up to 240 calories per hour. Not an easy task.

That's where sports gels come in. Basically, they are just sugary syrups, often caffeinated, that are easily digested for a quick mid-run energy boost.

- *Take with water.* They need water to break down, so take with 6–8 ounces of water. Sports drinks won't do the trick, since those extra carbs may be more than the stomach could absorb.
- *Experiment with the different flavors.*
- *Aim to take one every 45 minutes to an hour.*
- *Consider alternatives.* If you can't tolerate sports gels, experiment with other low-fat, easily-digested foods, like energy bars. There are even chewy bite-sized blocks and jelly beans especially for athletes.

Back to Where It All Began

I was glad to have worked my way through my disappointment with Steamtown so quickly, because my charity teams were making their final preparations for their own races. It wouldn't have helped them much to have a despondent coach.

First up was a return trip to Dublin. I was thrilled to be back; Dublin had become one of my favorite cities, and this time I knew exactly where I wanted to go and what I wanted to do. There was my favorite fish and chips stand next to the Jury's Hotel, and a pub in the Temple Bar district that had the best traditional Irish music. I also wanted to visit a great sweater shop I discovered on the previous trip, and revisit the beautiful Book of Kells at Trinity College.

And then, of course, there was also the race. This time we got lucky with the weather; skies were gray, but there was none of the rain and wind that had vexed us all the year before. All team members crossed the finish line without any significant problems, making me a happy coach indeed.

After the race was over, I set out with a woman I was dating and a few other people for a side trip to western Ireland, to visit Galway and the surrounding areas. The Irish countryside is starkly beautiful, with a checkerboard of stone fencing surrounding small, romantically weathered castles. We visited the Cliffs of Mohr, with its sudden and dramatic 700-foot drop. I was brave and cocky until we neared the cliff's edge, and then I chickened out like all the other visitors and got down on my belly and crawled to the edge to peer over the side.

I also learned the origin of the intricate piping patterns on the traditional Irish sweaters that I had bought. Traditionally, each clan was known by a particular pattern knit into their sweaters, much like a heraldic coat of arms. But instead of just being for show or vanity, these patterns served a grim purpose—they enabled the quick identification of drowned fisherman when their bodies were recovered. This was a harsh reminder that for all the beauty of the land, this could be a difficult and unforgiving place to live.

My Ireland trip drew to a close, but I wasn't ready to go home. I was about to meet up with another of my charity teams for a different adventure. We were going to visit the roots of the marathon, to retrace the steps taken by the ancients. We were going to Greece to run the Athens Marathon.

The racecourse would roughly follow the original route Phidippides supposedly traveled, from the still open and wind swept plains of Marathon, around the burial mound underneath which lay the remains of soldiers who fought that battle so long ago. From there, the route passed through the Greek countryside from town to town, until it reached its finish in the heart of Athens. It felt like a homecoming of sorts to me, though I'd never been there before. It was a race that I'd known for a long time that I would have to run.

Although cloaked in myth and legend, this event was still an actual race, and organizers would have to overcome the usual logistical problems. For years, the knock against the Athens Marathon was that it failed to provide enough water on the course. In 2001, the organizers finally solved that problem, placing drinks every 5 kilometers, and adding a few more water stops for good measure.

But we also had some unexpected water; the torrential downpour we missed in Ireland caught up with us in Greece. Most runners sought shelter in a nearby stadium construction site. Eventually, with clenched teeth and muttered curses, we all made our way through the downpour to the starting line. The race I had dreamed about for years was about to begin.

Running in the rain is not really such a bad experience. Even if it wasn't raining, we would all be soaked eventually by our own sweat. Our concern was really for our feet. When socks get wet, there's a greater chance of getting blisters, and a bad blister could ruin the most well-prepared athlete.

That day, things were not looking so good for our feet. Several sections of road were flooded under several feet of water. Some runners tried to cope by using garbage bags as waders, but discovered that the bags quickly tore and let water in. Others charged through, and either soaked their shoes or had them sucked off their feet by the thick mud below. Most of us just circled as wide as possible around these little lakes, climbing around grass and bushes. In the end, it didn't matter what each of us did; we were all going to get drenched by race's end. I was as soaked as I'd ever been, and that includes swimming.

The race presented other surprises as well. Athens is famous for its pack of wild, though mostly friendly, dogs. I had seen them and been trailed by them throughout the city, but I didn't expect to see them on race day. But there they were on the course, eyeing us curiously. Several of them decided to run alongside us for several kilometers. I was leery at first—even a friendly dog may be tempted to bite a runner—but they were as amiable and uncomplaining as any companion I've ever run with, and I was a bit sad when they decided not to go all the way with me to the finish line. They made a much better impression than the famous cats of Rome, who were nowhere to be found on race day.

Finally, the rain tailed off as we neared the outskirts of Athens. The traffic thickened, and stores and stop lights appeared. Near the 18-mile mark, we hit the big hill—there's always a big hill, remember?—and then we descended into the city for one of the most glorious finishes in marathoning: a loop on the track in the 1896 marble stadium that hosted the first modern Olympic Games. As the stadium came into view, my pulse quickened, and I picked up the pace for a strong finish. The course brought us closer to the stadium, and then ... led us past it. We had to run a little farther down the street and double back to the stadium. I felt like one of my canine companions might feel if a juicy steak waved in front of his nose, only to have it yanked away at the last second. It was a deflating moment, but when I finally did enter the stadium minutes later, my loop on that historic track made up for all the difficulties I'd had to overcome that day. It was my 66th marathon finish, and it was as sweet a moment as I'd ever had in road racing.

Running Tip #12

Running Etiquette

- *Stay to the right.* It's the rule with cars, and it should be the rule with people, too. Let faster runners and cyclists pass.
- *Don't run more than two people across.* If you hog the road, you're asking for trouble.
- *If you need to slow down or stop, step to the side.*
- *Be responsible for your own needs.* If you see someone else's cache of water or goodies sitting by the side of the road, don't touch it. They'll be counting on it being there when they need it. Choose training routes that pass by water fountains or convenience stores, or plant your own provisions by the side of road.
- *Be an honest racer.* If you're not a 5:30 mile, don't line up in the front of the pack before a race; you'll only get in the way of the faster runners. Plus, it's no fun getting passed.
- *Go the extra mile.* We're all part of a fitness community, and we should act like it. Wave and say hi to other runners, and offer extra water or goodies if you have them handy and someone looks like they could really use it. But be respectful of others; friendliness in the running community is not an invitation to distract or harass other runners.

As my marathon tally rose, I never gave up trying to understand my passion for the marathon. I knew instinctively that my running was meaningful in a way that I hadn't yet been able to explain, but now that I was recruiting and training team participants for my charity fund-raising teams, I knew that I had to find a way to articulate my reason for running 26.2 miles.

Information meetings usually began in the evening, after I had left my regular day job and my work as a lawyer. I began with the easy stuff, speaking about the joy of experiencing your body moving easily and powerfully, of the need to break through assumed or self-imposed limitations to discover the true potential hidden within all of us. I spoke of the satisfaction found in accomplishing the seemingly impossible, of proving wrong all those people who doubted not that it could be done, but that *they* could do it. I told them of my belief that everyone ought to have something they do that causes them to lose track of time, whether it's music or art or reading. For me, it's running. I rely on that quiet time to balance out the other demands on my life. I told them it might be the same for them as well.

Warmed up, I then spoke of the rewards to be found in accomplishing a difficult task. In a high school mythology class, we had been assigned Joseph Campbell's *The Hero with a Thousand Faces*, which explains the common threads of humankind's hero legends. The hero, Campbell explained, always sets out on a quest, separating himself from the ordinary routines of everyday life, and ventures to a land of danger. He confronts a great challenge, and after emerging triumphant, he returns home with a boon for mankind, whether fire, the Golden Fleece, defeat of the Minotaur, or great wisdom.

That is the hero's tale, I told my audience, and that is the tale of the marathoner, because the marathon is a heroic journey. Setting ourselves apart from our neighbors through our months-long ritual of training and sacrifice, we face the challenge of race day, when we test our resolve and preparation over miles of arduous roads, emerging, we hope, at the finish line, having gained wisdom about ourselves. Upon crossing that line, we are all of us transformed, having sensed our own power and determination, capable now of being masters of our fate rather than passive spectators.

I told them how running seems to bring out the best in all of us. I told them about Grete Waitz, the nine-time winner of the New York City Marathon. In 1993, Grete was in New York just as a friend of the race, and to support her husband, who was running. While she was there, she met Zoe Koplowitz, a marathoner who suffers from multiple sclerosis, and who competes while using crutches. It usually takes Zoe about 24 hours to finish a marathon, by which time there is hardly anyone at the finish line. Grete promised Zoe that she would wait for her at the finish line.

In the early hours of the morning following the race, Grete ran out to the finish line to see if Zoe was there yet; Zoe was close, but hadn't yet come into view. Then Grete discovered that there weren't any more finishers' medals left. Horrified and embarrassed, she ran back to her hotel room and grabbed her husband's medal, telling him "you don't really need another one," and made it back to the finish line in time to put it around Zoe's neck when she crossed it.

I told them that I often think of that story, about the caring of an elite runner for all the other brave people who attempt the marathon, and of the courage of a challenged runner like Zoe Koplowitz, whose achievement makes me thankful for simply having the opportunity to train and race. I don't know if running attracts good people, or if running makes people good, but there is a shared sense of understanding and respect among marathoners, a camaraderie forged by sweat and effort and sacrifice.

This is the marathon experience, I told them, and it is wondrous. I recalled for them the running of the 100th Boston Marathon in 1996, when defending champion Uta Pippig faded back behind young and strong Tegla Loroupe. It soon became apparent that Uta's difficulties were caused by the onset of menstruation and related intestinal problems, but Uta would not give in to the pain and discomfort. She gritted her teeth and flew past Tegla in the last few miles, en route to another first-place finish. That was as heroic an achievement as I've ever seen. When once asked why she runs the marathon, though, Uta simply answered, "I make the marathon beautiful for myself and for others. That's why I'm here."

I repeated that word, "beautiful," and looked out on the puzzled faces in my audience. Pain itself isn't beautiful, I said, but there is a beauty to effort, to perseverance, that marks it as special, as near as we may come to perfection.

I told them, too, of my own marathoning history. This is always a tricky business because I wanted to inspire them, not intimidate them. Many people find it easy to draw a distinction between what I've done and what they can do, saying that I must have some special gifts that enable me to accomplish these running feats. I told them that if I have any special gift, it's just stubbornness. There's nothing special about me that enables me to run so many races. My body might be a bit more durable than others, but there's really no reason why most of them couldn't run the same races that I do. All they need, I told them, is the determination to try. And despite my own experience, most people find that one marathon is plenty!

Some people nodded their heads, and some seem moved. Others sat politely in mute attention. Many of them joined our teams, and many did not. I always came away from these meetings with mixed emotions, feeling that I touched on something important, but that I'd circled rather than pierced the bulls-eye. I didn't manage to get to the heart of it; I couldn't fully explain what I felt. It was a frustrating, tiring business.

One moment crystallized my thinking. I had returned to Rome in 2002, and I had just finished pacing a group of my Team Diabetes runners to the finish line—marathon number 68 for me. Their day was over, but mine continued, as I ran back and forth on the course to cheer on the rest of my team and all the other race participants. I awaited two young women in particular: members of my team who were pushing against the clock. The race director, I knew, would shut off a section of the course at an appointed hour in order to let the city reclaim its streets, and the remaining runners on the course would have no choice but to cut the race short. It was a bum deal for those who had worked so hard and been struggling for so many hours, but there was no possibility for appeal. As I waited, I realized that my last two team members had not made the cutoff. They would cross the finish line, but they would not have completed 26.2 miles.

After the race, all of our teams from across the country returned to our host hotels, freshened up, and then gathered in the evening for a celebration dinner. There were smiles by the hundreds, and stories of obstacles overcome, random moments of hilarity, and new friendships forged. Above all, there was the electricity of accomplishment and pride. Whatever else may ever be said of them, they were now and forever marathoners.

But my two young women were not there. They were still upstairs in their shared room, and would not join us. Their marathon had been one of sacrifice and persistence without reward. They felt that they had nothing to celebrate. When I realized that they hadn't come down, I went up to talk with them.

I knocked on their door, and they let me in. I sat down, and asked how they were doing. Their words tumbled out in a flood, mixed with tears of frustration and anger. They spoke of their bitter disappointment, of the months of hard work they had poured into their dream, of their confidence in their ability to realize that dream if only it had *not been stolen from them,* of their dread of having to explain their failure to friends and family when they returned home. I sat and listened and tried to think of a way that I could tell them that there was nothing to be upset about, but I could not. It would be a lie.

But I did have something to say. I told them of the history of the race, of Phidippides's 25-mile journey, of the modern Olympic Games and the 1.2-mile accommodation to the British Royal family. I explained that the modern marathon is an exact distance, but that there is nothing sacred or immutable about the number 26.2. By itself it is without meaning; we alone give it meaning.

I spoke about time. I explained that my best time in a marathon is not the race in which I ranked highest; on that grand day in Detroit, I finished far behind the lead pack of runners, but I have never run faster. In other races, such as in Bermuda, I ran slower, but I finished higher in the final tally because my competitors were slower still. On which day, I asked them, was I the better runner? Of which day should I be proudest? I told them of my race in Pittsburgh, where I fought through heat and dehydration to finish over an hour slower I expected to. Rather than being despondent, though, I was thrilled with my performance that day, because I felt that I had shown courage.

So, I asked them, if distance doesn't matter, and time doesn't matter, what is the marathon about? What remains? In the end, what matters?

I spoke more about Detroit and Pittsburgh. Anyone can run well on a day when everything is in magical alignment, when your training has peaked, when injuries have been held at bay, when the course and the weather are perfect. Then performance is easy. In Detroit, I simply ran, like a machine. But in Pittsburgh, on the day when things were most difficult, when it would have been easiest to quit, that was the day when I asked more of myself than I thought I was able to give. It is in that kind of moment that glory can be found.

But in Rome, these two women had been denied their moment of glory. I told them that I knew that their victory had been stolen from them. But they had not given up. They had struggled, and had not turned away, even when they knew that they would ultimately not make the cutoff time, and would be rerouted on the course. There was no shame in what they had done, and their accomplishment was not lessened by the race director's decision. I told them that they had not completed a marathon; that was a simple fact that none of us could ignore. But they had not quit. They had transcended distance and time, and found something greater than just crossing a finish line; they had discovered the depth of their own power and determination. There would be other finish lines if they wanted them, as there were for me after my first disastrous marathon attempt, but they were already heroes, because they had journeyed and sacrificed and brought back the wisdom of self-knowledge.

We sat a while longer, and finally I stood up to leave. They thanked me earnestly, perhaps more for recognizing and validating their pain than for any other solace I tried to give them. As I walked away, I thought about what I had said, and tried to hold onto those thoughts the way you try to hold on to a dream upon waking. I felt that I had touched on something. This time, I had not become lost in a fog of words. This time, perhaps, I had moved just a step closer to finding the answer to my question.

In the meantime, I kept racing. Having tasted racing on foreign soil, it was all I really wanted to do. In March 2002, I raced Rome again, and then in April, I flew to Paris. I was certain that there was no better way to see a city than by running through it, and if there was one city that was big enough and beautiful enough to amaze runners over 26.2 miles, I was sure it would be Paris. But on race day, as I joined the 20,000 other runners gathered in the shadow of the Arc de Triomphe, I wondered whether it was fair of me to hold this race to such a high standard. It was a living city, not a museum showpiece, and this was a race, not a luxury tour. I tried to temper my expectations. There would be good parts and bad parts, I reminded myself, and all that I could be certain of was that eventually, if I kept moving forward, I would reach the finish line.

I needn't have worried. The City of Light turned out to be as glorious as I'd imagined it would be. After racing down the Champs-Élysées, we toured the parks and streets of the city, and then raced along the Seine. The Eiffel Tower loomed in the distance. It was breathtaking. Along the way I saw couples running in wedding attire, and heard shouts of *"Bon courage,"* and *"Allez! Allez!"* meaning, "Go! Go!" I later read in the *New York Times*[7] that spectators had taunted runners by shouting "Only 500 kilometers left!" and "Run faster! They're about to open the street up to cars!" According to the *Times*, the French appreciate track and field stars, but feel an ambivalence bordering on disdain for middle-of-the-pack runners. But I didn't hear any of those catcalls. Or maybe it was just that I don't speak French. For me, at least, marathon number 69 was perfect.

After returning from Paris, I settled into the morass of heat and humidity that is D.C. in the summertime. With temperatures climbing up into the 80s and 90s, there wasn't much for a marathoner to do; it was too hot for race organizers to safely hold any long distance events in all but the most northern of cities, or in chilly San Francisco, which is no surprise to anyone who's been there in July. So summer usually stretches out into a long season of training and catching up with running friends. And of making plans for the smorgasbord of fall races.

My grandmother used to have a saying: you make plans and God laughs. She was about to be proven right.

---

7 April 14, 2002, p.10.

Running and Romance

I have to admit it: my love for running marathons required a certain amount of understanding from the women I dated. We marathoners are a tough group for nonrunners to understand. We train our bodies for our own health and vanity, and then race to prove to ourselves how tough we are. Every day's activities are planned around the run. Friends and families sometimes take a back seat. Like most marathoners, I didn't really see anything wrong with this. I thought it was fair for me to have a space in my life that was all my own. As long as I didn't ignore any responsibilities, I didn't see anything wrong with doing what I wanted to do.

Unless, of course, I wanted to share my life with someone else. Most women who at first were attracted to my passion for running soon tired of my priorities. My getting up at 5 A.M. to run or meet with personal training clients, and fading by 9 or 10 at night, didn't help either. Eventually, they all asked why I couldn't just sit down and relax.

On occasion I dated another runner. It seemed like the natural thing to do: find someone who shared my passion and interest. All of my friends expected this of me; what could be more natural than for a marathoner to be involved with another marathoner?

As it turned out, it wasn't really that simple. Learning to date and train with someone as active as myself raised new issues. We all define ourselves in many different ways. For me, being a marathon runner is a big part of who I am. The athletic women I dated felt the same way, but sometimes their emotional lives were more complex. One woman in particular that I dated had always been the athletic alpha partner, faster and fitter than her dates. In this important arena, success defined her as a person. Things were different when I came along. Suddenly, she wasn't the one who could run or bike farther and faster, and she wasn't used to that. Whether we realized it or not, we weren't just romantically involved, we were competitors. Even as she tried to hide it, resentment and anger grew, and spilled out in small ways, and I didn't know how to handle it. After all, *I* didn't feel the need to compete with *her*. But it was easy for me to feel this way, since I wasn't the one having my self-image challenged. Would I feel comfortable if she was a better runner than I was? I'd like to think so, but I don't know for sure.

Ultimately, that relationship didn't work out, and not just for that reason, but it did play a part. I knew that things didn't have to be like that in every dual-athlete relationship; there were plenty of successful running couples out there. It just wasn't happening for me. But that was okay. I didn't feel the urgent need to settle down anyway.

But I did want a special person in my life someday, and to have a home and family: the whole nine yards. Suddenly, that person entered my life. Or rather, re-entered. It was Stephanie Kay, the former high school classmate from Boston whom I had tried to contact years before. Our class was now about to mark its twentieth graduation anniversary. Some class members had set up a Web site, and e-mails were flying in all directions. I thought I'd give it one more shot, so I sent her an e-mail. She wrote back. I answered, and then so did she. She told me that she had gotten my message years earlier, and had wanted to call me back, but that my message had been lost at her office. We now exchanged phone numbers, and had hours-long conversations about running and art and anything we could think of. One night, as we spoke on the phone, we hit a natural stopping point. There was just nothing else that came to mind to say. I expected her to wrap things up, but instead she waited on the phone for wherever our conversation would go next. It hit me right then: she liked me.

It was a long time coming, actually. I first met her back in 1976, when we both entered junior high school together in New York City. I was just twelve, and was immediately smitten, but at that tender age I was too shy and inexperienced to know what to do about it. So I did nothing.

The years passed, and although I never managed to ask Stephanie out, I did manage to become friends with her. Finally, we were in twelfth grade—seniors at last! Our senior trip was a ski weekend, and one night, as several of us were relaxing after a long day of skiing, I managed to finally ask her for a date. Sort of. I asked if she'd like to take a walk in the woods with me. With hindsight I can see how this could have seemed a little too bold. Stephanie must have thought so, because she politely declined. Later, she wrote some nice things in my yearbook, but signed it "wuv." Sadly, the replacement of that "L" with a "W" told me all that I needed to know about her feelings for me.

And now, all these years later, we were talking, and then making plans to meet up in New York. Then she visited me in D.C., and I visited her in Boston. By the time the reunion came around we were a couple. Little by little her "W" turned into an "L."

I had come to think of D.C. as my home, but the more time I spent with Stephanie in Boston, the more I grew to love it there. Which is not to say that every visit was like a fairy tale come true. For example, that summer I went up to visit her for the July 4th weekend. We avoided the throngs of people mobbed along the Charles River to watch the fireworks and hear the Boston Pops, but the next morning was clear and beautiful; a perfect day for an easy 8-mile run along the river. Evidence of the previous evening's celebration was everywhere, although cleanup crews were already hard at work emptying overstuffed trash cans and picking up litter, oblivious to the runners and cyclists flying past them.

Along the bicycle trail sat row upon row of portable toilets, put in place over the previous several days to handle the crush of revelers. Now, like cannons left on a battlefield, they sat silent, but apparently still usable. I don't usually have access to such conveniences except on race day; my training runs are often marked by moments of brilliant improvisation in dealing with bathroom issues. But now, faced with such opulence, I decided to use one of the silent soldiers.

I swung open the door on the nearest Porta-Jon. Just as I was getting comfortable, I heard the sound of a truck nearby. Very nearby. Suddenly I felt the stall move. I jumped to my feet and grabbed at the door, but it was pinned shut by the long metal arms of the truck's hydraulic lift. I was trapped!

I wasn't sure whether to laugh or scream. I opted for shouting, and after several tense moments of yelling and peering out of the mesh screen at the top of the stall, I finally caught the driver's attention. He motioned to me to stay put—where would I possibly go?—and he moved the truck so that I could free myself from my little prison. As I resumed my run under the bemused gaze of the driver, I wondered whether anyone would believe what had just happened to me. What if I couldn't get the driver's attention? Is there a secret Porta-John burial ground? Would it be more than a days' run from where I was staying in Boston? Would Stephanie recognize me if I even made it back to her? Would she want to?

But luckily, I made it back to Stephanie safe and sound, and we continued our courtship.

And that's how I found myself one afternoon at the top of Old Rag Mountain in the Shenandoahs, about to get down on one knee. It was a beautiful, sunny day, with a nice crispness in the air. I had packed a lunch, including chocolates with strawberries, and a bottle of wine. And a diamond ring. My plan was to find just the right spot; someplace sheltered from the wind, but bathed in sunshine, with a sweeping view of the valley below. And I found it. Everything was perfect. I began to set out our lunch.

Just then a young woman and a few men passed by. We exchanged hellos, and then I heard a loud thud. The woman had fallen heavily while jumping from one rock to another, and had twisted her ankle badly. Right next to our spot. I suddenly had a vision of all my carefully laid plans going up in smoke. I reached into my bag for an ace bandage.

"Would you like to wrap your ankle, so you can *get going*?"

"No," she said. "But it hurts so much, I'm feeling nauseous."

Nauseous. Right next to our perfect spot. I waited twenty years for this moment, and now this woman is going to throw up on us.

"Would you like some water, so you can *get going*?"

"Ugh," she said. "I'm seeing spots."

Spots. I couldn't believe it.

"That must be the altitude," I told her. Look, I know the Shenandoahs are not the Himalayas, but I was improvising. "You need to be at a lower altitude. You really should *get going*."

Finally, I realized that this woman wasn't going to be able to move anytime soon. Her friends were helping her, so I wasn't needed, but I would have to change my plan. Luckily, Stephanie and I were able to find another suitable spot, and this time there were no interruptions when, all these years after I had asked her to walk in the woods with me, I asked her my second bold question.

And this time she said "yes."

Running Tip #13

Strength Training

There are runners who believe fervently in strength training, while others argue just as strongly against it. I'm a believer; strength training helps maintain good bone density, and running efficiency, and keeps injuries at a minimum.

- *Invest in some expert advice.* Paying a personal trainer to show you the right way to do your exercises is money well spent.
- *Always change your routine.* This keeps you and your body from getting bored, and provides the best stimulus to your body for adaptation, so alternate between free weights, cables, machines, and body-weight movements.
- *Work the core.* Any exercise that forces you to balance will work muscles crucial to your running, including your abdominals, lower back, glutes, and hip stabilizers.
- *Do complex movements.* The more joints you get involved, the more muscles you'll be training. So forget bicep curls; do some squats and push-ups.
- *Don't rest; alternate body parts.* You've got the endurance for this, so use it, and get your workout over in lightning speed.

A Race Like No Other

My fall 2002 racing campaign began with a solid run in the Toronto Marathon in September, followed by the Portland Marathon in early October, which enabled me to add Oregon to my list of states completed. Portland's race was as scenic and well-organized as any of the other dozens of marathons I'd run, but what stood out in my mind was a short, brutal climb up and over a short suspension bridge, and the tiny redwood saplings the volunteers handed out to finishers at the end of the race. The rest of the country had not yet added "carbon footprint" to their lingo, but Portland was way ahead of them.

Two weeks after crossing the finish line in Portland, I flew out to Amsterdam with a small team of Arthritis Foundation charity fundraisers. Little by little, I was working my way to Europe's greatest cities, and each one was proving to be more astonishing than the last. I loved Amsterdam for its streets and canals and museums, and yes, even its red-light district and marijuana-selling coffee shops, though I was too shy and conservative to do more than quickly walk past either. More to my liking was the wonderful Van Gogh Museum. There was also the famous Rijksmuseum to stroll through, as well as a somber visit to the house of

Anne Frank, the young victim of the Holocaust whose memoirs touched the world.

But I had other things on my mind as well. I was especially looking forward to the race; Amsterdam's marathon course had once held the marathon world record, and was reputed to be as beautiful as it was flat and fast. But the day before the marathon I fell ill with a bad cold, and on race day I felt miserable. Still, after traveling all that way to be with my team and run the race, I wasn't about to let a cold stop me.

The cold had other ideas. By the halfway point, I knew that I wouldn't be able to run the entire race, and that I'd be lucky to even finish as a walker. Still, I pressed on, running as much as I could, and walking the rest. As I stumbled on, I tried to appreciate the beauty of the course. It had meandered through the downtown area, then wandered to the outskirts of town, passing along a river and old windmills. It's often difficult to be objective about a racecourse when you've had a rough day; it's too tempting to think badly of a race in which you performed badly. But in Amsterdam, it was easy to see that despite my own difficulties, it was a wonderful race. I only regretted that I wasn't able to make the most of it.

Even in my depleted condition, however, I found myself trying to push as hard as I could. Seeing other walkers brought out my competitive juices, and I silently took aim at each one directly in front of me, quickening my pace to catch and pass them. It might sound compulsive, but this helped me feel like I was still part of a race, even as my expected finishing time soared higher than I ever thought it could be. When at long last I crossed the finish line, though, I wasn't concerned about my time; I was just thrilled that I had managed to go on when it would have been so easy to quit. It was a lesson I had learned before, but which was worth learning again: some of my best moments aren't my fastest moments.

Marathon number 72 was in the books.

Two weeks after running Amsterdam, I ran the New York City Marathon again. I had beaten my cold, and was ready for a real race.

But even with all I had experienced in fifteen years of racing, there were still some things to learn. For example, I had believed it to be impossible to urinate while running. To the extent that I had ever thought about it—and I know that by thinking about it at all I am among 1/100th of 1 percent of people on the planet—I had thought it was like keeping your eyes open while sneezing: theoretically possible, but not likely to be seen in my lifetime.

As it turned out, I was wrong. The race had just started, and all of us in our tens of thousands were huffing our way up the Verrazano Bridge, when I noticed some runners to my right who were transfixed with something just ahead of us. They seemed amazed. I saw why: a woman wearing nylon shorts was letting go as she ran. Besides being inconsiderate of those of us behind her—and was there ever a better incentive to pick up the pace and pass someone?—I couldn't imagine running 25 more miles on a crisp November morning in those soaked shorts. But maybe she had once had a bad Porta-Jon experience, too.

But that wasn't my problem. In fact I had few problems at all that day, and I was rewarded with a finishing time almost an hour faster than I had just posted in the Netherlands.

And then two weeks after that, I ran a local race in Maryland. It was a cold, wet day, and when I crossed the finish line, I was relieved to see that the race organizers had put out soup and pizza to revive us. I was famished, and stacked three slices of pizza one atop the other, downing them all at once like a big hoagie. I'm glad the race photographers didn't capture that moment.

Two weeks after *that* race, I returned to Hawaii with another charity team to run the Honolulu Marathon. On the flight home, I thought about how, after fifteen years of marathoning, my body seemed to need less and less recovery time. I didn't know exactly how this had happened, but my body had obviously adapted on a very fundamental level.

The marathons kept coming. Number 76: Miami; number 77: Boston, number 78: Kona, Hawaii.

Ah, Kona. A race obviously dreamed up by a sadist who knew nothing about running. It was held on the Big Island of Hawaii, which sounds like a tropical paradise to anyone who hasn't been there. To those in the know, however, most of the island is a hot, barren lava field. A friend of mine had run it the year before and had lost eight of her toenails due to swelling of her feet during the race. I had already weathered plenty of hot-weather racing, so I knew what to expect and how to handle it, but for the uninitiated—that is, for the virgin marathoners on my charity team—it was a brutal awakening. I tired to help them understand what they were up against, but no amount of talking was going to fully prepare them for the broiling moonscape on which they found themselves. I stayed on the course helping our runners—and anyone else I saw in difficulty—until our very last participant crossed the finish line. As much as I love the marathon, I think the best that could be said of this one is that we all managed to get through it.

After Kona, I believed that I had pretty much figured out the marathon. The scenery might change from race to race, the temperatures and elevation might vary, and the crowds might differ in size and enthusiasm, but the overall experience would usually be the same. There would be an adrenaline rush at the blast of the starting gun. There would be early optimism, shouts of support, and periodic aid stations. There would be eventual fatigue, and perhaps blisters. There would inevitably be a moment of truth, accompanied by a wave of determination, and then perseverance, culminating with euphoria at the finish line. This is the beauty of the marathon—its predictability, and its simplicity. You just run 26.2 miles as fast as you can, and if you do it right, there are usually precious few shocks along the way.

Or so I thought. Then I read about a marathon that is different from all the others, the name of which brings a smile to the face of those who are in the know: the Marathon des Châteaux du Médoc, or as it is more commonly and simply called, Médoc. If the marathon is the serious-minded older sibling of running, then Médoc is the wild child, looking for the nearest party. In a sport defined by discipline, Médoc is the Dionysian exception: a race that is more revelry than competition.

Created in 1985 as a tour for a group of athletic wine connoisseurs, the race is a September jaunt along roads and trails, past fifty-nine vineyards in Pauillac, in the Bordeaux region of southern France, by the shores of the river Gironde. To say that it is just a race through wine country, though, is like saying that Mardi Gras is just a celebration of Fat Tuesday, because the organizers have turned the marathon into a uniquely local creation; a celebration of the senses. It has become famous for wine, food and music stations along the course, and for the outlandish costumes worn by its participants. Even the race materials caution you to think of it as more of a tour than a competition. It is truly what Ernest Hemingway named Paris: a moveable feast.

I first learned about Médoc in the mid-90s in a newspaper article that took a "look what those crazy foreigners are up to now" approach to reporting on the race. The race was described as being more notable for the quantities of wine and oysters consumed than for fast times produced. While most marathons are a 26-mile adventure, Médoc sounded more like it needed a twelve-step program, but I was more intrigued than dismayed. I knew that some day I would have to experience it for myself.

Several obstacles became immediately apparent, starting with simply getting into the race. Like most chronic marathoners, I had become accustomed to having to compete with other applicants to get a number in the most popular races. Over the years, the Marine Corps Marathon began to fill up more and more quickly, and soon would close out within days of being open, while New York required split second timing just to get a race application considered. Still, these races offered enough slots to give most runners hope: 18,000, 25,000, or 35,000. Not so with Médoc. The narrow lanes along which the course meanders makes a huge field of marathoners impossible, so the race is limited to only 8,000 participants. It is also an immensely popular race, and registration closes out quickly. To race Médoc, you have to commit early and keep your fingers crossed.

In April 2002, when I traveled to Paris, I thought I had managed a particularly good coup at the marathon expo: I convinced a race official at the Médoc Marathon information booth to let me reserve a block of one dozen slots for my running friends and myself. I thought it would be an easy sell back home. The race official put his initials on an application and told me to send it in with payment for the reserved slots as soon as possible. I was so pleased with my good fortune that I sent in the money while I was still in France. But when I got back to the States, a voice mail message was waiting for me that said, in a thick French accent, that there was a problem with my race application. Not trusting phone contact, I sent an e-mail explaining the arrangement I had worked out with the race official. All settled, I thought. Then I received an e-mail in return telling me that my demand to talk to the race director was refused. I was confused. Obviously, this was going to be more complicated than I thought, especially since I didn't speak French.

As I tried to sort out the application process, I also began to consider the logistics. There weren't any direct flights from the United States to Bordeaux. The best that I could arrange was to fly direct to Paris, and then either take a connecting flight or a bullet train to Bordeaux. And on arrival, the difficulties don't end; Pauillac is far from the Bordeaux city center, and lodging there is very limited. The only workable option seemed to be to stay in the city and arrange for a driver to take me for the nearly hour and a half long ride to the race start.

Ultimately, my plans to run Médoc collapsed that year like a house of cards. Still, I had caught the scent, and I would not give up hope. And then suddenly, in 2003, the opportunity arose: Jenice Cunningham, a coach and team coordinator for the Arthritis Foundation based in Atlanta, was putting together a team. I knew Jenice from the Honolulu, Dublin, and Amsterdam marathons. Jenice had worked out all the details, and she had called me to find out if I wanted to come along. I answered yes before she was even finished asking the question.

With the logistics all taken care of, I settled into deciding on a training plan. Knowing that Médoc is no ordinary marathon, I wondered if I needed to alter my usual routine. Speed work is usually a part of my regular marathon preparation, and speed can pay off handsomely in Médoc, where I had heard rumors that the winner in each age category receives his or her weight in wine. I'm not an elite runner, though, so a fast marathon would leave me without the winner's prize and also without full enjoyment of the race's amenities. Even if I could somehow miraculously take first place, I didn't think I would be able to survive the reward, even with the help of my friends. I decided on a more leisurely approach to the race. I crossed speed work off my to-do list. So far, so good.

The next issue was thornier. How does one prepare to drink wine during a race? I considered adding alcohol to my training regimen, but I was unable to find any advice on how to do this. Should I slowly increase my intake week to week, along with my mileage? Would it matter what kind of wine I trained with? I scrapped the whole idea; I just would build up a solid running base and let the race-day drinking take care of itself.

Although I couldn't find any information on training for Médoc, I did find plenty of advice on how to actually run the race. The first suggestion I came across was to skip wine altogether for the first half of the race, on the theory that if I should then encounter any ill effects from wine tasting, I would be close enough to the end to successfully make it across the finish line. The second tip was to not actually swallow the wine. Instead, I was told to just swirl the wine in my mouth like a professional taster, and then spit it out. This would theoretically give me the pleasure of experiencing the wine without actually getting drunk, the reasoning being, I presume, that being drunk diminishes the chances of crossing the finish line. A third idea was to simply run the race in a straightforward, no-funny-business manner—no wine, no food, no partying. Then, after coming across the finish line, I could make my way back on to the course to eat and drink to my heart's content.

These all seemed like very well-reasoned strategies. Naturally, I ignored them all. I had decided against running Médoc carefully and strategically; that just didn't seem to be true to the spirit of the race. Spitting out wine must be a kind of heresy in France, and as for backtracking the course, when my legs cross a finish line, they know the race is over, and they don't like to run after that. I decided to experience the race fully and let the chips fall where they may.

There was, however, one more issue I would have to consider before making my way to the starting line: what to wear. Usually this is a simple matter: shorts and singlet in warm weather, graduating through different combinations until I came to tights, gloves and a hat, with a long-sleeved top and jacket, in the coldest weather. Médoc, of course, demanded a different approach. The race materials not only mentioned that most participants wear a costume, but also promised an extra prize for all participants who did so.

What's that old phrase? In for a penny, in for a pound. Everyone in my group—myself included—decided that we would go the extra mile, so to speak, and wear a costume. But whatever we chose would have to be not only eye-catching, but practical as well. After all, this wasn't just some Halloween bash or a Thanksgiving Turkey Trot; we would have to wear this costume for 26.2 miles. With that in mind, Jenice's group agreed on the perfect outfit: grass skirts and leis over our running duds. I daringly cut the skirt down to make it more suitable for running— almost a grass miniskirt, really. I smiled at the incongruity of seeing it lying next to my usual race gear, but I began to relax. All the big issues were now decided.

Finally, September rolled around, and I found myself boarding a jet for a red-eye flight to Paris. I arrived almost too tired to appreciate the gleaming glass and steel of Charles de Gaulle airport as I made my way to my connecting flight. In the months since I committed to the race, international events had stormed onto the front pages as we moved closer toward war with Iraq. I wondered whether the rift between the U.S. and French governments would affect my travel and race plans, and whether Americans would no longer find themselves welcome in Bordeaux. I've long believed in the spiritual healing power of a marathon, but this was a tall order. Could wine, food, and running bring us together? I'd soon find out.

My flight landed in Bordeaux without incident, and if I had any doubts about where I was, they were quickly dispelled as giant bottles of cabernet sauvignon stared down at us from atop the baggage carousels. After a short ride to our hotel and a quick check-in, several of us went out for a walkabout.

Bordeaux seemed to be in the early stages of a renaissance, with ongoing restoration and construction projects throughout the city center. Its old-world charm was still evident, though, as cafes, restaurants, and shops lined the streets in centuries-old stone buildings, all leading down to the wide Gironde River. The streets looked impossibly narrow, and the traffic was choking, but to us, it was a beautiful place. We were even able to find a place that served pizza—or, at least, a version of it. And better still, we located a nearby supermarket for loading up on water and fresh fruit.

The following morning we piled into our chartered bus for the hour-long drive out to Pauillac for the race expo and number pickup. After entering the athletic center that served as race headquarters, we encountered a small sample of what to expect the next day, as an older gentleman in full American Indian costume stared us down at the entryway, and made folks jump by periodically letting out a short war whoop. Being a city boy, I admit to only a sketchy knowledge of Native Americans, but even I knew this was very odd. It would prove to be only the first of many such moments.

We proceeded to get our numbers, shirts, and race timing chips. Having a chip in a race like this seemed out of place; it was one of the few telltale signs that this was an actual competition at all. We then made our way to the modest Médoc Marathon expo. A few other races, including the Chicago Marathon, were represented, and among the race memorabilia that was available for purchase were bottles of wine with the race logo emblazoned on the label. There was also another uniquely Médoc concession tucked in among the stalls: a costume seller catering to those who hadn't yet settled on a race day outfit. As I looked over the racks of Viking, maiden, and clown costumes, I realized that my team's Hawaiian ensemble would probably seem very conservative compared to what we would see the next day.

I mulled that over as we went back to Bordeaux and spent the day lounging around waiting for our pasta feed. The race organizers put on their own prerace dinner—complete with copious amount of *le vin*, of course—but we opted to be closer to our hotel and an early bedtime. Though the race was scheduled to start at 9:30 A.M., the long drive necessary to get there required a predawn departure. Far from being annoyed, I was almost soothed by this return to a slice of my usual prerace regimen.

The next morning I scarfed down a light, high-carb breakfast, then boarded the bus and settled into a doze as the sun rose over the French countryside. The air was crisp and just a bit cool, with temperatures nudging into the 60s.

Stepping out of the bus in Pauillac, I couldn't help but think of the colorful world into which Dorothy's house fell in *The Wizard of Oz*. All around me were odd characters in running shoes; mimes, devils, cavemen, bunnies, pirates, prisoners sporting a helium ball and chain, cats and mice, and all manner of cartoon characters. There was face paint galore, and even teams of runners pulling theme carts, like mini floats in a Thanksgiving Day parade.

I had read that 70 percent of the participants were costumed, but on race day it felt like a much higher percentage; it seemed not just like many people had a costume, but rather that virtually everyone had one. Dressing in a plain running outfit suddenly seemed like a mortal sin, and I was glad that my team had at least made an effort, humble as it was. As I walked past a row of portable toilets, though, I wondered how all these odd and otherworldly people would manage the details and necessities of running a race. No matter; we were a colorful group, and we were having a good time.

In fact, we were the most self-aware race group I'd ever seen. In the minutes before most races, runners seem lost in their own thoughts, full of nervous energy about the challenge they would soon face. In Médoc, though, the prerace mood was festive; it was all about people-watching, preening, and enjoying yourself. There were dancers gyrating on platforms above the crowd, and everybody was posing and snapping photos of those around them. A Japanese group, dressed as samurai, even had their own camera crew following them around the starting line to record their encounters with other outlandish runners. It all reminded me of the crowd I'd seen at Grateful Dead shows years ago, which was so happy to just be there that watching the band almost seemed like an afterthought. Watching us laugh and point at one another at the starting line, it was almost easy to forget that we would soon be running a marathon.

But there was indeed a race, and suddenly we were off. We wound our way out of town, past scenic storefronts and booths offering food and wine-tasting, and past cheering supporters. We made our way toward the vineyards, and soon came upon the first official aid stop, just a few kilometers into the race. It was amply supplied with water, cake, cookies, raisins, dried apricots, and even prunes—prunes, for heaven's sake!—but no wine. In fact, there was no wine at any of the early aid stops. I wondered whether the race directors thought it best to protect us from ourselves. As the sun poked its way though and the temperature began to climb, I began to think this might not have been a bad decision.

Kilometer 9 brought our first wine-tasting opportunity. I was treated to the unusual sight of tables lined up with glass after glass of dark red Bordeaux. Never has being a runner seemed so rewarding! I slowed to a walk and lifted a glass. As I savored the first sip, I knew that I wouldn't remember the taste of the wine or even the vineyard, but I'd certainly remember the sensation. I tossed the glass in a receptacle and resumed running.

As we made or way past the châteaux and back into the fields, I saw a number of runners split from the pack and head out between the rows of grapes. It took me a moment to realize that they were taking bathroom breaks. A runner would not be surprised at such behavior, but I bet that wine connoisseurs would certainly be shocked.

We continued through the French countryside, passing the occasional stone châteaux and cyclists on holiday. We ran on paved roads, but more frequently on dirt paths alongside the vines, the pounding of our feet kicking up the soft, powdery dirt into low clouds. We didn't come across another wine-tasting stop until kilometer 16, but there were plenty of aid stations along the way offering refreshments and cool, wet sponges. The sun was shining brightly by this time, and I was starting to wonder about how the heat would affect our ragtag group. As if on command, some dark clouds rolled in, bringing along a welcome sprinkle of drizzle that cooled us off and quieted the billowing dust around our feet. The drizzle continued, however, and grew in strength, and soon became rain. Usually a cause for disgruntlement, the rain instead became a cause for more drinking.

At some point along this part of the marathon I had the most unusual sensation; I thought I saw flowers blowing around me, as if a herald were scattering petals in my path. Perhaps I was having a bad reaction to the wine. But no. Slowly recognition creased my bewildered brain—my lei had broken, and was quickly dispersing itself. I gathered up the loose ends and tied them together tightly. Just as my grass skirt had been shortened, my lei was now a streamlined version of its former self.

We also began to come across bands along the course offering up some musical distractions. Oddly enough, when I passed a couple of them, they were playing old American country and rockabilly tunes, like "Blue Moon of Kentucky." Not exactly what you'd expect to hear a band playing in France, but sometimes it's better to just appreciate a moment than to ask why and how.

After the second wine stop, the tastings came more frequently, and I stuck with my promise to taste each and every wine that they put in our path. Soon I lost count, but I knew that in all, there would be twenty-one wine-tasting stations. I've never been a math whiz, but even I could figure out that with there being only two wine stops in the first half of the race, there would be quite a bit of catching up to do. I mustered my best bit of marathoner's determination for the task that lay ahead.

As I continued on my way, I also realized something else about the course: its sheer beauty. I knew that it wasn't just the alcohol talking as I wondered whether this might not be the most beautiful marathon course I've ever run. It wasn't just that there were breathtaking sights along the way, although there were plenty of those. It was the absence of something; the inevitable marathon dead zone, the dry spot to be found in all races, where we labor though industrial parks, past train tracks and factories and parking lots, with no supporters to cheer us on, and no eye candy to distract us from our boredom and suffering. Boston has such a zone, lined by railroad tracks. So does the New York Marathon, in Queens, before hitting the Queensboro Bridge. And so do countless other races. But in Médoc, I realized, there was nothing but row after row of grapevines, full with their dark fruit, and beautiful châteaux lording over their fields.

The beauty of the course and the glory of the wine couldn't stave off the realities of running a marathon, however, and despite my leisurely early pace, I began to slow in the second part of the race. I won't blame it all on the wine, not when there were also some other obstacles I could point my finger at, like the food. At one station I took a bit of unidentified food and shoved it into my mouth. After all, no one would put out food on a marathon course that would be bad for us, right? Wrong, I realized too late. Wrong, wrong, wrong. Of all the foods in the world, the only one that I truly hate was liver. What I had now in my mouth was some type of liver-based lunchmeat. Yuck. The memory of it still haunts me, and has led me to instituting a new racing rule: put nothing in your mouth that you can't identify. My mother later insisted that she taught me that rule years ago, though I'm not so sure about that.

The race continued onward, past kilometers 25, 30, and 35. Then, at kilometer number 38, with just four kilometers to go, the race let loose, like a child that's been quiet too long and needs to scream. First came the oysters, piled ostentatiously on serving tables. A teammate of mine later told me of a writer's observation: "Oh, the courage of the first brave soul to slurp an oyster!" On that day in Bordeaux, I can tell you, there were plenty of brave men and women, and I struggled to be among the bravest.

Next up was a steak station, where bits of grilled beef on sticks were served up to runners. I took just a small piece to taste, then moved on to the next station just down the road, the cheese tables! And after that, more wine! I gulped and chewed and gulped some more, and then, as I slowly fell back into an easy running pace, a little voice somewhere deep inside began telling me that my gluttony wasn't such a great idea. I slowed down a little more as the oysters began to talk to me, and I reminded myself that I only had a little over 1 kilometer to go. I also said a little prayer of thanks to the race directors for not putting the oysters in the first half of the race.

One last unexpected race amenity awaited runners who made it this far: face paint. For those who had been too shy to wear a costume, or who had somehow lost it along the way, there was a chance for last-minute redemption. A couple of volunteers were quickly dabbing color onto runners on request. I opted for some black and red stripes down my nose and across my cheeks. All I can say is that it seemed like a good idea at the time.

And finally, the finish line was just up ahead. As I crossed through, I was given a backpack with the race logo on it, and a bottle of wine to put in it. For my costume-wearing efforts, I was also given a fanny pack bearing the race logo. And last but not least, I was pointed toward the finisher's tent, where wine and beer were being freely doled out. Perhaps not surprisingly, I had had enough by this point, and as appreciative as I was of the postrace offerings, I decided to head to the bus instead. And probably not in a straight line, either, despite my best efforts.

The afternoon was spent recovering from the race, followed later by more wine and food. The next day, we all decided to partake of the vineyard walk offered to race participants, featuring—you guessed it— more wine and food. A highlight was the lunch tent set up at the end of the tour, where oysters and other fare were doled out as a French chanteuse belted out old American tunes and various national anthems. Somehow, I wasn't at all surprised. By this time, I had learned to expect the unexpected.

After the race, we took a train back to Paris—still drinking along the way, of course. We then spent a few days drying out and sightsee-ing. As I gazed at the now-familiar Eiffel Tower and wandered the Latin Quarter, I tried to put the race in perspective. It seemed to fit into no readily available category. It belonged in a category all its own.

The winners of the marathon, incidentally, posted times of 2:32:52 for the men and 2:56:27 for the women; entirely respectable finishing times that seemed incongruous with my own experience. My finishing time was just about the slowest I've ever had—let's just say it was between four and five hours. Still, it was good enough to put me first in my little group; this was probably more of a reflection of the party instinct of my group than my own speed. But my slow time seemed to show the truth behind the race's motto: below an image of an apparently snookered runner weaving from pillar to post is the phrase "Médoc, Le Marathon Le Plus Long Du Monde," "Médoc, the Longest Marathon in the World." While it might have felt like an ultramarathon, I knew that Médoc is not really a race to be measured in time, or perhaps even by distance. It really was like no other race in the world.

As much fun as racing in Bordeaux proved to be, it wasn't the only excitement I had running that September. There was Hurricane Isabel to consider. It started as a small updraft as water evaporated over warm south Atlantic waters. The updraft gathered strength and grew into a tropical storm, and then flexed its muscles and grew into a Category 5 hurricane, with winds raging at 160 miles per hour. Inexorably, it moved toward the Carolina coast, and up toward Washington, D.C. Naturally, I took that as a sign to lace up my training shoes for the run of a lifetime.

As the storm drew near, batteries and bottled water were cleaned off store shelves, and schools, as well as federal and local government agencies, announced that they would be closed. Thursday—hurricane day—started out gray and windy, and I felt a sense of expectation among those out on the streets, rushing through last-minute preparations. As the day ebbed into evening, the winds picked up to a howl, and rain swept through in waves. The storm was drawing near, and it was almost time for me to go.

It was 9:30 P.M. when I finally ventured outside. The first thing I noticed was how very warm it was. It must have been in the upper

80s, and I immediately regretted bringing a light jacket. The rain had let up, and the winds had died down a bit as I ran southwest toward the Potomac River. If there were a front-row seat to the storm, it would be on one of the city's bridges, where wind can whip over the open water like race cars at Daytona.

As I ran down the city streets, I passed shuttered and boarded businesses, but also some open bars and restaurants, catering to the adventurous, the bored, or the addicted. There were already a few trees down, and debris littered the road. A handful of taxis roamed the streets, and there were a few police cruisers out, but little else. I ran down the center of M Street in the Georgetown district, one of the busiest thoroughfares in the city, and I was all alone. It was the first time I'd ever been able to do that. I felt giddy with power; this storm was not as bad as I thought it would be. Clearly, Isabel had lost a great deal of her punch as she made her way inland. Just then, a branch swatted me across the back of my head, as if to remind me that the storm had not yet lost all of its teeth.

I turned onto Key Bridge and looked across the Potomac River toward Virginia. I was about a third of the way across when the big winds hit. I was blown from side to side of the walkway like a pinball, despite my best efforts to run a straight line. As wind whipped my face, I found it difficult to breathe. It was exhilarating, but also terrifying, and it occurred that it wouldn't take very much more wind to send me hurtling over the railing for a hundred-foot plunge into the river below. I made it to the other side, then turned to head back home. My ambitious 12-mile course had been cut to a short 5-miler, but that was enough of a taste of the hurricane for me.

As I neared my apartment, the storm picked up in intensity, as if to say that it had only been toying with me so far, and that it was now ready to really play. Rain began to pour down again, and the wind increased. I raced toward my building and burst through the doors like it was the tape in a 5K race, then stood there, dripping and panting as the storm raged on the other side of the glass door like a lion in a cage. By that time, Stephanie had moved down to D.C. and was living with me. She just handed me a towel and shook her head.

By morning, the storm was all but spent. I ran different trails during the following days to assess the damage. Fallen trees across one of my favorite bike paths made for a unique climbing-running duathlon. Friends in the suburbs reported that their power was out, and would be for at least another week, from what they'd been told. Still, the city had been lucky to escape with relatively little damage; it has been far luckier than many other coastal towns. And I was lucky to have unwittingly found a relatively gentle hour during the storm to squeeze in my hurricane run.

Running Tip #14

The Bathroom Break

One thing that sets runners apart is the utilitarian view we take of our bodies. We see them as machines, built through training for high performance. Our need to relieve ourselves before a race is usually no more embarrassing to us than a need to check the oil in our car. This might put us at odds with the rest of the civilized world, but we're okay with that. Still, there are basic guidelines to follow to avoid any problems in this area.

- *Deal with bodily needs before the race begins.* All major marathons provide hundreds of Porta-Jons at their race starts, but before a race, the lines to get in one are usually very long. Minimize your need for them by cutting off the fluid intake a full hour before the race start. Wait until just 5 minutes before the race is to begin, then gulp down 6–8 ounces of water or sports drink.
- *Don't be too shy during the race.* Marathoners tend to act with unspoken cooperation during a race; we keep an eye out for places other runners choose to use. But sometimes, a race course simply doesn't provide any secluded spots to take care of business. Like Superman without a phone booth, I've sometimes found myself looking in horror at fields without trees and city streets without dark alleys, and those are somehow also the spots where the crowds of spectators seems most dense. In such situations, do what you must. Remember: during a marathon, the regular rules of proper public behavior don't apply.

Running Tip #14

If you doubt me, think of marathon world record–holder Paula Radcliffe, who, en route to winning the London Marathon in April 2004, crouched down on the course to relieve herself. She apologized afterward, but runners knew no apology was necessary. We understood.

A Bit of Hardware

By 2004, I had run eighty-four marathons, and my collection of medals was something to see. My first medal was earned in the Marine Corps Marathon in 1987, and though I was fiercely proud of it at the time, I can now admit that it was a cheap little thing. It was fashioned to resemble a dog tag, but looked like it had been pulled from a cereal box. As the race matured over the years, though, and received corporate sponsorship, its medals improved, and now they're smart, gleaming works of running art.

Twelve years later, when I crossed the finish line in Antarctica, I didn't get a finisher's medal at all. I wasn't concerned, though, because all of the runners were told that medals would be mailed to our homes later. Sure enough, it showed up in my mailbox a few weeks after I'd returned home. It was the biggest, heaviest, and gaudiest medal I had ever seen. I was thrilled; it was a tangible reminder of where I had been and what I had accomplished. But receiving a medal was not a surprise; most marathoners—even many elite runners—work so hard with so little tangible reward that we have come to expect, even demand, that we be given a finisher's medal upon completing the course. And in commenting on a race, a description of the medal is often right up there with reviews of the course and the race support. And woe to the race director who fails to deliver; he will not be spared the wrath of the runners.

There have been several races where I crossed the finish line and did not get my expected award: in the Northern Central Trails Marathon in Maryland I was given a cheap glass mug, which was also the reward handed out one year at the Houston Marathon. The race director in Virginia Beach was even stingier; there, I was only given a finisher's certificate. Although I never uttered a word about it—at least, not to race officials—someone clearly did, because most of these races now offer finisher's medals. In fact, race directors now go above and beyond the call of duty, offering finisher's medals that are getting ever bigger, shinier, and gaudier. Proof once more that it's possible to have too much of a good thing.

Medals have now become so popular that many races of less than marathon distance award them to their participants. Nestled in my collection are medals from the World's Best 10K in San Blas, Puerto Rico, the Amish Country Half-Marathon, the New York City Road Runners New Year's Eve Midnight 5K run, and the Virginia Beach Rock 'N Roll Half-Marathon. I had run each of these races as hard as I could, and felt that I had earned each medal, and yet something was not quite right about receiving that hardware. Perhaps I had become a snob, but I felt that only races of marathon distance or more ought to award medals.

Eventually, the question came up of what to do with them. Originally, an ordinary nail in the wall was good enough to hang them on. I graduated to a bigger nail, and then a hanging display rack I picked up in a yard sale, designed to hold baseball caps. Finally, I just dumped them all into a cabinet drawer.

Packing them away, I found myself rating them. My Boston Marathon medals were my favorite, each one a symbol of high achievement. They knew their value too; no shiny gilded affairs, these. The

Boston Athletic Association opts for pewter, with its emblem, a unicorn, in relief on the front. It's the marathoning equivalent of a pinstripe suit.

In contrast was the playfulness of the Disneyworld Marathon medal. It was an oval with two smaller ovals affixed at the top, giving an approximation of that famous mouse's head. On the face of the medal was a likeness of Mickey himself, tearing down the road in singlet, shorts, and running shoes. The Las Vegas Marathon medal is in the shape of a roulette wheel, appropriately enough. I've also got a ceramic medal, and even an embroidered one.

The ribbons on which the medals were attached reflect each race's personality as well. Their colors range from black to purple, white, green, red, and orange, and in combinations from traditional red, white, and blue to all the colors of the rainbow. The ribbon for the Marine Corps Marathon medals are red and gold, the colors of the Corps, while the Honolulu Marathon medal came on a string of puka shells, and the New Orleans Marathon medal hangs from a string of Mardi Gras beads.

And then there were the shirts. For some reason, most races have traditionally distributed T-shirts bearing a race logo to all race participants. Early on, they were all cotton, but now most races provide technical racing shirts instead. It might be a good way to tell the world that you had done something extraordinary, and it's certainly a good way for a race and its sponsors to get some cheap promotion, but at some point, enough is enough. Every year or so I've had to cull less desirable shirts from the herd, setting them aside for donation to a local homeless shelter.

But there is another kind of memento that I covet, the ultimate kind of racing hardware: an actual award. After I had finished my first marathon, my father was very proud of me. By the time I finished my second one, though, he asked when I would win one. Win? Not likely, I told him. I was a good runner, and usually finished in the top 10 percent of most race fields, but the difference between being good and being elite is huge. As I explained, if I was rested and warmed up at mile 25 and jumped into the race with the members of the elite pack, who had already been running for 2 hours or so, they would easily blow right past me and leave me in the dust. I hated to disappoint Dad, but I told him that I would *never* win a marathon. Simple as that. Just finishing was an accomplishment in itself, and running as hard as I could every time was my victory.

Of course, that didn't mean I couldn't dream a little. I didn't expect to win any races outright, but just placing in my age group would be nice. I achieved a little recognition in a race at Dewey Beach, Delaware one year. It was a 10-mile race with an interesting side competition called the Pump 'n Run. Race volunteers weighed participants, and then loaded up a bench press—full body weight for men, two-thirds of body weight for women—and participants benched this amount as many times as they could shortly before running the race. One minute was then deducted from their finishing time for every repetition they were able to do on the bench.

I signed up for the Pump 'n Run, and bench-pressed my body weight twenty-one times. I then went out and ran a strong race. When it was all over, I discovered that I had won my age group. It was my first award, and even though all I received was a commemorative T-shirt—another T-shirt, for cryin' out loud!—I enjoyed hearing my name being announced, and taking those few but glorious steps forward to claim my prize.

I wasn't completely surprised by my little victory, though. Back in high school I had enjoyed lifting weights with my friends, and I had never given that up, even as I took up running. I might not have been the fastest runner or the strongest lifter, but I can run very fast for a weight lifter, and I am very strong for a runner. The Pump 'n Run rewarded this kind of balanced fitness, and I appreciated that.

But still, I had not won an award for being the fastest runner on race day. My trophy cabinet was still bare.

Then came the Hog Eye Marathon in Fayetteville, Arkansas. Marathon number 85. The night before the race, my friends and I went to a famous local steak joint, Doe's. Supposedly it had been a favorite eating spot for the press corps who followed Bill Clinton on his campaign tours.

They serve two kinds of steak in Doe's: one-pound and two-pound. I showed restraint and ordered the one-pound. It was as good as word of mouth had said it would be. I knew that come race time, the steak would still be with me, like bag of wet cement in my gut. But I wanted to enjoy this time and place with my friends, and one never knows when such a moment may come around again. After eighty-four marathons, I bet that my body would find a way to handle it.

The next morning, though, I worried less about that steak than about the driving rain and wind outside. At the sound of the starter's gun, I set out with several hundred other runners on a very hilly out-and-back course. There is something about truly horrible conditions that focuses the mind, and soon I found myself enjoying the challenge in a crazy kind of way. I wouldn't be out running a marathon in the first place if I didn't like a challenge, and the weather was just one more obstacle to conquer. I gritted my teeth and ran on.

Eventually, the course led us back to town square and the finish line. I collected my medal and then lingered indoors to warm up and have something to eat. When the race results were posted on the wall, I went to check my official time and discovered that I had finished second in my age group. I was going to win an award!

I'm embarrassed to say how excited I was. Dad passed away in 1989, but if he were still alive, I know that he would be thrilled that I had finally won something, even if it took me 85 marathons to do it. My award was a hand-made ceramic plaque, with the race name and logo drawn into it. Aesthetically, it's not much, but to me, it's beautiful.

Looking at all my racing hardware, I'm reminded not only of my years of marathon running, but also of one of my great fears for the future: that some day, all of these medals—and my few awards—will be in a box at a yard sale somewhere, three for a dollar. As I handled some of my medals, I noticed that some of them had already started to corrode. I realized that I didn't have to worry about that far-off yard sale; apparently, my medals wouldn't even last long enough to make it there. What if they all disintegrated little by little? Or what if they were lost in a fire? What was I without my medals?

I knew that if all my medals disappeared, I would feel the loss of the tangible proof that I had led a runner's life. But I realized, too, that they didn't really matter that much. With or without them, I knew what I had achieved. Truth be told, I hardly ever look at any of them anyway; they are to me like the gold in Fort Knox, more of an idea than a physical presence in my day-to-day life. I ran the marathon to discover the depths of my own determination and perseverance. I didn't need a medal to tell me who I was.

Meanwhile, I had other things on my mind that summer. It was June 2004, and Stephanie and I were about to be wed. Even we were surprised at how quickly our relationship had moved along, but though we had dated a little more than one year, we had known each other since we were twelve, so we really felt like we had known each other all our lives, which was more or less true. It was as if we were each getting to know someone we were already very well acquainted with. We had shared history, yet separate lives; wonderful and varied life experiences, yet the same background. As we liked to say to each other, it just made sense.

On the morning of our wedding I woke up early and went for a run—no better way to burn off some of the jitters I felt. I showered and dressed, and drove down from our hotel to the site we had picked: a castle nestled in the Hudson Valley in upstate New York. I marveled that so far, things were going perfectly. Just as that thought went through my mind—hanging there, like a thought balloon in a comic strip—someone asked me if I had the rings on me. I froze. They were still back in my hotel room. Oh, crap. Crap, crap, crap. Un-freakin'-believable.

I jumped in my car and raced the five miles back to the hotel, cruising through stop signs and red lights, almost hoping that a cop would stop me so that I could explain my dilemma and get a police escort. That didn't happen, but I did make it back to the chapel in time, and the ceremony went off without a hitch. After the reception, husband and wife made it back to the hotel room, exhausted but very happy. We celebrated by opening a bottle of '93 Château Lafite Rothschild I had brought back from Médoc. Despite the shaky start, it turned out to be a wonderful day.

The first thing people now want to know about Stephanie was whether she was a marathoner. The answer is no. At first, Stephanie was concerned that I might pressure her into running a marathon, but I told her I could care less whether she ever ran one, and I meant it. Sure, it would be great fun for me to run a marathon next to my wife, but I didn't marry her in order to fulfill that dream; I married her because I love her for who she is, not for what she might become.

Still, Stephanie is very fit. She's a bit of a gym rat, really, which is important to me because I want to be with someone healthy, someone who I can grow old with, someone who can still see life as a great adventure well into our senior years. But run a marathon? Nah. There's plenty of stuff I have no interest in doing. Bungee jumping, for example. I have absolutely zero interest in that.

If Stephanie were to tell me that she didn't think she *could* do it, though, that would be different. Running has taught me to not automatically accept limitations, whether imagined or imposed by others. I don't believe anyone should automatically expect and accept failure, especially not in regard to the marathon. Finishing a marathon is within the reach of anyone with the determination and courage to *just try*.

When we first started dating, Stephanie actually did show some interest in trying to run. Her plan was to run as far as she could and see how that felt. I saved her the suspense and gave her an immediate answer: if she ran for as long as she could, she would only guarantee that she would be tired and miserable when she finally stopped.

Over the years, I've seen the same pattern among people who hate running: when they gave it a shot, they almost always went too far or too fast. The trick, I told her, it to not run until you're exhausted—leave that for the marathons! Instead, I told her to run until she felt fatigued but comfortable at the end. If she didn't want to hate running, she'd need to keep it manageable.

And that's what she did. She began with some walking and easy running on the treadmill, and little by little she worked her way up to running for a half hour straight. In time, she stretched it to an hour.

In November 2003, we took our vacation in New Zealand, which we found to be a magical, wonderful place, filled with beaches, gorges, smoldering thermal springs, and breathtaking mountain ranges. The Kiwis don't take any of this for granted; I'd read that if there's a dangerous, difficult, thrilling way of getting from one point to another, they do it. Naturally, I thought, there must be a marathon. Sure enough, there was, right in the capital city of Auckland, along with a 10K race. I signed up for the marathon, and with my encouragement, Stephanie signed up for the 10K. It was the first race she'd ever entered.

On race morning, I set out before dawn to get to the ferry that brought the marathoners across the harbor to the starting line. It was a beautiful course: almost pretty enough to keep me from cursing the brutal headwind I ran against over the last few miles of the race. As I neared the finish line, I wondered how Stephanie had done.

The race finished in a park, and it didn't take me long to spot her across the open field. As I waved to her, I ticked off items on my mental triage checklist: she was upright, she was walking, and she was smiling. When I got to her, I gave her a big kiss and asked how it went.

"Great," she said. "I finished in just under an hour."

"That's a great time," I told her. "You should be proud."

"Yeah, I am," she told me. "But around mile four, I thought, *Well, wouldn't a cup of coffee and a newspaper be nice right now?*"

So, there might be no marathon run together for us. Or maybe there will be. Either way, it's okay; Stephanie had proven—as much to herself as to me—that she could run one if she wanted to. But running isn't her passion, it's mine. Her passion is for art, both as a painter and a teacher. I love that she has such strong opinions, dedication, knowledge, and talent for it. That kind of passion is, to me, the fullest embodiment of what is best in our nature. Our appreciation for each other's passion is more important to us than being able to fully share in the object of each other's joy. We each feel deeply about something, and are willing to risk something of ourselves for it. That alone makes us kindred spirits.

We do actually run together sometimes. I think of these runs not just as workouts; they're couple-time, when we share stories or ideas, or just enjoy a break from the rest of the world. Instead of being in competition with our relationship, running has, I think, strengthened it.

After all these years, I think I finally got it right.

Running Tip #15

How to Do the Thing You Love with the One You Love

Training with your romantic partner is not impossible, but if you want to make it work, it's a good idea to follow some basic guidelines.

- *Put the relationship first.* Running with a mate can be tricky. The key is to not do anything to demean or demoralize your partner. So forget your training schedule. If you push too hard, he or she will get very cranky. The point is to demonstrate what you already know: that running can be fun. Do your hard workout earlier or later in the day, or on another day altogether.
- *Make your run together your entire workout.* Don't use your run together as a portion of a longer workout. That implies that the run was inadequate, which could undermine your mate's confidence. So start and finish together.
- *Make sure your partner has the proper gear.* Chances are your nonrunning mate will show up for your first run together wearing cross-training shoes, a cotton T-shirt, and sweatpants. In other words, all the wrong things. If you think missing your anniversary led to a big fight, see what happens when running with you causes your mate to have chafing and blisters. So go shopping together for proper clothing and good running shoes.

→

- *Figure out what works for your partner.* It's your job to show your partner a fun time; if he or she enjoys the run, he or she will be back for more.
- *Don't be the boss.* After years of running and racing, it's easy to think we know everything about running. But if you tell your partner what to do, you reduce him or her to an underling. So don't order; create a dialogue instead. He or she will probably follow your advice anyway, but that will be his or her decision. It makes a difference.
- *Don't forget these rules on race day.* When your partner is ready to try a first race, be supportive. Offer to run a race with her or him, at her or his pace. But remember: this is your mate's race, not yours; you're just support crew with a number. If your partner would rather run without you, decide together where you'll meet afterward, and ask what you should bring for after the race.

Good Things Come in Small Packages

My next marathon was only a few weeks after I got married. I met up with Dave in Calgary, Canada, to run a marathon. The race was held in conjunction with the annual Stampede Rodeo—not really a sport that I could identify with. But stranger to me than the idea of roping cattle was the gold band that I fingered on my left hand during the race. I quickly got used to it, though, which I took to be a good sign, and when I crossed the finish line, I received a large western-style belt buckle on a ribbon as a medal, which seemed a fitting memento for that particular race.

That was marathon number 88. When people heard that I'd run that many races, they'd usually ask me which one was my favorite. I didn't know what to say. There were obvious contenders, like New York, Boston, and Paris. I did love them all. But like a child in a candy shop, I just couldn't decide. Finally, I came upon an answer that was honest: my favorite marathon is … the next one. People smiled, but it was really a dodge, and we all knew it.

Little by little, I started to narrow the field, if not to a particular marathon, then at least to a category. The big races were the ones that people were most familiar with. These behemoths were cities unto themselves, and they were like huge running festivals. They were *events*. But with the bright lights and press coverage came the uglier side. These races were demanding, high maintenance mistresses, requiring one to fight for entry, to battle for hotels and flights, and to wake up early to rush to the starting line to wait with tens of thousands of other runners for the start, and then pick one's way through the crowds at the finish for family and friends, all lost in a sea of sweaty bodies. These races were memorable, but they often seemed like so much *work*.

That said, big-city marathons should not to be missed, and I returned to them again and again. But were they my favorite races? Not necessarily. There was something more important than the flash of the big-city races; I learned to love the allure of the small-town marathon. Modest, unassuming, more friendly and personal, these were the races I truly enjoyed. Still, people didn't seem to completely believe that. I could see it in their eyes. Sure, they seemed to say, that sounds nice, but you'd never turn down the New York Marathon for a race in, say, Idaho, would you?

Wouldn't I? I decided to put it to the test. I needed to add Idaho to my list of states anyway, so Idaho it would be for marathon number 89. The Mesa Falls Marathon in Ashton, to be exact.

First, I had to get there. Whoever said that it's the journey that matters, not the destination, never spent a lot of time waiting around in an airport. As soon as I went online to book my flights for the race, I realized that things would not be as simple as I expected. There weren't any direct flights from D.C. to Ashton, and among the circuitous routes that were available, there were precious few options.

But that was okay; I hadn't expected booking my flights to be a run in the park. Ultimately, the ones I chose would land me in Idaho well past sunset on the day before the race. No problem. I could handle that, too. There was no commercial airport in Ashton, which meant that I would have to rent a car in Idaho Falls and drive an hour to get to my destination. Still not a problem; I've had to do that before in other big-city races. I would miss the prerace pasta dinner and all the camaraderie that's usually found there, but that wasn't the end of the world, since there would be plenty of time to meet people on the course during the race.

After spending nearly the entire day outbound waiting for flights and making connections, I finally arrived in Idaho Falls. It was a tiny airport, but that was a good thing, since there was no need to take a shuttle to an off-site baggage claim area: I could just step down onto the tarmac, walk into the terminal, get my rental car and go. Except that despite having made a reservation, no one was available at the off-site office to set me up with a car. Quicker than I could say "grrrrrrrr," though, I rented another car from a friendly young woman at a competitor's sales desk, and was soon on my way to Ashton. Still, none of these transportation problems would have happened in Boston, Chicago, or New York. Advantage: big-city marathon.

An hour later, I was driving down ID-47 in Ashton, Idaho, also known more simply as Main Street. I was glad for the sign postings, because I easily could have missed it. With a population of 1,129, there wasn't going to be a lot of street life anyway, especially not around midnight, which is when I arrived. The marathon Web site had listed available lodging, and I opted for the Four Seasons Motel, which was said to be near where the runners were to line up for transport to the starting line on race morning. When booking the room a few weeks earlier over the phone, the clerk told me almost apologetically that the price would be $45 per night. I magnanimously told him that would be perfectly fine. As I edged down Main Street in the quiet darkness, I discovered it on my right, one of those wayside-type inns with parking spots in front of each room. There was a note affixed to the front door of the office addressed to me, letting me know which room was mine, and that it had been left open for me. This would NEVER happen in New York. Not on marathon weekend, not ever. Not even anywhere within 100 miles of

New York. I smiled with relief; at this hour, every moment was precious, and the sooner I could lay my head on a pillow, the better.

I ambled over to my room, swung the door open and found ... pretty much just a room. It was nothing fancy, but it was certainly serviceable. A clean bed, a TV, and hot and cold running water. Gazing out the door, I realized that the local high school's parking lot, where we would board buses for transport to the race start, was literally right across the street. At least I could sleep to the very last moment, and needed only to make sure I had all my running gear on as I stumbled out the door.

The alarm woke me from a deep slumber, and I looked out the window. Still dark outside. Nothing unusual, since many races have a predawn starting time. There were already two school buses idling in the parking lot, with a handful of runners milling about. Only eleven racers participated in the race's inaugural running in 1997, and the field ballooned to forty the following year.

From what I could see while peering out that window, it hadn't grown very much since then. There were only a few hundred runners, apparently no media representatives whatsoever, and precious few spectators. Still, I don't think I'd ever before had such a comforting prerace moment. I'd had some close calls in the past getting to the starting line in time, but this would not be one of those days.

Fifteen minutes later, while identifying constellations in the clear sky, I walked up to the folding table that served as headquarters for race-day packet pickup. The temperature was in the upper 30s, although warmer weather was predicted for later in the day. Race Director Dave Jacobson checked my name off the list and handed me my packet and a smart-looking polo shirt with an embroidered race logo. "You," Dave told me, "are the first person from Washington, D.C., to run the Mesa Falls Marathon." That meant I would hold the course record for a D.C. marathoner just by crossing the finish line. I began imagining my press release as I trotted back across the street to my motel room to drop off my shirt and goody bag.

Climbing aboard one of the buses minutes later, I peered toward the back for the one thing worth its weight in gold to a runner before a race: a bathroom. There it was, tucked away in the corner. Breathing a sigh of relief, I settled into one of the plush seats, felt the warmth flowing upward from the bus's heaters, and unwrapped my personal "breakfast of champions": two energy bars and a sports drink.

The bus was buzzing with conversation, and soon I met all the runners seated around me. There was a father-daughter team, and quite a few out-of-town runners. As it turned out, though, no one had traveled as far as I did. More than one person wore confused expressions when they found out where I was from; they seemed to find it hard to believe that anyone would come so far for such a small race.

As I sat talking with my new neighbors, I realized that very few of them were first-time marathoners. In fact, several of the runners had already completed over 100, and one runner had completed over 200. Apparently, I was no longer the craziest person in the room. This highlighted a characteristic of smaller races that I soon came to appreciate; the average depth of experience among the participants in small marathons seemed to be vastly greater than that of the people to be found in the typical big city marathon. This meant that I'd be able to tap into the collective running wisdom of this group throughout the day about various other marathons, and, more importantly, get valuable information about the marathon course from people who had run this race before. As the bus pulled out of the parking lot for the 45-minute ride to the race start, I fell into a light sleep.

The bus groaned through a turn, and my eyes fluttered open. The sky was slowly beginning to brighten, and the bus, having left the highway, was coming to a stop next to, well, next to nothing, really. We were in the middle of nowhere. There was no building or man-made structure to be seen anywhere, apart from the road we drove in on. I didn't know it at the time, but we were in Targhee National Forest, by the Island Park caldera. We were at an altitude of 6,142 feet, roughly one mile above sea level.

The air felt crisp and clean as I left the bus and moved toward the impromptu starting line along with the rest of the runners. In New York, sheer luck gets you close to the front of the pack; in Boston, it's proven speed. In the Mesa Falls Marathon, however, all you need to do is step forward and pick your spot.

I chose to stand behind some of the faster-looking runners; close enough to feel the excitement of seeing open road ahead when the race begins, but not so close as to give myself illusions of being an elite racer. Dave Jacobson led us through the traditional prerace remarks, and then, without fanfare, sent us off.

This small phalanx of runners moved briskly along the asphalt as snippets of conversation broke out here and there among us. At that altitude, I knew I would be laboring to maintain my usual pace, so I tried to rein in my legs, which were feeling particularly springy. The course would eventually bring us down to an elevation of 5,260 feet, for a net drop of 882 feet, so I wasn't worried about a slow start; I would have plenty of opportunity to pick up the pace later on.

I followed the pack through a left turn, and found myself on a wide dirt road, heading deeper into the wilderness. Full daybreak was upon us now, revealing rolling hills on both sides of the road, covered in brush and short trees. Up ahead, I was told, there would be wonderful views of the Grand Teton mountain range. One thing I knew not to expect, though, were spectators cheering us on in the coming miles, but with all of the great scenery around me, I was starting to think that they might not be missed.

It was at that moment that I realized we were not quite as alone as I thought. Strange noises echoed from distance. There were wild animals out there howling at us. Another runner then told me that he had seen a moose in the first mile of the race. Despite its great size, the beast disappeared soundlessly into the brush. These other animals, however, did not seem quite as shy. A volunteer at mile 8 told me that coyotes and wolves had given him the eye as he set up our refreshments earlier in the morning. I felt an instinctual moment of panic, but then I realized that these animals were probably more afraid of us than we were of them. As long as I didn't drift so far back of the pack that I'd seem separated from the herd, I knew I'd be safe. Just as I relaxed, the howling subsided, as if on cue.

Just then the Tetons came into view, bathed in bright morning sunlight. They were indeed magnificent, even if we were too far away to fully appreciate their sculpted beauty. Then the fickle road turned us away from this sight and plunged us into the woods. We were led onto a bike path, which emptied onto a small scenic overlook. Hundreds of feet below us and perhaps a half-mile away, the Snake River plunged off what appeared to be a wide, stone tabletop. It was the race's namesake, the Lower Mesa Falls. I paused a moment to fully take in the beautiful view. Reluctantly, I turned away and followed the race path back into the woods.

It was about this time that I fell into a conversation with Matt, whose race turned out to be a family effort. Matt's sisters and cousins were providing vehicular support—"support" in the sense of screaming and yelling from an open van door during a slow drive-by.

"Know those folks?" I joked.

"Yeah," he admitted sheepishly. "My brother and cousin are out here also somewhere, running their first marathon."

Matt already had a little marathon experience, having run the Roxbury (Idaho) Marathon. "Now *that's* a small race," he told me. "Just twenty-two runners." I guess he entered the Mesa Falls Marathon to see what it would be like to do a big race.

At mile 13 we came to a short stretch of paved road that led us to Bear Claw Junction, which was the starting point for the half-marathoners. Some marathon runners don't like having fresh legs suddenly thrown in alongside them at a race's mid-point, since it can throw off their pacing. As for me, on that day at least, I was glad to have a little more company as we descended into the brush and found ourselves once again on a dirt trail.

The path on which we were now running was narrower than the road on which we had started, but it soon revealed itself as one of the most scenic stretches of any marathon I've ever run—four beautiful miles along Idaho's Warm River. Our trail was halfway up the side of a valley, providing commanding views of the river below and the valley around us. The weather had warmed, the sun was shining, the trees and bushes were lush and green, and the river was an inviting blue. Matt told me that there was no truth to the river's name, however; the Warm River was frigid this time of year. No matter; it *looked* inviting. I found myself gliding along the path, lost in runner's nirvana. I told Matt that even though this was just his second marathon, nature and the race director had conspired to give him a grand treat. He would see many wonderful scenes if he continued racing, but there might never be another moment as perfect as this one.

And suddenly it was gone. We came off the trail and returned to asphalt roads, rolling through rich Idaho farmland. The views here were less spectacular, but no less interesting, at least for this city boy. I had been warned by several runners, though, that there would be a big hill coming up shortly at about mile 18, so I girded myself for the worst. There was a hill all right, but it was not a heartbreaker, not in the Boston mold. I threw my mental lasso around the runner in front of me—fitting imagery for this part of the country—and labored up to the crest. With the hill now behind me, I settled in to a steady pace and started to think more about the finish line.

Houses multiplied alongside the road, farmland gave way to stores and short buildings, and I realized that I was on the outskirts of Ashton and nearing the finish line. The streets were quiet as I passed an auto parts store and a thrift shop. Up ahead on my right were grain silos, and I knew the end was at hand. There were some spectators cheering now, as a volunteer steered us through a right turn, and toward Ashton City Park.

As I crossed the finish line, I heard my name being announced—always a nice touch—and was awarded a finisher's medal. Marathon number 89 was over.

But things would soon get even better. Our goody bags contained a coupon, redeemable after the race, for a huckleberry shake from City Drug. I retrieved the coupon and set off for my hard-earned treat. Along the way I passed other runners who had already claimed their prize, and their smiles quickened my step.

City Drug was only a few short blocks away, but it was of another time and place. It was a small storefront shop, featuring a soda counter with stools. An older woman gave me a smile as I came in, and a young boy reached down below the counter and produced a genuine, prepoured huckleberry shake. I didn't even have to say a word; it must have been pretty obvious why I was there.

Stepping out into the street, I took a long pull on the straw, savoring the creamy coolness. As I walked back to the park, I shouted encouragement to the other runners nearing the finish line—"Get the shake! Get the shake!" Back at the park I found the race director, Dave, and thanked him for a top-notch marathon. The last runners were still more than an hour away from finishing—there would be 120 finishers in all—but Dave was already looking to the future. Heady with success, he was hoping to expand the race. "We can accommodate about 500 runners before we have to have any restrictions," he said. It sounded like an explosion of runners, but it would still just amount to a small 5K field back home.

I picked an inviting patch of sun-warmed grass near the covered picnic area and settled down for the awards ceremony. The winning times were 2:51:12 for the men, and 3:12:27 for the women. Very respectable times, but far from the otherworldly ones posted by the world's elite runners at the big races. My own finishing time left me well behind the leaders, but as I watched them claim their prizes, I felt that we were at least still members of the same species.

As the winners of the various age categories were honored, and random prizes distributed—everything from a heart rate monitor to beef jerky—I realized that many of these people knew each other, and had probably known each other for years. The camaraderie among them was palpable. I found myself daydreaming of having lived here, trained here, and raced here, so I could share in their jokes and stories.

Finally, all the awards had been claimed, all the prizes had been distributed, and it was time to go. I showered, gathered my things, and checked out of the Four Seasons Motel, saying good-bye to the owner's young son, who was manning the front desk. I drove back to Little Falls, dropped off the car, and boarded my flight.

Gazing out the window past the thin, wispy clouds to the farmland far below, I thought about the Mesa Falls Marathon, and the other small towns I had visited for marathons. Tupelo, Mississippi. Fayetteville, Arkansas. Tulsa, Oklahoma. And Wichita, Kansas, so quiet on a Saturday night downtown that I wouldn't have been surprised if the city rolled up their sidewalks after dark. These races all felt like family gatherings, with people working hard to make the events come off smoothly, for no glory other than to have managed to make it happen and to have shown a few hundred runners a good time.

Sometimes, though, things didn't go quite so well, like in Louisville, Kentucky, where a mismeasured course added an unnecessary mile to the race, leaving runners swarming like angry bees at the finish line. There were times when the aid stations were not well-stocked, when there were so few spectators and fellow runners that it seemed to be a race in theory only. But still, there was something to these races, an earnestness that seemed truer to the marathoning spirit than the marketing and spectacle of the big city races. And those huckleberry shakes, of course.

But would I really trade Ashton for the New York City Marathon? No. What is lost in numbers is gained in excitement; there is no phenomenon as startling as the sight of a huge mass of people running down the street, not in panic, but with joy and determination. But if I had only experienced the Big Race, I would not have a complete understanding of the marathon.

So, my favorite marathon? I still can't tell you. Perhaps I'm too greedy. I want them all.

Soon after returning from Idaho, I had another interesting running adventure in my own backyard. In the green spaces throughout Washington, D.C., creatures stirred, awakening from their seventeen-year slumber. Soon, they would arise in the thousands from their underground lairs, like graveyard zombies, and invade the city, filling the air with a hellishly loud buzz. They were short and squat with thick, greenish bodies and blood-red eyes, and they were called "Brood X." The city seemed transfixed in nervous anticipation, but was powerless to stop them.

Despite their ominous name and hellish appearance, they were, in fact, just insects. Cicadas. And rather than being worried about them, most people seemed intrigued. As zero-hour drew near, the local newspapers themselves became infested with articles about them. We were told where we could expect the highest concentrations, and how to protect trees with netting. There were even recipes on how to prepare them for dinner. But no one told runners what they could expect.

The days flew by, and every morning I stepped outside, only to find … nothing. As it turned out, not every neighborhood would get a visit from the Brood. Why were they snubbing me? This was expected to be a seminal D.C. event, and I wasn't invited to the party.

I realized that if I wanted to experience these pests, I would actually have to go looking for them. I had read that areas farther northwest that had older trees would be harder hit by the little buggers. So I laced up my running shoes, corralled a running partner, and went north, entering Rock Creek Park near the Carter Baron amphitheater.

We soon came across our quarry. We saw first one, then another cicada laid out on the ground in front of us. There were dozens more nearby. Then we saw one fly right into a parked car. It occurred to me that was the equivalent of failing to notice a skyscraper and walking into it facefirst. These were not bright creatures. We continued our run.

I soon became accustomed to seeing small black clumps whizzing around us. Their style of flying can best described as awkward and clumsy, even out of control. I wondered if perhaps they were screaming in panic as they flew past. Suddenly, a cicada dove straight at me. I ducked to avoid a head-on collision. I looked over to see my running partner twisting and pirouetting herself to avoid contact. It was then that we stopped viewing the cicadas as silly little aerial clowns and more as incoming missiles, and we began to wonder how much a direct hit from one would sting. Luckily, we made it home with that question still unanswered.

A few days later I ran a different route up near Glover Park. Hurtling down Massachusetts Avenue, I saw hundreds of little black corpses on the sidewalk. Revulsion soon tuned to curiosity, which turned to sadness. Seventeen years of waiting, for only a few days of life. Their silly little existence suddenly seemed more precious, making my own life that much more valuable, too. Their ungainly attempts at flight now reminded me of so many runners who trump their own clumsiness with sheer determination, and who, through their efforts, gain a type of grace.

The cicadas no longer seemed to me to be tiny invaders, but instead, in a way, little creatures with whom I could share a strange kinship. Not born myself with a natural runner's body or a smooth stride, I run fearlessly, just like the cicadas seem to fly, knowing that honest sweat has its own grace, and knowing, too, that my days here are numbered. Perhaps we weren't so very different after all.

Of course, my empathy has its limits. If ever I run into the wall of an office building by accident, I'm hanging up my running shoes for good.

Running Tip #16

Mind Games

- *Stay mindful of what you're doing.* It's like driving: you don't have to hold the steering wheel in a death grip, but you should be calmly aware of both your car and your surroundings.
- *Have a checklist.* Are you landing too heavily? Are you swinging your arms too far? How's your breathing? How's your posture? Become aware of your bad tendencies, and keep an eye out for them.
- *Manage your intensity.* Some runners visualize how strong they'll feel at specific, difficult parts of an upcoming race. Others repeat a supportive phrase like a mantra. I like to visualize catastrophe. It's actually not as crazy as it sounds. If I can accept the worst that could happen on race day, I've conquered my fears, and I can relax and just run. Find out what works for you. Your mind is a puzzle that can be solved, and once you find the right answer, you can achieve your best times.

There and Back:
Adventures in South Africa

I sat in the dark theater, gazing up at the image on the screen. It was of a man pumping his arms rhythmically as he ran over brown, unpaved earth. The man was Haile Gebrselassie, the great Ethiopian middle-distance runner, and the movie was *Endurance,* the film that chronicled his rise from poverty in Ethiopia to Olympic gold in Atlanta. The opening scene was of Gebrselassie on a training run, covering the African countryside with long, powerful strides, gliding over rocks and hills with no display of effort. He looked like a running god, and the land looked primeval. This, to me, was Africa.

But Africa was also a land of war, oppression, corruption, and disease. Alongside its great beauty sat great hardship. It was difficult for my mind to encompass the whole of it. I've often imagined the world as being crisscrossed with running trails, interrupted here and there by mountains and oceans. Some of them are paved and measured. Most are not. Some haven't even been discovered yet. But try as might, I couldn't quite fit Africa into my vision of the world; I couldn't imagine racing there.

Clearly, something needed to be done. Stephanie, always up for a good adventure, agreed. I went online, signed up for the Two Oceans Marathon, to take place on March 26, 2005, and booked our trip to South Africa. One way or the other, I was going to sort this out.

Our itinerary would be challenging. We were to fly to Johannesburg, then on to Hoedspruit for a safari, and then down to Cape Town, where the race would be held. All that sounded fine, except that our return flight was booked for the afternoon of race day. Not an ideal plan, but that was the only schedule that met all of the conflicting requirements of our work lives and the available flights and excursions, so that was the way it was going to be. If nothing else, the fear of missing an international flight would be a great incentive to run faster.

The conceit of our age is that we live in a world that is becoming ever smaller. Interconnected economies, e-mail and online services, and fast, relatively cheap flights make almost any part of the globe as close as your next-door neighbor.

Don't you believe it. Africa is still a long way from the United States. From our home in D.C., we made our way to New York for a flight to Johannesburg, with a layover in Dakar, Senegal. The entire adventure would require almost a full twenty-four hours, but instead of moaning about the discomfort of it all, I actually appreciated the difficulty involved. Something magical happens during a long flight to a distant, exotic land. The idea of adventure ferments in your mind until it is fully risen upon arrival, making you hungry for whatever you may discover. This process takes time, and as we boarded our flight at JFK airport, I knew we would have all the time we needed.

That was the emotional argument in favor of a long flight. The physical arguments weighed in against it. I tossed and turned in my seat, bent and straightened my legs in a futile attempt to find a truly comfortable position, all to no avail. There were some bright spots, though; plenty of good movies to watch, and one truly memorable sight—a predawn liftoff from Dakar, with a view of dozens of fishermen slowly heading out to sea in their small boats, hundreds of feet below us, as the dark blue of the sky bled crimson and orange. It was an impossibly beautiful moment. I settled in for the remainder of the flight, contemplating Africa.

Eight hours later, the sun was setting as we touched down in Johannesburg. We would be spending only one short night there before leaving first thing in the morning for another flight to Hoedspruit. As we drove from the airport to our hotel on the edge of town, any guilt I felt about not spending more time in Johannesburg was allayed by our driver, who, while insisting that security was improving downtown, warned us about the prolific and violent street crime. When apartheid ended and movement by nonwhites was no longer restricted, millions of people migrated to the cities with a dream of finding a better job. When those jobs did not materialize, the dispossessed survived as best they could, building shantytowns on the fringes of the city, and, in some cases, preying on those around them. Our driver said that some downtown hotels had closed because of the crime, to which the government responded by installing street cameras.

During the ride, our driver taught us a few basic words of Zulu, one of the nine African languages spoken throughout the country. Most South Africans speak several languages in addition to Afrikaans and English, including Zulu. It was very humbling. Like many Americans, I'm limited to English and a smattering of high school Spanish. Stephanie and I were entranced as he ran through several dialects, occasionally making clucking sounds that no Westerner could emulate. As we drove past some abandoned buildings and gold mines, I wondered at this unique place. *Egoli*, the Zulu name for Johannesburg—City of Gold.

In the morning I made use of the treadmill in our hotel for a quick run, not wanting to get lost on the city streets. On the television was Nelson Mandela, who, even in retirement, is generally looked upon as perhaps the world's foremost moral authority. He was onstage at a concert on Human Rights Day, the national holiday memorializing the murder of sixty-nine pepole in the 1960 Sharpeville massacre. Taking the stage after a performance by Annie Lennox, Mandela said that healthy women were also victims of the AIDS epidemic. AIDS was becoming a disaster of epic proportions in South Africa, fueled by misconceptions about its origin and how to cure it. Some South Africans even believe that the virus can be cured by sleeping with virgins. The day after Mandela's speech, the local newspapers reported that a man with AIDS was arrested for brutally killing his wife, his wife's child, and his wife's mother because his wife stopped sleeping with him.

A few hours later, Stephanie and I boarded a small plane bound for Hoedspruit. After our long journey the day before, we were happy that this flight would only last a single hour. As the plane descended, I nervously scanned the countryside for signs of an airport, but found none. Nevertheless, the plane continued to drop, and then we touched down.

Stepping out into the bright sunshine, I was struck by the unlikeliness of the place. The airport was a tiny military airstrip that was converted to civilian use. The terminal consisted only of a small building outfitted with a couch, several comfortable chairs, and animal prints on the walls. It looked like a room in which you might relax with a drink after a long day traversing the grassy veldt.

After collecting our bags, we stepped through the building to our transport, and immediately saw a waterbuck—a deer-like animal—leap across the road into the bush. We weren't even off the airport grounds and we'd had our first wild animal sighting. This was the Africa of our dreams.

The wildlife preserves of Hoedspruit are large, but not the endless open miles of our imaginations. Fences—some of them electrified—separated the various preserves. These areas are large enough to get lost in, and for even the largest animals to hide. With the beautiful Drakensberg Mountains as a backdrop, we made our way to our campsite within the

Gwalagwala game preserve. This was nothing like the scouting adventures of my youth. These tents are mounted on large wooden platforms, and enclose modern accommodations, including a bed, proper bathroom, and electricity. There was also a treehouse bar in which to meet other travelers, and an open-air dining area.

Our hosts were Dorian and Ann, a couple who had decided later in life that they wanted a change, and gambled on buying untilled farmland and converting it into a game preserve. It soon became apparent, however, that they were still trying to figure out their proper place in this environment. Ann had unwittingly managed to adopt several animals, including a young, wayward warthog, despite concerns that it might not be good for a wild animal to become too accustomed to being in close quarters with humans. Still, the little warthog had a certain charm, and it was fun watching him try to chew the elastic laces on my running shoes. He pulled back the laces several times, only to jump with a start when it snapped out of his mouth. After several attempts, he grunted and turned away, much to our amusement.

After settling in and having lunch, we set out for an afternoon game ride. Early mornings and late afternoons are the best times for viewing animals, when the sun is the least oppressive and the animals are more active. *Not unlike runners,* I thought, as we clambered in to the open Land Rover.

We had scheduled three game rides over the next several days, in search of the African safari Holy Grail—sightings of the Big Five: lion, rhino, elephant, water buffalo, and leopard. We managed to see all except the elusive leopard, and saw many others as well, including giraffe, hyena, cheetah, and impala.

The impala were perhaps the most memorable, leaping as if staying planted on the earth took more effort than getting airborne. Locals referred to the impala as their "McDonald's," which had nothing to do with fast food, but instead refers to the pattern made by the distinctive black streaks running down each of their haunches and their tails, creating nature's version of the Golden Arches.

I wondered what it would be like to have so much power in my legs, to be able to leap so quickly and gracefully. Watching wild animals filled me with a sense of awe, and also revealed the limitations of my own body. Humans are not the fastest, strongest, or most graceful creatures found in nature, and I could only imagine how pitiful even the fastest among us must look to the rest of the animal kingdom. I recalled reading, however, that humans can track and run down game on foot over long distances, due in large part to the amazing shock-absorbing properties of our feet. We might not be the fastest, but as long as we can keep the game in sight, we can eventually overtake it, like the proverbial tortoise beating the hare.

This all reminded me of some trash talk I had recently engaged in with a friend at a local gym. He was younger than I, very fit and athletic, and had just started running. He boasted that he was already a faster runner than I was. I assured him that I could beat him. He told me that he was faster than I was in the 5K. I told him that might be true, but I'd race him in a 10K. He said he could still beat me at that distance. Maybe so, I replied, but if it took a half-marathon, a marathon, or a 50-mile ultramarathon, I would eventually beat him. I could run all those races, and I would eventually win. He was silent after that.

Not everyone among our group seemed enamored with the aesthetic beauty of the animals in quite the same way. One great big strapping fellow—a former rugby player—seemed to look at nature as one big all-you-can-eat smorgasbord. He talked a great deal about the South African taste for meat. From wild buck—especially one type called "kudu"—to crocodile and ostrich, South Africans will eat it all, as long as it once moved. They are carnivores with a capital "C." My wife is no vegetarian, but she was astounded. "Don't you ever eat any salad?" she asked. Winking, our companion said, "When we want vegetables, we eat chicken." I suddenly wondered whether a prerace carb load might be harder to find than I thought.

Managing a game preserve isn't all fun, though, as Dorian told me. He pointed to a young giraffe that was limping. His right hind leg was marred by a gaping wound, and his footprints were marked with spots of blood. He had been attacked by a hyena. As we watched the suffering animal, we wanted to help it, but that is not how things are handled on a game preserve. To maintain the balance of things, the animals must be left alone in all but the most extreme circumstances. The hyenas have to eat also, of course. It seemed cruel, but this was nature's way.

At our last evening there, we sat once again under the stars, drinking South African wine, eating a delicious dinner that did, thankfully, include some fresh vegetables, and compared stories with our fellow travelers. Several of them were South Africans on holiday, and they were open about their feelings about their country and recent events. Their mood seemed hopeful, although they had their doubts about particular politicians. Their criticisms seemed reaffirming, though, because not one of them stated any disillusionment with the overall direction their nation had taken over the previous decade, or even with much of what the current administration was trying to achieve.

Eventually the conversation drifted around to my upcoming challenge, and everyone wished me good luck in the race. The Two Oceans Marathon seemed to be quite well known; even people who were not runners were quite familiar with it. Finally, the dessert was over, the last of the wine had been drunk, and it was time for Stephanie and me to get our things together for our flight out the next morning. We would be departing Hoedspruit for Cape Town, and suddenly the race, which had not seemed real before, loomed large.

Cape Town is a beautiful, wondrous city, embodying much of what is best and worst about South Africa. Nestled between the sheltered waters of Table Bay and the majestic heights of Table Mountain, Cape

Town has a long and checkered past. Phoenicians and Arabs thought it had magnetic powers that would draw ships to their doom along its rocky coast, and the Portuguese explorer Vasca da Gama sighted it as he rounded the Cape of Good Hope in 1498. The town was laid out in 1652 by the Dutch East India Company as a replenishment station for its fleet. The local population mostly succumbed to smallpox brought inadvertently by the colonialists, and the surviving indigenous population mostly worked as poorly treated laborers.

In 1795 and 1806, the British invaded South Africa, and by 1843, it had annexed large parts of the country. Clashes with native Zulus and the rising population of Dutch-speaking farmers, known as Boers, led to the Anglo-Boer Wars of 1880–1881 and 1899–1902. The British crushed the Boers with a scorched-earth policy, burning farms and establishing the world's first concentration camps. Eventually, over 136,000 Dutch Afrikaners were imprisoned in these camps, in which more than 26,000 women and children died from typhoid, dysentery, and neglect.

The Union of South Africa was formed in 1910, and the policy of oppression against the native population reached full fruition in 1948 with the creation of apartheid, a complex system that separated the races by law. Apartheid weathered international boycotts and domestic protest and violence, until President F. W. de Klerk unexpectedly abandoned it in 1990, and began negotiating with Nelson Mandela, his formerly jailed adversary. Mandela's African National Congress then won South Africa's first full and open election, and South Africa's journey from darkness was completed when president-elect Mandela announced that "Never, never, and never again shall it be that this beautiful land will again experience the oppression of one by another."

Cape Town reflects all of this history. From its 300-year-old Castle of Good Hope, to its beautiful architecture and manicured gardens, Cape Town shows the best of its colonial past. But then there is District Six, the vibrant port area that was bulldozed in 1979 and declared "whites-only."

Loud protests followed, and the area was kept barren. Today a museum commemorates the destruction of this neighborhood. And there is also Robben Island, an Alcatraz-like penal colony sitting in the bay, where Mandela and others spent years imprisoned for dedicating their lives to fighting apartheid.

Stephanie and I settled into our hotel room overlooking Greenmarket Square, built in 1710 and still used daily as a popular flea market. One evening, we were serenaded by a free jazz concert held there. From our window we could see the square, nearby churches, and the looming mass of Table Mountain, draped in the morning hours with clouds. Over the next several days we would visit all of these sights, riding a cable car to the mountain top, wandering the through towns and visiting museums. Still, my mind kept turning to the marathon.

The Two Oceans Marathon is actually poorly named; it is not a marathon at all. Rather, it is a 56-kilometer ultramarathon, with a half-marathon option also available. The most striking feature of the ultra is its course profile. Starting with a small hill early on, the race meanders over flat roads for the first 28 kilometers, but then it takes a nasty turn as it makes a precipitous ascent of Chapman's Peak at kilometer 34. It then screams back down over the next 6 kilometers, and, at the point when a regular marathon would be over, begins a steep ascent of Constantia Nek. It's the kind of course profile to strike fear even into the heart of an experienced marathoner.

I was concerned about the race, and decided that seeing the beast might allay my fears. Stephanie and I decided to take a tour of the Cape of Good Hope, and the driver readily agreed to drive along as much of the race course for us as he could. Soon, we were driving up to Chapman's Peak, called simply Chappies by the locals. Even in a microbus I could appreciate the steepness of the climb. After severe rock falls plagued the area, the road up Chappies was closed and the course was altered to skirt around Chappies from 2000 to 2004.

I could see why so many runners were disappointed. The view was amazing. The road hugged the pale orange cliff-side, providing a beautiful view of Hout Bay to the west. Our driver pointed out the 1,560 meters of fencing and the concrete canopy that had been installed as part of the new safety measures that allowed the race to return to Chappies in 2004. The netting looked quite fragile to me, though, and I imagined struggling up this road on race day, conquering Chappies, and pausing to celebrate one of the greatest moments of my running life, only to be clunked on the head by a falling boulder. I made a mental note to remember not to pause here on race day if I could help it.

Finally, Stephanie and I found ourselves at the Cape of Good Hope, the storied tip of Africa, where the rough waters of the Atlantic meet the warm waters of the Indian Ocean. We stared out over the open expanse of water before us, and marveled at how far we had come. Ahead of us still was a visit to a penguin colony at Boulders Beach—yet one more sign that we were far, far from home. But standing at the Cape seemed to be the crowning moment. There was, finally, nowhere farther to go.

After feeling like the race would never come, I suddenly found myself picking up my race packet at the University of Cape Town the day before the start. I meandered through the expo, had a pasta dinner in the hotel restaurant, and then settled back in our hotel room with some good reading: the racing instructions. Among the papers included was a booklet entitled "Information and Statistics." It was an absolute compendium of minutiae about the race. There were 7,830 participants registered in the ultra. There were nearly four times as many male ultra runners as female, though there were 339 husband and wife teams. I was disappointed to see that there was no statistic on divorces caused by racing together.

There were also three runners going for their thirtieth finish, and twenty-four runners who would be celebrating their birthday on race day. The oldest registered runner was seventy-six, and the youngest was nineteen. Sixty-three countries were represented, although only 360 runners were from overseas, and only thirty-three were from the United States. I realized then that the worst I could do as a finisher would be to place thirty-third in my category—not bad for bragging rights back home, as long as there were no follow-up questions about the number of runners.

A few scant hours later, I stood in front of the hotel with some other runners in the predawn darkness, waiting for transport to the starting line at the University of Cape Town. The others were visiting Germans. One, in fact, was here on his honeymoon. I wondered whether he had even bothered to tell his bride that he was racing, or whether he was hoping to finish before she awoke. As the van sped along the highway, we talked about our hopes for the race and offered each other energy bars.

The van dropped us off on the main commercial street near to the University, in the suburb of Newlands. I wished the Germans good luck and joined the throng of runners making their way to the starting line. Despite the darkness, it was already quite warm, and I quickly shed my throwaway long-sleeved shirt. I settled into a spot in the crowd behind the starting line, and listened to the last-minute instructions that bellowed from the speakers. The various countries represented were named, to sporadic cheers and applause, and certain notable runners were introduced. The crowd then sang the traditional African song "Shozaloza."

Finally, the announcements were over, and I felt my body tense as I awaited the start, my finger poised on my watch's start button. The gun roared at precisely 6 A.M. I surged forward with the crowd, buoyed by a familiar wave of adrenaline. The asphalt below my feet, smiling faces and cheers of the onlookers, the sight of the runners around me, and even the smells of the race all seemed familiar. The gap in my worldview quickly closed, and Africa, wonderful and exotic, also became, for me, simply another place to run.

As we streamed along the dark city streets, I thought about my race preparation. I had trained for the Two Oceans Marathon as I had trained for the JFK 50 Miler: by including a full marathon in my final long run. This time it was the Virginia Creeper Marathon, a beautiful race in that state's southwest corner which I ran with my friends Dave and Renata. It was my ninty-sixth marathon.

The Two Oceans Marathon has a unique system for awarding finishers' medals. Rather than dividing the field into elite runners and everyone else, the organizers reward different levels of achievement. Runners breaking the 4-hour barrier in the race earn a silver medal, and those breaking 6 hours earn a bronze. Previously, the race had a 6 hour time limit, but now runners who beat 7 hours earn a blue medal. However, many veteran marathoners still consider 6 hours to be the "official" time limit. Factoring in my recent training, jetlag, and the great unknown of the two ascents, I pegged myself as coming in somewhere between 5:15 and 5:30, placing me solidly in the bronze group. In those first few minutes of the race, I calculated the pace necessary to hit my goal, and settled back into an easy stride.

As the sun broke the darkness, I looked at the runners around me. Although they looked like any race field I would find back in the United States, I quickly noticed one key difference: their conversations. Many spoke in the native tongues of South Africa, and even when their conversation dropped into English, the clipped cadences of Afrikaans or Zulu remained. Despite this language barrier, I still felt our bonds as runners, and enjoyed the voices around me.

Passing the first refreshment station, I realized another novelty of the race: there were no rows of cups, as are found in most other races I've run in the United States and abroad. In Cape Town, volunteers handed out water and sports drink in sealed plastic pouches. I ripped a hole in the pouch with my teeth and squirted the water into my mouth.

Newlands gave way to Kenilworth, which became Plumstead, and the city melted into open spaces and small towns. I spotted the pacer for the 6-hour finishers' group, and I reasoned that as long as I keep that group behind me, I would be certain to have a bronze finisher's medal. I passed them and didn't look back.

Being new to the race, I asked several other runners about the course as we ran, and was introduced to another unusual feature of the course: all runners who persevere through ten editions of the race are awarded a permanent blue number to mark their achievement. For me, this meant that veteran ultramarathoners were easier to locate and probe for words of wisdom. They seemed more than willing to oblige.

We entered the town of Lakeside, and then Muizenberg, which gave us our first views of water. This is False Bay, and beyond it the Indian Ocean, the first of the two oceans for which the race is named. The road fell before us as we passed old stone homes in St. James and Kalk Bay, and then, as we entered Fish Hoek and turned inland, we were greeted by a young couple painted entirely in green, cheering us as we streamed past. The views were beautiful and there was still plenty of energy in my legs. These were the good miles.

As I felt energy surge through me, I spied a runner up ahead holding a banner aloft. I wondered if he could possibly be the pacer for sub-5-hour group. No, it couldn't be. But it was. I caught them and stuck to them like glue. As we ran, I asked the pacer about the South African racing circuit. Although the Two Oceans seemed to be a challenging course, he told me that many runners use it as preparation for the Comrades Ultramarathon that follows several months later in mid-June.

Wow. Using a brutal 56-kilometer race as a training run for a more difficult race? There were definitely some tough runners out here.

We ran through Sun Valley, and entered the town of Noordhoek, at kilometer 28, the halfway point of the race. Craft shops and restaurants lined the road, eventually giving way to trees and parkland. Chappies lay just ahead. Our pacer announced that it was time to go to work.

The Chapman's Peak Drive, the race route, was opened to the public in 1922. A popular tourist and sporting destination, it actually consists of two peaks: "Little Chappies," at the 30 kilometer mark of the race, followed by "Big Chappies" 4 kilometers later.

Stands of trees thinned and then disappeared altogether, and the grass melted away as we began our first ascent. The sun was shining brightly now, but I felt comfortable and strong as we followed the road upward. The incline actually felt like a nice change from the earlier flats, and I was surprised at how good I felt. Soon the pace group crested the first summit, and we eased into a short easy stretch of road before the next peak. Talking to the pacer, I learned that the difficulty with Chappies is often not the actual climb, but rather the quick descent that follows, which can wreak havoc with the quads. But other than keeping proper form and trying not to go too fast, there wouldn't be much I could do about that. After all, I never expected to get through this race without some pain.

My thoughts were interrupted by the pacer's announcement that we would resume climbing around the next curve. Feeling confident after conquering Little Chappies, I surged forward ahead of the pack, and after rounding the corner, was able to see the road ahead as it wound its way to the top of Big Chappies. The ascent was over 2½ kilometers, but the views were even more spectacular than they had been from the van window a few days earlier.

Finally, I was at the top of Chappies. Fear that had been gnawing at me since signing up for the race melted away. The climb of Constantia Nek still loomed ahead, but with 17 kilometers left to go, things were looking very, very good. My legs swallowed the descent without a problem, and I said a silent farewell to Chappies as we entered Hout Bay.

Hout Bay was the site of a battle between the Dutch settlers and a British naval force in September, 1795. The Dutch were victorious in a battle that resulted in little loss of life, and cannons used in that victory still guard the town to this day. The proud residents of "the Republic of Hout Bay" have maintained a tradition of firing a cannon as the lead runners enter the town, though I was too far back of the lead pack at that point to hear anything other than the sound of thousands of feet slapping the asphalt. But the spectators and refreshments along the streets of Hout Bay were still a welcome sight.

At about this time fatigue began to seep into my legs, and my earlier soaring confidence started to leak out. I realized that I would probably not be able to maintain the sub-5-hour pace, but I resolved to stay with the group to the 42.1 kilometer mark. I would not have a sub-5-hour finish this day, but making it to the regulation marathon distance with this pack would be my moral victory.

Time ebbed past as I continued to press forward, clinging to the pace group. Finally, I saw an inflated archway spanning the road up ahead—it was the 42.1 kilometer mark. I had earned my victory in the race-within-a-race. As I crossed the timing mat set up near the distance marker, I fought the urge to consider the race finished. The visual cues all said that I'd completed a marathon, and my body certainly felt like it had finished a marathon. Like trained dogs sensing when it is time to go home, my legs were sure that it was time to downshift into cool down mode. Not yet, I told them. There was one last big challenge immediately ahead: Constantia Nek.

With a climb of 215 meters, Constantia Nek is actually the biggest hill on the course, higher even than Big Chappies. But it's also a completely different hill than Chappies. Gone were the cliffs and commanding bayside views; here, the roadside was thick with trees and dotted with residences. The race organizers, knowing that this was where the most suffering would occur, squeezed refreshment stations closer together here, and spectators lined the roads in groups to cheer us on.

At first, the climb didn't seem bad at all. But just as I started to relax, the road suddenly soared up toward the treetops. I had earlier resolved to run the ascents, but this stretch of road made me break that promise, and I briefly joined those who were walking the worst parts of the climb. The strained faces of the runners—runners in name only at this point — mirrored my own determination. Finally, I could see the top of the hill just ahead, and, like a swimmer reaching for poolside, I surged forward with one last push and crested the summit. Constantia Nek was history. Only 10 kilometers left to go.

With all of the fearsome hills finally behind me, I settled into the final task of finishing the race. I shortened my stride and searched for my last reserves of energy as I ran the rolling hills of Rhodes Drive down to the open, sun-drenched avenues of Kirstenbosch, where the glorious Gardens are found. There was now less than 6 kilometers to go. The bright sunlight pulled sweat from our bodies, but I saw no quitters around me. Up ahead was the sweeping turn known as "Harry's Corner," named for a course marshal who manned that corner for years until his death.

The crowd of spectators thickened as we entered Rondebosch, and with it, the university and its football field, where the finish line waited. Mustering the last of my strength, I sprinted to meet it. My final time was 5 hours 15 minutes, the exact time that I had originally hoped for.

As I slowly moved through the crowd, my newly awarded bronze medal hanging around my neck, someone pressed an application for the New York City Marathon into my hand. I continued moving, grabbing fluids and a goody bag, and made my way to the steps leading out of the university and down to the main thoroughfare, to catch a city bus back to Greenmarket Square. As I sat on the bus, an anomalous figure among the Sunday riders, I considered the race application in my hand. I had traveled so far, had experienced so much, but this piece of paper in my hand shrunk all that, shrunk the world. It was as if I had journeyed to the farthest reaches of the North Pole, beyond the edge of civilization, only to find a note from my family waiting for me. And then I realized what I'd always suspected was true: the world is indeed a matrix of running paths, all connected together, stretching from Haile Gebrselassie's flying feet to Chapman's Peak and over to Central Park in Manhattan. In a few short hours I would board a jet back to the States, but standing there with that paper in my hand, I knew that I was already home.

Only one final thing to resolve, though: did this race belong on my list or not? It was billed as a marathon, so that would seem to settle the issue. But it was not the standard marathon distance; it was about 9 miles longer, so it was an ultramarathon. As much as I would have like to have counted this race toward my 100, I knew that could not be allowed. I had now officially run ninety-six marathons and *two* ultramarathons. End of discussion.

Running Tip #17

Trail Running

- *Keep your weight over your feet and shorten your stride.* This will allow you to shift your weight quickly if your footing is unstable.
- *Don't zone out.* Running a trail requires focus and concentration, since a sudden misstep can lead to a debilitating injury. But focus isn't fear. Look at trails as puzzles to be solved.
- *Get the right gear.* Trail-running shoes are best because of their thicker outsoles and better traction. Bring a mini first-aid kit and water; there are no fountains in the woods.
- *Be safe.* Trails, even urban ones, are much more isolated than roads. Use common sense: don't run with an mp3 player or in the dark, since you need to be aware of what's around you, and run with a friend if possible.

Almost There: Marathon Number 99, Wilmington, Delaware

On the morning of May 15, 2005, Dave and I stood in front of Frawley Stadium in Wilmington, Delaware. We were among a small group of people shaking their legs nervously, pacing back and forth, and tying and retying their shoes. I was at another starting line, waiting for the signal that would launch us forward.

We were lucky to be there. Earlier in the morning Dave and I had checked out of our nearby hotel and got in our car for the short drive over to the start. It was about a mile away, a distance that we could easily have jogged or walked, which is exactly what we should have done. Driving on unfamiliar roads, though, we somehow wound up on the entrance ramp to I-95, the major interstate that runs through Wilmington. Peering out the window, I could see people gathering at the starting line as it receded into the distance at 55 miles per hour. I was annoyed, but it wasn't a major problem; we would just get off and turn around.

Except that we couldn't. After getting off the highway at the very next exit, we realized that we weren't near an entrance onto the highway heading back. We had to try our luck on local roads, and ended

215

up having to stop off at a gas station to ask for directions. With scant minutes to spare before the start, I couldn't believe what a mess we had made of things. There was silence in the car as we made our way back, and only after we parked with enough time to walk to the start did we finally relax. Even after all these years of racing, I couldn't take anything for granted.

The prerace dinner had not gone smoothly either. The brochure promised pasta with vegetables and chicken for all runners who attended, which sounded great, but whoever had arranged the meal clearly did not understand the crowd that would be showing up to be fed. A pasta station was set up with chefs cooking up meals to order; a nice touch, but not a very efficient way to feed hundreds of people. As time slipped by, runners grumbled on line and started to fill up on bread and dessert. I managed to finally get some pasta, but it was an unwelcome detour from my prerace regimen.

Despite the setbacks, I felt relaxed at the starting line. I was finally right where I was meant to be, feeling good and loose. It was a warm day, but not a bad one for racing. Clouds lingered from the rain that had blown through overnight, and a light breeze stirred the air. The deputy mayor made a few brief remarks, and a young lady sang "The Star Spangled Banner." And then we were off.

The course was mostly flat, consisting of four loops along the waterfront, the stadium, and an outlet shopping mall. I set out at a comfortable pace, sticking with Dave for a time until he dropped back. I set off on my own, lost in thought, reminiscing about my eighteen years of marathoning. I thought about the ambulances I'd seen out on various racecourses. There is a dark emptiness that marathoners feel anytime they see or hear an ambulance, and I've seen too many of those over the years. I've also seen runners throwing up, lying flat on their backs on the asphalt, and sitting dejectedly on curbs. One friend running the Marine Corps Marathon on an unseasonably hot day made it as far as mile 23 before she collapsed, only to awaken in a medical tent, buried under bags of ice. She recovered fully, but it was a very close call. I thought about how lucky I've been over the years to never have needed those ambulances, and to have escaped major injury. Despite the great demands I had put on my body, it had never broken, and had never given up completely.

I hadn't bothered to look at my watch as I crossed the first two mile markers, which was unusual for me. I suddenly wondered if I could manage to avoid looking at my watch for the entire race. Could I stand not counting the seconds and minutes as they passed? I wanted to be able to do that, to run the race by feel alone, as an experiment in "Zen running." As I finished the first lap, though, I passed beneath the official timing clock, and couldn't help glancing up. Just that quickly, my little experiment was over.

And then came the difficult miles, which every marathoner knows are out there somewhere on the course, the miles that test our will. Four laps in Wilmington were like the four laps of a mile on the track: the first lap is filled with energy and hopefulness; the second lap is for settling into a strong pace and holding it; the third lap is where the pain and doubt set in, when so much running is behind you, but where the finish line is still so far away; and the fourth lap is for just hanging on, where you try to not spoil all the hard work that preceded it.

I ran the race like I was running a hard mile, feeling all the ups and downs of my journey. Each lap on the course had an out-and-back portion, meaning that I was able to see many of the runners in front and behind me. I saw Dave on each lap, as well as the lead runners, striding easily like gazelles. There was a man running in pink tutu; Dave later accused him of lacking the proper respect for the race. I didn't mind—at least it was a distraction.

Finally, I set out on the fourth and final lap. I came upon an older man standing by himself on a street corner, wearing a shirt and tie. He was handing out free bottles of water, and near as I could tell, was not a race volunteer, but just a local resident who thought we needed and deserved to have some support. I took a bottle and thanked him, and then doused myself, feeling the coolness bring strength back to my tired muscles, even if only for a few moments.

Four laps provided enough time for the runners and the race volunteers to come to know each other, even if only in passing. As I passed one volunteer at mile 24, I told him that I hoped he wouldn't take it the wrong way if I said that I was happy not to have to see him again. He laughed and told me to get going.

And then, finally, the finish line was just ahead. As I crossed the line, the official clock overhead read 3:35:07. I had run my 99th marathon 10 minutes and 23 seconds faster than I had run my first one. The Me-That-Is had beaten the Me-That-Was. Someday, I knew, I would no longer be able to beat the Me-That-Was. But that day had not yet come, not in Wilmington.

And now, after all these years and all these miles, there was just one more marathon to go.

Running Tip #18

Eat to Run, Eat to Live

- *Eat a balanced diet:* 65 percent complex carbohydrates, 25 percent lean protein, 10 percent fat, preferably unsaturated vegetable fat, like olive oil.
- *Avoid processed foods and fried foods, and limit your intake of sweets.*
- *Aim to eat a good variety, especially fruits and vegetables.* The brightest and most colorful pack the biggest punch.
- *Graze.* Have something every two hours or so to avoid hunger and binging.
- *Take a daily multivitamin.* How many of us really have a perfect diet? No one I know. So cover your bases.
- *Don't skip breakfast.* You might lose more fat that way, but your workouts will suffer. With your tank full, you'll train better, race better, and lose excess pounds anyway.
- *Watch your portion size.* You should be able to fit most meals in the palm of your hand.
- *Read food labels.* You might be surprised at what's in there. Generally, if the list of ingredients is more than four or so lines long, it's not really food anymore.
- *Low-fat desserts aren't necessarily low-calorie!* These products often still have lots of sugar, so eat sparingly.

Marathon Number 100!

Back in 1987, my supply of running gear consisted of a simple pair of running shoes, a cotton T-shirt, and gym shorts. Nearly two decades down the road, my closet looked much different. On the floor were several pairs of running shoes, costing over $100 each, that were ultra-light and packed with all manner of hi-tech wizardry. On an overhead shelf were neatly folded shirts made of space age breathable fabrics, sporting evocative brand names like Gore-Tex, Dri-FIT, and CoolMax. On a rack hung several breathable, wind and water resistant jackets, and on another shelf sat my wrap-around sunglasses that block out UV rays and random ambient light.

Strapped to my wrist was a watch that could count and store up to 100 interval splits, although it was considered a dinosaur because it couldn't also measure my heart rate, or triangulate with orbiting satellites to record my route and speed. Of course, if I wanted to measure my route, there were now several Web sites that allowed me to precisely calculate the distance I ran, indicating elevation changes as well. In a drawer sat my mp3 digital player, although I usually didn't bring that along on my runs, since I feared getting too dependent on it.

My kitchen had undergone some changes as well. Although I still stocked whole-grain cereals, lean meat, fish, low-fat dairy, and unprocessed fruits and vegetables, I also now used engineered food, such as energy bars, sports drinks, and gels.

Change had also come to the races I ran. Online registration had largely replaced the ritual of mailing in a check and a race application, and the electronic timing chip is now used not only in major marathons, but in races of all distances. And the races themselves have grown larger than I ever thought possible. A field of 20,000 marathoners is now common, and the largest races are nearly double that size.

None of these changes had come about overnight, even if it felt that way to me. But as much as both my own life and the world of marathoning had changed over the years, one thing was constant: more than anything else, I just wanted to run.

And so I had. Now, impossibly, improbably, Dave and I were both about to take our final steps toward achieving our long-held dream. One hundred marathons. Over the years, I kept running, trying not to focus too much on that distant goal. So much could have gone wrong, but now it was really about to happen. I suddenly felt more nervous about it than ever. Which race should it be?

I pored over marathon listings, compared different race courses, and contemplated logistics. Finally, Dave and I made our choice. After coming so far, we wouldn't cut any corners now; we were going to run one of the most grueling races in North America: Grandfather Mountain. Set in the Blue Ridge Mountains in the town of Boone, North Carolina, it represented everything I loved about the marathon. It was beautiful, but after starting at 3,333 feet, it climbed almost 1,000 feet to the peak for which it's named. But it wasn't the net elevation gain that made this race so ominous; there were also numerous drops and climbs along the way. The course elevation profile posted on the race Web site looked like a shark's toothy grin. And to top it all off, the final 4 miles to the finish line were almost entirely uphill.

It was a race that was guaranteed to plumb every runner's well of courage and resolve. But to those who made it to the top came bragging rights, and the sense of accomplishment that only comes from facing a dragon and staring it down. I had learned the hard way over the years never to take a marathon for granted; there were simply too many things that could go wrong. But with Grandfather Mountain, even careful preparation might not be enough. If I could conquer this course, I would have truly earned my record.

Dave agreed that this would be a fitting capstone to our 100-marathon quest. Our friend Renata and another marathoner, Greg, committed to joining Dave and me for our milestone adventure.

Our first challenge would be simply getting there. We opted to make the seven-hour drive the day before the race. When we finally arrived at our hotel on the outskirts of town, we dragged our stiff and sore bodies out of our car and acknowledged to each other with silent looks that this was a less-than-ideal way to prepare for a race.

We were quickly distracted by the strange, mournful sound of a hotel guest practicing her bagpipes in the parking lot. It turned out that the Scottish Highland Games were also being held that weekend on Grandfather Mountain. They were the second largest such games in the world, and the marathon was actually being run in cooperation with them; runners who survived the climb would finish with a victory lap around the competition field, and were welcome to stay afterward and watch the rest of the day's events. This was clearly going to be a race to remember, if only I could make it to the finish.

We went to Appalachian State University to pick up our race numbers and official T-shirts, and to scout out the start of the race, which would be on the university's track at Kidd Brewer Stadium. We then spent the rest of the day wandering around downtown.

Boone was clearly a college town, with cafés and coffee shops lining the main street. It had apparently experienced some recent growth, but it still managed to retain much of an older, enduring charm. I wandered into a small barber shop for a haircut. This had become a little tradition of mine; I had originally started getting haircuts on race weekend simply to kill time and get a chore done, but I also got a little psychological boost from the grooming, since a haircut left me feeling lighter, leaner and faster. I also found that getting a haircut is also a great way to get to know a town if you can get the barber talking. The barber shop in Boone proved especially friendly, and I soon knew not just everything about the town, but all about the barber's own family as well. By the time I stepped back out to the street, I felt that I really knew the place.

On race day, we joined a small but determined group of 400 runners. At the sound of the starting horn, we set off for a single lap around the track, and then exited the stadium for a lap of the parking lot. In any other race, I would have been antsy to hit the roads and get to the meat of the race, but here I knew what lay ahead, and I wasn't in any such hurry.

Finally, we left the university grounds. We cruised past a row of fast-food joints and restaurants and ran toward the town of Blowing Rock. From there we turned onto the scenic Blue Ridge Parkway, and began the climb toward Grandfather Mountain. Here, hills were measured in miles, not feet or yards, and the lush green beauty of our surroundings failed to completely distract any of us from the difficulty of our climbing. I found myself pushing off from my backside with each step, as if I were ascending a ladder instead of running a race.

As I pushed on, I fell into conversation with several other runners. There were clearly a lot of race veterans in this crowd. These runners seemed to love the race not despite the hills, but because of them. With each conquered hill, I began to understand why. Year after year, these runners hurl themselves against the mountain, and are enriched by the experience. The hills stripped away all other concerns, and left us focused on achieving one simple goal: making it to the top. In the process, it would reveal our worst or best selves.

The hills came and went with jarring regularity, until I became accustomed to their rhythm, as if I were standing offshore and weathering a steady surge of waves. Suddenly, the road turned into a gravel and dirt path that rose before me like a wall. It looked so utterly preposterous that I laughed out loud, but I had no choice but to grit my teeth, churn my arms, and attack. With each step I became more determined not to stop running. It was as if eighteen years of marathoning were distilled into this one moment, and I needed to prove that my will was stronger than this latest obstacle. I had decided that if I could make it to the top of that hill, I would finish the race and could claim ownership of my dream, but if I failed, it was all a hoax. It would all come down to this.

Having raised the stakes to that level, I couldn't let myself fail. I sucked in great gulps of air and drove my legs and arms. My eyes blurred with effort; I felt like I was climbing this hill more than running it. A voice in the back of my mind told me that it would be okay to stop, but I pushed that aside. The crest of the hill was now just a few steep yards ahead. No matter how much it hurt, I couldn't stop now. After eighteen years of running, I could not let it end here. Push, I told myself. Push!

And then I had done it; I was king of the hill. I still had miles left to go, but I knew the race was effectively over. Whatever lay ahead, it would not, could not, defeat me.

Still, it could hurt. The final few miles were mostly uphill as promised. The very last stretch passed the aid tent where food and drink were available for finishers—a cruel sight for runners who hadn't yet crossed the finish line. The road rose up toward the make-shift arena; it was an incline that earlier would have worried me, but I had come too far now and conquered too much already. I crested Grandfather Mountain, and entered McRae Meadows. Passing through the crowd, I entered the arena for my victory lap on the dirt track, buoyed by the applause and cheers of the spectators. I pulled my form together and asked my tired, sore legs for just one more effort, a burst of speed to give the spectators something to cheer about. Just a few more minutes of agony, and it would all be over. My legs agreed, and they propelled me across around the final curve and across the finish line. I checked my watch: 3 hours, 46 minutes, 25 seconds. Eighteen years after my first marathon, I had finally arrived.

One hundred marathons. It was done.

Dave came in a short time later, and I and cheered him as he, too, crossed the finish line. He had reached his 100-marathon milestone as well. We had run some thirty marathons together; a friendship forged on roads and trails, spanning more race miles together than most runners compile in their entire lives. That crazy idea we had concocted years earlier had somehow come true. Now we grinned, shook hands, and hugged.

Now that my race was over, I felt fatigue, but mostly relief and joy. Not just for having survived one of the toughest races in the country, but to have had the right combination of determination and luck to have reached my goal. Dave and I gobbled down some peanut butter sandwiches, grabbed some drinks, and settled into the stands to watch some of the Highland Games as we waited for Renata and Greg to come into view. On the field, athletes were doing something that could only be described as a telephone-pole toss. Just watching them made my back ache, and I realized that in this crowd, running a marathon probably looked like a tame thing to do.

Finally, our little group was reunited, and we made our way to the Scottish Clan reunion area, where booth displays honored different family lines. I didn't expect to see any tables for Clan Horowitz, but Dave found some distant brethren.

On the long ride home, we had plenty of time to consider what we had achieved. In the coming days, I thought about all those race miles, and tried to wrap my head around the immensity of it. I had raced in fourty-six states, thirteen countries, and four continents (not including my ultramarathon in South Africa). I had run up and down mountains, across deserts and lava fields, through forests, vineyards, and cities. I had met many extraordinary people, and witnessed the very best of human nature. I had, I believed, lived life to the fullest.

But did I remember it all? Such a strange question. I certainly remembered each marathon, but did I remember every minute of each one? No, of course not. My 100 marathons had cumulatively taken about 385 hours to run. That's over sixteen days of non-stop, round-the-clock racing. Who can recall every minute of a single hour, let alone sixteen entire days? But still, I was surprised at how few minutes I did recall. I remembered certain moments from each race when I saw something interesting, or when I crossed the finish line, but all the other moments were lost to me.

I have memories, however, that are untethered to any specific race. I experience random flashbacks of running beneath sun-dappled leaves along a tree-lined street, or past a row of shops, and I can't link those memories with any particular race. It's a bit like finding an old photograph wherein you recognize yourself, but not all of the people around you. You knew them once, but no longer. It's an uncomfortable, disconcerting feeling.

Equally disturbing was a realization that I had midway through a recent race. I suddenly knew that I'd soon forget most of what I was seeing around me. I ran past ordinary office buildings and plain houses, thinking, "I'll forget that one, and that one, and that one, too." It was as if I was erasing my life almost as fast as my mind was recording it. Then I realized that this realization applied not just to my racing, but to our lives in general, since most of our day-to-day experience is lost to us as time goes by. Perhaps that's for the best, since our memories would be a chaotic sea of details if our minds didn't filter out unimportant minutiae.

Still, I wouldn't trade a single minute of this racing life, whether I remembered each of them or not. But what could I do for an encore? The answer was as simple as it was predictable: check the calendar and fill out my next race application. There were four states still remaining for me to conquer to be able to claim having run marathons in them all. Then the Canadian provinces—of which I'd already done three—and then the last three of the seven continents I hadn't yet raced on. Then there were dream race destinations, like the Himalayas and the Machu Picchu trail, and beautiful cities around the globe that boasted breathtaking marathons, like Prague, Madrid, Venice, and London. There would never be a shortage of marathons that could quicken my pulse and capture my imagination.

I thought about an advertising campaign put on not long ago by a major running-shoe company. It featured the slogan "There is no finish line." But rather than finding myself inspired, I was demoralized. Without a finish line, I had no sense of accomplishment, no valid way to measure my journey. Without finish lines, my running would consist of endless miles, as devoid of perspective as the emptiness of space, as empty of joy as boundless time. I need finish lines as much as I need the seasons, a calendar, and a watch. But these finish lines are not ends; they are only a brief rest stop before the next race. I had now crossed one hundred of these finish lines, but the journey wasn't over; I'd already begun planning my next 100.

Running Tip #19

The Last Supper

The best race preparation can be undermined by bad eating decisions the night before a race. Don't make that mistake.

- *Eat early.* You don't want to feel bloated at the starting line.
- *Don't over-eat.* Carb-loading doesn't mean carb-gorging. Eat a relatively light meal early, and have a light snack before bedtime.
- *Avoid foods you haven't tried before.* Choose a carb, like pasta, rice, or bread, and a protein, like lean meat, skinless poultry, or low-fat dairy. It doesn't have to be bland, but don't be adventurous.
- *Hydrate!* Avoid alcohol and caffeinated drinks.

Why Run the Marathon? Bell Lap: Running & Remembrance

In middle-distance races held on a track, race officials let the runners know when they're on their final lap by ringing a bell. This is the bell lap, the lap that determines the winner. It's the lap that counts.

I'm now in the bell lap of my story. I have traveled all over the world, running marathons, celebrating life. Along the way, I've pondered why I ran. I reached my goal; and I've told my story, but I still have one last chapter to write; I still need an answer to that question: why run the marathon?

I thought about a recent trip I'd taken back up to Queens, New York, to visit friends and family. That Saturday morning, I set out on a run. It was early, and after stepping out of the apartment where I'd been raised, I began running down the old familiar streets of my youth, past stores where I held after-school jobs, past school yards where I used to spend long summer days playing handball and stickball. I ran past Alley Pond Park, where my friends and I would occasionally do short runs on a bike trail through the woods. Back then, our 3-mile run seemed like a tremendous achievement.

I left the park and headed west on Union Turnpike, a major thoroughfare that ran past the apartment complex where I lived. Every weekday morning from age twelve through eighteen, I would board the Q44 bus on Union

Turnpike for the 6 mile ride to the train station, where I would take the F train to the N train to the uptown 7, exiting at 96th Street for the short walk to my school. It was an hour-and-a-half commute, but that didn't seem unusual to me. Everyone in New York commutes.

As I ran down the avenue, I thought about my father. He used to take the Q44 bus also, getting off earlier to transfer to another bus to nearby Jamaica Avenue and the clothing store where he worked. After I moved to D.C. and became a runner, I ran along this bus route when I was visiting. I'd try to keep pace with each bus as it passed, looking to see if my father was on board, on his way to work. He always stood toward the back of the bus, a figure in a dark raincoat, looking out the window, leaning in to get a better view, looking for me as I was looking for him, waving at me as I waved back.

My father and I, like many fathers and sons, weren't very close, though I think we both wanted to be. We had difficulty talking with one another, of finding common ground. This chasm grew when I went to college and entered a world that he had no experience with. It would be many years until I began to understand that he showed more character through his daily sacrifice for his family than I would ever learn in school. It is a lesson that I continue to learn. But on those runs back home, I didn't yet understand these things, so the brief morning encounters we had, with me on foot and him peering through the bus window, were one of the few ways we had of connecting.

My parents were actually very proud of my running. Even Dad, who never let on when he approved of anything his children had done, bragged about me to his coworkers, and when I gave him a plaque with mounted photos of me crossing the finish line, he showed it to anyone who would be foolish enough to agree to see it. Dad wasn't an athletic man; in fact, he was often quite overweight. I had the feeling that my running somehow balanced the scales for him, that by producing someone who could accomplish these things, he had shown that it was in him somewhere as well.

Then, in 1988, right after I graduated from law school, I decided that I wanted to go skydiving. It sounded like a fun thing to do. My parents weren't so proud of that decision. They thought me foolish for wanting to throw myself out of a plane after all the hard work I put in to getting through law school. It was all fine and good to run marathons—even if I didn't win any of them, as my dad once pointed out—but at least that was safe. You get tired, you stop. Easy. But what sane person jumps out of a plane?

We never agreed on it, but one sunny day, I did it anyway. It was a static line jump, like in those old World War II movies where paratroopers dove out the door and their chutes opened automatically, except in my case there was no diving. Each of us crawled out to the edge and then slid out the door, hanging onto the strut of the overhead wing, waiting for the signal to let go from the jumpmaster, who sat just inside the door. I was third of three to go, and after sucking in engine fumes as our plane circled, climbing and dropping, I was more than ready to jump. I crawled out and looked up for the instructor's thumbs-up sign. He gave it, and I let go.

I didn't get a free fall, didn't get to assume the arch position that the instructor had us practice earlier. As it turned out, my chute opened almost immediately after I let go of the plane. But I did get some fine gliding time under the canopy, circling left and right as I tugged on the toggles above me.

I slowly drifted down to the target landing spot on the field. I misjudged my distance from the ground, though, so I landed hard and rolled instead of stepping gracefully back onto the earth. Not perfect, but good. And very fun.

I called my parents afterward. I hadn't told them that this was the day I would be jumping; no point in having them spend the day gazing at the clock, wondering if I'd splattered yet. They were relieved that I got through it okay, and that I had gotten it out of my system. Except that I hadn't. My jump was fun, but a free fall, well, that would be something else altogether. I needed just a few more jumps to graduate to that level. It would be easy.

My parents didn't share my enthusiasm. In fact, Dad started a letter-writing campaign against it. Well, he didn't actually write any letters. Instead, he clipped articles on gruesome skydiving accidents and sent them to me, without even attaching a note. Stories like the one about the skydiver who got tangled up in a plane's fuselage and had to cut himself loose from his chute to save the plane, while dooming himself. I wondered where he found these; I had never seen a single one on my own.

I knew that I'd have to deal with this sooner or later, or one of us would crack. I needed a plan.

Here's what I came up with: while Dad was always overweight, he would occasionally add on an extra twenty pounds or so, which he would drop as soon as his coworkers started teasing him about it. He'd gotten big again recently, and wasn't losing weight, despite the teasing. So I offered Dad a deal: no more skydiving if he lost forty pounds and kept it off. There seemed to be no downside there for me; if he agreed, he would either lose the weight, but probably put it back on later, freeing me from my bond, or he wouldn't lose the weight, and would have forfeited his right to campaign against me, since he knew exactly what he had to do to get me to stop. Brilliant.

Dad agreed to the deal. Then he quickly lost the forty pounds. That surprised me, but I was okay with it, because I knew that the game wasn't over yet. Then something unexpected happened; he seemed pale and tired easily, and Mom said that he was getting night sweats. That wasn't part of my plan.

We talked Dad into seeing his doctor, who took blood samples and ordered some tests. I figured Dad's crash diet had left him with some type of anemia, and the doctor said yes, that there was evidence of anemia, but he also said that there was something more. He wanted to take some tests. So Dad took off a week from work and let the doctor poke and prod and stick him. After all that, the doctor announced that he wanted to do a bone-marrow biopsy.

For me, that was the first sign that something might be seriously wrong.

I went up to New York that weekend, right before the biopsy was scheduled to be performed, to spend time with my parents and with my younger sister, Dori. My older sister, Marlene, was abroad traveling, but we were keeping her updated. While I was home, we just relaxed, and spent time poring through old photographs. We found some of Mom and Dad's wedding shots, and laughed at Dad's terrified expression, looking at us across the decades with great big eyes.

I was back at work on Monday when I got a phone call from a neighbor telling me that my dad was ill, and that I needed to come up immediately. I called my mother to find out exactly what was going on, and she could only say, "He's gone, he's gone." Finally, she told me that Dad had just collapsed and died. I jumped on the next flight to New York.

I sat gazing out the window, tears welling in my eyes, waiting for the flight to be over, but wishing that the plane would never land. An elderly woman sitting beside me started up a conversation. More than a decade later, I still wonder whether she somehow guessed what had happened, and was just trying to distract me.

She asked what I did for a living. I told her that I was an attorney. Looking at my hands, callused from working out in the gym, she said, "there's no shame in being a workman, you know."

"Yes," I said. "I know. But I really am an attorney."

After I arrived in New York, I kept wondering what it was the doctor had been testing for. I finally called and asked. Lymphoma, he said. Cancer. He was sure of it, and only ordered the biopsy to confirm it. Dad would have been dead within two years, he said. He was surprised at my dad's sudden death, but he said that perhaps it was for the best.

My dad dropping dead was for the best. I rolled that one around in my mind for a while. It was hard to accept, but I knew he was probably right.

But here's what I'm not supposed to tell you: a day or two after I had returned home, I took a late-night walk with my mother. She seemed to want to say something, so I asked her what was on her mind. She told me that on the day Dad died, he had been nervous about the biopsy, and had asked her to lie down with him. Mom paused and looked me in the eyes. "You know what I mean? *Lie down.*" The dime dropped, and I got it.

"Afterward," she continued, "he got up and went into the next room and collapsed." She looked me in the eyes, deadly serious. "Do you think I killed him?"

Good god. Can you imagine? Bad enough to have to think about my parents having sex, but now I had to imagine Mom killing Dad in the sack. *Well,* I thought, *maybe she did. Good for him. Good for her. Good for the both of them! What a great way that would be to go: spend a week at home, have your son come in for a visit, make love to your wife, then go into the next room and check out. That's a pretty sweet deal.*

Of course, I didn't say any of this to my mom. I told her, "Of course not. When it's your time, it's your time, and nothing you did with him could have changed that."

Which might be true. Or perhaps not.

Meanwhile, I was comforted, too, by the realization that my parents had always wanted it to be this way. Not at that exact moment or in that way, but in the scheme of things. Children bury parents; that's how it was supposed to be. Any time we heard about a child dying first, the expression on my parents' faces betrayed pain for the grieving parents that they didn't even know. Looking back, I realized that my parents had, knowingly or not, prepared me for this moment all my life.

I had it in my mind that burying my dad was a very personal thing, and I didn't want a stranger to do it. In Jewish funerals, the immediate family and closest friends each toss a shovelful of dirt on the coffin after it's been lowered down into the earth. After that, workers generally come over and shovel the bulk of the dirt into the grave. It seemed too impersonal to me. Burying my father was my last act of devotion to him, and I wanted to do it myself. My mother and sisters understood, and gave their consent. I then asked my family rabbi if it would be allowed. He warned me that it would be hard work. I smiled, and explained to him that I was in pretty good shape.

And that's how it went. For years afterward, when I ran down Union Turnpike, I couldn't help but glance up at each passing bus, looking to see if my father was on board. I know it makes no sense, but part of me imagined that it would still be possible to see him standing there, waving at me, if only I could run fast enough and catch the right bus. My running would bring him back to me.

I think now about all the other places that I had run over the seasons and the years, the people I met, the person I was, and the person I had become. Running seems to be the thread that connects it all, a line to all that was and all that is; a strip of asphalt thousands of miles long, on which I'd run all the workouts and races of my life.

I wonder what the Runner-That-I-Was would think about the Runner-That-I-Am, and I imagine that if I run really fast, I would be able to fold the years and catch sight of the Me-That-Was. We'd lock eyes in passing, and he'd nod slightly and tip his hand, the runner's greeting that says, "I know you; you are one of us."

My mind floods with the memories of my running in D.C. I recall crossing Key Bridge during a driving rainstorm, and the sweltering heat of the 14th Street Bridge in late summer. I recall the reflection of myself on an office building's gleaming window during a 10K race, and the potholes I've scrambled over, and occasionally stepped into.

I think again about the marathon, and again about the question why. I've lived with the marathon for nearly two decades; it has become a part of my being, my personal culture. It is no longer just something I do; it is a reflection of who I am. The great Czech Olympic champion Emil Zátopek said that if you want to win something, run 100 meters, but if you want to experience something, run a marathon. I've wanted the experience, and I've discovered that each marathon is a life-journey all its own, filled with expectation, disappointment, realization, and, sometimes, triumph. It has become the measure and mirror of my life.

I think again about Burt, my personal training client who passed away. I think about how the muscles we fought so hard to strengthen have now melted from his bones, and that I may be the only one who knows how hard he struggled to improve himself. But I know that Burt labored not just to gain strength and fitness; what Burt gained in the gym was a sense of purpose. His struggles were a demonstration of his character and his faith in the wonder of life. I think, too, about my two team members in Rome, and how we talked about the meaning of the marathon, of the arbitrariness of the number 26.2, of the relative insignificance of finishing times.

Finally, I had my answer. I knew why it was important to run the marathon. The race distance matters, but only because it takes 26.2 miles to strip away the falsehoods and comfortable compromises of daily life. My finishing times matter also, but only as a reflection of my effort. I know that I will eventually lose my speed, and that someday I will get old and die. But during the time I am here, I will find a deeper satisfaction and meaning to my daily routine; I will find a way to connect to the animal that I am, and to make a statement about what kind of person I am, and what I stand for. It doesn't really matter that I will slow and weaken. There is a kind of glory to be found here, a glory earned through sweat

Why Run the Marathon? Bell Lap: Running & Remembrance

and effort, from a stubborn refusal to give less than your best. It is the reward that dwarfs all the medals tucked away in my drawer. It is why I run the marathon.

Here's a story: during the 1968 Olympic Games in Mexico City, the winner of the marathon had already crossed the finish line over an hour earlier when John Stephen Akhwari of Tanzania entered the stadium. Akhwari was limping, and his leg was wrapped in a bloody bandage. Akhwari slowly made his way around the track to the finish line, as the few spectators who remained in the stands applauded his efforts. Afterward, a reporter asked Akhwari why he hadn't just dropped out of the race, since he clearly had no chance of winning. Akhwari paused, and then said, "My country did not send me to Mexico City to start the race. They sent me to finish." It was the greatest last-place finish ever, and perhaps the most succinct expression I'd ever heard of the marathon spirit.

Everyone needs a place to make their stand, to declare their character through their actions, to say "this is who I am and what I believe." For me, that statement begins with a race application and a pair of running shoes. We marathoners are the people who suffer and persevere. That is who we are.

As I write these words, I look over at Stephanie. Soon after we married, we talked about whether we wanted a child. We were both accustomed to an adventurous lifestyle, and we were reluctant and even scared to take on the burden of parenthood. Even if we wanted one, we knew that the odds were against us. We were both forty, which we knew was a problem. Friends our age had gone to extraordinary lengths to conceive, using fertility drugs and in vitro fertilization. We fully expected that would be our lot as well, much as we hoped to avoid it.

We finally decided to try to start a family. Actually, it would be more accurate to say that we decided that we didn't want to *not* have one, which was what we thought would be the result if we put off making a decision any longer. Since we were sure that we would have difficulty getting pregnant anyway, we made an appointment with a clinic. Stephanie showed up for her appointment on time. She'd missed her last period, but she wasn't concerned. These things happen occasionally. The doctor did a few preliminary tests, and then came back with surprising news: we didn't need his services after all. Stephanie was already pregnant.

We were dumbstruck. As Stephanie's belly swelled, the reality of our situation slowly sunk in. In time, we found out that we were going to have a boy, and we began the ritualistic collecting-of-things that all expecting parents go through. I trusted her to decide what we needed; I hadn't even heard of many of the things that she told me were essential, and even holding them in my hands left me with little clear idea of what to do with them.

The one thing I did take responsibility for, though, was the choosing of the jogging stroller. After extensive research, I bought a model that just screamed speed. It looked like it was setting a PR even when it was standing still. I felt ready for our son.

As we got closer to our due date, I thought more about what kind of father I wanted to be, and I began to feel hopelessly ill prepared. How had my father handled it, and his father before him? I hoped that my instincts and basic common sense would carry me through. And I also counted on close supervision by Stephanie.

One thing I did feel confident about, though, was my determination to be a running father. If children really do learn best by example, then my little boy would learn that it's perfectly natural to run on a nice day, and to enter a marathon and finish it. He would watch his old man compete, and see that hundreds and thousands of other dads and moms did the same thing. He would grow up thinking that there was nothing extraordinary or unusual about this, and that he could do it, too, if he wished. He could do anything he wanted, if he did the work.

As I glance over at Stephanie's belly now, I think of the lessons I learned from my father, and I think of how I will some day be regarded by my own son when I'm gone. I hope that he'll recall the passion with which I pursued my dreams, and understand that in my running, I was trying to explain to him my understanding of life, and how to live it. This is the gift I wish to give to my son.

My 100th marathon has now come and gone, less a finish line itself than a marker on a path. More are planned, and after that, more will hopefully follow, stretching into the distance like light posts on an endless highway. As each one comes into view, I will greet it and test myself against it, pushing muscle and sinew against time and distance. If ever I should forget who I am, and what I believe, I only need to run that path, and in my running, I will find my way back to myself, and discover once again who I am.

Epilogue: Bumps in the Endless Road

In November 2004, a story was reported in the back pages of *The New York Times* that was of great interest to me.[8] Dr. Dennis M. Bramble of the University of Utah and Dr. Daniel E. Lieberman of Harvard had published a paper hypothesizing that ancient humans were physiologically predisposed to be long-distance runners.

The scientists had begun by analyzing the evolution of our physique. As early as two million years ago, humans developed an upright posture, long legs, shorter arms and a narrower ribcage and pelvis. We also lost our fur, which allowed us to develop sweat glands and prevent overheating during intense exertion. We developed a ligament network to keep our heads steady while running, and a muscle and tendon network along the back of our legs, including an Achilles tendon, to store and release great amounts of energy—enough to propel our bodies forward quickly with power. And then there's our highly-developed backside, which stabilizes our midsection during running.

---

8 "Even Couch Potatoes May Have Been Born to Run," by John Noble Wilford, *New York Times*, November 17, 2004.

All of these traits are conducive not just to walking, but to long distance running, and apes don't share any of them. Bramble and Lieberman speculated that running would have increased the early humans' chances of survival, as they could cover large areas of African grassland in pursuit of food.

Apparently, then, we are all born to run.

Of course, I knew that already. I was once told that there's a German word, *tatesfruedig*, which roughly means the joy of doing that which you can do well. A cheetah loves to sprint because it is built to sprint, and a monkey loves to climb because it is built to climb. My running wasn't an aberration; it was an expression of my genetic heritage. It was something I was born to do.

So I kept on running. I ran marathons in Montana, Alaska, and North Dakota. In late September, with the birth of my son just days away, I returned to the Marine Corps Marathon yet again. And then, on November 12, 2005, I experienced something more miraculous than a marathon finish line: the birth of Alex Michael, named in honor of my grandfather and Stephanie's dad. I cut his umbilical cord and then later laid my hand across his tiny body. There was no amount of thinking that could compare to the reality I saw before me. It was magical and humbling. I thought about my life, and I felt like I was the luckiest man on earth.

Then things became unhinged. A dear friend of twenty years died of breast cancer. A cousin died from lung cancer. And then hardest of all, I had to watch my mother's health suddenly spiral downward, despite all the treatments recommended by the best doctors we could find. Mom was obese and had diabetes, which I knew was a time bomb waiting to explode, but there was little I could do about it. As a coach and trainer, I felt particularly responsible, but I couldn't force her to save her own life, and after a while, I decided not to spend whatever time we had left together fighting with her over this. But now her problems gained a velocity I never could have imagined: she experienced full renal failure and had to go on dialysis, then she contracted pneumonia twice and a vicious intestinal infection. Fear and various drugs addled her mind, and a foot infection forced her doctors to amputate her leg. The lone bright spot for us was the look on her face when she held tiny Alex in her arms for the first time.

Her health continued to decline. Every time the phone rang, I feared the worst. My sisters and I shuttled Mom between hospitals and nursing homes, and we realized at some point that she would never return to her old apartment. We were still hopeful of her recovery, and had just filed the paperwork to move her into a home that could properly care for her. My sister Marlene was visiting us in D.C. with her two children when we got the phone call from New York. Mom's blood pressure had suddenly plummeted, and she had needed to be resuscitated twice. She now had a tube snaking down her throat, delivering oxygen, and her heart was beating only because she was being fed drugs intravenously. Her doctors wanted to know if we wanted to give them the order to stop resuscitating her. They wanted to know if we were ready to let her die.

Marlene had been on a grand tour of Europe and Asia when Dad fell ill. When she called us from Istanbul, we told her not to worry, but that she should sit still for a while and keep in touch. There was no need to panic, after all. Everything would be okay. And then Dad suddenly died, as you know. Marlene immediately got on a plane heading home, and spent that twelve-hour flight weeping and growing the guilt she would carry forever for not being home when her daddy passed away.

As I looked at Marlene now, I knew that more than anything else, I didn't want Mom to pass away without Marlene being at her bedside. So the answer was no. We would not give a do-not-resuscitate order. We told the doctors to keep the meds flowing. We were on our way.

When we reached the hospital, Stephanie took Alex and Marlene's children back to Marlene's house, where Marlene's husband Jerry was waiting for them. Marlene and I went up to Mom's room in intensive care. Our sister Dori was already there, with red-rimmed eyes. She had been there for hours.

We went right to Mom's bedside. She looked back at us, wide-eyed, gasping for air as a tube hung from her mouth. Her gaze shifted, and I realized that she was looking back and forth across the room. Back and forth, again and again. I wondered if she knew we were there.

We stepped into the hall to speak with the doctors on call. They told us that the only thing keeping Mom alive was the medication they were pumping into her veins to maintain her blood pressure and heartbeat. Mom's body had already begun to shut down; the flow of blood to her remaining leg had virtually stopped. After absorbing this information, we returned to her room. I pulled back the blanket and looked at her right leg. Her foot was already turning black.

My sisters sobbed while they held Mom's hands and stroked her head. I stood at the bedside, waiting. Finally, we looked at each other, and started talking about what needed to be done.

How do you go about stating the obvious when no one wants to hear it? I was a lawyer, so I approached it in a lawyerlike way: I made the case. Mom could not live on her own without these extreme lifesaving measures, and what she had now was not living. Even if she were to somehow revive and not need life support, her remaining leg was rapidly dying, and would need to be removed. Would she be able to survive another amputation? We doubted it.

When we were finished reviewing the situation, we just stood there, not wanting to say what needed to be said. It seemed like we had been led into a Faustian bargain; in exchange for being allowed to be at her mother's bedside at her passing, we had to give the order to let her die. It was an awful responsibility, but as we looked at Mom, the reality sunk in. We realized that we really had no choice at all. It had already happened. We were there to just hold her hand and observe the passage.

We went back out in the hall and summoned the doctors. They told us that if we discontinued the medications, her heart rate would immediately begin to drop. She would probably only start to feel lightheaded, and then gently slip away. After all the months of physical and mental agony she had endured, it seemed only fair that she was at least given a peaceful end.

We had the meds cut off, and my sisters and I stood around her bedside, stroking her face and saying "I love you." I leaned in close to her cheek, kissed her, and whispered, "Be at peace," and then I glanced at the monitor and watched the drop in her heart rate. It fell slowly but steadily, from 119, to 107, to 98. My sisters cried more intensely, and held her hands tightly. Mom still looked up at us wide eyed.

84. 77. 65.

Her cheek felt cold to me, but as soft as it was when I stroked it as a boy. When I was very little I once told her that when she got old, I would get her a facelift. I don't know where I had gotten that idea. I wondered what she thought when I said it.

59. 53. 48. 42.

Her eyes seemed to lose their vitality. I wanted the moment to be over, and I wanted it to never end. I wondered what she was thinking.

36. 28. 19. 12.

Stillness.

After my mother died, I felt numb and detached. Even with Stephanie and Alex beside me, I was shaken by the sudden disappearance of so many people from my life. I didn't know what to do to make it all seem okay, so I relied on the one thing that had always provided me with support when I was troubled: I ran. I raced in Arizona, Florida, Wyoming, and still that was not enough. While Mom was ill, Stephanie and I had made plans to let her mother watch Alex while the two of us went to Mexico for a vacation—and a chance for me to run the Mexico City Marathon. After Mom died, I wasn't sure we should still go, but we decided it would be best for us to stick with our plans. More than anything, we needed some time alone. It was the right choice. We had a wonderful time, even if we missed Alex.

And still I kept running. On October 8, 2006, Dave and I completed the Mt. Rushmore Marathon, crossing the finish line together. We had added the final state to our list, and could now both claim to have run the entire country.

I didn't stop there; I added more and more marathons to my list, running them more frequently than I ever had before. And then I committed the cardinal runner's sin: I ignored pain, thinking it would just go away. It didn't. My body suddenly decided that enough was enough, and grounded me with a series of devastating injuries. Tenderness in my hamstrings, blinding pain in my Achilles tendon, and stabbing pain in my heel. My running came to a screeching halt. I was through.

After a series of X-rays and MRIs, I accepted that I would be off running, and that I would never again run the way I used to. I was allowed to cross-train, and I attacked the bike and weight room with a singled-minded fury, but I missed my running. The weeks passed, and I followed the doctor's orders religiously, but I was still grounded. I kept up a cheerful face for my charity running team and my friends, but I'd never before had to face a setback like this. After all I had just witnessed, I knew that not being able to run was hardly the worst tragedy one could face, but it was still a difficult blow to me. The one crutch that I had consistently relied upon over the years to help me through all my crises was itself in crisis. I felt lost.

In April 2008, I sat in an airport, waiting by a gate for a plane that would take my charity runners and me to Monterey, California for a race along the coast. They would run, but I would not. But I was their coach, and I was committed to helping them achieve their goals. It was all I could do. But in the airport at that moment, I just wanted to sit quietly and read. I didn't want to think about running.

"You ran the Dublin Marathon?"

"Huh?" I said, confused.

"Did you run the Dublin Marathon?" The tall man standing in front of me pointed at my backpack. "It says so on your bag."

"Oh, right. Yeah, I ran that a couple of times. It's a fun race."

"Do you run a lot?"

"Well, not right now, but I used to." And so I told him about my races. Eventually I told him how many I'd run.

"You should write a book."

"Funny you should say that."

"Wait a minute," he said, getting up. "I gotta get someone." He came back with a few people and introduced me. We all sat there and talked running. Races we'd finished, races we'd dreamed of doing, the great moments and the horrible ones. And little by little, I began to feel better.

"Good talking with you," the first man said. "You're an inspiration."

An inspiration. That was funny. They hadn't known how depressed I was just a few minutes earlier. And now like a summer storm, it had blown away. Talking with them, I felt my hope rekindle, and I suddenly knew that these injuries—these terrible but completely common injuries—would pass, and I would solve the puzzle of my body and find a way to run again, to race again. Despite all, the road was not ended and I was not finished. Everything in my life would be all right.

I was still a runner.

By the Numbers

1 Marine Corps Marathon, Washington, D.C., November 8, 1987—3:45:30

2 Marine Corps Marathon, Washington, D.C., November 4, 1990—4:08:00

3 New York City Marathon, November 3, 1991—4:11:12

4 Shamrock Marathon, Virginia Beach, March 20, 1993—3:45:33

5 Pittsburgh Marathon, May 2, 1993—4:25:42

6 Columbia Birthday Marathon, Maryland, September 19, 1993—3:35:00

7 Northern Central Trails Marathon, Maryland, November 27, 1993—4:00:17

8 Boston Marathon, April 18, 1994—3:57:38

9 Vermont Marathon, Burlington, May 29, 1994—3:40:33

10 Grandma's Marathon; Duluth, Minnesota, June 19, 1994—3:47:38

11 Atlantic City Marathon, New Jersey, October 16, 1994—3:39:52

12 New York City Marathon, November 6, 1994—3:42:33

13 Richmond Marathon, Virginia, November 27, 1994—3:35:38

14 Philadelphia Marathon, November 20, 1994—3:43:44

15 Las Vegas Marathon, February 4, 1995—3:58:26

16 LaSalle Chicago Marathon, October 15, 1995—3:21:28

17 Marine Corps Marathon, Washington, D.C., October 22, 1995—
4:27:55

18 Schweizer's Delaware Marathon, December 10, 1995—3:34:12

19 Disneyworld Marathon, Orlando, January 7, 1996—3:26:55

20 *Charlotte Observer* Marathon, North Carolina, February 17, 1996—
3:28:48

21 Music City Marathon; Nashville, Tennessee, March 16, 1996—
3:38:39

22 Cleveland Marathon, May 5, 1996—3:44:39

23 Mayor's Midnight Marathon, Anchorage, June 22, 1996—3:19:41

24 Marine Corps Marathon, Washington, D.C., October 27, 1996—
3:37:46

25 Atlanta Marathon, November 28, 1996—3:32:05

26 Kiawah Island Marathon, South Carolina, December 14, 1996—
3:23:47

27 25th Olympiad Memorial Marathon, St. Louis, February 23,
1997—3:48:51

28 Ridge Runner Marathon, West Virginia, June 7, 1997—3:40:57

29 San Francisco Marathon, July 13, 1997—3:32:00

30 East Lyme Marathon, Connecticut, September 28, 1997—3:12:57

31 Detroit International Marathon, Michigan, October 19, 1997—
3:08:59

32 Vulcan Marathon; Birmingham, Alabama, November 8, 1997—
3:31

33 Mardi Gras Marathon; New Orleans, Louisiana, January 17,
1998—3:45:02

34 Lincoln Marathon, Nebraska, May 3, 1998—3:18:05

35 Heroes Marathon; Madison, Wisconsin, May 24, 1998—3:10:09

36 Sunburst Marathon; South Bend, Indiana, June 6, 1998—3:36:50

37 Pikes Peak Marathon, Colorado, August 16, 1998—6:58:00

38 New Hampshire Marathon, October 3, 1998—3:46:00

39 Louisville Marathon, December 5, 1998—3:30:22

40 Houston Marathon, January 19, 1999—3:25:14

41 The Last Marathon, Antarctica, February 13, 1999—5:10:00

42 Los Angeles Marathon, March 14, 1999—3:27:25

43 Boston Marathon, April 19, 1999—3:09:00

44 *Deseret News* Marathon, Utah, July 24, 1999—3:54:00

45 Tupelo Marathon, Mississippi, September 5, 1999—3:32:13 (19/120)

46 Berlin Marathon, September 26, 1999—3:26:17

47 Marine Corps Marathon, Washington D.C., October 24, 1999— 3:21:15 (with a borrowed number—sorry, Mr. Race Director!)

48 New York City Marathon, November 7, 1999—3:34:51

49 Seattle Marathon, November 28, 1999—3:32:34

50 Jacksonville Marathon, Florida, December 18, 1999—3:24:15

51 Myrtle Beach Marathon, South Carolina, February 5, 2000— 3:15:00

52 B&A Trail Marathon, Maryland, March 12, 2000—3:40:01

53 Boston Marathon, April 17, 2000—3:11:44

54 Portland Marathon, Maine, October 1, 2000—3:22:04

55 Beijing Marathon, October 15, 2000—3:31:01

56 Dublin Marathon, October 30, 2000—3:27:45

57 Honolulu Marathon, December 10, 2000—3:25:37

58 Bermuda Marathon, January 14, 2001—3:23:37 (16/287)

59 Desert Classic Marathon; Phoenix, Arizona, February 18, 2001— 3:44:01

60 Rome Marathon, March 25, 2001—3:49:38

61 Boston Marathon, April 16, 2001—3:19:05

62 Vienna City Marathon, May 20, 2001—3:41:37

63 New Mexico Marathon, September 9, 2001—3:33:00

64 Steamtown Marathon; Scranton, Pennsylvania, October 7, 2001—3:20:14

65 Dublin Marathon, October 31, 2001—4:07:00

66 Athens Marathon, Greece, November 4, 2001—3:23:00

67 Honolulu Marathon, December 9, 2001—3:48:34

68 Rome Marathon, March 24, 2002—3:49:38

69 Paris Marathon, April 7, 2002—3:52:43

70 Toronto Marathon, September 15, 2002—3:28:10

71 Portland Marathon, Oregon, October 6, 2002—3:38:00

72 Amsterdam Marathon, October 20, 2002—4:27:00

73 New York City Marathon, November 3, 2002—3:37:00

74 Marathon in the Parks, Maryland, November 17, 2002—3:57:21

75 Honolulu Marathon, December 8, 2002—3:47:29

76 Miami Tropical Marathon, February 2, 2003—3:16:16

77 Boston Marathon, April 14, 2003—3:22:00

78 Kona Marathon, June 21, 2003—5:21:00

79 Pikes Peak Marathon, Colorado, August 17, 2003—7:24:00

80 Médoc Marathon; Bordeaux, France, September 6, 2003—4:41:18

81 Wichita Marathon, Kansas, October 19, 2003—3:35:47

82 Auckland Marathon, New Zealand, November 2, 2003—3:39:00

83 Tulsa Marathon, November 22, 2003—3:28:00

84 Barbados Marathon, December 7, 2003—4:38:00

85 Hog Eye Marathon; Fayetteville, Arkansas, March 28, 2004—3:43:58

86 Boston Marathon, April 19, 2004—3:34:00

87 Vancouver International Marathon, British Columbia, May 2, 2004—3:25:43

88 Bunco Calgary Marathon, July 11, 2004—3:55:57

89 Mesa Falls Marathon; Ashton, Idaho, August 28, 2004—4:00:42

90 Des Moines Marathon, Iowa, October 17, 2004—3:20:34

91 Marine Corps Marathon, Washington, D.C., October 31, 2004—
3:28:33

92 Marathon in the Parks; Montgomery County, Maryland, November
14, 2004—3:45:01

93 White Rock Marathon; Dallas, Texas, December 12, 2004—
3:32:58

94 Las Vegas International Marathon, January 30, 2005—3:36:59

95 George Washington Birthday Marathon; Greenbelt, Maryland,
February 20, 2005—3:49:40

96 Virginia Creeper, Abingdon, March 13, 2005—3:49:36

97 Ocean City Marathon; Ocean City, Maryland, April 16, 2005—
3:53:00

98 Vancouver Marathon, British Columbia, May 1, 2005—3:57:19

99 Coventry Healthcare Delaware Marathon, Wilmington, May 15,
2005—3:35:07

100 Grandfather Mountain Marathon; Boone, North Carolina, July 9,
2005—3:46:00

Acknowledgments

To borrow a well-used phrase, it takes a village to publish a book, and I was lucky enough to have a particularly great bunch of villagers to help me turn this idea into a reality. First, thanks to my agent, Lauren Abramo, for her support and ever-helpful guidance. Thanks also to Bill Wolfsthal and Sarah Van Bonn at Skyhorse Publishing for their patience and vision, and to Jan Seeley and Rich Benyo of *Marathon & Beyond* for a decade's worth of friendship and encouragement. I still remember the first article query I sent over to Rich: I suggested a word limit, and he e-mailed back that I shouldn't worry about that; I should just write all that I needed to say. It's a freedom I've never taken for granted, and which I hope I haven't abused.

Thanks to Dave Harrell for being a big part of my story, and to Renata Carvalho for running and racing with me and for offering me valuable advice after reading the first draft of this book. Thanks also to my pace team organizers, who have invited me to enjoy a new side of marathoning: Josh Leibman of FunnerRunner and Marathon Memories, and Star and Darris Blackford and the entire Clif Bar Pace Team family.

Finally, a world of thanks to my sisters, Marlene and Dori, and their families, all my friends and colleagues, and especially to my parents, who I wish could have been here to see this.

About the Author

JEFF **HOROWITZ** is a certified personal trainer and running coach, living in Washington, D.C. He got hooked on marathoning in 1987, and in addition to his own running, he has coached hundreds of others to run their first marathon while raising money for various charities. When he's not busy doing these things, he's also an attorney, columnist, husband, and father to little Alex Michael, who pleased his daddy by quickly learning how to say, "Look, I'm running!" Visit Jeff at www.runtothefinishline.com.